Mind Sharing

Michael O' Doran

Table of Contents

Preface

Have you ever awakened from slumber and thought that: *Was it a weird dream? It didn't seem like that was me in that dream. I don't remember all the details, but it didn't seem like anything in that dream was me.*

Definitely not me.

I began wondering what would it be like if I could remember everything about my dreams. What if I was someone else half of my day? What if there were a finite number of minds in the universe that needed to be shared? What if I was able to see into another man or woman's life in my dreams? What if there was some sort of way to tap into that? Maybe the ancient medical arts of the native Americans had the clue? What if I could change my personal attitudes through herbs? What if those same native Americans had the potion to see through the eyes of another person in your sleep?

That was me on April fourteenth, twenty-twenty. While most people were gathering their taxes, I was writing the first chapter of "Mind Sharing."

I began crafting the book you are about to read. I sat down at my computer and, like many times before, I just began to type. I stopped to see if there were ways to affect the compassion of an individual through herbs. I couldn't find anything, so fiction had to do.

I thought I needed a character that you would hate in the beginning. How do I achieve that? He needs to be a bigot. No one likes a bigot. He needed to be cranky. He needs to be out of touch with the world and live in a very small box. He needs to have a certain abrasive attitude. He need only care about himself, on the surface.

Then I thought, a medicine man could change all that and more. Would a medicine man do such a procedure on this fellow? Not likely, so let's alter the story and "Mind Sharing" began to take off.

As I researched locations in Arizona, the Navajo and their customs, their names and their ways, I found them compelling. They are honorable people who deserve more recognition. My time and experience while living in Colorado taught me much about the area and its food. That led me to search for certain cuisines. I found similar places in Arizona, and I have introduced them to you. I hope that one day you'll seek these places and see if I was right about the tasty delights they offer.

The story left Arizona when I introduced the "hitman" Tony Palumbo. We land in Chicago, where crime today is at an all-time high, and the authorities there are overwhelmed. That is where most of the story takes place. I hope you'll recognize some of the things I tell you about and maybe even take a tour, a ride from Chicago to Saint Louis.

Saint Louis is the town I was born in. It's where I grew up. I know that place better than anywhere in the world. Saint Louis has some of the best people. You will not find a more friendly place. We briefly stop in St. Louis to meet Mike O'Keefe as he is faced with a horrendous murder perpetrated by Tony.

This account convinces law enforcement to investigate the dreams of our witness, Stewart.

So often, we see books and movies about criminals and their ways of life. I had to create a criminal in Tony who had an illicit lifestyle. You will not hate Tony, and in some cases, some people will envy him. Stewart envies him momentarily then his deeds cause Stewart to turn on Tony.

My hope is that this book will entertain you, introduce you to new ideas, and get you thinking that perhaps the mind is more than a resident. Perhaps the mind is something more malleable, more elusive or even more powerful than ever considered before.

Chapter One: Leaving New Jersey

"This plane is taking forever to take off," Stewart thought as he sat alone on the tarmac.

Stewart Miller, an accountant from Edgewater, New Jersey, was not known for his demeanor. He was not known for his patience. Stewart was not known at all or loved by many.

Stewart was on a plane headed to Arizona to visit his sister, Sheryl. Hania, his sister's husband, passed away two weeks prior. Hania, a Native American, had found a white woman against his tribe's culture and married her. Taught in the cultural ways, Hania was thc premiere medicine man for the tribe. The shame was his medicine could not predict the end of his life.

Stewart lacked the strength of physique, character, and presence. The lonely staff accountant never had a relationship with a partner of any kind. Stewart seemed like that weird fellow you heard about on the news. You know, the ones, the murderer who always kept to himself.

"He was a quiet man."

Inside, he reeled from his loneliness. It angered him that friends eluded him. It infuriated him that his only sister moved thousands of miles away. He was incessantly crabby, and that made him constantly annoying. His miserable existence was lathered with hatred. Nothing made Stewart happy.

So, sitting on the tarmac of the airport, awaiting takeoff, got Stewart's blood boiling. He considered the opportunity of lashing out at the airplane staff. He began formulating the words and was about to deliver them as soon as someone happened by.

A ruckus in the front caught everyone's attention. It seemed one more passenger was allowed to board the plane. He watched intently for the culprit so that he might have an opportunity to hurl insults. He was poised as the stewardess escorted the newcomer onto the plane. One stewardess ahead and one behind, they made their way down the aisle. He didn't know that the empty seat next to him was the only one available. So, as the stewardesses approached, his selfishness built. He feared his flight would be interrupted by some chatty bimbo or some smelly kid. Still, he didn't see the passenger as the stewardess kept leaning in the way. He didn't notice that passengers were showing the newcomer attention. He wondered if this was a celebrity or a sports figure. Maybe a dignitary. His interest piqued as the group got closer.

A peek at the passenger told him it was a woman. As the group got closer, more people fussed about her. She was waving and shaking hands with the passengers. She was smiling and nodding at the many onlookers. Stewart didn't recognize her. He never really cared about a celebrity or sports figures, so he didn't understand the commotion.

The group arrived at his row. The flight attendant opened the overhead compartment, removed Stewart's small bag, and handed it to him.

"Can you hold this for a second, sir?"

Before Stewart could answer, it was on his lap. The attendant tucked the woman's bag into the space and backed away, forgetting Stewart had his bag on his lap.

"Excuse me, Ma'am. Can you put this back?"

"I'm sorry, sir, there isn't any space up there. You will have to put it under your seat."

"Are you kidding? I was here first."

"Sir, please, hers is much bigger and will not fit under the seat."

"Miss, really? I was here first. Find her another place to sit."

As the woman began to sit, Stewart began to stand up to the attendant, nearly bumping into the woman.

"You must put my bag back."

"Okay, sir, give it to me."

The attendant took the bag and searched for a place to put it. The woman sat down next to Stewart. Stewart watched the attendant check various compartments until, four rows back, she found a place to put his carryon. Stewart was miffed. He tried to stand, but just as he unbuckled his seatbelt, the captain's seatbelt sign went on. The flight attendant vanished towards the back of the plane, out of sight.

Now Stewart had to contend with this somebody who he didn't know. Her perfume overwhelmed the air, and it was choking him. He reached up and turned all of the fans onto her. She reached up and redirected them towards him. He repeated, and she repeated until she gave in. It took six times each. She shook her head and leaned away from him. He wondered who she was and why she was not on a plane with first class. He wondered why they had to sit her next to him.

A different flight attendant came by to check the seatbelts. Stewart hadn't re-buckled his. "Sir, please buckle your seatbelt." Stewart ignored her. "Sir, your seatbelt!" Stewart looked out the window as if he had not heard her. "Sir, please. Sir, fasten your seatbelt."

She raised her voice and leaned in. He still ignored her.

Then, the woman sitting next to him elbowed Stewart in the ribs.

Stewart said, "Hey, what the fuck?"

She replied, "Didn't you hear the flight attendant? Fasten your fucking seatbelt!" People overhearing this nearby applauded when Stewart finally complied.

The woman next to Stewart then asked the attendant, "Is there any chance I could move?"

The attendant replied, "I'm dreadfully sorry, this was the only seat available. Let me see if another passenger would be kind enough to do that for you."

Then, the stewardess walked to the front, picked up the microphone and began speaking. Stewart expected the standard seatbelt safety story, but instead, the attendant said, "Attention passengers, as many of you have already noticed, we have a celebrity in our midst. She is a film and TV star, friends with Courtney Cox, and many more. She's fun, funny and gorgeous. Jennifer has asked to move to a different seat because the fellow next to her is not being very nice. As you all know, our seats are assigned, and she's not going to be able to move. We hope you all have a wonderful flight, especially you, Miss Anniston."

It seemed the attendant was now miffed at Jennifer Anniston for asking to be moved. The weight shifted away from Stewart, and he was happy. He hoped the stewardesses would continue the baton of insults toward the lady. He leaned his head against the window, closed his eyes, and hoped for sleep.

Jennifer was no longer the center of attention as the flight attendants went through the various safety protocols. In her head, she mocked them and remembered the Saturday Night Live skit from her friend Helen Hunt. She remembered the "Buh Bye" parts and began to giggle to herself.

Stewart couldn't sleep as the plane was rising to its cruising altitude. The pressure made his ears hurt, so he stretched his jaw to no avail. He, like many, hated this part of flying. He wondered if anyone liked the pressure and pain. He wondered how flight attendants put up with it day in and day out. He pondered all of this while staring out the window onto the city below.

As the plane rose past the clouds, Stewart lost interest in the window. Feeling her gaze on him, he turned to Jennifer sitting next to him; it was a painful, eye-stabbing glare, more like hatred and disdain.

Their eyes met, and she said, "You are an angry little man, aren't you?"

Stewart didn't respond. He turned back to the window, closed his eyes, and thought about her statement.

As the plane descended, the pressure built in Stewart's head, and he woke from the long flight. He moved his jaw repeatedly to open his ears, and finally, they popped. Then he noticed the plane was lower than the clouds, and it seemed it was beginning to land. He heard the landing gear open and the whistle of the rudders, so he knew the time was coming near. He wondered how he slept the entire four hours when he had never slept on a flight in his life. He looked around. It seemed everyone was waking up from a nap. Jennifer was wide awake, reading a fashion magazine.

The plane landed. One of the attendants brought Stewart his bag, and he rested it on his lap.

"Welcome to Phoenix, y'all. The temperature is ninety-two degrees, the sun is out, and there is a breeze from the West moving at about ten miles an hour. The captain will be turning off the fasten seat belt sign... In case y'all didn't notice, we had a celebrity among us, Miss Jennifer Anniston. It is the airline's policy to allow certain people immediate departure from the plane, and Miss Anniston has asked that y'all give her a chance to disembark. We ask that everyone in the first twenty-two rows please stay seated until she has made it past your row. As a thank you, she has purchased vouchers for y'all for a free round-trip flight on our airline. That includes row twenty-three, seats A, B, C, and D." Stewart sat in seat F.

Jennifer was looking right at him as the announcement came to an end, and the passengers cheered. This was so typical of Stewart's life. He had been left out all too many times. She smirked at him, and he turned away, back to the window. Story of his life.

Chapter Two: The Pickup

Stewart made his way to baggage pick up behind a slow-moving older couple. Every time he tried to get around them, one would veer into his path. His patience grew thin. Just as he arrived at the baggage claim, he got around the woman, only to stand and wait. As bags made it onto the carousel, his patience thinned out even more. One passenger after the other took their bags and left. The crowd shrunk to only him and no luggage. He had been looking around for any evidence of his mistake. He remembered the announcement that his flight was to pick up their bags at carousel four, and he was at carousel four. The U-shaped carousel was connected to carousel number three by a door. The door was on the opposite side of where Stewart had been waiting. He was certain something nefarious had happened to his and only his bag.

His blood began to boil. He stomped to the opposite side of the carousel to see nothing on the floor, nothing on the carousel, no bag. Nothing for Stewart. How could he be the chosen one whose bag would be lost?

He remembered the curbside baggage drop-off. He had handed the clerk his bag but didn't tip him. He thought the guy makes more in tips than I do every year. He watched as the baggage clerk set his bag off to the side. He had just figured it would make it onto the appropriate cart and then to his destination. He figured it wrong.

Earlier, back in New Jersey, Lenny, the baggage, handed the bag to Steve, the handler. With it, Lenny said quietly, "Lose this one." Steve smiled, nodded, and placed the bag onto a cart. Steve went from pile to pile, placing noted bags on his "Lose it" cart as if they were headed to the right destination. After the morning rush, Steve managed his cart to a loading dock, completely undetected, and into a van. Every morning, the van filled with "lost luggage" departed the airport. Every Friday afternoon, Lenny and the baggage clerks would meet at their regular hangout and Lenny would distribute the week's take. Some weeks, there was not much, and other weeks, the group would haul in thousands in cash from hocked jewelry and goods. The clothes would end up at thrift store drop-off locations. They felt like modern-day Robin Hoods.

Stewart made his way to the lost luggage office to file a claim.

Meanwhile, Stewart's sister sat in the heat in her CJ7, top gone, doors gone, under the roof of the parking lot. The breeze was just enough to prevent her from perspiration. She was reading a book and patiently waiting. She had nowhere to go and was not in a hurry. She was excited about her brother as she had forgotten his demeanor.

The clerk in the lost luggage office was Latin American with broken English. Stewart struggled to understand her. She finally gave him a form to fill out, and he complied. In the interim, she did a computer search for his bag and didn't find it delivered anywhere. On the form, it asked for a valuation of the goods inside of his bag. He claimed twenty-five hundred dollars. She looked at the form and asked him to explain what was in the bag worth that much. He made up a few items on the list she required. She looked at the list, typed it into the computer, and then walked to the printer. She had Stewart sign the paper, and she tore off a check and handed it to him. He left thinking, I should have said five thousand.

He walked out to the parking lot with just his carry-on. It had his sundries, his underwear, and a few nonclothing items. Sheryl had told Stewart where to find her. He followed her instructions perfectly, and there in front of him was an old, faded Jeep. It was rough. The light blue paint was almost white. It was void of a top, and he could see through the missing doors that his sister sat in a multicolored sundress. The stripes on the sundress reminded him of a Mexican rug. Red, green, yellow, purple, and orange vertical stripes in many thicknesses curved around her fit body. She heard Stewart before she saw him. Over her right shoulder, she got the first glimpse of him. Stewart was in faded blue jeans and a heavy brown sweatshirt with a hood. His shoes were slip-on so that he could remove them easily at the TSA. They were brown, scuffed, and old-looking. His hair, a greasy gray and brown, complimented his gray eyes. He looked sick and tired. He always looked angry, so Sheryl was not surprised at the look on his face. The odd thing was this time, he was not angry. Stewart had just scored twenty-five hundred dollars for a few old clothes and some shampoo. He figured the actual worth to be less than three hundred.

Although Stewart didn't see his sister as attractive, she was. Unlike him, she always smiled. Her eyes were bright blue, and her sun-bleached blond hair refused to gray. Her lifestyle with her recently departed husband had them hiking through the desert and up into the nearby mountains. Her skin was gently tanned and void of wrinkles. Her beauty and style offered a natural appearance as she skipped to Stewart to hug him. Her momentum, as she jumped into his arms, had the pair spinning around. He had not been this happy in forever.

She was a candle in his dark life.

"Where is your luggage?" she asked as they walked back to the Jeep.

"It got lost," he said. "It is a good news, bad news thing."

"What do you mean?"

"Well, they gave me a check for twenty-five hundred dollars," he said as he climbed into the passenger seat and tossed his carry-on onto the floor in the rear of the Jeep.

"Really, you had twenty-five hundred dollars' worth in your luggage?"

"No, not really. I figured a little extra for my trouble."

"Stewart! A little extra? What does that mean? You bilked the airline out of what, two thousand dollars?" she said, miffed.

"Can we just get going?"

"Stewart, I'm appalled," she said as she began backing the Jeep up. Then, into gear and off they went.

"Sheryl, you know I never have any good luck, and people always shit on me."

"That does not matter. You gotta be honest, brother!

Karma's gonna get your ass. Just you wait."

"Sis, you look good!"

"Fuck you, changing the subject!" she said as she exited the airport parkway onto the highway.

"Still have a potty mouth, I can see."

"It's a sign of intelligence, asshole."

"Oh, keep telling yourself that."

"Fuck off. How ya been, dickhead."

"Good God, you have not changed a bit."

"I know, a pretty face and a dirty mouth made me a popular cock sucker back in the day."

"Will you stop, please?"

"Nope, it's who I am."

As they got onto a highway headed south, the heat of the road was making Stewart very warm in his hoodie sweatshirt. "Sheryl, could we go to a Goodwill or something so I can pick up some appropriate clothing?"

"Yeah, who the fuck wears a sweatshirt in Arizona in the springtime?"

"Shut up. It was like sixty in Jersey when I left. I was gonna change, but they lost my luggage, remember?" he said with a tone.

"Oh, there's the condescending Stewart tone I was expecting. That only took three minutes."

"I guess I gotta speak like you. Fuck off, bitch!"

"Awesome, now you're speaking in my native tongue," she said as she slapped his shoulder with the back of her hand.

He laughed. "Seriously, Sheryl, I need some clothes."

"Can you wait until we get to the house? Hania had a bunch of clothing. I'm sure most of it will fit you. He was taller, stronger, and fucking gorgeous, but that doesn't matter."

"No bitch, it's hotter than Satan's bathroom out here."

"Satan's bathroom? What the fuck?"

"What? You like Satan's sauna better?"

"Ha, ha, ha, yeah, that's much better. I know a place; hold onto your ball sack, we'll be there in a few," she said, laughing.

She got off the highway onto a side street in what looked like a depressed part of town. She took a route unfamiliar to Stewart in silence. He wondered about his safety until they arrived at a fenced compound. A guard stood watch at the eight-foot-high gate. He recognized Sheryl immediately and waved her in as it opened.

She passed by, and he said, "Good afternoon, Ms. Sheryl."

Stewart was puzzled as she responded, "Hi, Johnny. Sorry, no time to talk, my brother here has an apparel emergency."

He laughed and said, “Hi Stewart, pleased to meet you. Go on in.”

She drove past the chain link gate onto a parking lot. It was unknown to Stewart why a Goodwill would be gated. Etched on his face was disbelief. They pulled up to an unmarked double glass door. A few old-looking cars spotted the parking lot. She threw the Jeep into gear and shut off the engine. Leaving the keys behind, she leapt out of the Jeep and headed towards the door.

Tinting didn’t allow Stewart to see inside, but he followed his sister. Once past the glass, he found himself in what looked like the original “Outdoor Man” store from the show “Last Man Standing.” Few people were in the store on a Monday afternoon. He looked around at merchandise from all eras, new and old. Used clothing hung on racks next to brand-new clothing. He spied the walls and saw rafts, canoes, signs for shoes, baseball, basketball, golf, and many other outdoor activities. On an upper floor, he saw fishing and hunting gear. Sheryl led him to the clearance rack, knowing Stewart was that kind of shopper. He found a few pairs of shorts, some T-shirts, some camo clothing, and then he went to the shoe department. His arms were full, and he had changed his clothes into cooler options of a blue t-shirt and khaki shorts. He grabbed flip-flops and hiking boots. He found a barrel hat, a brown cowboy hat, a big belt buckle and jeans. With arms full, he went to check out.

Sheryl had left him behind in the men’s department as she headed to the back office. “Hi Bill, are you guys having a good Monday?”

“Hey, Sheryl,” Bill responded, getting up from his chair for a hug. He met her in front of his desk, “Sorry to hear about Hania. He was a good man. What brings you in on your day off?”

"I just picked up my brother at the airport, and he needed a few things. Seems his luggage was lost."

"Oh, he's here now, I'd love to meet him."

"Yes, he is. Bill, I must warn you, he's nothing like me. He's out shopping. Something he hates. He probably hates everything in this store. If you insist, I'll introduce you." She turned and headed out onto the showroom floor. When last she saw him, he was at the front, so she figured he hadn't gotten anywhere. She walked up to the front, Bill in tow, and there was Stewart with his arms full, waiting next to the counter to pay. She was stunned.

"Looks like you found a few things."

"I did. This store is fantastic. What is it?"

"I'll tell you later. First, my boss, Bill, wanted to meet you."

"Boss? You didn't tell me you worked here. Hi Bill, I'm Stewart, pleasure to meet you."

Sheryl was thinking, who stole my brother?

"Well, it's a pleasure to meet you too, Stewart. How long have you been in town?"

"I'm not sure. The heat is gonna drive me home sooner than the bad food and the crime, I'm sure. I ain't never seen a store caged like a prison. You must have some nasty ass people living in this Godforsaken neighborhood,"

There he is, Sheryl thought.

Stewart continued, "What's the point in having such a place amongst these despicable people anyway? I bet you gotta have armed guards walk you to your car. What are they? Spicks, Chinks, Niggers, or towel heads?"

"Excuse me, Sheryl and Stewart. I have to get back to work." Bill walked away disgusted.

"What the fuck was that Stewart? You trying to get me canned?"

"What? I was just talking to him. Bill, right? He seems like a nice black fella."

"He is. Shit, Stew, you still got that racist pole up your ass. When you gonna lose it?"

"Racist? I ain't no racist. You know, when a bad guy is a bad guy, he's usually not a white guy."

"Did you fucking hear yourself?"

"What? That's what Granddad always said," Stewart barked.

"Right, and Grandpa was gunned down in a KKK demonstration in the seventies. He was a fucking self-proclaimed white supremacist."

"He never hurt anyone."

"Not that we know."

"He never," Stewart said with a declining voice.

"Shut the hell up, Stew. Let's get outta here."

They walked to the counter, and Sheryl took out a badge or card or something. The clerk scanned it and rang up the goods. "That'll be eighty-two, eighty-eight."

"What the? Only eighty-two..." Stewart said in surprise. "Can we come back here when we have more time?"

"Sure Stew."

Stewart paid the clerk. Took his bags and left.

"Shit Sheryl. I forgot to pay for the clothes I'm wearing. Should we go back in?"

"No, you didn't. I pointed at them and she got 'em."

As they got into the Jeep, she opened a box in the back.

"Put your bags in there."

He followed orders, and she closed the box. She started it up, and off they went to her place.

The change of clothing didn't solve the heat problem for Stewart. As the sun beat down on his greasy head, beads of sweat formed on his nose, forehead, under his man boobs, and his armpits. The seat offered a mesh back, and the wind from traveling cooled his back. The skin behind his knees began to form a stream down his calf into his sock. In only five minutes, he felt as if he was on a rotisserie from hell. The discomfort steamed his attitude and elevated the Stewart-ness that Sheryl expected.

"What is it about this place that you like? It's springtime, and it is sweltering."

"Stewie, it's beautiful once you get used to it."

"Used to it? I don't think the lizard can get used to it. Ever watch those National Geographic shows where they must lift their feet because of the heat? I bet they would move to Jersey if they could. This is fucking miserable."

Sheryl knew the rest of the ride would be the same if she didn't change the subject. "So, how was your flight?"

"Are fucking kiddin' me? It was fucking miserable. Some celebrity bitch held up the plane. Then they sat her smelly ass right next to me. I don't understand what the big deal is. She was good-looking and all, but come fucking on."

"Who was it?"

"I don't know. Some chick named Jennifer."

"Jennifer Lopez?"

"No, another Jennifer."

"What'd she look like?"

"Well, brownish hair with some blonde. Blue eyes, I think. Kind of big tits."

"Jennifer Lawrence?

"No."

"Jennifer Love Hewitt?"

"Who the fuck is that? Who the fuck are any of them?"

"You need to get out more, Stew. Jennifer Garner?"

"No, who?"

"Jenny McCarthy?"

"Oh, no, I know that one. Wow, no, I would'a like that."

"Ya know, we could go on and on with the Jennifers. Do you have any other evidence?"

"Evidence? What is this a crime?"

It's a crime you don't fucking know who the bitch is, she thought.

"She was married to some dude named Brad."

"Are you fucking kidding me? You don't know who Jennifer Anniston is? Haven't you ever watched 'Friends' or 'Horrible Bosses' or a thousand other movies?"

"What's her name?" Stewart asked.

"You are a fucking idiot, Stewart. That was Jennifer Anniston. You rode on a plane next to Jennifer fucking Anniston. Do you realize eighty percent of the male population in this country over the age of forty would give their right nut to be next to her?"

"She was on my left."

"You are a fucking idiot. What did she say?"

"She called me an angry little man. I fell asleep after drinks were given out, and when I woke up, we were landing."

"They put your ass to sleep so you wouldn't bother her, that's fucking precious."

"They let her off, and the bitch gave everyone in front of her and the people next to her a free round trip from the airlines."

"Not you?"

"No, not me. She just smirked as they made the announcement, got up, and walked off the plane. Oh, and she said, 'Buh Bye,' as well. What was that?"

"I think it's an old Saturday Night Live reference. I thought it was Helen Hunt."

"Helen, who?"

"Never mind. What else happened on the flight?"

"Nothing, remember I fell asleep."

"So, tell me, anything else new?"

"No, my life is a plethora of events so exciting they cannot be collected into any sort of list or story. Is your interrogation complete, officer?"

"Is this your style of humor, dumbass?"

"Yeah, I thought it was funny."

"It's not."

"Okay, then what about you? What's new?"

"Well, my husband died. Remember that little cock sucking detail on my life?"

"Um, yeah, that's why I'm here."

"So, why then, haven't you said jack shit about it, you insensitive prick?"

Sheryl turned off the main road onto a dirt road, kicking up dust behind them. Stewart looked around at the vast emptiness of the desert. He wondered how long a person could live or why a person would live in such a nasty place.

"What?" Stewart said.

"Are fucking kidding me? Where the hell have you been, Stewart?"

"Why do you live in such a fucking ugly place?"

"Ugly? You don't have a clue, motherfucker! Answer the question."

"Honestly, Sheryl, I was afraid to ask."

"Afraid? Afraid of what?"

"I didn't want to see you cry. I haven't seen you cry since Mom and Dad died."

"You mean since Mom died."

"Right, since Mom died. That was terrible. I was hoping we could avoid emotion."

"You are a French peach, Stewart. You come here for what? You wanna avoid emotion in what is likely the most emotional time in my life. You selfish fuck."

She slammed on the brakes of the Jeep. The dust followed and engulfed the air, causing Stewart to choke and cough.

"Get out! I mean it, get out."

"What the fuck, Sheryl? We're in the middle of the Goddamned desert. I'll die from this heat."

"No, you won't. You'll die from the cold. Tonight, it'll be fucking freezing, and I'll come back to this road and retrieve your scrawny ass body and bury you in a pit somewhere or leave you for the buzzards to eat. They need to eat shit, too. Now get the fuck out of my Jeep."

"Jesus Christ, Sheryl. You gonna let me die out here?"

"Yes, you motherfucker, then I won't have to deal with your bitching ass anymore. Get the fuck out."

Stewart got out of the Jeep, stunned. Sheryl drove about fifteen feet away, turned left off the road, and began driving in circles around him, covering him with dust. He was bent over, coughing and covering his eyes. After several donuts around him, she took off up the road over a hill and out of sight. What Stewart didn't see was her throwing a bottle of water out the back of the Jeep before she crested the hill.

When the dust settled, he wiped his eyes as best he could. Once his vision had returned, he looked in the direction she had left and began walking. It took him almost half an hour to crest the hill that looked less than a half mile away. The distances in the desert seemed deceiving to him. Before he reached the hill, he found the water. That brought him hope. Hope that his sister would be parked on the side of the road soon, waiting for him. He walked another hour and still no sign of her. The heat from the desert seemed to be diminishing. The sun was inching towards the horizon, and nightfall was soon to be upon him. He had finished the bottle of water hours prior. He began to question his life. Could his sister be so tainted by him to leave him stranded? Could he be so wretched for her to want him dead? Could his life be so worthless to leave in the desert to spoil? Was this his final resting place? He was so thirsty, but he kept walking. It was nearly dark when he found a second bottle of water. At first glance, in the dimming of the day, the water seemed yellow. It was hotter than the first. The plastic had swelled as it was only half full. The sun was nearly gone, so Stewart squinted at the liquid. He wondered if it could be something else. He knew the only way to know for sure was to open it and smell or taste it.

Reluctantly, but with great thirst, he twisted off the cap. He waved his hand above the bottle to push any aroma towards his nose. This motion got no results. He quickly waved the bottle under his nose – nothing! Was it safe? What was in the bottle? Was it water? He was so thirsty. He brought the bottle to his nose without breathing and then pulled it away. Still no aroma, no smell, nothing. He thought, *okay, this must be water.* He put the open bottle to his dry, parched lips and opened them slightly. Raised the bottle, allowing a few drops to enter his mouth, then immediately spit it out. *So, that's what piss tastes like. That's fucking disgusting. Who pisses in a bottle in the fucking desert?* He thought for a minute, then answered himself. *A woman does.* He threw the bottle, and as it flew away, it sprayed him with urine.

The sun had all but disappeared, but with the moon, he could see the road. He felt the temperature dropping as his sweaty clothing charged the cold. It had been three hours of walking. Now dark, he wondered if he would survive. He heard a howl. *Shit, was that a wolf?* Then another. Now, it sounded like a pack of wolves. They were far off to his left. To his right, he saw a faint light and a city ahead of him. Were the city lights his destination? More wolves, now closer. *What would kill me?* His mind wandered to snakes, wolves, the cold, or thirst. He thought about his childhood. He thought about his work. He thought about how wretched a man he must be for his sister to leave him in the desert to die. *Oh, what I'd do to have that bottle of piss.*

The light to his right was closer. The howling grew closer. *Shit, I stepped on something. It's fucking dark. I got nothing. Wait, what's that? Is that a car coming my way? Hurry, these wolves are getting closer. It's a car. No, it's a truck. It's coming closer, I'm saved. Fuck, it turned.*

"No, no, come here. Don't fucking turn."

Wait, it stopped. Lights came on. I need to get there. The fucking wolves are coming. I'll run. I can't run in flip-flops, shit. Whose idea was flip-flops anyway? Ew, I stepped on something again. What's out here? The light. It's still on. The car or truck, what is it? Shit, the light went out. And now the car, where is it? Wait, I see red lights. It's leaving, wait, here I am!

Stewart lost all hope. The light is gone. The car is gone. It's so far away. He kept walking. Wait, what's that? The light came back on. Look, more lights. I'm saved. No. No. Come this way. Shit, they went the other way. Wait, they're turning around. Did they somehow hear me? They're coming and coming fast. Shit! Really fast. I should hide. What if they're drug runners or something? Fuck they're almost here. Do I flag 'em down? Do I run?

Wait, they're slowing down. It's a car, alright. No, it's a Jeep. No. It's my fucking sister.

"Get in the Jeep, asshole," Sheryl demanded

"You left me out here to die," Stewart screamed.

"Shut the fuck up," she blasted back. "You gotta be the slowest walker in the world. No one takes four hours to walk four miles."

"What do you mean four miles?"

"It's only four miles from where I booted your scrawny ass. Here, have some water," she said, handing him a bottle of water.

"Four fucking miles. You left me for fucking dead."

"Right, and when I came out to get the pizza from the delivery guy, I heard coyotes howling and figured you'd shit your pants by now. Then I thought, you're so weak they'll probably eat your ass. I had to come and get you. You're an ass wipe, a dickhead, a motherfucker, but you're still my brother."

"I don't know whether to thank you, Sis, or beat your head in," Stewart said with a nasty tone.

"You better thank me because beating my head in is not an option for you. You should've taken an hour and a half tops to walk those four miles. Fuck there's only a half mile left, and you still ain't there. I've half a mind to make you walk the rest."

"I'm sorry, Sis," He almost whispered.

"What did you say?" She turned to him, surprised.

"I said, I'm sorry, sis," he responded a little louder.

"I thought I heard you say that. Can you repeat it?"

"No, that's it." His tone returned to normal.

"Okay. Well, thank you. I've never heard you say you were sorry."

"Well, the four hours in the desert gave me time to think." It really did. He thought.

They pulled into Sheryl's driveway. A sign outside was not lit up, saying, HANIA, Healing Man."

Once inside, Stewart smelled something that resembled pizza. He walked into a waiting room, there was a receptionist desk with a sliding glass partition. It looked like most doctor's offices. It was not as clean as a regular doctor's office, but the chairs and layout felt like a doctor's. Sheryl led him to a stairwell door. She opened the door and turned on the lights.

"Hit that lights switch on the way in," she said, pointing to his left. He did as commanded, and the lights in the office were extinguished. Sheryl led Stewart down a flight of stairs to a dwelling under the doctor's office. The first room they came to was a living room. It was like most. There was a TV mounted on the wall, a couch, and several chairs. There was a wet bar against the wall, and to his right, she led him to the kitchen. It was a nice kitchen. She had gas appliances, marble countertops, and large cabinets, but it was western looking. Knotty pine wood embraced the marble. The lighting was dim; she turned it up to bright. The can lights filled the kitchen workspace.

"You took so damn long I didn't know what to cook, so I ordered a fucking pizza. Do you still like meat?" she said with wonder in her voice.

"I thought you were a vegetarian?" he said sarcastically.

"Where the hell did you get that idea from? I was married to a fucking doctor, medicine man, Indian fucking hunter. Either I ate meat, or he'd fucking starve me."

"Oh, I stand corrected."

"Good, now sit your corrected ass down, and let's eat some Goddamn pizza."

Stewart grabbed a piece of pizza and went to take a bite.

"Wait, muthafucker!"

"What?" he said, visibly surprised. "Grace! Have you no spirituality?"

"You still pray?" he wondered.

"Seriously, Stewart, you don't even know me." She said with her head twisted on her neck.

Sheryl said a prayer, and it went like this, "Hey God, it's me, Sheryl. My brother is here with me. See him? He's a dickhead. You already know that. Well, he's here to console me, and so far, he's fucking failing. Sorry about the language. You know me, God. You know my mouth, and you know my heart. Right now, what you can hear louder than my words is my fucking stomach growling. We're hungry. So, thank you, God, for this food. Without you, we have nothing. And with nothing, we starve, so thank you for this pizza. Next time God, Stewart is buying, 'cause I can barely afford this shit, uh, Amen."

They both dug into their pizza. After Stewart's first bite, he said, "This ain't bad, but it ain't..." he said chewing.

She interrupted him, finishing the sentence, "It ain't Joe's Pizza on Carmine Street in NYC."

They both laughed. Stewart said, "You remembered, oh, and you remembered NYC, just like Dad used to say."

"How could I forget? Dad would take us into the City for what fucking ever. We always ended up at Joe's. Why do you think Mom never came?"

"Remember, Dad was a dick like me?"

"Yeah, no, he was a sweet man. You just pissed him off like Mom did."

"You didn't know him like I did. You ran away when you were twenty and married this Indian Chief."

"Uh, no, he wasn't an Indian Chief. He was a doctor."

"Right, a doctor."

"Right, a doctor! He studied real American medicine and tribal medicine, and he blended them to make people well. He used herbs more than FDA approved meds, and that's why the tribe loved him so. He kept 'em all healthy. Now he's gone." Sheryl held back her tears.

"What do you think of this pizza anyway?"

"It's pretty good. After four hours in the desert, I was considering eating a Gila monster."

"That's for dinner tomorrow," Sheryl said, smiling.

"Ha, ha!" Stewart said sarcastically.

"No. I have a great recipe for lizard. You'll love it. It tastes..."

In unison, "Like chicken."

They both laughed.

"Seriously, we eat some weird ass shit here, but it tastes awesome," Sheryl said with a gleam in her eye.

They ate the entire pizza and had a few beers. Stewart was beginning to crash. "Hey, you look tired. Wanna shower? Follow me."

He got up and walked with her down an ordinary hallway to a room. "This is your room; you have your own shower. We are on a well and septic out here, so it takes a bit for the water to warm up. Use as much as you want. It feels so soft; you'll love it." She pointed to a door next to the bed.

He walked into the room. Sheryl had put his bags from the store on the bed. It was adorned in a Southwestern motif. He felt like a cowboy in Indian territory. He reached down, thinking the multi-colored blanket would be stiff and scratchy, but it was soft and smooth. He pressed on the bed, and it felt firm. He thought, *I like a firm bed.* He opened the bathroom door to expose the same accompaniments in style. He realized he was in Arizona, and that's the way things are. He started the water and then he heard a knock on his closed door.

"Hey, I forgot to tell you. There's a pillowcase under the sink for your dirty clothes. Put them in there. I'll collect them in a day or two and wash them all before you leave. Which reminds me, did you know when you're leaving?"

"No, I was thinking maybe a week."

"No rush. Just tomorrow, the clinic upstairs will be seeing patients still. They start at about eight a.m. If you are awake, I will introduce you to the staff early. Once they get started, you can't talk to them until the day is done."

"Sheryl, are we... on the reservation?" he asked, looking at the closed door.

Sheryl wondered why she was talking through the door and answered, "Uh, no. They didn't allow him to put his practice on the reservation because he was using American medicine. They funded the practice but wouldn't allow it on the land. It's kind of weird how it all works. They own the practice, the US government funded it, and we, no, he just worked it. He also saw patients who weren't Native Americans. There weren't many, but that was our main source of income. I worked back in that small town at that store. I'll tell you more about the store later." She never did.

Stewart showered and climbed into bed. When he woke up the next morning, he didn't remember any of his dreams, but he could hear the clinic above him. Without natural light, it was easy to sleep late. He felt more rested than he had in as long as he could remember. He went out to the kitchen and found a note.

It read: Stew, I should have told you I have got to work today. I'm on the schedule until four, so I should be home around five. I will call you later, and we can talk about dinner. Love, Sheryl. Ps. Make yourself at home.

Stewart was lost for a Moment. It was as if he'd been dropped into a foreign country where he didn't speak the language. He didn't think he could leave the building. He didn't know where anything was, and he was not all that great at food preparation. Back in New Jersey, he would start his day with a trip to the local bagel deli for breakfast. He would hop on the ferry into the city and get lost in the sea of humanity. Here, he felt like a hostage on an island. He looked around the kitchen. As usual, there were knives, a stove, the microwave, a sink, all the usual kitchen suspects. *Where was the coffee pot? He thought. No coffee pot?*

Okay, then, I need some water. Where are the glasses? He started opening cabinets in search of a vessel to drink water from. To the left of the sink, he found both coffee cups and drinking glasses. *Hmm, coffee cups but no coffee pot. It's gotta be here somewhere.* Eventually, he found the coffee pot, the coffee, and everything he needed to make it. After the coffee was made, he drank it while he microwaved a bagel and cooked two eggs. He left the mess on the counter and in the sink for his sister. He found the TV remote and settled in for a day of channel surfing.

Around noon, his cell phone rang.

"Hello."

"Stewart, did you find something to eat?"

"Who is this?"

"Huh?"

"Who is this?"

"Did you find the TV remote?"

"Are you watching me?" Stewart asked, confused.

"Did you find the coffee pot?"

"Who is this?"

"This is Bill, Sheryl's boss. We're playing a joke on you. Here she is."

"What the hell was that? It was like you guys were watching me," Stewart said in his best New Jersey accent.

"I knew what you'd fucking do. You lazy motherfucker."

"Thanks. That was fun, now what?"

"Well, I thought I was going to get off at four, but a girl called in sick, so I have to work a double. At the front desk up in the clinic is Tricia. She's real nice. Go see her."

"Why?"

"Well, I was thinking maybe you and her could come here, and we could do dinner around six."

"I'm confused. Why?"

"Well, you gotta eat, you don't cook, and she lives in this direction. She'll give you a ride, hang out with you unless you piss her off or you can wander around this deadly hood."

"What's plan B?"

"Plan B? I have no plan B. If you wanna eat, it's plan A. You got a problem, here's the solution. Ride with Tricia or fucking starve. In the meantime, read a book and use your brain. There are tons in Hania's den. I'm going to tell Tricia you're riding with her; she'll be fine with that. Gotta go, see ya later."

Chapter Three: The Book

He felt his usual dejected self-pity moment that was induced by his attitude. He pressed the end of his cell phone and placed it next to him on the leather couch he was sprawled across. The TV was blaring again as he switched to an episode of "Friends." There on the screen was the woman from the airplane. He didn't recognize her at first. Then, in a clear-headed moment, ah, that's her! I can't wait to tell Sheryl about that.

Bored with "Friends," he turned the TV off. He rose from the couch and wandered to the kitchen. Nothing to eat. He went left towards his room, stopped, turned around, and then went back through the kitchen to the hallway opposite his. There were two rooms down his hallway and two rooms down the other hallway. The first room was the master bedroom. He tried the door.

It was locked. She locked the fucking door on me. *"What's she think? She thinks Ima snoop around in her room."* Then he went to the second room. Sheryl called this room Hania's den. It seemed like a library or an office or even both. The opposite wall to the door had a very large landscape photograph of the desert. Each adjacent wall was nothing more than floor-to-ceiling books. In the center of the room was a conference table and, further from the door, a desk. The drawers in the desk were locked, he tried them. Eight comfortable chairs surrounded the oval-shaped oak conference table. The bookshelves matched the wood color and materials. The floor was a Berber crème colored carpet. He felt the texture with his hand and wondered if it was wool. He began on the wall to the right of the door, looking at the books. Some paperbacks filled the shelves, but mostly hardbacks.

He grabbed the first one he came to. Not bothering to look at the title or author, he opened it. He realized the binding was too tight to have been read. He giggled. He had books on the shelf just for appearance. I wonder which one he's actually read. Scanning the wall, he was not impressed. Then he turned around to peer at the other wall. He was looking for the most worn book he could find. He had no idea what could happen next. At the same level as the desk, to the right, was a very thick book. The edges seemed handmade. The leather looked like suede. There was no Dewey Decimal label or title. The top edge was worn as much as the bottom. It was undoubtedly the most intriguing book on the shelf.

Stewart had to look at that one first.

It took two hands to take it off the shelf. Stewart carried it to the conference table and set it down. From the front, he still could not tell the origin or information held inside. There was a Navajo word on the outside *biiji.* He couldn't pronounce it. Inside the book was a combination of Navajo writings and pictures as well as English words. The book seems to be divided into three sections: anthropology, psychology, and medical. There were descriptions of herbs, mixes, chants, and hand tremor methodology. There were indistinguishable documents in the book, extra handwritten pages copied pages, and drawings, yet none of it was professionally printed. It was bound with leather laces and smelled of linseed oil and ragweed. It looked ancient and felt fragile but massive and vital at the same time.

Some of the distinguishable words included recipes to alleviate arthritis, abdominal pain, and chest pain. There were allergies listed with solutions to overcome them. Healthcare maintenance seemed predominant throughout the English descriptions. There was a section on childbirth and pregnancy. There were solutions for ailments ranging from the common cold to upper respiratory and sinus infections. Then, he came to a section mostly in Navajo. Footnotes in English gave him the understanding he was in the psychological section. Unity and harmony were keywords to the Navajo. It seemed when you were in harmony with the universe, your health would be well. If your emotions were in harmony, your health would be well. If your mental health was strong, so too would your physical health. There were chants and prayers to heal the mind, and there were herbs to change the mind. It seemed depression and anxiety in the native American culture are no different than in the rest of the country. The Navajo dealt with conditions both with their own healing properties and with modern American medicine when necessary.

Stewart kept paging until he found a handwritten page titled: "Changing Minds." Some of it was in Navajo, while other parts were in English. The description was in English. It read, "Try this combination only when a patient has extreme conditions the following: Anxiety, depression, hatred, anger, selfishness, self-centeredness, lack of remorse and more. What's the 'and more?' Maybe this could make me happy. Perhaps this would help me make friends and find interest in other people. Nah, it'll never work."

He tried to make out most of the process but got lost on the Navajo. Bored, he got up, looked at more of the bindings, and then gave up on the room. He left the book open to the page of mind changing and went back to the living room. He lay on the couch, turned the TV on, and within minutes, he was asleep.

Chapter Four: Dinner for Three

Stewart awoke to the phone ringing and someone knocking at the same time. He answered and could hear Sheryl's voice, "No, he hasn't answered his – oh,

Stewart Tricia is at the door. Can you let her in?"

"I was sleeping," he said groggily.

Annoyed, she said, "Lucky you. You need to get going. I only have an hour for dinner, and you guys need to be here."

"Okay, okay. Bye," he responded, equally annoyed.

"Wait!" she spoke.

Click. He was gone.

Stewart walked up the stairs to greet Tricia. It was a good thing he was holding onto the handrail as she was beautiful to him. She had curly multicolored hair, brown eyes, and a party smile.

"Come on, dude, let's get this party goin'," she said with a festive smile.

She didn't look her age or act it either. She grabbed him by the hand and dragged him out the front door. She threw him out and turned around to lock up. She was full of energy. He feared he would not be able to keep up.

As if she read his mind, "Don't worry, Stewie baby. No one keeps up with me. Will you dance with me? Can you be my heartthrob?"

Stewart watched in amazement as she controlled the world right then and there.

"Come on, Stewie, let's go," she said as she danced to a late-model Mustang convertible. With a beep, the doors were open, and before he knew it, the ragtop was down, and they were headed down the highway. He didn't complain about the heat. He kept his eyes forward. She rambled on about this or that, but he couldn't pay attention. His mind was on the mental vision of watching her dance over to the 'Stang.

Swaying hips, twisting, turning, and bouncing around. She left an indelible mark on his head. He sat thinking and savoring the images. This was new for Stewart.

She drove fast. He could hear the highway whine. The wind was strong, so when they finally stopped, his face was numb. She hopped out of the Mustang at the restaurant and said, "Let's go, city boy, time to fress."

Fress? What's that? He didn't ask. He was afraid. She ran around the car up next to him and grabbed his arm. Arm in arm, they approached the door. She stopped and waited. He stopped. Oh shit, I'm supposed to get the door! His hesitation was too long; she opened the door herself un-lathered. She bounced inside to the hostess stand and stopped.

The hostess looked up from the floor plan and

Stewart said, "Three for dinner, please."

"Follow me."

The hostess led them to a round corner table. It was seating for six. Tricia slid onto the booth like bench around to the middle. Stewart was confused until Tricia patted on the seat next to her. He slid in next to her.

The hostess asked, "Betsy is your server tonight; she'll be right with you. Can I get you guys something from the bar?"

Tricia said, "I'll have an Ultra."

Stewart answered, "Make that two."

What's an Ultra, he wondered.

Stewart looked around the place. It was dark with soft music playing, and most of the tables looked like the table they were at; round tables for six, with only a couple at the table. White linens and black napkins were at each place setting. Goblets sat on the tables. A small crystal chandelier hung over every table. He thought this place would fit in a mafia movie, but it doesn't fit the Southwest.

Betsy brought two beer bottles on a tray with two frosted pilsners. She poured the first one and placed it in front of Tricia, then she poured the second one and placed it in front of Stewart. *Shit, an Ultra is a beer.* Stewart was never a beer drinker. He hated beer. He picked up the glass and placed it on his bottom lip.

"Wait," Tricia said with a misunderstood come-and-get-me smile, "Toast to new friends!"

Then they tapped glasses, and he tried to take a drink. One sip made his face compress. Tricia saw it and laughed inside.

Then she said, "You didn't know an Ultra was a Michelob Ultra, did you?"

"No. I had no idea,"

"You don't like beer, do you?"

"No. Not really," he said with a grimace on his face.

"That's okay, I'll drink it. Do you want something else?" Tricia offered.

Betsy was still standing in front of them, "Sir, I can get you something else, that is, if you'd like?"

"Well, yes, I'll have gin and tonic with a twist."

"Do you have a preference for gin?" Betsy asked

"No, your house gin will do fine."

She thought, *Ew!* Then she said, "Ýessir, right away." She left, taking the beer with her.

Stewart looked down in embarrassment. Tricia poked him and said, "It was cute. You're ordering the same thing as me, like we're on a date or something."

Now he was really embarrassed and responded, "Yeah, that was funny, wasn't it."

"No, it was cute," she said with that same misunderstood come and get me look.

"I haven't heard that in forever."

"Thanks. When do you think Sheryl will be here?"

"Oh, she's not coming."

"Whaaaa!"

"No, she can't get away for dinner, never does. It's just you and me, baby."

"You mean like a date?"

"Ha, ha, ha, yeah, like a date. Sorry, yeah, a date. Stewart, please don't get the wrong impression. I'm your sister's best friend. I'm married, and I've been married for twenty-seven years, but to three different men. Ha, ha, ha, no, just kiddin'. Same guy, my grade school sweetheart. He'll be here any moment."

Stewart hated meeting new people. It brought great anxiety. He especially hated meeting men married to the woman he was sitting next to. He said, "Oh great, I can't wait to meet him."

"Maybe someday. He's not coming. You ever heard of Area 51?" she quipped back.

"Yeah. Does he work there?" he said with some disappointment.

"No. But he's heard of it," she responded, looking down at the menu cover on the table.

Betsy arrived with Stewart's drink as he was laughing at Tricia's last statement.

"Here you are, sir. Have you made up your minds for dinner, or would you like a shrimp cocktail to start off? I must tell you, we have colossal Gulf shrimp flown in daily for our world-famous shrimp cocktail. They're the best."

Tricia responded, "That sounds great, doesn't it, Stewie?"

"Maybe if I wasn't allergic to shellfish," he said, hoping she wouldn't order it.

Tricia then said, "How about spinach, artichoke dip, and pitas?"

"Oh, yes, that's one of my favorites," Stewart answered with a smile.

Betsy left, and the couple picked up their menus. Stewart opened the appetizers and found the shrimp cocktails were forty-five dollars each. The spinach artichoke dip was twenty-seven. Nacho chips and queso cheese were fifteen. Then he looked at the rest of the menu and began tabulating the dinner. In his mind, he had calculated a possible four-hundred-dollar meal. He scanned the menu for the cheapest thing. It was a cheeseburger and fries. Thirty-two dollars for a cheeseburger and fries. *It better be the best ever!*

"I'm thinking cheeseburger and fries. What are you thinking?"

"Oh, no, you have to try the filet. It is a melt-in-your-mouth steak. You can cut it with a fork, and it's just fantastic," she lavished while licking her lips seductively.

It should be at eighty-seven dollars ala-cart.

"You go ahead and get that; I think I'll stick with the burger."

Betsy returned and took their order, "What is your pleasure, ma'am?"

"I'll have the twelve-ounce filet," she said with a glimmer in her eye.

"Good choice. What temperature do you like?" Betsy asked graciously.

"Medium rare. I'd like a loaded baked potato and asparagus," Tricia continued.

"Sounds terrific. Would you care for a garden salad or a Caesar salad to go with dinner?"

"Oh yes, I almost forgot, a Caesar with extra croutons," Tricia concluded.

"Perfect, and you, sir?"

"I'll have the cheeseburger."

"Oh, I'm so sorry, that's not on our menu any longer."

"Is there something else?"

"Hold on, let me look. I had my heart set on a thirty-two-dollar cheeseburger, not a hundred-dollar steak.

Did I say that out loud?"

"Um, yes, you did," Betsy said.

"Don't worry, Stewart, this is on me," Tricia offered.

"No. Oh really? Oh, I guess I'll have the Chilean Sea Bass, rice, and vegetable medley with the Garden Salad and Ranch dressing," Stewart said with excitement.

Betsy nodded and walked away.

Tricia said, "It feels good to get what you want, doesn't it, Stewart?"

Stewart raised his glass and toasted, "To new friends. And, yes, it does. Thank you."

She smiled as if knowing something, "No. Thank you."

Stewart looked at her, puzzled.

She said, "I'm just glad to make a new friend."

"Oh yeah, me too," he said, thinking, this is going to cost her big.

Betsy arrived with the dip and pita wedges.

"Wow, this is really good," Stewart said.

"Yeah, this place is the best. Were you close with your sister when you were younger?"

"We were. We're only eighteen months apart, so our childhood was a lot of fun," he responded, chewing.

"Funny, she hasn't ever mentioned that. What kinds of things did you guys do?" Tricia asked.

"You know, the regular kid stuff. We played in the woods back home, swam in the creek, and we would swing on the rope swing."

"You swam in the creek? How deep was the creek?"

"There were spots where it was really deep, ten or fifteen feet, I don't know," he answered, wondering why she had asked.

"Hmm, Sheryl can't swim."

"What. Yes, she can," he exclaimed.

"No, I have a pool, and she'd stay in the shallow end. She's deathly afraid of water."

"No. No, not Sheryl," he insisted.

"Scout's honor," she said, holding up three fingers.

"I was a scout, were you?" he asked with a sarcastic glare.

"No, my brother was. He's not like you, sorry, was not like you."

"Was? I'm sorry," he said, feeling ashamed.

"You honestly don't know, do you?" Tricia asked.

Stewart was attacking the dip, but then he stopped.

"I don't know what?" he said as he finished chewing.

He paid full attention to her as she spoke.

"My brother was your sister's husband. You didn't come to their wedding. You and your parents haven't recognized my brother for a long time. I remember your father calling him a savage, and your mother said nothing. It killed Sheryl, so when you said you were coming to visit her for the first time since they met, well, you can imagine what she thought. Why do you think she left you in the desert yesterday? I told her to leave you out there to die. Now that I've met you, I can't see the person I thought you were. Not yet, anyway. Oh, I'm sorry, I speak my mind. I shouldn't have said anything."

All of a sudden, the dip tasted terrible.

Betsy arrived with the salads and placed them in front of each of them. Stewart had lost his appetite.

Tricia started eating her salad.

She turned to him and said, "Listen, I have had this pent-up inside of me for years and years. I have needed to say it. Don't let what happened back then affect the future. Let's forgive and forget and enjoy this meal."

Stewart felt better and began eating. The ranch dressing was the best he'd ever had. Then, the rest of the meal arrived. His fish was phenomenal, as were the vegetables. Stewart was thinking it was the best meal he had ever had. During the meal, the conversation continued lightly. More drinks were brought to the table. The Ultra was affecting her head, and the gin was getting to Stewart as well. They were laughing and telling stories. The food was all but gone when Tricia changed the mood.

"You know, my brother truly loved your sister. He was a very good man. They were great together. Their love was unlike anything I had ever seen anywhere. Do you even know how he died?"

"No, I haven't asked," Stewart admitted.

"What? You don't even care about how he died!" Tricia exclaimed.

"I didn't say that," he barked back.

"Words not said don't change the implication of the silence."

"What do you mean?" he genuinely asked.

"When a person doesn't ask such an important question, it implies they don't care to know," she said with a slightly raised voice.

"I didn't want to upset Sheryl."

Tricia cried out, "Are you fucking kidding me? Ask your fucking sister. Jesus Christ, man, grow some balls. I'm sorry. I loved my brother and my sister-in-law. They constantly ached from the lost love from you and your parents. Now, you don't even ask. Ask her!"

"Okay, okay, calm down," he said, patting his hands in the air in front of her. He was more concerned about causing a scene than her emotions.

She looked him right in the eyes, raised her voice, and then said, "You are right. I should calm down. I think I should be calm. Maybe I should take a nap!"

"Please lower your voice."

She looked around, and people were staring at her, "Yes, yes. I'm sorry. I should. Yes, let's have dessert and calm down."

She began waving her hand above her head to get Betsy's attention, and Betsy rushed right over. "May I help you, Ma'am?"

"Yes, we'd like dessert."

She ran through the dessert choices, and Tricia ordered a chocolate suicide cake and a double Baily's Irish Cream. Stewart ordered decaf coffee. Then, the conversation turned calm. Betsy returned almost immediately with the cake, and it was gone before they knew it. Stewart had not had such a fabulous meal since, well, ever. He was so grateful that she was buying it.

"Well, Stewart, that was terrific. And you should know that this is Phoenix's finest restaurant. I'm so glad your sister suggested it."

"Me, too. Thank you very much. I'm fully impressed. This was amazing, and despite the rocky conversation early on, it has been a delight."

Betsy brought the bill and placed it in front of Stewart. He slid it over to Tricia, and she reached down for her purse. She opened it up and gasped.

Stewart said, "What's wrong?"

"Oh, my, Stewart, I'm so sorry, it seems I left my credit card at home. I do that so often. All I have is like forty dollars, and well, I need gas in my car to get home and back to work tomorrow. I'm sorry, I can't help out with the bill."

Stewart was stunned yet again. This time, with a check of more than three hundred and fifty dollars. With the tip, he thought, it would be over four hundred dollars. It was.

Tricia sat back, satisfied by the night. She had gotten her due and voiced her best friend's pain. The conversation was nil. Stewart sat ruminating over the bill and how he was hornswoggled. *It was a good thing he had gotten the luggage money,* he thought.

Within minutes, Sheryl showed up, and she slid in next to Tricia, "What'd I miss?"

Stewart answered with an elevating voice. "Well, earlier, she read me the riot act for not coming to your wedding, for not asking you how Hania died, for not being involved in your life, for not visiting earlier, for not knowing who she is, and that was just the beginning. Am I really that terrible?"

"Sheryl, before you answer, let me out. I've done my part," Tricia said.

Sarcastically, Sheryl responded, "Really? You gonna abandon me now?"

Tricia snapped back, annoyed with Stewart and taking it out on Sheryl. "Well, yeah, you're a big girl. You've been a big girl most of my life. You wear big girl pants; put 'em on. Now, will you excuse me, please?"

She started to slide Sheryl's way, but Sheryl didn't move. So, she tried to slide Stewart's way, and he didn't move either. She realized she was stuck, so she crossed her arms and sat back. "If we're gonna do this, Ima need another drink."

Just then, Betsy showed up. "Oh, a late arrival. Can I get you something to drink or a menu?"

Sheryl answered, "Give us another round. I'll have a shot of Tequila and an Ultra."

"Sounds good! Give me a shot, too." Tricia said.

"Nothing for me," Stewart said, "Wait, maybe water with lemon."

"Fine, water with lemon, two Ultras, two shots of Tequila, any brand?" Betsy asked.

"Any brand as long as it's Patron," Sheryl said.

"Silver?" Betsy asked.

"Silver sounds great," Sheryl responded. Then she went back to Stewart and Tricia, "Should we go through this point by point?"

Stewart quickly began talking, "No, Sis. Look, I'm a product of my environment. You know Dad was a total bigot, and so am I. You know, Mom was assaulted by more men of varying ethnicities than most women encounter, which made her who she was. You escaped that world over thirty years ago. I stayed back and took care of them."

"Fuck that. You sponged off them and even lived in their house, where I got shit from them for the last thirty years. All I got was forgotten. Even when I came to

Mom's funeral, you and Dad treated me like an outsider. Then, when Dad died and I came to visit, you were not very consoling. You acted like I had no claim to him, Mom, or you. You treated me like the savage that you guys called my late husband. Now you expect to pop into my life, and what? You want me to be 'Sis' again. What the fuck is that? You and that attorney, what the fuck was her name, Lisa Barnes? Yeah, she was the root of all evil, and you played right along with her. Or did you? Maybe you are as evil as her, or maybe she's not evil, and it's just you. One thing I will say about you is you have been like this since you went to that stinking college. What the fuck happened to you there?" Sheryl stopped talking and took a deep breath, looked to her side and then down.

Stewart waited. She stopped, and he began speaking, "Oh, is it my turn? Lisa Barnes was an angel sent from God, so it must have been me. I admit I haven't been the best brother or a decent person. I've been known to take advantage of situations and people, but I always considered it a defense. Since coming here, I'm beginning to realize how much I hate myself. You have opened my eyes, both of you."

Tricia jumped in loudly, "Bullshit! You're just saying that to her so that you can save face. Sheryl is a genuinely great person with a heart of gold. When she escaped the clutches of New Jersey and came here, her real self-emerged. You, on the other hand, are a spoiled rotten little man."

Stewart made a mean face at Tricia, squinting his eyes, and then barked at her, "Oh, thanks for that, Captain Obvious. Now clammer down. This is between me and my sis."

Tricia was visibly upset when she retorted, "Clammer? What the hell does that mean? I asked to leave, so with me here, I will chime in whenever I fucking feel like it. Time for more tequila. Where the fuck is Betsy Wetsy?"

"Girl, we all think you've had too much. I'm just getting started, so I think I'll have another," Sheryl said, finishing her Ultra and waving in the air and catching Betsy's attention from afar. In a loud voice, "Can you bring me another shot and another Ultra?"

Everyone in the restaurant heard Sheryl. Betsy went to the table directly.

Betsy asked, "Anyone else?"

"I need more water," Stewart ordered with attitude.

Tricia raised her hand, but Betsy ignored her,

"Coolio, be right back."

Sheryl continued, "You know, Stew, this has been boiling inside of me for years. Maybe you don't deserve this because you seem to be trying to be a decent guy right now. I've had decades of hurt; shit piles of hurt that haven't fucking been dealt with. One thing is I. Never. Got to. Tell Mom or Dad how. I. Felt. I never got to say goodbye. To, either. Of them. I never got the love you got even though you treated them like a piece of shit compared to me. When Dad lost his mind and forgot the present, I could have had some. Of his love. I could have been present for him to ease his pain and fuck, yours too. You didn't let me do that. Who the fuck were you not to let me do that?"

The emotion of the release pushed her from anger to tears. Tricia put her arm around her, and Sheryl buried her head on the table. Tricia stroked her head as she cried. Stewart sat in stunned silence.

"Maybe now it's time to go," Tricia said.

"I think you're right," Stewart agreed.

Sheryl sat up, "No. It's not time yet. I'm just getting started. Can you explain yourself?"

"No, I cannot."

"You had no argument?" Sheryl questioned, throwing her arms up in the air.

"None."

"You leave me empty then?"

"Why do you say that?"

"Think about it, Stewart. For years, I've wondered. For fucks sake, Dad died over a year ago. Before that, I wondered what the motivation for hate was. I wondered what the fuck I did to you, to him, and to Mom. I've racked my brain trying to figure it out. The only thing I can think of is that I fell in love with an amazing man. This man was someone who truly loved me. This man would have done anything for me and the people he loved. Did you know what this man did? He died for his tribe. You haven't fucking asked me how he died. I'm not sure why. Right now, I don't care because I'm going to tell you. My husband died a hero."

"No, Sheryl, he doesn't deserve the story, your brother is an ass," Tricia said.

"Maybe, but in my husband's honor, I will tell it."

"Go ahead then," Tricia said.

"First. It was over a month ago. Why are you just now coming to Arizona? Never mind, that's not important now. Just sit back and shut up until I'm finished.

"One night, we were in the clinic when a group of bikers stopped in front. One of them came in and asked if the doctor could help a comrade who was injured. The man had been stabbed and was losing a lot of blood. I went out with Hania, saw the injury, and ran back in to get gauze to stop the bleeding. As I was coming out, they were helping the man off his bike. I handed Hania the gauze. There were about twelve of them. Hania told one of the guys to hold the gauze on the wound and bring him inside. I heard one of the guys tell another,

"'If Kit dies, we're going to have to kill everyone here.' The biker's name was Kit. He had long blond and gray hair and looked to be about sixty. He was skinny, really skinny, with lots of tattoos, not that that's a problem. We run into that all the time. His tattoos were prison tats. He had three teardrops under his right eye and six hash marks on his left bicep. He was covered in skulls and crossbones, as were most of the rest of them. Like the rest of them, he was wearing a dirty white t-shirt, blue jeans, biker boots, and a matching vest. Most of them wore some kind of head dressing like a hat or bandanna. They smelled of road, sweat, whiskey, and cigarettes. We often helped bikers in need, but never a group like this.

"Hania worked on him for a few hours and even gave him blood we had stored. It didn't help. He was too far gone. He died.

"They blamed Hania. They started calling him names, wielding knives, and threatening him. It had never been so tense. One of them grabbed me, put a knife to my throat, and told Hania it was him or me. Hania was defenseless. Just then, three of his tribe came in. I suppose sensing the danger, they showed up. There were five of us and eleven of them. The tribe had guns pulled, so it looked like it was going to end there. The leader of the biker clan calmed his men down, and they agreed to leave with no one being hurt. So, they filed out to their bikes. Leaving Kit's behind. They told us to keep it for payment. It was strange.

They went from killing us to paying us with the bike. It wasn't over. I was standing in the doorway when the shooting started. Hania was in front of me. He was the first hit. He fell on top of me, covering me. I couldn't see very much; I just heard shots. Lots of shooting. It was a massacre.

"In the end, there were three dead bikers, Hania, and all the guys who came to his rescue. I think they thought I was dead, too, because I acted dead and was covered in Hania's blood. I was fucking covered in my husband's blood. His dead, lifeless body on top of mine, I could barely breathe, and certain someone would still shoot me. Brothers Ahiga and Atsa and their friend,

"Bidzii are all dead on the ground. The Fighter, the Eagle, and the Strong One, murdered by rouge bikers. I lay there hoping Hania was still alive. My arms were trapped under his weight. I wiggled one free to check his pulse. It was no use. I used that free arm to push his body off me. At that point, I didn't know what to do. I didn't know who to call. That part isn't important. You know the story. The tribe has been great to me even though I'm an outsider."

"I think that's our cue to leave," Stewart said, getting up.

"Are you that fucking insensitive? Did you hear a word your sister said? Do you have no comment?"

"I do have a comment," he said. "That was the worst story I've ever heard. I'm beyond the ability to make conversation as my conscious left me midway through. I was taken to the scene, saw the blood, heard the shots, and felt the pain. How can anyone give justice to a story like that with a comment? Now, if you don't mind, I'd like to take my sister home. I believe I have some time and love to make up." He slid out of the booth. Sheryl did the same, and then Tricia followed. Tricia stumbled when she got to her feet, so Stewart helped her to her car and put her in her passenger seat.

Sheryl jumped into the Jeep and said, “Follow me. We’ll get her drunk ass home.”

Chapter Five: The Next Day, A Rekindling

Deep in a cave, it is hard to see light. The same goes for Sheryl's house. Stewart had no sense of time when he woke up the next day. Without ambient sunlight, everything in the world seems to pass on by. Stewart could sleep the day away and not even know it.

Sheryl would not allow that, though. She set the alarm for six in the morning, woke up, and showered. She went to Stewart's room around seven, woke him, and told him breakfast would be ready in a half-hour. Stewart got up, showered, and was at the table at seven-thirty. He was still groggy, a little hungover, and certainly his crabby self. Sheryl had a cup of coffee poured in front of him as he sat down.

He added cream and sugar, stirred, sipped, and said, "Ahhhh!"

Sheryl returned to the stove, then back to him, delivering two eggs over medium, three pancakes, and three crisp strips of bacon, just the way he liked it.

"How did you know I would like this breakfast?"

"I figured everyone does," she replied with a sideways grin.

"But the eggs are perfect," he said, smiling.

"That's how I like 'em. I remember Dad liked 'em that way, and you're basically him."

"I'm not sure if that's a compliment."

"It's really not. I loved the man for most of my formative years; I wanted his love for most of my adult years. So, yeah, I knew what he liked; I remembered," she looked down in sadness.

"I'd like you to consider something, Sheryl. I'm going to ask you to hold your comments until I'm finished. Can you do that?" Stewart asked with a stern but caring tone.

"Yes, I can. Go ahead."

"No. Wait. I'm serious. I have been giving this a lot of thought, and even though my head is full of gin, I think I can get it straight. I just asked you not to comment. Let me finish."

"I said, go ahead!"

"So, Mom and Dad were a product of their environment. They were brought up by people of a certain time period. Their ideals, influences, and lifestyles were representative of that time period and the generation before them. You and I made a choice in life to either follow their logic, lifestyle, and environment or change. You had the ability to change. I didn't. Mom was sick when you left to marry Hania. She didn't tell anyone, not even Dad. The MS took a long time to affect her day-to-day activities, and she hid it from us all. Dad was working for the transit. Then I started working for Price. A few years after I started at Price, Mom became an invalid and was unable to work. Dad quit his job to care for her. I became the sole breadwinner in the family. I didn't get the life and freedom you got. Yes, Price paid me well, but it went to Mom's medical bills, the mortgage, food, and all the rest. I never dated. I never had a social life. I never had friends. I worked, came home, and took over for Dad. Yes, he was angry. It seemed to him, God stole the best years of his wife's life and his, too. He was sad. He was weakened. He was a bigot, as he saw others who didn't work as hard as him, have more on the tit of the government.

"He was a tiger with stripes. Those stripes were deep. They were not on the surface and couldn't be washed away by the changes in society. He had seen too much injustice allegedly directed at him and Mom. They say there's no such thing as racism against white people, that only white people are racists. You know that's bullshit. After Mom died, Dad tried to get his job back at the authority. By then, they had filled all the positions with blacks and Puerto Ricans, and there weren't jobs there for white people. His friends there were laid off to be replaced by niggers and spicks. I know, I know, you hate that language, but understand where he came from. Maybe that wasn't true; maybe it was. I have no idea, but Dad believed it. Since he said it every day, it was hard for me to fight. I believed it.

"I watched the culture of Price change. I watched the diversity destroy what we had there. I watched as all the traditions of the company went away to be replaced with sensitivity shit. I couldn't change Mom, Dad, or myself. I watched as the city we lived in diversified into a rat hole. I watched as crime, gangs, murder, and robberies got out of control, and the people blamed the police. What the fuck was that? The same people trying to uphold the law and protect law-abiding citizens were vilified and became the enemy of the people. Now, Sis, you cannot change the stripes on a tiger when you keep painting them darker with reasons to hate. Yes, we had reasons to hate. We lost our neighborhoods. We lost our schools. We lost our churches. We lost our grocery stores. We lost, and no one cared. Pizza places were being replaced by Middle Eastern establishments, and the old folks who could, fled. Home values dropped like a rock, and Dad couldn't sell to move out. We were stuck in a rapidly diminishing neighborhood, and it was all for the sake of diversity. In an effort to be nice, they destroyed the city. I never got it. Maybe I will someday.

"When Great Grandma and Grandpa came to this country, they had to work and fight to get anything, fuck, everything. Today, someone sneaks in and steals an identity, and the government pays them more than Dad got for his retirement. He got seven-hundred dollars a month, and because we lived in the same household, that was it. The wetbacks next door don't work. They have two brand-new cars, the best new phones, and the best clothing. Dad wore rags until he died. So, yes, I'm angry. I'm angry at the establishment and the political bullshit that ruined our community. So, when you left and married Hania, it was another loss for Mom and Dad. I don't know where he got that idea, but Dad always called 'em savages. He always said a savage stole his daughter. Again, his words, not mine. For me, I lost my sister. I know I could have reached out to you, but then you'd ask me about Mom and Dad. They would've found out, and then it would have caused strife amongst us all. I could not betray them. They counted on both of us. You chose this, and I chose them." Tears fell on her face as he was speaking. He saw them but continued stabbing her with his words while she bled tears the whole time. To her, it was as if he had no feelings.

"Is that it? Are you finished? I'm not sure if I should tell you to leave and never come back or if I should hug you for your honesty."

"If there's nothing else in my life, I'm always honest. It is almost never popular, but I'm honest. I'm sorry if I hurt you in what I said. That was not the point. I needed to explain."

"I understand. I guess I need to hug you, come here."

They hugged. Holding each other, Stewart began to cry. He was inaudibly sobbing and mumbling. The hug went on for what seemed like forever until they both stopped crying.

Then Stewart said, "Can you help me?"

"What do you need?" she choked out the words, paused, and continued, "I mean, sure, what do you need?"

"I was looking at the books in Hania's office and found his medicine man guide. I found something that might help me be a better brother and a better person and maybe even improve my life. I was wondering if you could administer it on or for me."

"What is it?"

"It's a behavior-changing process. I think it'll improve my temperament. I think it might change the way I see people and things."

"Stewart, I'm not a medicine man. I'm not allowed to use the book."

"Well, okay then, you're stuck with the asshole brother that I am."

"Putting it that way. Let's see what we can do. Show me."

Stewart took Sheryl into Hania's room, and she sat in his chair. It was the first time she had sat in his chair since he had died. She could feel his spirit, his emotion, and his love. The lump in her throat grew to choke her until she burst into tears. It was the first real explosion of emotion over her husband's death. She had kept it together. Now, her wailing was uncontrollable, and Stewart did not know what to do. He stood next to her and stroked her head. He said nothing until he remembered hearing someone say, "There, there." So, he repeated it over and over until her wailing turned to sobbing, which turned to sniffling, which turned to silence. He felt that his words did something. He was wrong; her tears ran their course.

In front of her was a box of facial tissues, so she wiped her tears away and blew her nose. Once her eyes returned to focus, she looked at the nearly saturated page before her. It gave her the step-by-step process for changing Stewart's personality. She was able to discern some of the Navajo words and so she prepared a shopping list. She hoped it was right.

"Wanna go fucking shopping?" she asked with less enthusiasm than he had hoped.

"Yeah, Sis, let's do this," Stewart said enthusiastically, filling in the gap of what she had left.

The next day, she mixed the ingredients and began the process as per the instructions. She administered peyote to him, he ingested it, and she began to say prayer and chant. His mind began to become altered as he started to feel high and dizzy, and then he laid down on the nearby couch and fell asleep. Many hours later, he woke up.

Stewart stumbled to the bathroom, washed his face, brushed his teeth, and stumbled back into the main living quarters. Sheryl was nowhere to be found. He tried her room, and well, there she was, sleeping. He looked at the clock beside her bed, and it said eleven. He thought it was eleven in the morning since he had fallen asleep around seven in the evening on what he thought was the day before. He discovered later that it was eleven in the evening the next day.

Stewart left his sister's room and proceeded out to the living room; he found a spot to sit on the couch where he had just been asleep, and he turned on the television. Instantly bored, noticed it was quiet on the main level where the clinic operated. Stewart went over to the stairs to listen for voices and wondered where everyone was at eleven in the morning. Quietly, he crept up the stairs and opened the door. It was dark in the office. At the front door, it was the dark of night. Astonished, Stewart thought for a second. How long was I asleep? Did I? Could I have slept twenty-eight hours? He had never slept so long in all his life. He felt rested, energetic, and didn't feel stressed or angry. How did that work? He went back inside to the living quarters and sat in front of the TV and watched hours of reruns of "Friends" until Sheryl woke up the next day.

Sheryl woke up at about eight in the morning when she heard the workers rustling about in the clinic above, and she could no longer sleep. She dressed, washed her face, brushed her teeth and hair, and then went out to the kitchen, where Stewart was making breakfast. She immediately smelled frying bacon. Sheryl was shocked as she had never seen her brother cooking breakfast.

"Are you hungry, Sis? You still like your eggs like I do? Ima make bagel sandwiches, want one?"

"Who are you? I guess the sleep did you good. When did you wake up?"

"Breakfast?" Stewart offered.

"Oh yeah, thanks, that's nice," she said with a smile as she sat at the table.

Stewart began explaining his night, "I woke up around eleven last night. Ya know that 'Friends' show is pretty good."

She giggled to herself, "Yeah, it is. How are you feeling?"

"I feel great. Seriously, whatever you did, it healed me!" he said with a newfound attitude.

"Cool. Maybe it has. I'm not sure it works like that, so I think we should do it a few more times. The book says five days in a row at the minimum," she answered with some authority.

"Oh really? I was thinking about heading home tomorrow. I guess I can stay. I have like a year and a half of PTO."

"PTO, what's that?" she asked genuinely.

"Paid time off," he answered without condemnation.

"Oh, wow, really?"

"Yeah, I haven't had a vacation or sick leave in nine years," he boasted.

"Does that really add up to a year and a half?"

"No, I was exaggerating," he answered, smiling. Changing his tone to thoughtful, "I toasted the bagel. Is that alright?"

"That's fine. How did? Where did? Bagel? Where did you get bagels? And when?"

"I got them this morning when I went out for eggs and bacon. Sammy's bagel shop is a few miles away. I left around seven, found a bagel place, and went to a food mart," he said.

"How did you find that?"

"I Googled it, got the address, and drove there," he replied.

"You drove there? How?"

"I borrowed your Jeep. Oops, was that okay?"

"Who are you?"

"What do you mean?" Stewart asked.

"Stewart, I think this stuff is working," she said in surprise. "You wouldn't have ever gone out of your way for me," she continued with a huge smile.

"I hope it lasts. I would like to be a nice guy for a change. You know that saying, nice guys finish last?"

"Uh-huh."

"Well, there's this gal at work who is always telling me that she'd like to find a nice guy like Brian at work. He's married. I hope to become more like Brian."

"There's a gal?"

"Uh-huh, her name is Emily. She's a few years younger than me. In my opinion, she's the best-looking gal at the office. She talks with a lisp, and I think it's cute. A lot of the guys make fun of her, so I play along, and I do it too. I don't want to, but I cannot let on that I like her."

"No wonder she's hoping to find a nice guy. Guys have been mean to her because of her lisp. Some people are so rude when it comes to disabilities," she said as if admonishing his own behavior.

"Disability? What? Until she opens her mouth, no one says anything about her. She doesn't say much. She's very quiet. I think she's very insecure. What I am saying is when it comes to women, I'm the insecure one. You know, I haven't had a date since high school, and that was a mess. I suppose that's what set it off," he spoke with embarrassment.

"Set it off? What do you mean?"

"Oh, nothing," he replied, wishing he hadn't said it.

"Uh-huh, you ain't getting away with that. Come on, what do you mean?" she said, insisting. She got up from the table and went into the kitchen.

"Well, I went out with this girl. She was a sophomore, and I was a junior. I had gone out with her a few times when, shit this is embarrassing," he said looking away then back.

"Come on, Stewie, you gotta tell me now," insisting further.

"Eggs are ready, let's eat," he said, avoiding the question.

They brought their plates to the table and sat. They ate and continued the conversation.

"I haven't told anyone this. I'm embarrassed. Her name was Ashley, she was blonde with blue eyes, and she was on the girls' soccer team. She was really fit. I heard a great swimmer. We went to a movie on the first date. Nothing happened. I didn't even touch her. The next date, yeah, I got the gumption up for a second date. We had pizza at Joe's, then another movie. She held my hand in the movie. I kissed her goodnight. I felt so awkward. I was terrible. So, on the third date, we went to a party. Some of the guys from her class came over to me and said if I didn't get at least a blowjob, I was a loser pussy. I guess I was a loser pussy. I thought she was a good girl, so I broke up with her. I never trusted a girl again."

"Really, that's it? You were embarrassed about that?" she said, squinting at him.

"I suppose, now, that seems like nothing," he said, looking down.

"I'm not sure why you never trusted a girl again."

"Me either," he said, knowing why.

Sheryl didn't dig any deeper. She knew her brother had put everything into trying to date that girl in high school. He didn't encounter another girl or woman to replace the girl he had such affection for. Now, Stewart was interested in Emily.

"You should look Ashley up," she said honestly.

"I found out recently that Ashley was a good girl and the guy who said that about her had a crush on her. She didn't like him, so he disparaged her for nothing. He married one of my classmates. He approached me at the reunion three years ago and told me he lied to me. Scott had carried that lie for thirty years, and apparently, it ate him alive. At that point, I tried to find her. I found out she had passed away," he said, beginning to cry but trying to hold back tears. "It has taken me this long to let go and find interest in Emily.

I hope she'll be interested in the new me."

"Wow, Stewart, I never knew you were so smitten by Ashley. I vaguely remember you talking about her now that you mention her. Since I left that year to find myself, I wasn't there for you. I'm so sorry. Speaking of 'new you,' are you ready for another go-round? I figure if you sleep as long, you'll wake up in the morning. How about if we do it around two this afternoon?"

"Yes, sure, two is fine."

Twenty-two hours later, Stewart woke up at nine in the morning. He was rested and felt happier than he could ever remember. He went out to the kitchen to find that Shery had left for work. His day was filled with rerun television and pacing until Sheryl arrived home that evening. By then, his good attitude had been deflated by boredom, and the usual Stewart had returned. Sheryl was worried as it seemed her treatments were temporary.

"Stewart, hey, Stewart, come into the kitchen," she called out.

Stewart was in his room trying to nap. He thought a nap might get his good attitude back, but it did not. Annoyed, he answered, "What? I was trying to nap. Why you gotta bother me?"

"I'm going to mix up a stronger batch of peyote. I think it's too weak and is temporary," she offered, trying to console him.

"I don't give a shit what you do. I just wanna be left alone," he answered with disdain.

"Yes, sir, a more potent batch is on the way," she said with her voice fading into thought. *Fucker better improve.*

Sheryl went to the kitchen and looked at the recipe. She didn't know what would make the mixture stronger. So, she figured, fermentation might do the job. Each day she had created a new batch. On this day, she took the batch outside into the Arizona heat in hopes of quicker fermentation while Stewart parked himself in front of the TV as he was on season three of Friends. While most people would laugh at certain parts, he just sat with a puzzled look upon his face. The day turned into night, and the night into the next day.

Stewart arrived in the kitchen earlier than the previous days to find Sheryl drinking coffee. "Would you like some coffee today, Stewart?" she asked, just to be cordial.

"Not today, not ever as long as you make it," he answered with an obvious sharp tongue.

"Okay, well, feel free to make your own. While you're at it, take that peyote too, and I'll see you tomorrow."

Stewart dumped a half pot of coffee down the drain and started a fresh pot. He ingested the peyote with pain as the taste became extremely bitter. He sat on the couch, and before the coffee was finished in the Mr. Coffee, he was asleep. Sitting straight up in the chair, he had passed out like a drunk in jail. He immediately started dreaming.

Chapter Six: The Dreams Begin

Stewart had not had his eyes closed for a minute when new visions started in his head.

It was daytime, and the sun was shining in through a window. He could see tall buildings through the window, so he knew he was in a high-rise apartment. The place was messy. He could smell the dirty clothing on the floor, and he could feel himself breathing. He couldn't move. Even though he could see, he could not move his head to look around. Nothing moved, but the light from the window seemed bright and unexpected. Stewart felt like he was semi-conscious but unable to interact in his dream.

The same scene remained in his head for what seemed like hours. He watched as the sun began to set in the window. Finally, there was a change of scenery. The room began to get dark, and then he couldn't see anything. Still paralyzed, Stewart felt helpless. The darkness brought more rest, but his consciousness was still clear.

Light! Turn off the light, he thought. It was very bright. He could not adjust it. He could see the room; he was moving now. He could see everything. Sitting on the nightstand was a pistol. There were open curtains in the room, and an adjacent room had a bathroom.

I'm walking into the bathroom. Whoa, penis! What? That's not mine. Shit, what's this? I'm pissing, but I don't feel it. I hope I'm not pissing myself. I can hear it. Mirror. Where is the mirror? I wanna see myself. Okay, shower. I'm getting in the shower now. Nice. I still don't feel it. Damn, the shower is loud. Lather. Right, lather up my body. Oh, oh no, penis again. It's clean already. Stop cleaning it. Good. Rinse. Dry. This is not my body. Where am I, and why can't I wake up? Wake up, wake up, wake up. Nope, not gonna wake up. Mirror. Fogged. I can't see me. Bed. Girl in bed. She's sleeping. Not anymore. Okay, then. Here I go. What am I doing? I'm kissing her, and she's kissing back. I see nothing. My eyes must be closed. I can't feel anything. What's going on? Wake up, wake up! I can't wake up. Skin. Her skin, her belly button. Wow, her skin is tan; no, it's not tan. It's cocoa colored. No, that's tan. Oh, I'm going down, no tan, no hair. Um, yeah. I can't close my eyes. Oh, my, what am I doing? She's moaning loudly. This is weird. What's going on? Oh, she's arching her back and squirming. Wow. Hello. Stop, no! What the hell? Oh, joy, she's screaming. I think she just came. Now, what am I doing? Penis, again. Oh, good, lord! It's inside her. I'm actually fucking her. Okay. Close my eyes. I can't. I can see it all. Should I count? No, that's stupid. I can't feel a thing. That looks really good. She's screaming again. I think I'm moaning; yeah, I'm moaning. Oh, I'm getting louder. Louder. She's louder. I'm louder. Oh shit! I think we just came together. Now, I'm lying on her. My eyes are closed. I can't feel a thing. Why can't I wake up?

"I can't breathe, Tony move. I can't breathe."

Stewart thought. *Who was that? That voice. So sweet. Who was that?*

"Okay, baby. Gimme a second."

"Why?" she asked.

"I'm still hard. I wanna go again."

"No, you gotta go to work."

Stewart thought, w*ho are these people? Who is Tony? Where the hell am I?*

"Fuck work. All I ever do is sit and wait."

"But you get paid, and if you wanna get laid, you gotta get paid."

"Bitch, I ain't done fuckin' you."

She pushed me off and said, "I'm done, so are you!" *Then she gets out of bed. I watch her as she walks to the bathroom. Her body is perfect. She stops to stretch, and I can see every rib. Her ass is tight as she walks away without a jiggle. Her breasts are ample and supple at the same time.*

"Wait, I'm talking. Bitch, come back here. Okay, fine, I'll come and get you."

Stewart thought, *I am following her. She's giggling. We're in the bathroom now. Wow, I'm fit. I still can't see my face. Oh, I'm picking her up under her thighs. And now. I'm back inside her. Yes, indeed, I'm pressing her against the wall. Good lord, she's very tiny. I close my eyes. I wonder if the neighbors hear us. I'm grunting, and she's moaning. Cool, she's coming again. Uh-oh, me too. Okay. Wow, what the hell is going on?*

"Shower time, baby. Will you join me? You made me dirty?" she asked me.

I answered, "Yeah, I will."

The water is on. Wow, she is beautiful. She kind of looks like Raquel Welch. Crystal blue eyes and reddish-brown hair. God, the curves. This shower is immense. Where am I? Why is everything so clear? Why can't I wake up? Wait a minute, great, I'm washing her now. I like this. Damn, those tits. And her nipples, nice. This seems so real. Nipple, in my mouth. Why can't I feel that? My hands, they're all over her body. Wow, what a body. She's rinsing. What a sight! Well, now she's washing me. I lift my arm, looking at my muscles. Shit, where did I get those? Oh, my belly, so flat, a six-pack. Yes, I'm dreaming. She's washing my core. I'm moaning again. No! She stopped.

Tony said, "It's clean now. Get out of here so I can finish."

Stewart thought, *I just got out of the shower. The mirror is fogged; I'm drying. White towel. Are we in a hotel? I look into the bedroom. Looks like a hotel room. I look around the room. It has to be a hotel room. Where am I? Wait, no, there's a hallway. Pictures. There are pictures on the wall. Wait, look at them. I couldn't look at them. I'm in the kitchen now. High ceiling, very high ceiling, like a warehouse-type loft. Wood beams painted black. Black marble countertops, stainless steel everywhere. Stainless cabinets. Who does stainless cabinets? Did I dress? I don't remember dressing. Where am I? Look at that view out the window of this city. Where am I? Well, it looks like I'm thirsty. I'm opening the refrigerator and getting a Bud Light. I hate beer. I'm drinking a beer. Good, I don't taste it. I'm going back to the bedroom. I can see myself drying off my arms and legs, they are not mine, but oddly, they are mine. My feet, and yup, that's my package. Don't over dry it. It looks so much bigger than I remember. Why is it different? Why am I different? Why can't I fucking wake up? Okay, good, underwear drawer. Lots of underwear in that drawer. Weird ones. Leopard skin?*

Me? Yeah, no. Black, perfect. What? Bikini briefs. Who am I? Okay, to the closet we go. Suits. I have lots of suits. Blue shirt? Alright, that sounds good. Shiny blue shirt. Silk, I wonder? I can't feel it. I can smell it, though. It smells stale. Okay, yeah, I need cologne. I sprayed something; hmm, it smells good. Polo, yeah, I like Polo. Pants, everyone needs pants. I need pants. Blue jeans. Yeah, I like those. Really? White socks? I didn't expect that, back to the closet. Walk in, his and hers. I wanna see hers. I guess I ain't looking there. Boots, I bend over for boots. Look at all the boots. Brown cowboy boots, those there. Damn, snakeskin. Are you kidding me? Who am I? I suppose I am finished in the closet. Uh-huh, there's the bed. I'll sit and put on my boots. It sure is quiet in here. Wait, no, I still hear the shower. She's still in the shower. I wonder what her name is. Maybe it's

Raquel. I hope it's Raquel.

Tony spoke loudly, "Hey baby, I'll be leaving in a minute. You gonna be here when I get back in the morning?"

"Nah, I'm going back to my place. I'm going to go to bed after I go out with the girls for a while," she answered him from the shower.

"Where are you going?" he asked.

"We'll be at 'the Underground' prolly until two-ish," she hollered back. Then she walked out of the bathroom completely naked, with her hair dripping on the floor. Tony got up from the bed, and she returned to the bathroom. He followed her.

Stewart spoke to himself, *"Prolly? Is that a word? Does she mean probably? Damn, she looks good wet. Look at her, eh? I looked away. Look back. Come on, look back. Oh, there I am. In the mirror. Black hair. Long. I need a comb or brush. Brush the hair. Damn, I'm a handsome guy. Who am I?"*

Tony turned and left the bathroom, saying, "Okay. I gotta go, I'm late."

"Brush your hair, shithead. You look like a dog," she said, laughing to herself.

"Oh, you're right. Thanks, Jen."

Stewart said to himself, *Jen? Her name isn't Raquel. Another Jen. What's my name? That's right, she called me Tony. I look like a Tony. Why am I so conscious, but I can't control any of this? Seems so real. Cool, one more look at her before I leave. I got my wish. Yum, she's standing in the open shower doorway, tan, beautiful, seductive, and still naked. Stop. Don't leave. Douchebag.*

Tony left the apartment down a light blue and dark blue hallway. The carpeting was a checkered pattern, and the lighting was dim yet stylish, with wall sconces every twenty feet. Stewart was watching as he came to the elevator, and he pressed the down button. *Did I press the down button, or did Tony? I wonder where we're going, where I'm going? The elevator smells funny. I wonder why I can smell it in my dreams. I don't remember any of this ever happening. I have never dreamed like this. Wake up, I wanna remember. I'm in a parking garage now. Smells like sewage. Yuck, where are we, am I? What the fuck is going on? Wow, my car is a Range Rover. That's nice. I guess I was carrying a bag. Yeah, put it into the back seat. It looked like a gym black leather bag. It seemed heavy even though I couldn't feel it.*

Shit! Turn that crap down. Apparently, I like rap music. I can't turn it off. What the fuck! Stop it; it hurts my head. I'll think of something else. I can't think. That's awful. What do they call this music? It's a real catchy tune; 'fuckin bitch gonna suck my dick as whores like it, she's a whore in all the ways.' Who writes this shit? I wanna wake up.

We're here, I'm here, wherever here is. What's this? Sign says 'Acme Medical Supply.' Really? I work at a cartoon medical supply. It looks like I have a key. Glass doors and windows lead to nothing. There isn't a receptionist's desk, just a phone on a table. This is weird. Here's a solid steel door. Another key. Dark, antiseptic hallway. I feel like Maxwell Smart. Another door. Another key. Okay, here we are, an elevator. Down? Really? I thought we were on the ground floor, but we went down. The door opened. Looks like a hospital waiting room. Did we just go to a hospital? To a hospital waiting room. There are so many chairs, but no one is here. Why are we picking that one? Weird. I'm the only one here. Why am I the only one here? Now we're talking. I have a cool cell phone. Okay, contacts, "S" Steve, dialing... It's ringing.

I guess that's Steve's voice, "You there? You're late."

"Really? Late to sit here and maybe go somewhere?"

"No, we have one in the OR at Mercy right now. Go there, and you have a heart for Northwestern Medical, you have lungs for Northwestern Hospital, they've been extracted. So have the kidneys for university; at university, they'll take the remains out. When they are done, go back to Mercy, where the undertaker will pick the body up. Talk to Doctor Li, she's expecting you. All the rest looks legit. She'll get it already for you. Got it?"

What the fuck? Stewart thought.

"Yeah, got it. Are you expecting any more?"

Steve said in a hurried, mean voice, "Well, you may have a deal yourself if you think you're ready."

Stewart thought, *A deal? What's that? I wonder what he means by a deal.*

Tony answered, "I think. Yeah, I'm ready."

"Okay, text me when you're done at Mercy, and I'll give you the details if there's another job."

"Got it, boss," Tony said.

So, here I am, waiting for body parts from an OR to deliver. Hmm, looks Like I'll play Candy Crush on my phone. Shit! I listen to rap while I play Candy Crush.

What the hell is wrong with me? Why can't I wake up? If I'm in a hospital, why isn't there anyone else here? What did Steve mean, a deal? I need to pee. Wake up, wake up. Damn, it hurts. Why doesn't this Tony guy feel this?

"Oh, I woke up," Stewart said out loud as he woke up.

Stewart thought, *What time is it? Eight-thirty. Seemed later. I need to pee. That was weird. I remember everything about that dream. Bathroom, bathroom. Yay. Wait, what's this on my pants? Shit, no, fuck, I came on myself. I had a damn wet dream. Ew. Gross. I need to change. I hope Sheryl didn't see that. I'm not going to ask. I think I'll stay up awhile. That way, I can avoid that dream if it continues.*

Stewart decided to shower and change his clothing. The images in his head of the alter-him were stunning, but the real Stewart was scrawny. He looked at himself in the mirror after showering. He was disgusted by his lack of muscle tone. He wanted to be more like his alter self. He put on fresh clothes and went out to the kitchen. Sheryl was standing in front of the stove, warming dinner up.

"Stewart, you had some dream there. At first, I was worried about you, but then you started to moan and talk in your sleep. I wanted to make popcorn and watch, but instead, I left you to your sex dream. Was it good? Looked like you liked it. You're really gross, brother. I bet you're hungry, stud. That was so funny," she winked. "I wish I had videotaped it. Maybe next time I will. You were fucking in your sleep. Rubbing all over the couch, writhing like a fucking dog in heat. Was she good? I bet that Ashley chick was hot."

"Her name was Jen," he blurted back. "She looked like Raquel Welch. Fuck you, I ain't kidding." *What am I saying? It was just a dream. Shut up!*

Sheryl laughed very hard, and Stewart was completely embarrassed. He left the room and waited in the hallway near his temporary bedroom door, awaiting her calmness.

He walked back to the kitchen. Sheryl said, "I bet you're hungry, champ, wanna eat?"

"Actually, yeah, I'm hungry and still very tired. Whatcha got?" Stewart responded.

"I made stew. Buffalo stew, ever had it?"

"Can't say I have. Does it taste like beef?" he asked.

"No, well, sort of. I like it better."

"Sure, I'll give it a whirl. You gonna join me?"

"No, I ate while watching the show," she said, giggling.

"Oh God, sis, really?"

"Yeah, it was fucking awesome. I'm so glad you got your rocks off. Did you learn anything from that dream?" she continued with great sarcasm.

"I think I learned more than I wanted to," he said with a weird smile on his face.

She put a plate down on the table and sat with a cocktail. Stewart sat in front of the plate and consumed every morsel. She said, "I guess you hated it. Do you want more?"

"No, that was perfect. Sis you are a culinary expert. Keep this up; I may never leave."

She thought, *Oh shit.* "What do you say? We'll go into the city and go to a bar. I'll call Tricia and see if she wants to join us."

"Sheryl, it's like nine o'clock."

"And?"

"It's late."

"Uh, no, it's early. Let's go, it'll be fun. You and I have never done that; maybe I can get you laid for sure."

"Where did you come up with this talk? Don't you have any respect for your gender?"

"Dude, if you respected my gender, I'd answer that. Just come on, let's go have some fun."

"Okay, but I told you I'm tired."

"Hold on, there's some shit in Hania's medicine cabinet that'll wake your sorry ass up." She went to the medicine cabinet and brought out a jar with a gooey paste in it. She could not pronounce what was on the jar, but she knew what it was. She went to the kitchen and got a paper towel. She dipped it in the goo and then rubbed it on the back of his neck. It smelled of mint. He didn't mind as it was warm and smelled good to him. "There now, you're a walking fucking Mojito. No hot chick could fucking resist you. They'll start at your neck and then lick your whole fucking body, thinking that's everywhere once they start. Instantly, he began to feel more awake."

"Okay, let's do this."

"You'll likely be the DD, as that stuff won't allow you to get drunk until it wears off. Then you had better be near a toilet or a bed. If you've been drinking a lot and it wears off, you're likely gonna puke. I'll laugh my fucking ass of if that happens. If not, you will fall flat on your face, and that'll be equally hilarious. Either way, we have six hours."

"Six hours? Are you sure?"

"Yes, exactly six hours, well, unless."

"Huh, unless what?"

"Unless you overexert yourself, then you could shorten the duration. If you're as boring as fuck, like you normally are, you may not fucking, sleep for a week," Sheryl said, laughing.

The top was on the Jeep, and they rode into town with air conditioning. Sheryl had not been out since Hania died other than to commiserate with close friends. Tricia was waiting inside at The Gopher Hole, drinking an Ultra. Sheryl hugged her, and she hugged back, whispering something in her ear. Then she hugged Stewart and pushed him back. "No, you didn't!"

"No, I did," answered Sheryl.

"Stand back, Stewart, before I eat you alive."

"See, Stewart, I told you."

"Fuck girl, why'd you do that? Ima be all over him now."

Stewart was silenced as Tricia wrapped a leg around him and nestled into his neck. She was almost licking as she did tiny kisses.

"Sis, I thought you said this was to wake me up?"

"Well, bruh, are parts waking up, like earlier in your fucking, and I do mean, fucking, dream?"

"Good Lord!" Tricia was making Stewart squirm as her tickling on his neck was driving him a little bit crazy.

Then she pushed him away. "Sheryl, bathroom, Now!" Tricia said.

They left Stewart standing alone inside the bar. He looked around and heard music playing from a jukebox. He saw a band setting up in the near distance. He assessed the crowd. There were three to two women over men. On either side of him were collections of three women standing and chatting.

Tricia and Sheryl got to the bathroom. "So, you told him that stuff drives women crazy, right? And he bought it, right?"

"I did. I was hoping it would bring him confidence."

"He smells like a fucking Mojito, why would that bring him confidence?"

"I can't tell you. The least it will do is make him stay sober so we can get trashed."

"Right, as long as it's only six hours."

"I know, we have until three something."

"Three something? You better get more specific. You know what happens after six hours."

"We better be tucked into a bed somewhere by three."

"He thinks he's tucking me in tonight. Well, he ain't fucking me tonight," Tricia said, laughing.

"Let's go, he's been out there too long."

"What's your problem? He's a grown-ass man."

"No. Not really. He's never been laid."

"Fuck me running, he's a fifty-year-old fucking virgin?"

"Well, he has had his nut cracked, but not on a pussy. He had a wet dream on the sofa earlier tonight. I fucking watched the whole thing. He was a fucking animal on the pillow. I had to throw it out. Nobody wants their brother's cum on their pillow."

"What in the holy hell?"

"He was completely clothed. But it came through. It was funny and gross at the same time. I'm thinking that wasn't the first time that happened, poor fucker."

"Yeah, that's a poor fucker, alright."

"Come on. We gotta get back to him."

As they approached, Stewart was conversing with a woman a few years younger than him. She was marginally attractive with brown and gray hair. She had a few extra pounds and was dressed like she just came from a rodeo. She was wearing pointy boots, very tight jeans, and just a jean vest. Tricia recognized her immediately. She walked up and whispered something in her ear, and she turned and walked away.

"Hey, what was that about?" Stewart cried.

"There are tons of girls in here better'n Margie. She's been fucked by every guy in Scottsdale since she moved here, bout finished with this town, too."

"What'd you say?"

"Can't tell you, it's a girl's secret. Besides, I already staked my claim on you for the night. Can't wait to get you where I want ya," she stopped talking and began laughing very hard. People started looking at the three of them.

"Sis, what's her problem? I thought she was married."

"She is. She's just fucking witcha."

Just then, a short woman with reddish brown hair came by. As she passed, she could smell the mint, and she turned toward Stewart. Took a deep breath and continued over to a table with three other women. Stewart's attention was on her. Their eyes hadn't met, but he watched her walk away. She reminded him of Jen from his earlier dream. He undressed her with his eyes. When she made it to the table, one of her friends asked, "So, what's up with the nerdy guy at the bar?"

"Can't tell ya, but he had a scent, kind of minty, like a Mojito."

"Minty? Like a Mojito, I gotta go see that."

Before the one woman sat, the other got up and walked past Stewart. She turned and mouthed to her friends, "He does smell like a Mojito." Then she returned to the table to be replaced by one of the other women at the table. All four took their turn walking and sniffing Stewart. They returned, mesmerized and laughing. The scent did something to them.

As the night wore on, more people came into the bar. It got warmer, and Stewart began to perspire. His perspiration caused the mint scent to enhance its strength. More women happened to sniff him until the first one staked her claim. She had wandered by three times, expecting Stewart to say something, and she had lost her patience. She touched Stewart's arm, and he turned toward her. Like his dream girl, she had reddish long brown hair, but she had green eyes. They locked eyes, and without thought, Stewart said, "Hi, my name is Stew."

She responded, "Like buffalo stew?"

He laughed, "I had that for dinner."

She said, "I haven't eaten yet."

Tricia and Sheryl were astonished. They had no idea that the mint would seriously have that effect on women. Tricia exclaimed, "What the fuck!"

"I know, who the fuck knew. I need to make a female version so I can get laid, too."

"Girl, you ain't got no problem with the men. They're falling at your feet since my brother died."

"I know, but they're all drunkards and drug addicts," Sheryl said.

"Sorry, my cousins are like that. You are fuckin funny, sis. Love ya. Will you look at your brother go? That one is eating out of his hand. Looks like we're finding another road home."

"They are all eating out of his hand. I wonder if the other stuff I'm doing is making a difference?"

"What are you doing? What the fuck, girl, tell me," Tricia said.

"Does he seem different since you met him the other day?"

"Well, fuck yeah. He's somehow sexy. He seems nicer and has more confidence."

"What the fuck did you do?"

"You can't tell anyone."

"Oh shit, now you gotta tell me."

"Seriously, I'd get into a lot of shit if you tell any, one."

"Hey, it's me. Have I ever told any of your secrets?" Tricia insisted.

"I don't think you have."

"I haven't."

"Besides the gooey shit on his neck, I have been doing mind-altering. He was such a dick and wanted to change, so I made some peyote and did a few chants."

"Oh, my God, you didn't. Do you know what'll happen if the elders find out about that? You'll be excommunicated, and you'll be fucking homeless. They will kick your right to the curb." She paused and then continued, "I gotta tell them, sorry."

"You are kiddin', right?"

"No, it is my responsibility to tell them. I need to preserve the traditions our family had fought to save, and you have fucking besmirched the name Navajo. Why didn't you ask my husband to do it? What if you did it wrong? What the fuck Sheryl!"

The music seemed to get really loud in Sheryl's head. She was trying to think. She couldn't. She needed to stop the train before it ran over her. "Tricia, you hold the key to my survival. Are you truly going to let me go like that after all our history?"

"Sheryl, I have an obligation."

I might need to kill her. Sheryl thought. *I can't do that. I suppose I'll have to accept my medicine.* "Do what you have to. But can I just ask one thing?"

"You can ask."

"Can you wait? Can you wait until I get my affairs in order?"

"I'll give you a month."

"Thank you, I guess. Okay, can we stop talking about this and have fun for the night?"

Tricia thought she took that well. "Yeah, let's rock this town. Hey, your brother is dancing. You said he didn't dance."

"He doesn't dance. Really, he can't fucking dance. He looks like Ellen from Seinfeld, dude! I gotta help my brother."

"Wait, no, that chick is totally digging it. Let him be."

"Right. Yeah, we should let this all play out."

The music changed, and Stewart stopped dancing. His partner stopped as well. He said, "Should we get another drink?"

She answered, "I think that's a good idea. What say we go over to one of those dark booths and get to know each other better."

"Yes. Sure, let's do that."

They made their way through the crowd to an empty booth far away from the dance floor and the bar action. A waitress came over, "Hi, lovebirds. Can I get you something? Do you want a menu?" They looked at each other and smiled. Something had certainly changed in Stewart.

"I think we'll take a menu and a few drinks. What'll you have, darlin'?" Stewart responded.

"I have a hankering for a Mojito, and can we get some of your famous nachos? Skip the menu," she said and then whispered in his ear, "don't worry honey, a few drinks won't satisfy my desire for your Mojito."

Stewart held back his excitement on his face but thought, *wholly crap.* "I think I'll try a Bud Light."

"Okay, nachos superior, a Mojito, and a Bud Light."

Stewart's new friend turned to him and said, "What did you say your name was sweetheart?"

"I don't remember exchanging names; mine is Stewart. Some people call me Stew, and others call me Art. Not sure why. You can call me whatever you like."

"I think I'll call you Mo. It's short for Mojito, you, the delicious wiry man you."

Is this a setup? No one's ever been like this with me.

"Okay, and what should I call you?"

"Well, my name is Jennifer. It's spelled weirdly. I'm not sure where my parents got it from. Most people call me Jen or Jenny."

How can this be? She looks almost like the Jen from my dream. What the fuck is going on. "Are you from here?"

"No, I'm from Utah. I moved here for a job in 2007. I was married, and we bought a house for more than we could afford. You know, like most people. Then, we lost our jobs, our home and our marriage. We loved the Obama administration. I got divorced in 2015. Sorry, I got political. What about you?"

"I'm visiting my sister. I live in New Jersey. Her husband recently died. She's over there. See her. She's the one in the flowered top," he said, pointing in Sheryl's direction.

"She's really pretty. Who is her exotic friend?"

"Oh, that's Tricia. That's her sister-in-law."

"She looks pretty, too."

"She's married to a medicine man, just outside the reservation."

"A real medicine man? I never met one of those."

"Yeah, my sister was married to her brother, who was also a medicine man."

"Are they real?"

"It seems so." *I wouldn't have believed it if this wasn't working on me,* he thought.

The small talk continued as she got closer and closer to him. The drinks kept coming, the food came, got consumed, and was replaced with more drinks. They began making out in the booth, and their hands were roaming over each other.

"Look at your brother over there, that's disgusting."

"What the fuck? You'd be doing the same thing if you could."

"Not with him, I wouldn't."

Just then, a cowboy-looking fellow walked up and said to Tricia, "Excuse me, ma'am, might I have a word with your lovely friend here."

They both looked up at the man standing more than six feet. Tricia answered, "What do you need with her, cowboy? Ain't you got some horses to wrangle?"

Tricia had no place in her life for cowboys neither did Sheryl.

"Excuse my friend, what she was trying to say is get back on your fuckin' horse and ride on outta here before I find my Indian ass bow and put a fuckin' arrow in your chest. Do you not have any respect for the native culture around here?"

"Sheryl, don't you fucking recognize me? It's Earl. I'm Hania's third cousin. My mom and Hania were medical students together. She works in Scottsdale at regional. I just came over to say hello. Aunt Tricia, your potty mouth is gonna get you in trouble someday."

"Earl, what the fuck. You are all grown up. The last time we saw you was at the family thing in oh eight. You were just a kid back then, fuck you're still a kid but a man and a kid at the same time. Now go away; you're making me all hot and bothered. I don't need any half breed boy hanging around my stables. My girl Sheryl ain't interested in a boy-man, not tonight."

"What are you doing speaking for me, Tricia? If the boy wants to hang around an old bat like me, I'm not gonna stop him."

"Excuse me, ma-am, I wasn't thinking what y'all are thinking. I just saw you and wanted to pay my respects to my uncle. He helped me more times than I can count. He was a great man. His death is a tragedy, and me, and my boys, and I think there's a way we can help bring justice to his name."

Sheryl was surprised, “I think the police have it under control.”

“I don’t mean no disrespect, but these fellas are despicable. We know their gang; they have been terrorizing our people for a very long time. With your blessing or without, we plan to go after them and put an end to their reign. I just wanted you to know what we plan on doing.”

“Sheryl and I don’t want to know what you are doing. We expect the law to take care of the justice part officially. Right, Sheryl?”

“Right, You do what you think you need to do. We’d feel better if you helped the law do their job and not get into any trouble.”

“I was a ranger and a sniper in Afghanistan, they won’t know.”

Sheryl interrupted, “I don’t wanna know.”

“Gotcha, okay. Copy that, Ma'am,” he said, tipped his hat to her, turned, and walked away.

Sheryl and Tricia smiled at each other in approval. Then they looked back at Stewart and Jen, and they were gone.

“Where’d he go? He has my fuckin’ keys. How am I getting’ home, he better not’ta left.”

“Don’t panic. He’s gotta be around here somewhere. He’s a responsible guy. He knows we need a ride,” Tricia said.

“Are we talkin’ about the same guy? Stewart is the most selfish man I have ever met. He’s about to get laid, and that pecker of his is doing all the thinking right now. He doesn’t give a shit about you or me. The fuckin’ fifty-year-old virgin’s gonna get his dick wet. Fuck me runnin’ if he’s left?” Sheryl finished.

“Backwards, bitch, he’s gonna get his ass kicked by me and mine if that’s the case.”

They looked around the place. It was shoulder to shoulder. Each scanning in a different direction, overlapping and scanning the crowd. Neither saw Stewart nor Jen.

"Maybe we should spread out and see if we can find him," Sheryl announced.

"Did you hear yourself, Sheryl? You sounded like a wagon train leader. Stop it," Tricia said, laughing to herself.

"You know what I mean, bitch? No, you go that way."

"Stop," Tricia said quickly.

"What?"

"Does he have a cell phone?"

"Well. Yeah," Sheryl answered.

"Just text him."

"Uh-huh, I suppose I could try that," Sheryl replied with her face contorted.

Sheryl texted Stewart, "Where are you?"

"Look, he didn't answer. Go that way," she said, pointing toward the bathrooms impatiently.

"Wait, just wait a minute."

"Whaaa... Oh, he texted back. We're on the dance floor," she said surprised.

"See. Nothing to worry about," Tricia said with a smile.

"He texted back, at The Grey Room."

"What? They left and went to The Grey Room?" Tricia responded, annoyed.

"Great. Well, we Uber over there. No biggie," Sheryl said in a hurry.

"Right, we Uber over there, let's go, you call," Tricia barked.

"Me? Why me?"

"Isn't he your brother?"

"Yeah, but did you drive here?" Tricia asked.

"No, you fuckin' stupid or something. I told you I Ubered here."

"Oh. Yeah, that's right. I'll get the Uber," Tricia said acceptingly.

They contacted Uber and got a rideshare to The Grey Room. It was not nearly as busy, and the music had stopped. It was one in the morning, and there was no sign of Stewart in the place.

"What now, Sheryl?"

"Wait, he texted me a half hour ago and said they were coming back."

"Brilliant. He texted you before we Ubered?"

"Uh-huh. Shots bitch, you had me doing' shots. I can't fuckin' think right now."

"Text him, tell him to come and get us."

"Right, good idea. Let's go have another drink."

They went to the bar, and the bartender told them they had had enough and were given water. They took the water to a booth, where they sat and waited. They had less than an hour to get home before Stewart would crash. He came to get them, and he was sweaty. Tricia noticed first. Sheryl didn't notice. She was nearly out cold. The outside temperatures had dropped into the fifties, so there wasn't a reason for him to be sweating. Tricia asked, "Have you been dancing? Is that why you're a sweaty mess, and where's your bitch Jen?"

"First, she's not a bitch. She went home. I put her in a Lyft about a half hour ago. I have been running all over the place looking for you. Sheryl didn't answer my text, and I know we gotta get home before I die on the street. I think I might have burned an hour. I'm pretty fucking tired."

"Shit, let's git. Ima have to sleep at her place tonight, you don't have time to take me home. Wait, I could Lyft or Uber from here. No, I better not. I need to make sure she's in bed okay."

"Thank you."

They got to the Jeep and drove to the clinic just in time. As they walked into the place, Stewart started to stumble. He made it down the stairs and into his room. He kicked off his shoes and was asleep before his head hit the pillow.

Tricia put Sheryl to bed. Took off her smelly bar clothes and rolled her into the king-sized bed. She took Hania's side of the bed and fell into a deep sleep.

Chapter Seven: The First Crime

As soon as Stewart's eyes closed, he was asleep, and his dreaming began.

Where am I? This looks like a strip club. It is. Naked women everywhere. I wanna leave. Wake up, change dreams. I want out. Wait. Okay, a woman is coming up to me. She's leaning in. Wow, she is fine. Ew, a slut. Stop. Leave. No. Okay, she's taking my hand. We're walking. Where is she taking me? Oh, a black curtain. A small box with a bench, all black, very dark. Okay, yeah, I'll sit on the bench. I gave her money. How much did I just spend? Do I get a receipt? Hey, excuse me, but I need a receipt. That looked like one hundred dollars. Okay, the music is starting. She's on her knees in front of me. Oh. Okay. She's taking off her bra. That's nice.

A hundred dollars nice, no! Probably cost her thousands. It was a good investment. I still need a receipt. Okay, here we go. She's rubbing those silicone sisters on my knees, now my chest, oh, yeah, they are in my face. She smells like baby powder and flowers. Why am I doing this? This is dumb. Oh. She's done, she turned around. Cool, her ass is in my face. Right there in my face. Who likes this? Nice, she moved the string between her ass cheeks for a peek. No. No. No, don't put that in my face. Well, I seem to like it. No more baby powder and roses.

That was rank. Oh, cool, she backed away. She turned around, ouch. Wait, did I feel that spiked heel goes into my thigh? Reassess? No. That should have hurt. There ya go, she's hiking her leg up, spreading her thighs. Super, she pushed the thong away, and now I see it all. Did I really pay one hundred dollars for this? Oh, now she took it off. Naked girl. She turned again, sitting on me. Rubbing. Rubbing against my jeans. That cannot feel good for her. Rug burn? Jeans burn? No wonder it was so pink and inflamed. I wonder if that was makeup. Okay, rubbing, rubbing, more rubbing. Two minutes of rubbing, we're done. One hundred bucks, really? Hey, where's my receipt?

I guess I liked that. I need to compose myself in this booth for a minute or two. Do do do do do do. Do do do do do do. Do do do do do do. Jeopardy music in my head isn't going to make me move any faster. Come on, let's get out of this stinky place. What are we doing here? Let's go. Why am I dreaming this shit? Great, we're ready. Go ahead, open the curtain. Man, is it loud in here? I can see more. Not very busy. I like counting. One, two, three, four, five, okay, six, seven, and eight, over there, nine, then eleven. Man, this place is huge, with eleven stages. One great big stage in the middle, five poles. Five girls on it. Sure, let's go over there. Into a dark corner away from everything. Yeah, good choice. I like it. Wait, who are you?

"Billy, good seeing ya, buddy," *I apparently said.* "The boss sent you, huh? You got that deal for me?"

Billy responded by passing me an envelope. "Don't open it in here. The instructions are in there. His address and work address are in there. All I know is he's an accountant. Been onsite, and the boss wants him gone."

"Do you know his blood type?"

"What?"

"Never mind."

"So, you get fifty thousand up front and fifty when it's done. Boss wants a token. Mail it to the P.O. Box number."

"What token?"

"I usually give him a finger or a thumb."

"Got it, okay."

"So, Billy, why aren't you doing this one?"

"The guy knows me. Knows what I do. If he sees me, it'll all get spooked, and he'll run to the cops. He doesn't know you. And, Tony, next time we meet, let's do it in a diner during the day, not at six in the morning in a strip club. I need food, and these titties are pretty, and all, but a man can't eat a tit."

"Okay, Yeah. I just-"

"Don't think, let's go eat. Meet me at Eggy's on Benton. I like their pancakes."

Hey, look, the sun is coming up on the lake; go over there. I wanna see it. No. Man, I can't do anything I want in my dreams. Alright, no one is out in this town at six in the morning. Where am I? Lake, Look. Oh, Lakeshore Drive. I might be in Chicago. I have never been to Chicago. How can I get such clear details from a place I have never been to? Driving. Okay, Eggy's, yeah. Looks kind of nice. I wouldn't expect hitmen to meet in a place like this. A booth by the window, just like in the movies. We can watch people walking by. Menu. What are we getting? Eggs Benedict. Let's go with that. Where's Billy? He should have gotten here already. I guess... oh, there he is. These guys dress nicely for hitmen. Billy is wearing a very nice suit. I don't know suits much, but I'd say that's a designer suit. Maybe Armani. Maybe Polo. Looks silk. His hair is really kept. Black and slicked back like in the seventies. He's obviously Italian. Look at that nose and his skin tone. Yeah. He's Italian. I bet he's fit, too. Probably has to be ready for a fight. This is like the Godfather movie. Where's Pacino? He's gotta be here, too. Hey Mikey! Mikey! Vinnie! Tommy!

"Can I get you gentlemen something to drink, coffee, OJ?"

Waiter. I wonder if he knows we're hitmen.

"I'll have both, thanks, and for some reason, I want eggs benedict," Tony said.

"Coffee and a three stack, two eggs over easy, bacon crisp, and bring us one of those famous cinnamon rolls first."

"Yes, sir." He walked away and was back in an instant with a cinnamon roll and two plates.

Shit. That looks really good. Too bad dreams don't have taste. Wait. I think I can taste it. I can't move. I can't wake up. I can smell, see, and taste. This doesn't seem like a normal dream. What's happening?

"So, Tony, this guy. He has a family. You gotta take 'em all. The wife, she knows too much about the business. We think the kids know where he works, too. I'd suggest a gas leak. That is after you strangulate them all. There are four. Husband, wife, two kids. Girl and boy. Girl seventeen, boy fourteen. They all need to go. Make it look like a Clinton job."

"I thought it was just one. A hundred grand for four? I gotta blow the house and suffocate four people? How am I gonna do that? You know I have never done this before."

"Right. Boss is counting on you. If you do this right, there will be a lot more coming your way. He has me running ragged. Between you and me, he had me do that Seth guy for the bitch."

"I guess I can't use them for organ donors."

"No, man, that isn't what this is about. This is about taking care of problems. This guy is a problem to the organization, and he's got to go."

It looks like I'm about to kill a family in my dream. Who dreams of this shit? What happened to the meadow and flower dreams I used to have? How about the, falling from a plane dream? At least I can wake up from those dreams. Man, this breakfast is amazing. I can actually taste the eggs benedict. That's some good hollandaise. Here's a positive about these dreams. The food is incredible. Okay, so I heard Chicago-style pizza in Chicago is amazing. Let's go, Tony. I mean later. We're still eating this stuff. Coffee. Good. OJ, well, it's OJ. This is a great dream. Weird though. I'm not full. Pie Tony. Let's have pie. No. No pie? Okay.

"Tony, you got a week. The boss wants this done before the weekend. Five days. More like five days. You got it?"

"Yeah, I got it. What if I just blow the place when they're sleeping?"

"No, you can't."

"If you do that, somebody might survive. Gotta strangulate them all first. I say start with the boy."

"Don't the husband and wife sleep together?"

"Yeah, that's tough. You might need help."

"Help? Who can I trust?"

"Dude, no one. You clean up that loose end after."

"So, I recruit a friend and kill them too."

"See why I never asked for your help. I like you too much. Now you're one of us. I can trust you. Money is dope, man. I mean some serious fucking money. Better'n any money anywhere. You want ladies, the boss'll hook you up. You want blow? We got blow. This is the job, my man. Welcome to the job. Speaking of ladies, dump that Jen chick. She ain't no good. She's too smart. If she gets wind of this, we'll all go down. Dump the bitch."

"Got it. Okay. Money, blow, and bitches galore. Yeah, sounds dope, alright."

What? No more Raquel Welch? Shit. I liked that girl. Maybe I won't listen to that. Wait. What's going on? The detail is amazing, like a movie. It's better than a movie. I guess we're done here. Driving. Wow. The traffic sure has picked up. Oh. Parking garage. Do de do de? Parking. Remember the key. Oh, keyless vehicle. That's nice. The inside of this spectacular. I'm making a killing. Oh, that was funny.

Yup, black Range Rover. There's the elevator. Up, yup, up. Lobby. Busy, where are all these people going? Another elevator. Up. Hmmm hmmm.

Do de do de do, la la la. Hmm. Hallway, blue still, door, key, open. Ah, home. Refrigerator, milk, what, no glass. Ewww, okay. Close the door. Was it empty? Why did I leave it on the counter? Bedroom. We're going to bed. We're alone. It's bright in here. A remote. Really? Nice. The remote control and the windows are dark, shades of darkness and coolness. One button, and it's sleepy time. Great! Finally! Rest.

I'm in bed. Pillow, sheet, blanket, warmth, ahhh, sleep. Darkness. That's it, Tony. Let's go.

"Stewart, Stewart, wake up."

"What? What? I'm so tired. Please let me sleep."

"No, I need your help."

"Ugh, sis, what is it? Gimme an hour. Two tops."

"No, I need you now. Get up."

"But I-"

"I don't care. We gotta go."

"What is it?"

"Come on, here's coffee," she said, handing him a cup.

"Thanks, what is it? You're so cryptic."

"The elders. They are coming. You can't be here."

"What? Why?"

"Because I did that spell on you. They are coming to see you. If they figure this out, I'll be tossed out. Fuck, Bitch told me I had a month, what the actual fuck. Come on, you gotta go."

"Where?"

"Anywhere."

"Do you know a place that has Eggs Benedict?"

"That's weird. Yeah, sure, Mike and Ronda's, the place, has it."

"Well, thanks, anything else?"

"Here are my keys. Get dressed and leave."

Stewart was gone before the elders arrived. Mike and Ronda's, The place. It was a strip mall comfort food place. *She was wrong. No Eggs Benedict. Bagel yes. Eggs, check. Belgian Waffles, check; hollandaise sauce; no. I guess the best I can do here is bagel, egg, and ham. Hmmm, that guy has biscuits and gravy. I think I'll get that too. I'll sit here.*

"Excuse me, miss, can I order?"

"I'm sorry, sir, you're in Stella's section. Let me get her for you."

Stella, really, I got the old lady waitress. Might as well call her Flo. Wait, is that Stella? Here she comes.

Stella spoke in her broken English. Stewart couldn't identify her accent, "Good morning, zir, can I bring zoo zometing to drink, diz morning?"

"Well, yes, coffee, black, and so you have Stevia?"

"No zir, just de pink ztuff. I can bring z pink ztuff."

"No, black is fine. I'm ready to order. I want two eggs over medium, bagel with butter, bacon crisp and biscuits and gravy."

"Do zoo vant haze bonz?"

"I'm sorry, what?"

"Haze bronz. Zoo no, po-tat-oz"

"Oh, hash browns, yeah, sure."

Stella left and returned immediately with coffee. Minutes later, his breakfast arrived, hot and amazing. It was the best biscuits and gravy he had had in his life.

Back at Sheryl's place, Jonathan, the Navajo leader, arrived an hour later than expected. Stewart had just been served his breakfast and was almost finished. His hair, black and his brown eyes were kind, and his smile was genuine. He was the youngest-ever recorded president of the Navajo Nation. Sheryl was surprised to see him at her door.

"Hello, you are Sheryl, right? Might we have a seat in your living room? I'm-"

"I know who you are. My husband voted for you as President. You are Jonathan. Yes. Please, can I get you some coffee or tea?"

"No... no, thank you. I should not be here that long. First, I'm sorry for your loss. Your husband was a great man. He was one of our best. I don't know if you know this, but he and I spent many nights commiserating over tribal traditions. He wanted to stray and accept the Western ways more so than we did. You know as well as anyone this nation is a balance. We live under two sets of rules, and your husband toed the line far too many times. His practice has been under tight scrutiny from every administration since its inception. His generosity to the community was unparalleled. Too many of our people told stories of his love and caring. His death was a tragedy. I understand you were approached by a young man over the weekend. He vowed to avenge your husband and his name. Rest assured; the Navajo Nation does not condone such activities. We would try these men for murder alongside the United States if any harm were to come to those responsible. We believe in justice; yes, we do, but this is barbarism, and we will not stand for that. As for you, Ms. Sheryl, we know of your activity. We realize you are grieving. We understand your pain. We know that times like these require support from all sides, including your family. I know you've been told outsiders are not allowed in tribal-owned properties such as this. Rest assured; we will not take measures to eradicate your brother from the premises. May I remind you that we choose peace over anything? You, Ma'am, need all the love you can get. Even though we've only met a few times, I still consider you part of the family.

"Thank you, I appreciate that. Such kind words."

"Well, allow me to finish. As I said, this is Navajo property, and you and your husband have no claim to it. The senior doctor, whose name I've forgotten, shall take residence in this place on the first of next month. He needs to be present in case of emergency like your husband was. As for your residence, well, I apologize we don't have a place for you on the reservation. Since you bore no Navajo children and are not of Navajo blood, we will regrettably have to ask you to find other accommodation. I'm sure this is not a surprise to you."

"Paco."

"Excuse me?"

"The primary physician here. His name is Paco. And, no, I'm not surprised. I expected a letter. Your visit is more than I ever thought I'd see."

"Mark my words, Sheryl, Hania was one of our best. You do know what his name means, do you not?"

"Yes, it meant 'spirit warrior."

"Yes, he was known to all in the nation as one of the greatest spirit warriors. We appreciate all you have done to keep his traditions alive and to keep this place for the duration since his passing. We wish you no harm. As a recompense, we will be providing for your living so long as you shall live, no matter where. We will provide you with his pension equal to his monthly wages plus the value of living expenses in comparison within the city limits of Flagstaff. Naturally, you can choose to live anywhere but your stipend will be equal to a three-bedroom home with similar amenities in the area. We will pay for a home valued at no more than five hundred thousand dollars. You can choose to take a cash buyout for the home of the same amount and use it as you see fit. We will still provide you with the four-thousand-dollar salary per month with standard increases as time goes by. We extend our gratitude to you for your unwavering support of our brother. We know, I know, from our conversations, he loved you very much, and so does our community. Of course, we would love it if you found a place nearby to stay close to the nation. Oh, and I almost forgot. The belongings in the domicile are tribal. We would need you to leave everything intact except for the personal effects. His books are considered tribal property. You may take those things you might have given him. Those things given by the tribe belong to the nation. Please consider our offer of generosity and an additional one hundred thousand dollars for furnishings in your new place. I regret to say, your government will tax you on every dollar we provide. You will no longer get our tax allowances. What this means is we have calculated your after-tax reward, if you will, and adjusted our generosity to fit. On this gift, you will not see a tax burden. On the monthly retirement, you will. My apologies."

"Sir, Jonathan, can I call you that?"

"Feel free."

"Jonathan, that is more than expected. I don't have words to share my appreciation. I just wonder, how much time did you say?"

"Oh, I'm sorry. I thought I said at the end of the full month. This being April, you have until June one to find a new residence. We believe that there should be plenty of time. Expect to see the consistent direct deposits as before. I realize that Hania got annual bonuses, and I regret that those will end as well. You will get a prorated six-month bonus for the time you are here. I hope that helps with moving expenses."

"Thank you, Jonathan. I have to say, I was not expecting this visit, and I was not expecting such generosity. I will comply fully."

"There is one more thing before I go. It is a matter of the medicine you have given your brother. You have, haven't you?"

"Well, sir, yes. You see-"

Interrupting, he said, "That has to cease. I don't want an explanation. We cannot have the liability. You must stop. No questions asked. If you don't stop immediately, this whole deal is voided. You will be removed tomorrow with nothing. I trust you understand the gravity of this situation."

"Well, yes, sir. I do."

"Great, we are understood. Now, before I leave, I will need to take his book with me to ensure compliance. You know what book I speak of, correct?"

"Yes... yes, I do. I will go get it for you."

She went to Hania's den and found the book lying open-faced on the desk. The spell was rewritten on a separate page, and she slid it off the book and closed it. She lifted the old book carefully and carried it out to the living room. Jonathan was standing. He took the book from her and then asked, "Can you show me the peyote you were using on your brother?"

He set the book on the counter, an island in the center of the kitchen. She opened the book. Paged through until she reached the page. He said, "Thank you. Did you follow these instructions?"

"I did. I don't think I got the prayers right, though."

"This is why only Hania or Paco should have administered this. You see, it is very spiritual, and it takes the blood of a Navajo to connect with the spirit guides. They have the blood and the guides, and they have the skills. I certainly hope you have not damaged your brother, as this particular process is one of the most difficult ones. If you did it wrong, there could be grave consequences. Have you seen or heard anything that you might call out of the ordinary?"

"He slept a lot, I mean a lot."

"Dreams, has he mentioned dreams?"

"No, nothing about dreams."

"That is good. I will not go into the side effects of this procedure. Let's just be glad he hasn't seen anything unusual in his dreams. I'll take this and be on my way. It was so good to have this chat with you. Again, I'm truly sorry for your loss. If you see that young man, Elu, he goes by Earl, let him know there's no room for retribution in our nation at this time. Once again, it has been a pleasure, and I do hope you will stay nearby. Come enjoy family get-togethers and feel like you are always a part of our nation. With love, I bid you farewell."

"Thank you again, Jonathan," she said as she led him up the stairs, into the lobby where two armed men waited, and to the door where a car and two more armed men protected his vehicle. Three identical Chevy Suburbans with dark windows waited, running, for him to return. One of the men standing outside the center vehicle opened the back door, and he climbed in. Like a train, the three deep red vehicles took off.

She closed the door behind him and then sighed a huge sigh of relief and satisfaction. She thought*, wow, it looks like I'm set for life. I wonder how he knew so much. I know. Yeah. Spirits, they must have told him.*

As she was making her way down the stairs, she heard a knock on the door. She turned and went back up. Opened the door, and one of the men who had accompanied Jonathan stood before her. He said, "Ma'am, there is a matter of the handwritten paper on the desk. I will need to take that with me."

Astonished, she led him to the den and gave him the paper. He was gone as quickly as he arrived, letting himself out and locking the door behind him. Sheryl sat in Hania's chair. Upright, she looked around at the memories. She took a deep breath; she could smell his presence. The room smelled of stale tobacco from when he used to smoke. It smelled of his cologne engrained in the walls. She could smell the age of the leather in the chair and the old books. She put her hands flat on his black leather desk pad and closed her eyes. She hoped to feel his energy in the room. She could. She heard a whisper in her ear, "I miss you too."

A tear formed in her right eye. An old expression came to mind, *'If a tear forms in your right eye, it is joy. If in your left eye, it is pain.'* She smiled. She said in her thoughts, *I feel you, baby.* She heard back, "I will always be with you." She felt gratitude. She felt humbled that he was still there and had not moved on. She felt loved. Then, she could not breathe, as if someone was holding her tight. She fought the feeling until she heard him say, "Fear not. It is me. I'm hugging you."

The tears welled in both eyes. "Please don't cry," he said. "I will be nearby for you always." She could not help herself, so she wept, laid her head on the desk, and fell asleep.

Stewart returned with a carbon copy breakfast for Sheryl. He stormed into the room, singing a Led Zeppelin song off-key. His explosive entrance woke Sheryl from her nap. "Sis, I brought you breakfast. Are you hungry?"

"That was unusually thoughtful, Stew. Yes, I'm starving. What is it?"

"Eggs the way we like it, bacon, Belgian waffles, hash browns, and the best biscuits and gravy ever."

"Oh, you went to Mike and Ronda's, that's right. Didn't they have eggs benedict?"

"No, I had the same as what I brought for you. If you don't mind, I'm going to go back to sleep. I haven't been sleeping well. I've been having such real dreams.

Hopefully, they won't be as vivid now."

"Wait. You're having weird dreams. Tell me about them."

"I will if they continue. For now, I need more sleep. Gotta go," he said as he left the room, past the kitchen, down the hall to his room, where he dropped straight on the bed, shoes and all. He was asleep in seconds.

Sheryl didn't move for several minutes. She wondered if she had done something wrong. *His dreams. Should I tell Jonathan? Should I tell Paco?*

What do I do? She decided nothing.

Chapter Eight: Surveillance

Stewart's sleep was restful as he dreamed the usual dreams. Flying, riding in a car on city streets, conversations with strangers. Fragmented thoughts that seemed meaningless allowed him to find peace for most of the time he was asleep.

He was groggy but still asleep when he thought he felt someone in bed with him. He opened his eyes, and they were out of focus. It was dark in his bedroom, and he rolled over to feel a warm body next to him. *I'm still dreaming. Who is there? I wanna ask. Ask who is it, look. Oh. It's Jen. She's naked again. She's touching my chest. I don't feel it, I see it. Why can I not look where I want to? Hmm. This dream is so unsettling. Oh. Looks like she wants something again. This girl is insatiable. Oh. I'm pushing her away. Gentle, partner, she's a tender flower. Now I'm talking, "Jen, we can't."*

"Why Tony, I thought you liked it."

"That's not the point. I'm glad you are here, though."

"Why are you speaking in complete sentences? Is there something wrong?"

"Huh? What? No. Well, yeah. Jen, we should get dressed," he said, getting out of bed and putting on his pants with his back to her.

What, no underwear. What am I a Neanderthal?

She stayed in bed, the sheet covering the bottom half of her body. She was propped up on her elbow, laying sideways. Her hair draped over one breast while the other fell close to the flat bed sheet. She was a vision of sexiness, yet Tony ignored her. He turned and said, "You have to get dressed. We have to talk," he said as he walked out of the room.

Wait. What are we doing here? Did you see her lying there, dude? Come on, one more for old times' sake.

Since when do you have integrity? My dream guy has no integrity, why now? Come onnn.

Well. I guess I don't get my way. Now I'm in the kitchen. It's dark outside, and I'm making coffee. Who drinks coffee at this time of day? Let's go back to bed. She's there. Don't do it for yourself; do it for me. Wait. I stopped like I heard myself speak. No. There she is, dressed. She has my, sorry, his T-shirt on. That's not dressed.

"Jen, you know I like you a lot, right."

"Tony. Don't."

"I don't want to hurt you."

"Stop, Tony, stop."

"I don't want to hurt you, but I'm afraid what I'm about to say will."

"Tony, NO! Stop, I'll do anything you want."

"I don't want to hurt you, but I just don't see a long-term."

"No, I know this. No, stop, Tony. We can work this out," she was wailing.

Dude, really? We gotta do this?

"I just don't see a future together. I need someone I can have a future with."

Seriously now. You don't see a future. Oh. That's right, we gotta break up. Alright, I'll shut up. I'm just watching. Go on.

"You're done with me, just like that. You are done. What, did you find another girl? Some whore? Some slut who will suck your cock more than me, come on, give it to me, I'll suck it. Asshole. Why did I invest the last year of my life with you, you mutha-fucker."

Okay, a year. And we're kicking her to the curb? Raquel fucking Welch-looking hottie who says she'll suck my cock. Really, come on, Tony, get a pair."

"I'm so sorry Jennifer. This is just the right time."

"Was it because I went out with my girls last night? Did you follow me? What the fuck, you followed me.

You saw those guys talking to me. They meant nothing. They were just boys hittin' on me. Like it doesn't happen to you all the time. Bitches be all over you. I know you have been steppin' out on me. I ain't guilty of shit. I ain't never sucked another dick, no sir, only yours, since we met. You know I can have any of those boys, but I want a man, I want you. If you ask me to marry you right now, I'd fucking say yes. You said you wanted me forever just the other day. Now this. You fucking kick me to the curb. I don't even know you. You asshole, cocksucker, mother fucker, gimme a break. They didn't mean anything. I can't fucking believe this. Gimme another chance, Tony, come on. We can make this work. I love you. You told me you love me too. Now what the fuck. Okay. Okay, you can't have me. Nuh-uh, I'm outta here. Uh-huh, I'm fucking outta here. You ain't ever gonna touch this again. Good fucking bye. Ima pack my shit and leave. You'll be sorry, you muthafucker."

She left the room. Tony sat on his couch and stared out the window, silently looking out onto the night skyline. No words. Very few thoughts.

Jen returned with two trash bags, said nothing, and walked out the door, slamming it behind her. Tony never moved a muscle. He didn't turn to look at her as she left. When the door slammed, he took a deep breath and began to weep. She was gone. It was the best. She knew too much. This way, she would be safe. "Yes, I loved you, Jennifer. I really fucking loved you," he screamed out loud and then began to wail. It seemed this heartless guy did, in fact, did, have a heart.

He cried until he couldn't. He got up and went to the bathroom, where he blew his nose, gathered a few things from the kitchen into a cooler, and left out the door. Down the hall, onto the elevator to the parking garage. Once in the Range Rover, he turned off the music and drove in silence.

Stewart had the presence of mind to think while he was dreaming: *Where are we? Wait, where am I going? Suburbs. Okay, yeah, let's leave the Godforsaken city. There go the streetlights. Good thing this truck has GPS.*

Twenty minutes until we're there, turn here, turn there, I'm bored. What are we doing? Okay, times up, we're stopping. What time is it? We're parking on the street. Watching a house. This is exciting. Let's see. The two-story house, brick front, looks to be about four thousand square feet. Four car garage, nice. What do I know about square footage? White double door. Beautiful chandelier in the foyer window. Circle driveway. I wonder why there's no gate. Looks like a good place for a gate. Oh well, what are we doing here? This is boring. Feels like surveillance. Uh-huh, watching a house. Oh, joy, this is my dream. Could I... be... any... more... boring—a dreamer? Oh, okay, cool, binoculars. Yeah, a closer look at NOTHING! Wait, I see movement. It's a kid in the upper window. A girl. That was fun; she's gone. Downstairs windows. Those are great, all covered. What the fuck are we doing here, Tony. You gotta be impatient, I know I am. Okay, cool, we're getting out. No, back in, one of the garage doors is opening. Looks like we're off for a family drive. The lights are going out upstairs, now downstairs, okay Mom's coming to the car, kid one, kid two. Is that it? Looks like it, brake lights, reverse. There they go. Oh fun. We're following them. Turn, turn, turn, snooze, lather, rinse, repeat. Oh, a parking lot, Giuseppe's Pizzeria. Oh, here's my chance—Chicago-style pizza. What, no. We're passing the place. Man, you're no fun. Turn, turn... back at the house. Looks like we're going in. Oh, we have a key. How did we get a key? Must have been in the package. Alarm! Well, we have the code too. Time to look around. I suppose we have a few hours. Should we open some of this fine wine, Tony? Hey Tony, didn't you see that fine wine? Okay. Upstairs. Master bedroom. Master Bath. Kids rooms, we're done here. That was fun. Now, let's go back to the pizza joint. Oh, looks like we are. He's listening to me. Parking. Get out, come on, get out. Yay, we're getting out. Going in. Smells fantastic in here. Italian-looking hostess, "Yes, just one." *Wow, this guy can be ruder than me. Let her ask the question.*

"Your server is blah, blah. I know the drill. Just bring me a pepperoni pie for one and a Bud Light. Keep the buds coming, got it?"

Seriously rude Italian guy. It's no wonder he even had a chick, like ever. I suppose money and looks go a long way.

There's the family. They look so happy. I guess they're the ones we're supposed to kill. Good thing this is just a dream. How we gonna do it, Tony? We gonna shoot 'em all? Oh, that's right, we're gonna blow up the place. Can't be any survivors. And the dad needs to know his family is dying. This is gonna suck for him. Again, it's a good thing it ain't real. Is it?

The pizza arrived with the beer. The waiter poured the beer into a frosted mug in front of Tony, set it down, said nothing, then left.

It's square. Square pizza? It's a good thing I can't feel the heat. That's funny, I'm sorry, he's burning his mouth. Wow, now, this is good. Not as good as Joe's, but damn, this is tasty. I like it. The crust is different. The sauce is on top. Who does that? Well. I have had it sort of. I just noticed. Who does square pizza?

Four big pieces, three gone. I wonder how filling it is. Seems filling. We're eating pizza, beer number three, watching those people, oh man you know how to live. Last piece. You gonna eat that? Here comes beer number four. I wonder if we can drive. I know I wouldn't be able to. Beer gone. Wholly cow, I can drink. Good thing this is a dream. Boring dream, beer, I hate beer, pizza, not even Joe's pizza and watching this fucking family eat. Great dreams, Stewie. Oh. Looks like they're done. Leaving shit, she's a cow. That guy is married to a cow. The girl is hot. The boy looks like a dweeb like his dad. He's even wearing the same shirt. Why didn't I notice that before? It's gonna be hard killin' that girl. Nah, it's like a movie. Just a dream, it's all make-believe anyway. Let's go. Let's get the show on the road. Oh no, another beer. Really. It's gonna be like watchin' paint dry. Nothin' to see here, move along. Song. I need a song. I need a television. Something to look at. Oh, good, a cell phone. A call. Let's answer it.

"Hey, Toe knee, what's happening, bruh?"

"Oh, just sittin' at Giuseppe's having a few slices and a couple buds."

"Who's witcha?"

"Nobody, I'm eatin' alone. I dropped Jen tonight, feeling kinda down."

"Fuck man, why'd you do that? I thought she was the one?"

"Nah, she got super needy, ya know, all possessive and shit. Then she fuckin' cheated on me."

"No way, Jen cheated on you? That bitch, when?"

"Last night. She went out with the girls. I went to the bar she was at. You know the place. I forgot the name. Oh yeah, downstairs. This guy comes over. Buy her a drink. Before long, they're kissing and he's grabbing her all over. I followed them back to her place. I'm pretty sure she fucked him."

"Dude, that's terrible. Well, you did the right thing. I'm surprised, though. I thought she worshipped the ground you walk on. I guess not. But, you know people make mistakes."

"That ain't a mistake I can live with, she had to go."

That's a lie. Wait, is it? Did I miss something? No, no, I didn't, this is a dream and I'm making it up as I go along. Carry on.

"You need some company? You have been drinkin'. How many you down?"

"'Bout six."

"How long you been there?"

"'Bout two hours."

"Fuck man, I'm coming to get your ass, stay there."

"Yeah."

It seems my vision is getting blurry. Oh great, another beer. Number seven. Where's what's his name? Damn, am I slurring my thoughts? Did the alcohol seep into my dream? This is another weird side effect. This all seems so real. Okay, here comes a guy. Not what I expected. Tall. Curly hair, balding on top, kinda blondish, no red. He's fat, like two-fifty or more. Maybe three hundred, he's pretty big. What's his name? Did he ever say? Nah, he's not fat. He's picking me up, what, over his shoulder, no way. He gave the guy a hundred. Oh shit, I'm puking. Really? Yeah. I'm puking. He doesn't care. He has pants on. Oh, truck. Shit, truck bed. Good thing I don't feel anything, that's gonna leave a mark. I can't believe it, he tossed me in the back of his pickup. I can't see, but I think, yep, he just tossed his pants on me.

"Wipe your face with those, don't worry, I got another pair."

I bet it's cold. Well, his eyes are closed. He left a trail of pizza and beer all the way from the front door to the truck bed. What an awesome dream. Good thing it ain't real. Darkness. Unconsciousness. No more dreams except road noise. Weird. Now I don't hear anything.

Okay, deep sleep. Regular dreams…

Elu was accompanied by three friends. They entered "The Devil's Den" and headed up to the bar. Elu asked for a Coors Light, and the bartender asked him for his identification. He obliged, and the other three did as well. They all got the same beers and looked around for a table. There was one. It was a high-top table with three chairs up against the wall next to the pool tables. Nothing was on top of the table, so they walked towards it. Before they could reach the table, a bearded fellow in a vest intercepted the table and prevented them from getting to it. They turned back to the bar, and the space they had just been at was filled. Every other seat in the place was now occupied. They could tell they were unwelcome. All eyes watched them as they fumbled to find a place to drink their beers. They rested, standing next to the end of the bar. The Alman Brothers Band was playing on the jukebox. There was smoke in the air even though smoking was no longer permitted in public places. The crowd was speckled with white and black people. They were the only Native Americans. Still, every eye was planted on them as they stood uncomfortably.

One of the guys said, “Elu, let’s get out of here. This is really creepy.”

Another chimed in, “Yeah, everyone is watching us. It’s like they are all looking to kill us. What’s the problem?”

Just then, the bearded guy walked over. “Excuse me, but have you realized you ain’t welcome here?”

Elu spoke up, “Last time I checked it’s still a free country.”

“That may be so, but we don’t take kindly to your type in this place. Didn’t you learn your lesson a few weeks back when that Spirit guide of yours got his? If you want some of that, you stick around, and the boys here will give you a taste. This is just a friendly warning, chief; you better get your red ass outta here before someone scalps you and your pals. You got ten minutes. Drink up and get out.”

Elu said nothing. They finished their beers and walked out. Once outside, they convened. "Elu, what now? You wanna get dead? I know I don't."

"No, boys. We needed to see 'em. We needed to see what we were up against. We know how many there are and what we need to do. I think we just chain the doors and light the place up. What do you think?"

"Kill 'em all? They all ain't part of the gang. We can't do that," one of the guys said.

Elu responded, "We gotta do something. I think it's best. They would call it collateral in war. Those innocents are not innocent. Anyone in this place is guilty of something, they should all die."

"Count me out."

"Me too."

"Me three. No way I'm killing forty or more people to get eight. Come up with another plan."

"I got nothing else. It's either this, with you or without you."

They all agreed it was without them.

"I made a promise, Imma keep it. I told Sheryl I'd take care of it. Imma take care of it."

"When you gonna do it?"

"Right now."

"You can't do this right now. You don't even know if the guys who were at the clinic are even inside there."

"Look, Gus, we gotta take care of this for the pride of the tribe."

"No, Elu, Ms. Sheryl wouldn't want you to kill a bunch of innocent people. You know, I don't think she'd want us to kill anyone."

Another chimed in, "I agree, and I don't think Hania would want us to kill anyone either. Count me out."

The third one agreed as well, and it appeared the subject was closed. They walked to their vehicle. Once there, Elu went to the trunk, took out two chains and a gas can and went to the building. He went around to the back. The others waited, doing nothing. He came back around to the front of the wooden building, went inside with the gas can pouring onto the pavement, then came back out, wrapped the chain around the door handles and threw a match to the ground. In less than a minute, the place was fully engulfed with flames. They heard screaming as they drove away.

No one was injured. They all escaped out a third door. Elu had begun a war.

***

"Stewart, wake up. Stewart, come on, wake up," Sheryl insisted.

"Wha... Wha... What do... What, Sheryl, what?"

"We have to leave," Sheryl barked.

"Yesterday, you woke me and said I had to leave," Stewart responded groggily.

"No, that was earlier today. Come on, we need to go."

"Where? Where now? Isn't it the middle of the night?"

"No, no, it's morning," she said quickly.

"Oh. What time?" Stewart asked, trying to wake.

"It's after eleven. I have been up since eight."

"And you've had too much coffee. Okay, okay, hold on. Lemme get dressed. I'll be out there in a few minutes, please."

Stewart came into the kitchen. "So, what's the big hurry?"

"The president of the Navajo Nation was here yesterday. He took the book."

"He what? He took the book? Do you have the process?" Stewart said frantically.

"No, he took my notes," she answered back worried.

"You have nothing?" he retorted, beginning to worry. He continued, "Do you remember?"

"No, well, maybe, I don't know... Yes, I think so," Sheryl answered.

"Were you finished?" he questioned with deep concern.

"I don't think so," she said, wringing her hands.

"What can we do?"

"We still have some in the refrigerator. You can take it, I'll try to remember the prayers," she answered as she paced the hallway. She walked out of sight and then back again.

Stewart waited to see her again, then said, with little confidence, "I guess that's fine."

"Let's do it now," she said, pounding her hand against her thigh.

"Great, I'm all in," he said, thinking, I just woke up.

Sheryl gave him the peyote, and he stopped and said, "Wait, Let's wait until tonight before bed so I can sleep normally."

"Good idea! Can I ask you a question?" Sheryl asked.

"What kind of question?" he genuinely asked.

"What do you mean, what kind of question? Just a question," she continued.

"No, I mean a yes or no question or a question that needs an answer?" he said with a small smile.

"When did you become this way?" she asked, thinking, *have you changed?*

"Was that the question?" he asked, giggling.

"No. That was a question about you asking the question," she said.

"Okay, which question do you want an answer to?" he asked.

"I want to know if you'll answer a question if I ask you."

"I have already answered your question about a question," he said.

"Have you?" she responded.

"Are we not talking about a question?" he asked back.

"We are, but I haven't asked the question yet," she said shortly, getting frustrated with his humor.

"Why don't you just ask the question? Instead of asking if you can ask a question," he said with a smirk.

"What would you think if I moved back East?"

"Where back East?" he asked.

"Oh God, here we go. I fucking mean back home to Jersey."

"You wanna move back into Mom and Dad's house with me?"

"Maybe for a while. Until I find my own place, I used to be part of the Navajo Nation and now my ties are dead. They told me to stick around and that they'd like me to stay, but I don't think that's really what they want. Maybe you should sit down. Here, I'll get you a coffee."

He sat at the table and Sheryl mulled around in the kitchen. She brought him coffee and then said, "You know what? We should go get a green chili

cheeseburger. Have you ever had one?"

"No, what's that?"

"Well, here in the Southwest, there are these peppers that grow. Mainly in New Mexico and some in southern Colorado. The Hatches are the most famous. They harvest them in the fall and on almost every street corner in the cities, people sell 'em. You can smell 'em roasting from miles away. You go up to these tents and they have varieties available, like six or seven. From mild to scorch your ass hot. You can mix them up if you want. They take a bushel, and they roast them for ya."

"Wow, are they good?"

"Then people take 'em home, peel 'em and make a kind of chili sauce out of them."

"So, what's the big deal?"

"The flavor from these chilies is amazing, you gotta try one. Nowadays, restaurants make up batches of it and freeze it. That way, they can have it all year long. We gotta go to Mama's. Do you like hot stuff? Even if you don't, Mama's has some incredible burgers. My favorite is huge, it is the MOAB, 'Mother of All Burgers.' It has everything but the kitchen sink. One of Arizona's ten best burgers and it is practically in our backyard. Oh, oh and, plus, the best shakes ever. So, you heat up your mouth on the green chilis and then cool it down with the delicious shake. We gotta go!"

"Sounds interesting. I'm game."

"You don't sound as excited as me. It's not fancy, but golly Mike, it's fantastic."

"Who's Mike?"

"Shut up, let's go."

They pulled up to Mama's burger and Stewart was less than impressed. It looked like an old Dairy Queen or A&W Root Beer place. There was outside seating and a drive-up window around this old brick structure. A simple "RESTAURANT" sign adorned the roofline and Mama's logoed sign stood on a pole. This was a family restaurant with Mama and her two daughters working at the restaurant. Everything was fresh and the aromas were to die for. Inside, they went to the counter to order. Sheryl knew exactly what to order and Stewart took his time. They placed the order and sat. One of the girls brought them their meal on a tray and they began a taste explosion. Stewart got his chilis on the side and so when he forked a little onto a bit, he was stunned by the flavor. It was a taste he had never experienced, and he was pleased. They chased their burgers with chocolate shakes and left the place totally satisfied.

During the meal, there was not much discussion, nor was there much on the ride, both were thinking. Stewart was thinking about his dreams and Sheryl was thinking about restarting her life at age fifty-one.

The thought of living with Stewart could be the worst thing I ever do. He's so different from when we were kids. Maybe I could keep working on his fucking attitude and change him for the better. Maybe just being around me would help him. I so don't want to pack my things and leave. There is so much of this place I love. The rises and sets of the sun are delicious to the eyes. Did you hear you? That's a good one, I should say that out loud sometime. I love not having a top on my Jeep. I know I can only do this a week out of the whole fucking year. It's so cold there in the wintertime. Oh, wintertime, snow at Christmas. Why do I care I don't celebrate Christmas? Maybe I will. Maybe I can get back into the swing of the season. It's been so long since I Christmas shopped. And, oh, I get to hang out with my old friends. Damn, I wish I had not missed my high school reunion. I should probably join Facebook. Yeah, maybe. Well, I can have great Italian food again. Hmm, no green chili. I'll have to import it. Oh, the sunshine. I'm going to miss the sunshine. Wow, what a nice day today.

At the same time, Stewart was thinking:

What are we going to do, Sheryl and me? She's an emotional basket case. She cries at the drop of a hat. I guess I need to be careful with the hats. I hope it's true that time heals all wounds. I think it'll be good to have someone else in the house. It gets so lonely since Dad died. She never really liked Dad. He never really liked her. He might have loved her, but I don't remember them ever having anything in common. I wonder if she likes to fish. I want a boat. I wonder if she likes golf. I hate watching golf on television. I don't really like television. I like daydreaming. I have to get back to work. I wonder if I'll have a job when I go back. Yeah, it's only been three weeks. I told 'em I'd be gone for a month. Wow, that means I need to leave next week. I should tell her.

"Sheryl, remember when you asked me how long I'd be here?"

"Yeah, you said you didn't know."

"That's right. When I left Jersey, I took a month off. I didn't know how long we could stand each other. Well, I think things have gone pretty well these three weeks."

"No, two weeks. Count again, Mr. Accountant."

He thought for a minute and then said, "Wow, yeah, two weeks."

"Have you heard from anyone back in Jersy?"

"No. Well, yeah, my friend Bob did text me. Bob is a divorcee who was an aeronautic engineer. He worked on spacecraft for some company. He got divorced, retired, made some incredible investments, and now he's filthy rich. He plays golf three times a week, and the rest of his time is fiddling in his yard. He has a Tacoma and goes mudding. Sometimes, he takes me fishing. I think Bob is my only friend. You'll like him. He's much older than us, but he doesn't seem to like it. Do you think it's weird that you'll associate with someone fifteen or twenty years your senior now, but when you're fifteen, that guy wants nothing to do with you? It seems to me, Sheryl, that when you reach your middle age, it's a big club. We are all in the same boat. Pain, suffering, loss of loved ones. We can't do the things we used to be able to do, although I didn't do much. A sedentary life is our path. Some, like me, don't even leave the house. I don't even like going to the grocery store. Price now allows us to work from home, and there's no reason for me to go into the city other than to go to Joe's. I go once a week to keep my desk. I don't know why. My desk at home has almost everything I need. I get everything via email, and I rarely see a client face-to-face. Back when I started, I had to meet at the client's offices to go over books. Nothing was on the computer; we didn't even have such a thing as a laptop.

Sheryl had stopped listening back at the grocery store. She thought, *how can I deal with this, fucking on and on blabbering. Hania was so quiet. It will be nice to go to the theatre and to the movie openings instead of waiting. It'll be nice to have a schmear on a real New York bagel. It'll be nice to go into the city and see my old friends. God, I hope they're still alive. So many have died. Stewart told me Ashley had died. That's so sad.*

They arrived home. Stewart was a sweaty mess, and Sheryl was delighted with the cooler weather. To her, temperatures in the eighties were indeed cooler. They went into the clinic and down the stairs as usual. When they got there, Tricia was in her living room measuring. It was a tense moment. They said their hellos, and each went to their separate rooms. Stewart went straight to the shower, and Sheryl fell on the bed. She felt so betrayed by her friend that she started crying.

Stewart finished his shower, dressed in some of the cooler clothing he had recently purchased, and went out to the living room. Tricia had left, and he was alone. He took out his phone from his pocket and noticed he had missed a call from his friend Bob. He called him back.

***

Elu and his posy made it back to the reservation safely. No one would be able to find him. He thought all of the witnesses in the bar had died. So, when he laid his head to rest, he slept that night. When he woke up the next morning, it was a knock on the door. He answered the door, and the nation's police and the Flagstaff police were standing on his front porch. His Mom and Dad had gone to their perspective jobs, and so he was alone in the house. Bidzill has been a classmate of his and is now a police officer in the nation's police. Most people called him Benny.

"Benny, what's up," Elu said to Bidzill.

"Earl, I'm going to need you to step outside with me. We need to ask you a few questions."

"What's this about Benny?"

"Come on out, let's take a ride, and we'll talk about it."

"Who's your friend?"

"Well, this is Officer O'Malley from the Flagstaff Police Department. Come on outside, and we'll have a little talk."

"Alright."

He came outside, and O'Malley pounced on him. He threw him to the ground, handcuffed him, and lifted him up.

"Did you need to do that? He was complying."

"He's dangerous. He nearly killed seventy-two people."

"Allegedly," Benny said.

"Seriously, Benny, you saw the footage. Earl, Elu Hollister, you are under arrest for arson and seventy-two counts of attempted murder. You are going to federal prison for a hate crime, and you will die there, come with me. I'm going to read you your rights. You have the right..."

The war Elu started had ended without a shot. Three days after arriving at the county jail, he was stabbed and died.

Chapter Nine: The Crime

After several hours of "friends" reruns, Stewart was crazy. He had a "smelly cat" song in his head and needed a respite. He flipped through the channels and found nothing. So, he got up and went to Hania's den and looked for a book. On the shelf, he found an interesting little book entitled "Unlikely Angels." The book looked like it had been read a hundred times. It was a paperback book with a baby's picture on the front. He read the back cover and then decided to take it to the living room and give it a try. The story was about two boys who fell for the same girl. They were in grade school at the time, so later in life, when they were reintroduced, it was shocking to one of them that his long-lost friend had gotten the girl who got away. After a few encounters, one of the characters realizes he is better off where he is even though the torch has never been properly extinguished.

Sheryl came out to the living room to find Stewart reading this unknown author's book. She was surprised as it was her favorite book. She had read it at least fifty times in the eleven years she had it. She commented, "That's one of my favorite books. It is full of little life lessons. I wonder if that author has written anything else."

"I'm almost done, don't tell me how it ends. I like the dialogue in the book. I'd prefer a single point of view, but it is interesting how the writer weaves the perspectives. I think this would make a good movie."

"Ya know, I have thought the same. I could tell you almost every line. I got this book when I ordered some others from the publisher. They bundled five books together for the price of three. I didn't expect it to be so good."

"I'm almost done. What are we doing for dinner?"

"That's a good question. I don't have any plans."

"Tricia isn't really my friend anymore. She betrayed me."

"What, what do you mean?"

"She told the nation, and that's why the president came to tell us to leave. He gave us nearly two months, but still, if she hadn't told him... Also, it's why I can't finish your treatments."

"Was she your only friend?"

"Kind of, yeah."

"Hmm, let's go home, sis."

"I have lived here thirty-three years Stewart. She was my only friend," she began to weep.

Stewart put his arm around his sister in the kitchen, then hugged her and held her as she wept. He thought she might be lonely or maybe lonelier than me. "Let's change that."

"Don't worry, sis, we'll get to the city and get you reacquainted with all your old friends in no time. We'll be out partying and having a good time. I'll even go along with ya. You'll see; it'll all be fun and games."

"You know, Stew, I think you might be right. And, you know what else? I think you might be changing. I think what I'm doing might be working."

"You think. Thank you, Sheryl. I will say I'd like to go back to that bar again before we leave. Maybe that Jennifer gal will be there."

"I'll be your wing gal. Tonight?"

"We just went there two nights ago. Do you think she'll be there again?"

"Yeah, that's right, prolly not. But you might meet some other Arizona hotties there."

"Sounds worth the try."

They went to the two bars and found Monday nights to be a bust. They were home before ten in the evening. Sheryl said, "You wanna try the peyote again tonight?

I dialed back the strength. I think you only need a little."

"Okay, yeah, then we'll figure out our moving adventure tomorrow."

"I like that," she said and started the prayer as he consumed the mixture.

Within minutes, Stewart was groggy, and Sheryl helped him to bed. He could hardly stand or walk, and he ended up falling asleep on the bed in his clothes.

Oh great, we're back at the house, surveillance again. This is going to suck. I wonder how long we're going to sit here this time. It seems this dream is even clearer. It's like I'm really here. Hmm, still can't move anything. I hope I do more than just sit in this car.

Well, the lights just went out in the house. I suppose that's interesting. What's next? Come on, what's next? Let's do something. Here I sit. What a boring dream. My dreams used to have action in them. I guess I wait. This music, even soft, sucks. Sigh. Come on. This has to be the worst, most boring dream...

Okay, an hour has passed. Listen, Tony, do something already. Oh, okay, we are. Ski mask, on. Open the door. Closing it quietly. Trunk. Gun, yeah, we'll need that—weird looking gun, like a dart gun. Hmm... Propane tank? What's that for? I suppose we'll find out. Gas mask, yeah, everyone needs that. We're going around back. Sneaking in. Now we're talking about fun. We're in the kitchen. Stove. Gas. Blow out the pilot light. Oh, here we go. It seems I'm carrying the propane tank upstairs, I wonder. Oh. I put it down. The boy's room. Ouch, I just shot the kid with the dart gun. Now I'm reloading. The girl's room. Got her, too. What a beautiful house. Reloading. Down the hall, there's Mom. Got her. Reloading again. Now the accountant. Okay, we're pulling that one out quickly. I smell the gas already. That was quick. Okay, I'm on top of the accountant. I'm strapping the gas mask on him.

Attaching it to the propane. Turning it on. He doesn't like that. I can see the fear in his eyes. Why am I doing this? Oh, now Tony is speaking, "This is for stealing money from the boss. You and your family will die tonight." It took a few minutes, and then his eyes closed. Tony rolled off the man, put the mask on the sleeping woman and repeated the process. After three minutes, her pulse stopped. He took the dart out of her and put it in a pouch he had on his belt. That's a good place for it. I guess we're going to do it to the boy now. Yeah, it is his turn. He's so young and innocent. He's gone. The dart. Yeah, he took the dart. Now, the girl. Just kill the girl and get out of here, Tony. Tony began putting the mask on her and stopped. He set the mask aside and began undressing her. The smell of gas was very strong, so he stopped what he was thinking of doing. He put the mask on her, waited three minutes, checked her pulse and removed the dart.

We left the room.

Down the stairs, we go. Out the back. Back to the car. I don't smell gas any longer. Oh, we're going to sit here still. No. We're leaving. Driving. He's rolling down the window. Oh, a picture. No, a flare gun. Aim, window, shoot. Oh my God, huge explosion, big fucking explosion. Good thing that the house is so far from the street. Man, it rocked the Range Rover. It's engulfed in flames. I'm looking back. Wow. Huge fire.

We haven't been driving long. Why are we stopping? Oh. Gotta ditch the car. There's the Rover. Of course. We torch the car. Dart gun, check; propane tank, check; Gas can for the car, check; gas mask, check. All in the back of the Rover. Now, we take off the ski mask. Did he get the flare gun? Where's the flare gun? Dude, that's evidence against ya. Did you leave it? Looks like we're driving again. Where we going, killer? Nice, it's starting to rain. Driving. Driving. Turn. Turn. Turn. Stopping. Oh, perfect, a bar at four in the morning. Can't we just go to sleep dude. No. We're going inside. This is a rough place. Empty mostly. A shotgun kind of place. Tables are to the left, like two rows, and the bar is to the right. Hmm, we're passing the bar. Nod from the bartender. Oh, there's a back room. Knocking.

"State your name," *somebody on the other side of the door said.*

"It's Tony."

"Come in."

Oh, this is typical. A desk, a dude in a suit, black suit as a matter of fact. He told the chick to get lost. Nice guy. This dream is getting better. What's next, the payoff?

"It's done."

The guy is reaching into his drawer. Oh, an envelope. He's saying, "It's all there. Take it. Go. We'll be in touch."

We're taking it. Turning around, walking out.

"Oh, and Tony. Good job."

How did he know it was a good job? We just finished. Maybe someone was watching us. Oh. Wait. Tony stopped. I'm talking, "How did you know?"

"We watched the whole thing. Don't know exactly how things went down inside, but we assume, based on the tools you used, it was done and done right. Hope you made the bastard suffer."

"I did."

"Good. Get lost."

"Gotcha, boss." *Walking again, up the bar.* "Buffalo Trace, neat."

The bartender is pouring us a bourbon. I haven't had that one. Wow, tastes good. Gone. Here we go. Still raining. Now, can we go home and sleep?

Tony got into the Range Rover. He started it up and blared the rap music. Stewart's head was pounding in his sleep from the horrid music. He tried to think of something else. Fifteen minutes later, Tony was on the elevator up to his apartment. Once inside, he went to the bathroom and showered.

Oh, yeah, a shower, a bed and some sleep. Figures, we're pissing on the floor in the shower. Lathering, rinsing, I'm so tired. Bed. Eyes closed. Darkness.

Stewart's body was getting used to the peyote and his sleep had lessened as he woke at nine o'clock in the morning only ten hours later. He lay in bed thinking about what he had seen in his dream the night before. It all seemed so real, not like any other dream.

He got out of bed, showered, and went to the kitchen where Sheryl was sitting, drinking a cup of coffee. Her laptop was in front of her, and she seemed lost in it. Stewart came in, poured himself a cup, sat down, "What's up, sis?"

"Good morning to you, too. I'm looking for a job in Jersey."

"A job? Why? You can hang out there for a while. I still have some time. We can get you reacquainted with the area. I bet you'll see a lot has changed."

"Okay, a few weeks. I was just keeping myself occupied."

"Want breakfast? I'm buying."

"Okay then, we need to try out Casa Duarte's. Martanne's menu is superb; her pork green chili is to die for."

"Green chili, I'm game, let's go.

They rolled up to another strip mall. Casa was at the far end. The place looked nice from the outside, with seating for a few dozen on the patio. Once inside, the décor was Mexican, with paintings of the Virgin Mary, a few Catholic-looking pictures, and a cool black and crystal chandelier over the entrance. Hardwood floors filled the space, and against the windows were tufted faux leather oblong booths. The wood tables matched the floor color, and the walls were a warm, soft copper color, almost beige, almost orange. The art was framed with mahogany-colored carved frames as the appointments gave the ideal ambiance. From outside the building, the aroma was tantalizing, and as they walked in, they noticed a few people waiting. It was ten thirty in the morning, and the place was full on a Wednesday. The hostess told them it would be ten minutes in Spanglish. Sheryl understood, but Stewart didn't. The bar was empty except for individual men eating. They stood silently, looking around. Sheryl knew the taste and aroma would meet.

It was less than ten minutes, and the young girl led them to a table for two in the middle of the room. She handed them menus and walked away. They opened the menus and began looking. The hostess returned with chips and salsa and then asked if they wanted queso or guacamole. Sheryl answered, "Their guacamole is a phenom. Yeah, let's have some." Then she realized they were there for breakfast, but it was too late. She was gone.

The waitress came over, delivered the guacamole, and asked what they would like to drink. Sheryl responded, "I'll have coffee and spicy Bloody Mary."

Stewart said, "Same for me, 'cept, don't make the Bloody Mary spicy."

"Are you ready to order?"

Sheryl quickly answered, "No, please give us a minute." She walked away.

"Whatcha gonna get, sis?"

"I'm getting my favorite, 'tamale y huevo,' red chile beef tamale, hash browns, beans, cheese, topped with an over medium egg, onions and avocado. It is so good."

"I'm going to get the 'green chile omelet,' three egg omelet, with shaved ham and diced green chilies or the house green chile pork, green sauce and cheese.

Which one should I do: shaved ham or house green chili?"

"Me, I'd go with the house green chili."

"Settled."

The waitress arrived with the drinks, took the order, and vanished into the kitchen. The noise in the place was a mixture of languages, chatter, plates tapping together, forks on plates, and faint Spanish music in the background. Stewart was satisfied with his meal's mixture of Southwestern flavors and sat back feeling fat and happy.

"So, sis, I wanted to tell you about my dreams."

"I hope it's not like the wet one you had the other night."

"No, it was so strange. So real. In short, I murdered four people in my dream."

"You what?"

"So, apparently, in my dream, I'm like a hitman. I've been hired by the mafia to kill an accountant who's been skimming."

"That's interesting, an accountant that is skimming. You're not skimming, are you, bro?"

"No, I don't have account access, sis. I'm just a staff accountant. Anyway, my name in my dreams is Tony.

I'm like this stud Italian guy."

"What? You're not yourself?"

"Yeah, that's the weirdest part. I look in the mirror, I have long hair, a six-pack, muscles, and a tan. Other shit too that I don't really wanna explain."

"What, like you got a two-foot dick?"

"Not two-foot but huge, yeah. Remember, in my dream, I'm a total stud. So, in my dream the night before last, I staked out this house. I watched this family leave and go to this pizza place. Oh, if you are ever in Chicago, that's where this is set. You gotta try Giuseppe's Pizza. It's not Joe's, but it's fucking delicious."

"You could fucking taste the pizza in your dream?"

"Yeah, that's another weird thing. Since I have been taking the peyote, I can smell and taste it in my dreams. I see in color, and the only thing I can't do is move independently. Oh, and I can't feel pain or pleasure either."

"That is fucking strange, go on."

"So, the other night, I watched the family, then last night I returned to their house, gassed them all, and blew the house up. It was so real; I could feel the heat as I drove past."

"You blew the house up? How the hell."

"Well, when I first got to the house, I turned on the gas, blew out the pilot light, and let the house fill with gas. I was there about fifteen minutes; I suppose enough time to fill it with gas..."

"Then what'd ya do?"

"Well, then I went to this bar, met the boss, and got paid."

"And?"

"And then I went home, I mean, to the apartment I guess I have in Chicago. I showered and went to bed."

"Tell me about the shower."

"Really?"

"Well, fuck yeah, then tell me about the body again. Girl needs a fantasy."

"So, sis, do you think there's anything to this?"

"I don't know. Lemme google house explosion in Chicago and see what comes up." She grabbed her phone, went to Safari, and googled

"House explosion Chicago yesterday."

"Oh, shit, Stewart, it's fucking real. Listen to this, 'Family of four killed in a house explosion in Oak Park. The police are investigating a home explosion in Oak Park where a family, identity withheld, has died. Early this morning, the explosion from an apparent gas leak rocked the affluent Oak Park neighborhood. Neighbors were awakened by shattering glass that could be felt four square blocks away. The identity of the family is being withheld until the next of kin can be informed. More on this story in tomorrow's issue. In a perhaps related story, a car was set on fire ten blocks from the scene of the explosion. Police are investigating this suspicious car, which Lt. Grayson says was stolen earlier yesterday from a retail store in Lincolnwood.' You didn't tell me you torched a car, too."

"Oh yeah, I torched a car too. Sheryl, my dream was real. It really happened. What the fuck! I know the guy. I can finger him."

"Finger him, ha ha ha, that's fucking funny, now you sound like a hitman. Finger him."

"Seriously, I see him in the mirror every dream."

"Sheet, let me think. Hmm... you can't tell anyone."

"Why?"

"Well, if you fucking tell someone, then the tribe will know what I did."

"So, fucking what. This guy is a killer. I need to bring him to justice."

"Now listen to you. You sound like that guy from that show."

"That guy from that show? What guy, what show?"

"Lemme think, Timothy, Timothy, what's his last name, Timothy elephant, no Oliphant, right, that guy, Timothy Oliphant from the show, 'Justified.' Damn, he is hot."

"Oh God. Really? You're thinking of sexy actors, and I'm telling you I witnessed a real crime here."

"Who is gonna fucking believe you saw this in a dream?"

He sat back in his chair, looked around the room, and then down at his dirty, empty plate. He looked her square in the eye and said, "No one is going to believe it."

"Right. So, forget it. Maybe later, I can try something that might reverse it."

"You'd do that for me?"

"Well, sure, bro. I kinda got you into this, didn't I?"

"Not gonna blame you. I asked for something, and neither of us knew what was going to happen."

"I will say there have been a few improvements. I'd hate to reverse that."

"Seriously? What?" Stewart asked.

"Well, you never bought me breakfast, ever."

"You ask me instead of telling me. You were nice to the people in the bar, and that girl wanted you. Physically, you've changed. Your shoulders seem squarer, and your confidence seems greater. You are more conscientious and considerate. Before it was 'all about you.' Now, it's not."

He took a step back and said, "I didn't notice."

"Uh-huh, it's why I even gave it a second thought about moving back home with you. If you hadn't changed, I would not have given it a thought. I think we can have some fun now."

"I'm touched, sis. But what do I do about the murders?" he said with concern.

"Should we talk to someone?" she asked.

"Who?"

"Maybe a cop," she said, scratching her head and adjusting the hair away from her eyes.

"Do you know a cop?" he asked, resting his arms on the table and leaning forward.

"I met a few when Hania was murdered. Maybe I reach out to one of the nation's police. Yeah, let's do that. We're done here. Let's go to the station when," she said and then sat back.

"Sheryl?"

"Yeah!"

Stewart sat back as well and said, "We've both had three Bloody Marys."

"Oh, yeah, maybe tomorrow," she said, laughing.

Stewart laughed along, "Yeah, tomorrow."

"For now, let's go find you some souvenirs' to bring home."

"Sounds good."

They paid the server, left the restaurant, dropped the top on the Jeep, and headed up US 180 to the Grand Canyon. Along the way, they stopped at the Grand Canyon Outpost. It was at the intersection of US 180 and US 64. The sign said, "We have a little of this and that." That was what they found: beef jerky, local jewelry, t-shirts, and hats. Stewart bought himself and Sheryl similar western hats with cords to hold them down as they drove in the open air in a windy Jeep. Then they turned on US 64 and headed north. The terrain was flat, brown, and ugly. Up ahead, Stewart could see mountains and trees. They came up to some trees and began to line both sides of the road. They were in what seemed like a forest. The road got hilly. They pulled up to a building that appeared to be an old fort on the right. An adobe brick building on his left was a modern building that looked more like a hotel. Between the buildings was the entrance to the Grand Canyon. The colors of the rocks were more magnificent than he could ever imagine. Before the Jeep stopped, he jumped out and ran to the edge. She parked the Jeep in the nearest spot. She walked up, and a very old man began talking to her. She stopped to hear him. "Your husband," She quickly interrupted, "My brother." The old man continued, "Your brother did what everyone I see here does." He ran to the opening and was in awe. Flies could make homes in his open mouth. He looked left, and he looked right. Then, on the path, he dropped, sat, put his face in his hands, and began to cry. The old man continued, "He is stunned by how big the God of the universe is. He is stunned by how God can create such beauty and magnificence. Now look at him. He weeps like a baby because he feels so small."

Sheryl continued walking toward Stewart and then sat next to him. She asked, "Is everything alright?"

Between sobs, he answered, "Yes, I just feel so small."

She turned and looked back at the old man; he nodded. Then, she went back to consoling her brother until he stopped. One of the fire ants on the ground began feasting on Stewart's leg, and he immediately jumped up and began brushing ants off his bare legs. In the end, five ants got their teeth into him. It was his first experience with fire ants. Sheryl stood up with him, and together, they absorbed the colors until the light from the sky vanished. They turned, and under the streetlamps, they made their way back to the Jeep. They put the top up and headed back to Flagstaff.

Chapter Ten: Meeting A Navajo Cop

Stewart and Sheryl settled into bed early, and Stewart quickly fell asleep. His dreams seemed almost normal, but the main subject was still Tony. Tony's night was back at the organ transplant delivery waiting room. He sat all night without a single delivery. At the end of his shift, he went home and went straight to bed, allowing Stewart better sleep.

Stewart woke up at around nine again to Sheryl again at the kitchen table. He had fallen into her routine. Coffee, then breakfast out, then it was time to visit the Nations police department. With the top down on the Jeep, the ride to the Twin Arrows Casino substation was less than a half hour. When they arrived, the desk officer was kind and courteous.

"Good morning, folks. Is there something we can help you with?"

Sheryl responded, "Hello, we would like to talk to Lieutenant Chee, please."

"Do you have an appointment?"

"No. I'm sorry we don't," she answered.

"Is this an urgent matter because Lieutenant Chee isn't in right now," the man behind the desk answered.

Sheryl continued nervously, "Well, he helped me with a recent case, and I kind of know him. I suppose we can talk to another detective or officer."

"Might I ask what this is in regard to so that I can give you to the right person?"

Sheryl spoke up again, "Well, officer."

"Sorry, ma'am, I'm Sergeant Yazzie."

"Oh. Sorry, Sergeant. Well, I'm Sheryl Benally. I was married to Dr. Hania Benally. Some called him Dr. Henry. He was murdered a month or so ago, and my brother here came to visit me a few weeks ago. Since Hania was a medicine man and I still had his books, I cooked up some peyote for his attitude. It was a legal concoction, and it did something weird for my brother."

"Stop right there. You made a peyote?"

Sheryl confidently answered, "Yes."

"I think you should stop. You are tiptoeing on a slippery slope. Doing the work of a medicine man might be illegal," the sergeant warned.

"If it is, I'll take my punishment, but what I'm about to tell you is far more concerning."

"Okay, then proceed. I want to caution you, though. I may be able to use it against you."

Looking concerned, he said, Stewart stepped in and began, "Excuse me, sir, I'm not going to allow my sister to implicate herself, so allow me to tell you the issue."

"That's fine, sir. What is your name?"

"Me? My name is Stewart Miller. I'm visiting from New Jersey. I've been having some very strange dreams." The sergeant looked down and took a deep breath. "You see, since my sister helped me, I've been seeing the same person and basically watching his life. I have to tell you it is very real."

"I'm sure it is. Can you get to the point?"

He took a deep breath as the sergeant's tone heated his blood slightly. "I witnessed a quadruple homicide in my dream the night before last. We checked yesterday, and in fact, the dream was real, and the people are dead."

Rudely, the sergeant replied, "So now, you are somehow clairvoyant?"

"Right, the family was involved in a home explosion, and I saw it all."

"Just where was this alleged home explosion, and why are you coming here?"

Annoyed, Stewart continued, "We came to you because you likely believe in the works of the medicine man and the spiritual effects of some of the procedures. We thought if we went to the Chicago Police, they would just laugh at us. We expected more from you."

"This happened in Chicago. Well, sir, that is way out of our jurisdiction. I can't really help with that," he said as he began to move away from the desk.

Sheryl chimed in, "We were hoping you might give us some advice."

"Oh, I have some advice. It is; go home or go somewhere other than here and not tell anyone in law enforcement about this. Now, if there isn't anything else, I would hope you would please leave me be," he turned and tried to leave the room.

"Well, sergeant, thank you for your time. Might I just ask that you have Lieutenant Chee call me when he is free," Sheryl finished. She gave him her name and phone number, and they left.

The sergeant turned around and watched them as they walked out. Then he went over to a desk, sat and brought Google up. He did a search for home explosions in Chicago and found one had occurred in Oak Park, Illinois, a suburb of Chicago. He saw that four people perished and that the police didn't expect foul play. Then he saw that the adjacent story was about the car fire in the same vicinity around the same time. He picked up the phone and dialed Lieutenant Chee's number.

"Hello, Chee here."

"Lieutenant, this is Yassie at Twin Arrows."

"Yeah, Sergeant, what's up? How are Chenoa and the kids?"

"They are well. Kids are a handful, as you might expect. How are yours," Yassie answered, smiling.

"Bout the same, whatcha got?" Chee asked.

Yassie started, "You know the late Dr. Hania Benally. Some called him Dr. Henry and his wife, Sheryl?"

"Oh yeah, great people. I cannot tell you how many times that man saved my life and the lives of my family," Chee said gratefully.

Yassie continued, "Well, Sheryl Benally was just in here with her brother, Stewart Miller, from New Jersey. Seems she gave him some peyote and did some prayers, and it opened a sort of portal in his mind that he sees crimes in Chicago."

"I'd say it was farfetched if I didn't know them personally," Chee interrupted.

Puzzled, Yassie asked, "You know this Stewart guy?"

"No, I mean Sheryl and Henry. If Sheryl says, it happened, it happened."

Yassie continued, "Well, I went online and checked. Yes, a home exploded in Chicago. So far, they have ruled it an accident with a gas leak."

"What did this Stewart guy tell you?"

"He said he witnessed a guy kill the family," he said, questioning his own response.

Chee responded, "I think I need to talk to Stewart. Do you have his number?"

"No, but I have Sheryl's."

"I have Sheryl's. I'll call her and set up a meeting. Thanks for this. I'll take care of it from here," the Lieutenant said.

"Copy that, sir, talk soon."

"You take care of that family, and I'll see you at the picnic next weekend."

"Right, we'll be there," Yassie said, smiling.

The Lieutenant called Sheryl, "Hello Sheryl, this is..."

"Hi Lieutenant, I thought you would get back to me."

"Yes, can I meet your brother, say, at four at the Roadhouse?"

"You're coming down here?" Sheryl asked.

"Of course, I never miss a chance to go to the Roadhouse," Chee said with a grin.

"Okay, yeah, see you then," she ended the call and turned to Stewart. "Looks like the Lieutenant is going to meet with us after all. At four this afternoon. I wanted you to see the Roadhouse anyway. It's a place where you can grill your own meat right there in the dining room. It's very cool. The Route 66 Roadhouse is the whole name."

"Seriously? Will they grill it for me?"

"Yes, it's optional."

"So, if I get this straight, all there is to do around these parts is eat and drink."

"Pretty much. Let's go four-wheeling, wanna?"

"Why not? Let's do it."

Sheryl turned off on a dirt road and made a few more turns, and they were rock climbing before he knew it.

After a few hours in the sun, they went back to the clinic to get cleaned up. Stewart took an eventless nap, and then at three-thirty, they were on their way to the Roadhouse.

The Route 66 Roadhouse is an old metal building painted charcoal gray with a red gutter and fascia. Stewart could see himself in the mirrored front door as he approached. The deep red floor looked slippery as it was so clean, and the red neon surrounded the bar. Sheryl looked around for the Lieutenant but didn't see him. She figured he was running behind. She pointed out a round table near the billiards with round red vinyl and chrome stools. They sat, and a young lady named Sara introduced herself. Sheryl said, "I know you, you are Sakari. You're Hania's niece."

"Hi, Aunt Sheryl. How have you been? I'm so sorry to hear about Uncle Henry."

"Thanks. Me? I'm fine. This is my brother, Stewart. He's from back East. Gotta show him all the hot spots. How long have you been working here?"

"Well, not more than a month. My youngest just turned two, so it was time I found a good job."

"Did you ever think about maybe working in the clinic?"

"I thought about it. Are they hiring?"

"Should be. Tricia's gonna stop working. Maybe you can get her job."

"I'll look into it. Oh look, Officer Sam is here," Sara responded.

"Yeah, the Lieutenant is here to see us," Sheryl said.

"Hi there, Sam. Whatcha all want?"

"Hi Sara, I'll have a kill the keg pint," said Sam.

Stewart answered, "Water for me for now."

"I'll have a kill the keg too, pints, right?" Sheryl said. "Indeed."

"Perfect, gimme a pint," she said with a wink. "Lieutenant, allow me to introduce you to my brother Stewart."

"Hi, Stewart," he said, reaching his hand out for a handshake, continuing, "I'm Sam Chee. You can call me Sam, if you'd like."

"Thank you, Sam. A pleasure to meet you."

"Sheryl, how have you been? I bet it's good to see your brother here now."

"Me. I've been better. Gonna move on back to Jersey. I still have family there. Stewart and I need to rebuild some things. Yeah, it is good for him to be here now. 'Cept we got a problem."

"So I heard."

"Uh-huh, gonna let Stewart tell you all about it."

He turned to Stewart and said, "Don't get me wrong, son, I wanna hear all about it, but I haven't had anything to eat and have been saving my appetite for the best bacon cheeseburger in the world. So when Sara comes back here, we are going to order. You got it?"

"Yes, sir, Lieutenant."

"I thought I told you to call me Sam."

"I will. That was a demanding Lieutenant kind of statement, so it demanded the lieutenant response," Stewart said meekly and then began, "I got here almost three weeks ago, and I was angry and mean. Sheryl mixed up a potion of peyote and said a few prayers, and it helped my attitude. She thought I was leaving sooner rather than later, so she increased the dosage, and that's when she opened my mind to see this guy, Tony."

Sara arrived with the drinks.

Sam said, "Have you ever eaten here?"

Stewart said, "No."

Sam began, "Well, let me tell you. They have five items on their menu because they want to make them the best. I don't know how they do it, but they have the most amazing chicken quesadilla. Around these parts where people know their quesadilla, everyone says it's the best. The Bacon cheeseburger will make your eyes spin. It is phenomenal. Hell, I like it all."

Sara said, "He does. I have seen him almost eat the whole menu in one sitting."

Stewart said, "I'll try the quesadilla and potato salad."

Sheryl replied, "I do love the quesadilla, but today I feel like the Roadhouse Club."

"Great choice. Would you like potato salad, too?"

"Do you really need to ask?" Sheryl replied sarcastically.

"Sam, you want the usual bacon cheeseburger on the onion roll or the Kaiser? With the mixed cheese, too, right?" Sara asked.

"You know me too well. Yes, and the bow tie pasta."

"Got it. Coming right up."

Stewart continued, "After Sheryl gave me the peyote, I fell fast asleep and began dreaming. At first, it was like a normal dream, you know, the kinds of dreams guys have."

"Uh-huh, I think so," Sam responded.

"Well, I noticed the first night I could faintly smell stuff. The second night, I could smell and taste, and then, on the third night, it was like I was there. That was the night that Tony killed all those people."

"Now, how do you know they were killed? The official report says it was an accident."

"I saw it all. On the second night, we watched the family. We went to a pizza place. I could taste the pizza; it was so weird. I could actually taste the pizza. Tony burned his mouth, but I didn't feel that. Anyways, we sat and watched them then we went back and waited outside their home to see what time they went to bed. Oh. I almost forgot. Before we went to the pizza place after they left home, we went inside the house. He or we looked around. He, Tony, had a key, and he knew the alarm code. We checked out the bedrooms, the kitchen and the windows. Then we went back to the pizza place."

"Back to the pizza place?"

"Right, Tony followed them to the pizza place, watched 'em go in and then backtracked to the house. Once finished at the house, we went and watched them at Giuseppe's. They finished eating, left and we got back to the house and just watched until the lights went out. The next night, we waited until the lights went out. After an hour or so, we went in. Tony had a gas mask, a tranquilizer dart gun and a propane tank. He blew out the pilot light and turned the gas on. Then he went up the stairs and shot the boy, then the girl, then the mom. When he got to the dad, he shot him but only left the dart in him a few seconds, so he was conscious."

Sara arrived with the meals. She served Sheryl first. She looked at the stack of meat and toast and smiled. Then she set Stewart's quesadilla down. He inhaled, and he could smell the chicken and the spices. The tortilla was golden and spotty from the grill. When Sara put down the cheeseburger, Stewart eyed it up and down.

Sam looked at him and said, "Hey man, this is mine. You got the best thing on the menu, with potato salad. Just wait."

Sara giggled and asked, "Anything else?"

Sam said, "Another round."

Sara responded, "Are you off duty?"

He snapped back, "Are you my mother?"

They both laughed, and she walked away.

Stewart was very pleased with his quesadilla and, on his last bite, said, "Shall I continue?"

"Damn, son, you ate that quick. Please do. Yeah, go ahead," Sam responded.

Stewart started up, "It was really good. I couldn't put it down."

"Didn't I tell you?" Sam said.

"You did, and the potato salad. Who knew potato salad could be so good? Okay, here we go again. Tony put the gas mask on the man connected to the propane and turned it on. He looked right in the guy's eyes. I couldn't believe it. I saw the guy struggling in his head, but he was unable to move. Tony said, 'The boss hired me to kill you and your family because you took from him.' The guy died right there. I watched him die. It was terrible. Then Tony did the mom. The rest were asleep, so they didn't suffer, that I could tell. He was about to rape the girl, and then we smelled gas. So, we left. A few minutes later, he shot a flare gun through the window as we drove past, and the house exploded.

Tony drove a few blocks away, ditched and torched the car. The next day, yesterday, I told Sheryl about my real dream over breakfast and some Bloody Marys, and she looked it up. Sure enough, it was real. Sam, I remember all the details."

"That is quite a story, Stewart. What do you think I can do to help?"

Sheryl said, "We were thinking maybe you could guide us as to our next steps, Sam. You see, we didn't think a police officer in Chicago would take Stewart seriously."

"You are correct, Sheryl. If not for witnessing your husband's wonders myself, I wouldn't believe it. I'm not sure I do believe it. Stewart, what happened last night?"

"He worked at his usual job. He transports organs from what looks like a halfway hospital to other hospitals."

"Oh. He works at a place we like to call an organ mill. Most of the time, they are legitimate, but sometimes they're not."

"He took organs to hospitals, they were expecting him, so I'm thinking it was legit. Last night they didn't have anything to deliver. He complains there's not much action there. He works nights and sleeps during the day."

"Do you know his name and address?"

"I only know him as Tony. I've seen his place. It's a high-rise apartment building; I haven't seen the name or the address. I don't know his last name."

"Do you know the boss' name?"

"No, he just calls him boss."

"I don't have much to give the Chicago police. Maybe you can go to sleep and get some more information for me. Sheryl, you got any more of that peyote?"

"I do."

"I think you should give him some more so it doesn't wear off and get me some more details to take to Chicago. Once you know his name and where he lives, I can give that to them."

"So, you gonna help him?"

"Yeah, Sheryl. This looks like a bad guy doing some really bad shit. If Stewart can witness something or even get a plan in place before it happens, we can maybe catch him and the boss before they kill again."

"What's next?" Stewart asked.

"Like I said, when you have something, let me know. I gotta go. Where's Sara? I need to settle up."

"That's okay, we got this," Sheryl said.

"Thanks, I'll get it the next time," Sam said, getting up.

Stewart got up, as did Sheryl. He shook Sam's hand, and Sheryl gave him a hug and he walked out. They sat back down, and Sara came over to see if they wanted another drink. Stewart ordered a Bud Light, and Sheryl ordered an Ultra.

"You know this place has karaoke tonight. Wanna hang around and watch a little?" Sheryl asked Stewart.

"Sure, is it good?"

"You'll have to see for yourself. You already said yes, so we're here for a little while. What do you think of Sam?"

"He seems like a great guy. Why do you ask?"

"He's had some trouble with his wives, and he's been to see Henry a lot for the same peyote as you. That's why I knew he'd understand. The peyote helped."

"But the difference is Henry did it right," Stewart said.

"Yeah, remind me. I'm so sorry this has happened to you."

"So far, no harm, no foul. Maybe we stop a bad guy from being worse."

"Good attitude. Oh, the karaoke is starting. You wanna sing a song with me?"

"Are you crazy? I'm not going to get up and sing. What song, by the way?"

"How about 'Picture' by Sheryl Crow and Kid Rock?"

"That's an easy one, maybe. I have never done karaoke. I haven't sung since the third grade when I was kicked out of Catholic choir by Sister Marsha."

"You weren't kicked out?"

"I was," she said. I sang too loud. I was loud and proud."

"Whatever."

"Seriously, sis, I sang too loud. A choir can't have anyone singing louder than the rest."

"Okay, so we doing this?" she asked.

"Really, you want me to sing with you?"

"Yes, I'm going to go put our name in."

Two beers and some laughter and clapping later, it was their turn. Melissa, the karaoke hostess, brought them both a microphone. She smiled and repeated the song they were going to sing. The music started, and Stewart started singing softly, "Living my life in a slow hell, a girl..." the crowd cheered at the tone and pitch of his voice. Sheryl came in on her parts, and the two delivered a nearly flawless rendition of the song to cheering and applause. A few people even whistled. As they sat down, Sara brought two more beers.

Sara said, "These are from those folks over there."

She pointed, and they waved. Sheryl and Stewart waved back. Sheryl mouthed, "Thank you." Stewart had never felt so appreciated. He thought of another song to sing alone, and he went up and gave Melissa the song.

He came back smiling.

"What's with that smile?"

"You should've heard that karaoke girl. She said we did that song better than anyone she'd ever heard, and she's been doing this for over twenty years. I told her I wanted to do another song. I asked for; 'Hard to handle,' by Black Crowes. I hope it works out alright."

"This is fun, isn't it?"

"It is. I have never had so much fun. Thanks, Sheryl. You certainly have opened up my world."

"I'm glad, ya know, even though you guys left me high and dry, I never stopped loving you."

"I'm sorry about that. And, for the record, I never stopped loving you either. I just didn't know how to show it."

The Roadhouse was starting to thin out. Stewart had sung three songs, and he could see Sheryl was fading fast. He offered to drive home, and she insisted, so he did. She nearly passed out on the way back. He helped her out of the Jeep and down the stairs. The clinic would be closed until the afternoon since it was Saturday, so they could both sleep in. He took her to her room, and she fell on the bed. He took off her boots and rolled her under the covers, clothes and all. He turned around, stopped, looked back and smiled. He had gotten his sister back. He turned the light out, closed the door and headed to his room. Once in his room, he disrobed and climbed into bed. He laid there for a minute and then thought, peyote.

He got up and went into the kitchen. He had some peyote without prayers and headed back to his room. Back in bed, he fell asleep instantly.

Okay, I'm dreaming, and I really need to pay attention. Where am I? Surprise, it's ten at night on a Friday and I'm in a bar in Chicago. Hmmm, I'm in a booth away from most of the people. I'm looking down at my, sorry, Tony's phone. Oh. Playing that game again. Look up, Tony, look around. Nothing. What's up with this guy? Has he adapted to my personality? The music in this place isn't all bad. Got a little Bon Jovi "Livin' on a Prayer" playing. That's cool. I just noticed I have no peripheral vision. I can only see straight. Good, the game is over. This is a dark place. Dance floor to the left with a bunch of people dancing. Oh, it's a band doing that song. Lots of pretty people. I wonder why Tony is alone. Is he meeting someone? Nice song. 'hey, hey, hey, hey, wooooooah. Don't you...' This band is pretty good. Is that Jen? It is. She's with another guy. That's why he's alone. Tony is sad. Jen is looking really hot. Dude, you made a big mistake. I think he knows it. Look at her looking over here, shaking her money maker. You should leave. Tony, we should get out of here. Oh. We're getting up. Walking to the door. Did I do that? Did I influence him to leave? Scratch your face. Come on, Tony, scratch your face. Come on, listen to me, scratch your face. Okay, nope, you're not going to do it. I guess I didn't influence you after all. Tony, you passed Jen by without even a look. Oh, I have peripheral vision now. I can see some out of the edges of your pupils. Nice. Uh-huh, looking around much better now. Well, not much to see out here. Look back, Tony. I wanna see where we are. Come on, look back. No? Alright. Where are we going now?

"Taxi!" Okay, good, we're not driving.

"Where to?" the cab driver asked.

"Polekatz," Tony answered.

"Gotcha! Are you in town visiting?"

Tony didn't answer.

I wonder what polekatz is. Hmm, pole katz. Sounds like a strip club. Yeah, it has to be. Why didn't Tony answer him? That's rude. This is a different side of him. I wonder if we're trading personality traits. Cool, he's becoming me, and I get his good ones. Wait. I don't wanna become a hitman. Sheryl did say I was becoming more confident. I wonder what that looks like. Hmm, yeah, here we are, Polekatz, a strip club.

"Eleven fifty," the cab driver said.

Tony handed him a ten and a five and waited for the change. He took the bills and said, keep the change. The driver said, "Well, thanks, buddy." Then he drove away. Tony walked up to the door.

The doorman opened it, then said, "Tone-knee, how you doin'. Good to see you, pal. We got a great lineup tonight. From LA, we have Diana LaTease on the main stage at midnight. Our cover tonight is twenty dollars. She is worth it. Come on in. Tomorrow night, Veronica Vice will be here. Word has it she might show up tonight. Ask Jeff to introduce you to her if she does."

Tony paid the twenty dollars and went into the club. He looked around for a place to sit. The main stage had all the seats taken up to it, so Tony found a table a few rows back. It was situated between three stages so he could turn and look in either direction.

I don't know why you bring us here. This is like window shopping when the stores are closed. Ugh, the music right now is terrible. I'm so bored. I suppose there are worse things we could be looking at, like the Cubs or Blackhawks playing basketball. Yeah, I hate, hate, hate basketball.

The music changed to a big band, and all the lights fell except the lights over the main stage. From behind the curtain, there was activity. The first layer of curtains was opened, and a shapely silhouette stood with her hand above her head. On arm straight and the other bent to touch the crease in the elbow. The opposite leg was slightly bent, and the other straight. She began to move slowly. She was swaying her hips, exchanging leg positions. Her bent arm seemed to be stroking the straight arm. She stroked a few times until she reached her other hand and together, they fell in front of her. The light behind her extinguished, as did the lights above the stage. Only one light was on the stage. It was an upplight at the opening of the curtain. It was very dim, and she was only slightly visible. Her clothing was shimmering in the dim light as she swayed to the music. Her features and skin were still indistinguishable. She moved forward a half step on every fourth beat of the big band music as the light grew ever so slightly. Her face and skin were only slightly exposed, and then there was an explosion. The stage seemed to blow up, and lights flashed everywhere, but she didn't move. She had fallen into a heap on the floor. She was engulfed with light on her back. The music went silent. One single light above her now showed her. The music began again, slower from the start and increasing in speed as she added movement. She lifted her head to reveal her face. She began waving her arms and hands to the music as her body lifted from the floor. The light followed her from above, only embracing those areas that protruded. Her eyes were hidden, and her breasts were lit from above. Parts of her waist had light. The tempo of the music increased as did the volume, and with a single movement, she jumped, opened her legs and put her arms straight out, and all the lights came up. She was certainly a sight. She was the body of Carmen Electra, the strength of Gal Godot, the lips and eyes of Angelina Jolie all in one package. Her long white sequin dress lasted through the first song. During the second song, it was removed to show her curves. Her muscles were toned but not over-toned. She was fit without being muscular. Her skin was smooth, and the youth had yet to escape from her face. Her long brown hair was shaken in every which direction as she pranced around the stage, occasionally stopping to drop her hair onto a man's lap. She would brush it over his face, and he would smile and throw money. This went on for three minutes, and then the song changed. A more provocative song began playing and off came her bra. There seemed to be a gasp in the crowd. Men who waited for these breasts were delighted by their natural appearance and shape. Now, as she approached men, she would tug at them and wave them. More money hit the stage floor. She had but one more garment to remove. There were men lined up all around the stage, waiting for the prize. The song changed. It was time. She put her thumbs under each side of her panties. She bent down and shook her hair to the right as she contorted her body to the right and looped her head in a circle. She moved and planted both feet slightly apart and repeated the move with her head. She stopped in the center, head down and flung her hair back. She brought her feet together and pushed her thumbs down to the middle of her hip. She opened her legs again and swung her head around and around in a circle, two, three, four times. The crowd was fixed by her hair, not noticing that the panties had dropped to the floor. The music stopped. She stood in her star position, feet apart, arms out. She was completely nude. Applause was rampant, whistles and screams, hoots and hollers as she stood in her position. Flashes of cameras continued. The music began again, and she danced off the stage, back through the curtains and out of sight. A helper came out and collected the cash on the stage, and the DJ announced she would be back for another session soon.

Damn, that was fantastic. My heart is racing. I have never seen a show like that. Oh, we're moving. Tony, did you notice the door says, 'Private.'

"Tony, how the hell are you," a man in a black suit behind a desk asked. He got up and came around to the front and shook Tony's hand.

I guess they know each other, my bad.

"I've never been better, Jimmy. How are you?"

"I'm well. Is there something I can do for you?"

"You gotta introduce me to that Diana chick."

"I expected you'd say that. She's available for five hundred dollars for fifteen minutes and five thousand for an hour. It's by appointment, and as you might expect, the level of service varies based on the time. The fifteen minutes is on-site, and the five thousand is offsite at the end of her shift. I already have two one-hour appointments. Would you like to be put on the list?"

Yes, yes, oh yes, please. Come on, dude. Have you ever met a sexier woman? Come on, it's only money.

"I want to meet her first and see if up close is as good as what I saw from a distance before I commit."

"You can do that."

"Thanks, when?"

"Now."

"Great, let's go."

"Sure, five hundred dollars."

"Seriously, Jimmy, you know me."

"Right, but still, that's her rate, and you get fifteen minutes. You'll get a preview."

"What about the touch policy?"

"She will put your hands where she allows. You will be in private, and we will have cameras on in the room. You can do what she allows, and it's her domain. So, if she likes you, you will know."

Do it, Tony! Do it.

"Do I pay you or her?"

"You pay her assistant, her manager, her bodyguard. If you do something she doesn't like, he's gonna kick your ass."

"He might try."

"Tony, don't do anything disrespectful. It's only five hundred dollars."

"Got it, Jimmy, let's go."

"Go out to a table. I'll have Celeste come and get you when she's ready."

Oh boy, Tony, this is amazing. You go, boy. Okay, we'll wait. Ohhhh, I can't wait. Look at your watch. I wanna count the minutes. One Mississippi, Two Mississippi. This is going to take forever. Tony, just watch the other girls; that'll take my mind off what's about to happen. Look, Tony, come on. Stop looking at the table. What are you thinking?

Celeste came to get Tony. She led him down a hall past girls half-dressed to a door marked "Green Room." Once inside the door, he could smell her before he saw her.

What is that delightful aroma? Where is she? Oh, a room divider. Japanese-looking flowers and tigers. I always think of those together. Where's the dragon? Ya know dragons and tigers are besties in Japan.

A voice from behind the divider began, "Have a seat, darlin'. I'm putting on something delicious for you."

Delicious? Wow, I'm so excited. I wonder if I'm erect. Me, I probably am. Is he? She stepped out from behind the divider. Oh, my, God, look at her. She stood still in a silky red negligee that was tight where it needed to be. It was lace around her breasts, exposing her areola and nipples in view. She was wearing red stilettos, and seductively, she sauntered over to Tony. She put her hand out and said, "So, you're Tony."

Tony took her hand, kissed it and said, "Yes, ma'am, I am."

"We only have a few minutes to get acquainted," she said with a soft voice in his ear as her hand trailed from his chest to his side while she was circling him. Her hand continued to the small of his back, giving him a chill, then up his back to his left shoulder. She kissed his neck and whispered, "Do you like what you see?" Then trailed from the front of his shoulder to the center of his chest. She put her hands flat on his chest and leaned forward and licked his neck on his left side to the center, then over to the right, where she whispered, "Are we going to spend more time together, sweetie?" Then she gently pushed herself back, leaving her hands on his chest, extended her fingers and lightly slid them down his belly to his belt, where she stopped and slowly looked up at him.

"Yes, I'd like that, Miss Diana,"

"Oh honey, just call me Diana. Shall I give you a preview of what's to come?"

Tony moaned affirmatively.

She unbuckled his belt and undid his button, slid the zipper down and pressed the inside of her hand against his flat belly. Under his briefs, she slid her hand to his semi-erect penis. She pulled it above the lowering briefs and squatted down in front of him. She could see what was in store for her. She looked up at him, looking down, and she smiled, "This is a pretty one."

Her ruby red lipstick was dry, and she licked her lips in a circle, making them wet. Their eyes were connected as her closed, puckered lips began moving close to the tip of his head. The erection was growing as she got closer and closer. She backed up to see the length, looked back into his eyes and smiled, "Can I have this?" Tony nodded.

She looked at it again and slightly opened her lips. She moved closer and then softly touched her lips on the tip. Tony nearly fell over. She moved closer, putting the head into her mouth. He could feel her tongue making circles around it. Then she moved even closer, taking some length into her mouth. Half of him was in her mouth, then two-thirds, three-fourths, and it was gone. Her face was pressed full against his belly; she was looking up, but he could not see her. His eyes were closed.

Open your eyes, come on, man, open your eyes.

She put her hands on both hips and held him inside her mouth. All the while, her tongue was circling inside her mouth. He had never felt such a thing. She began to hum. Her vibrating throat caressed the head of his cock while her tongue circled. She could feel it begin to pulsate. Tony moaned in pleasure, and at the very moment, he would explode, she removed him from her mouth and pumped his cum onto her chest until he stopped. His fifteen minutes had ended sooner than he expected. She raised his briefs and pants, zipped them, buttoned them and buckled his belt. She got up and whispered, "I hope you'll have more for me later, and maybe we can make it last a little longer."

Then she turned and walked back behind the divider. Celeste opened the door, and Tony turned around. His shirt tails were hanging out, and so Celeste said, "Compose yourself, Tony."

Diana said, "See you later, sweetie."

Then Tony walked out. He nearly fell over from his lightheadedness as Celeste led him back to the main floor, "Would you like us to put you on her schedule, or did you have enough?"

"Did you see that?"

"Every bit, she's quite talented, isn't she?"

"So far. From what I've heard... you... will... not... be disappointed. We hear she's worth it. Oh, and she picks the guys. You've been picked."

"Yes, put me on the schedule. For now, I think I'll have a shot of tequila. Can you make that happen?"

"Patron, Silver?"

"Perfect."

Celeste was Johnny's girl, and everyone knew it. No one in their right mind made a pass to Celeste, not even Tony. She was a petite blonde with a round butt, oversized breasts and a thin waist. She might be Kim K's other sister. Her green eyes made her elusive, and she was properly dressed in a skirt and form-fitting sleeveless top. Her confidence was un-waivered as she spoke and walked away. Tony had been temporarily satisfied while the next candidate was ushered into Diana's room. He didn't get the same treatment and left dissatisfied. The door opened and closed for the five-hundred-dollar meetings, but only Tony was as impressed.

Celeste returned with a card for Tony, giving him the time and the address. He accepted it and put it into his coat pocket.

Eleven o'clock, really? We gotta wait that long?

Tony stood up, walked toward the door and out to the street. He gave the valet a five-dollar bill and said, "Cab, please."

A cab pulled up, the valet opened the back door, and Tony got in. He handed the cabby a card, and off they went.

Damn, where are we going? Why didn't you just tell the guy? I need the address. Well, now what? Great, we're closing our eyes.

Tony closed his eyes for the fifteen minutes it took to drive to his place. Stewart saw nothing. When they pulled up to the apartment door, it had begun to rain, so Tony kept his head down. He walked straight to the elevator and up. Once inside his apartment, he set the alarm on his phone for nine in the morning, crawled into bed and went to sleep. Stewart slept soundly. He woke to the sound of his sister singing.

"All we do crumbles to the ground though we refuse to see, dust in the wind. All we are is dust in the wind. Oh, ho, ho. Now, don't hang on..."

She must have her headphones on.

"It slips away. And all your money won't another minute buy Dust in the wind. All we are is dust in the wind..."

Stewart tapped Sheryl on the shoulder as she was dusting, "Hey, sis, is there any correlation between you dusting and that song?"

She laughed and said, "Ironic, isn't it."

He agreed and sat on the couch as she serenaded him with more Kansas songs. He closed his eyes and saw darkness. He wished he could be back in Tony's head. "Say, sis, do you think we can do another peyote tonight? It seems every time you do it, my senses get stronger."

"Yes, of course. But, bro, for now, what'ta ya wanna do?"

He said, "I wanna look at old pictures of you and Hania. I wanna get to know the Sheryl you've become."

She was floored. Her mouth agape, she tried to formulate a response. Tears filled her eyes, and then she said, "That... would...be...nice." She put down the End dust and the rag and hugged her brother. He held her tight, and she reciprocated until it seemed awkward. At that point, they both let go, and he sat down on the couch. Sheryl left the room for a minute as Stewart thought of all the hugs he had missed from his sister. She returned with a stack of albums, about three. She took out the top one and began, "This was before I left Jersey. When I was little, I kept all the pictures I could."

For hours, they reminisced over the pictures, they laughed, and they cried until they were both hungry. Sheryl made a meal, they talked until midnight, and she gave him more peyote. He went to bed, and when he closed his eyes, there was darkness. He slept.

Chapter Eleven: Another Dream

Stewart's sleep was interrupted by Tony's eyes opening. Tony was in the waiting room at his employer's. He was awakened by the receptionist, "Tony, Tony, wake up. We have some deliveries for you. Then you need to call the boss. He has more work for you."

"Okay, great thanks. When will they be ready?"

"Give us about an hour. Here's the destination," she said, handing him a piece of paper. They were like his last delivery work schedule. The same hospitals, different organs. The final destination was the same. He sat back and waited. He closed his eyes and dozed off again. Stewart slept soundly.

"Tony... Tony, what's wrong with you?"

"I didn't get much sleep. Sorry, you got it all ready?"

"Yes, it's in the van, marked and ready. Get going time is of the essence."

He nodded and rushed to the van.

The deliveries went off without any issue, and when he finished, he went back to Acme Medical and switched vehicles. He was on-call in the event of another organ donor delivery with an hour to arrive. He wanted to make sure he stayed within the appropriate distance. He met the boss at the diner like last time. Sitting alone for a few minutes, he ordered coffee, black and a cinnamon roll. The boss arrived with two other men who sat in a different booth. He stood up and reached his hand out to shake for the boss, but he ignored the gesture and sat down. Tony sat, and the boss began to talk, "You did well last time. We needed someone clean, and you are very clean. Nothing to tie us up. My boss has asked me to get you to St. Louis. We have a problem down there, and we need you to handle it. You leave tomorrow. Randall has the details. He will meet you at I-55 and South Bolingbrook, you know the intersection?"

"Yeah, I know it."

"We got a construction company there on the outer road. Go there. Randall will meet you. It's next to the Denny's there, right off the highway."

"Okay, what time?"

"Right now, you fuck. Get your ass on the road, go meet Randall. He's got the details."

"Okay, boss, gotcha." I wonder what his problem is.

"Oh yeah, one more thing, you ever heard of Fergusson?"

"You mean the town in St. Louis?"

"Yeah, Fergusson."

"Yeah, boss."

"That's where you're headed. We have a group of associates that aren't playing fair. You gotta show 'em what fair is, Capish?"

"Yes, sir. I got it."

"Good, finish your roll on the road. You gotta get moving, don't wanna keep Randall waiting."

"Okay, boss."

Tony left the cinnamon roll behind and headed to his Range Rover. He stopped for gas at the nearest station and then arrived at the construction company ten minutes later. There wasn't anyone on the lot at the construction company, and the fence was locked. He drove to the Denny's parking lot and waited. After a few minutes, two black sedans arrived at the construction company. One of the cars pulled up to the gate, and the passenger got out and unlocked the gate. Both cars pulled in. Tony left Denny's and followed them in. He parked near them and got out of the Rover. He walked to the vehicle that the passenger got out of. The driver of the other vehicle opened the door, walked over to Tony, handed him the keys and said, "Instructions are on the seat. Don't open them until you arrive at the Hilton by the airport in St. Louis. Use the Lincoln. You'll get paid when you return. There's enough cash in the envelope for expenses. Don't use credit cards and avoid interstate highways. Take the back roads from I-fifty-five in St. Louis. No highways once you're there, got it?"

"Yeah, I got it."

"Good, now go. What are you waiting for?" he said with an elevated voice.

Tony walked quickly to the Lincoln MKS and climbed into the cockpit. It had brown leather seats, a black leather dashboard and soft blue lighting. Real wood appointments on the doors and dash finished in mahogany gave the Lincoln a touch of class. He pushed the start button, adjusted his seat and mirrors and took off south on I-fifty-five.

Wake up, wake up. I gotta tell Sam. I gotta wake up and let someone know what's happening. He's gonna kill some more people. I need to stop this. Wake up. Wake up.

Stewart couldn't wake up. He tried repeatedly to no avail. He settled into the boring ride and tried to be unconscious. He was not resting.

This really sucks.

More than five hours passed when Tony arrived at the Hilton Hotel near the airport. Stewart had tried over and over to wake up but was not able to. The sun was coming up, and Stewart was exhausted. Tony stopped under the canopy, went inside and met a lovely black woman named Charise, "Hi, I have a reservation. The name is Steven Taylor."

"Yes, sir, I had you checking in last night with a late check-in. Here is your room key. The room is prepaid, and the pool is closed for renovations, our apologies. The exercise room is available with your room key. You are here for two nights, is that correct?"

"Yes, I presume."

"Perfect, if you'll sign here, you can be on your way." She handed him the paper and he began to sign Tony, then changed it to Steven Taylor. He went back to the Lincoln to park and collect his things. He took the envelope and the carry-on from the trunk and went inside. He nodded at Charise and made his way to the elevator. Once there, he selected the third floor. He got off the elevator and walked towards 311-321. He opened the door without looking at the number on the door, but Stewart had figured it was room two-twenty. It was a nice room, with a mini fridge and a microwave. The bathroom had a jacuzzi tub and a shower. He threw his bag on the bed and went into the bathroom.

Ew, there's the penis again. Why you gotta look at it when you piss? Okay, so you're proud. I guess I would be, too. Ew, gross, what's that smell? Damn, dude, you haven't showered since getting laid with that whore. Come on, clean up, buddy.

Tony finished showering in the bathroom. He dropped his towel as he made his way to the bed, collapsing on the king-sized bed. He was out instantly. Finally, Stewart could rest.

Sheryl had no reason to wake Stewart, so he slept until his body was ready to wake. It was almost five in the evening when he woke up. Sheryl was not home when he made his way to the kitchen. She had gone out and returned after seven with groceries and met Stewart at the bottom of the stairs.

Stewart began, "Hi, sis, where ya been?"

"I had some errands to run, bought some groceries. Can you help me get 'em out of the Jeep?"

"Sure, I'll go fetch 'em."

Stewart went and grabbed the remaining five bags and brought them down the stairs to the kitchen. Together, they unbagged them and put the items away.

Sheryl asked, "Are you hungry?"

"Nah, I ate a sandwich a while ago."

"Did you sleep?"

"Yeah, I just got up around five."

"Wow, really? What's going on?"

"Oh my God, I almost forgot. Where's my head? Shit. Sheryl, there's another murder about to take place in St. Louis tonight."

"Oh no, really? What should we do?"

"I was hoping to get up earlier, and for some reason, I had completely forgotten about it. We need to tell Sam."

"Right, tell Sam. Did you call him yet?"

"No."

"I will. Hold on. I'll dial and put him on speaker."

"Hello, this is Lieutenant Chee."

"Sam, it's Sheryl and Stewart, you're on speakerphone."

"What's up, guys?

"Sam, this is Stewart; I need your help. There's going to be a crime in Fergusson, Missouri, near St. Louis tonight."

"Okay. Where? and who?"

"That part, I don't know. You see, Tony got a package and drove a car to the Hilton Hotel in St. Louis. He hadn't looked at the details yet, so I hadn't seen it. Right now, he's asleep. It was at five this afternoon, three his time. If I go to sleep, I won't be able to wake up and give you any details. Well, maybe there's a way. Can you come here?"

"What are you thinking?"

"I'm thinking, if I go to sleep, maybe you can watch me. If I sleep restlessly or after a few minutes, maybe you can wake me to see if I have the details of the crime."

"That might work. If I call the police in St. Louis, they are going to think we're crazy."

"You have to be compelling."

"Right. Sure Stewart. I'm not sure why I believe you and this sort of shit. Imagine some random cop from the Midwest. The best we can do is try. I'll make a call on the way there. You should take some more peyote and go to bed."

"That's a good idea."

"Yeah, I'll give him another dose and send him to bed," Sheryl said.

"I should be there within an hour. Don't wait for me; we might miss something."

"Got it, okay. Talk soon. Stewart, I have some on the counter. Go ahead," Sherl responded.

"I will. I'm going to lay on the couch. That way, youse guys can sit comfortably around me."

"That's fine."

Stewart took the peyote and lay down on the couch. In five minutes, he was out. Sheryl sat and watched him, but nothing happened. On the outside of the clinic there is a doorbell that rings in the living quarters as well as in the clinic. It was installed for emergencies so that Hania could care for emergencies after hours when necessary. So, when the doorbell rang, Sheryl knew it was Sam. She went up to the clinic door and escorted Sam to the living quarters below. It wasn't his first visit to the living quarters below, as he had visited after the murders of Hania and the others. Sheryl and Sam exchanged pleasantries. Sheryl got Sam a drink of water, and they sat chatting and waiting for Stewart to show some reaction. Sam had a notebook and wrote down a few notes. He noted the time he arrived. He noted that he was waiting for Stewart to do something, and then he asked, "How long has he been asleep?" Sheryl answered, and he noted the time. Then he asked, "Should we wake him and see what's going on?"

"Okay," Sheryl said, and she tugged at Stewart to wake, but he didn't. She shook him, but he didn't wake.

"What do you think I should do?" Sheryl asked.

"I say, slap him gently."

"Okay, here goes." She slapped him, and he came to consciousness.

He was groggy, and when his eyes focused, he could see both Sam and Sheryl.

Sam immediately asked, "What's happening?"

Stewart responded, "Nothing, he's sleeping."

"Oh," Sam said, disappointed.

Stewart couldn't keep consciousness and fell right back to sleep. Sam sat back in the chair, as did Sheryl, and they were silent.

Sheryl broke the silence by saying, "I guess I'll turn on the TV, and we can watch something. Any suggestions?"

"No, it's your house. Your TV, your choice."

Sheryl flipped through the channels, looking for anything to keep her occupied. Sam took his phone out and began playing a game. Stewart slept.

An hour passed, and Sam suggested another slap. Sheryl slapped Stewart again, and he rose to consciousness.

"What are you seeing now, Stewart?" Sam asked.

"I can't believe you woke me then. He was reading the papers. He was looking at the pictures. Four black men, apparently in a gang. One is the leader, Mike Robinson, who goes by Micky. He's the main target. They crossed the mob, and they're buying directly from the Mexicans. It's supposed to look like a drive-by. He's set up a meeting, but you woke me just as I was going to see the place."

"Fuck really? Oh, Stew, I'm so sorry," Sheryl said.

Sam wrote down the notes, and Stewart continued, "There were a lot of weapons in the trunk of the

Lincoln. I got the license plate number, what was it, shit. I think it was two letters; one was an X, eight-seven-four, another number then a-c, an Illinois plate from Cook County. The car was a Lincoln MKS, and it was black. The windows are tinted, and Tony isn't alone anymore. There are three other guys with him. They have a black SUV and they rode together. I have not seen the plate on that one. I have seen the guys, though. One is short and heavy. He seems to oversee the three. They seem to be supportive guys. Like they are there to do the deal, and Tony is there to exterminate the black guys. All of them are in black suits with white shirts and black ties. It's like a Blues Brothers convention, except no one has a hat. They are at a parking garage waiting. I do know it is an abandoned shopping center parking garage. I think one said, 'Northwest Plaza.' Oh, the other two guys, Italian looking one is tall and big, while the other looks to be average height and weight. The black guys haven't shown up yet. I saw pictures and got that one name, but that's all I got. I should probably go to sleep and see what's going on."

"Yeah, you should," Sam agreed.

Stewart closed his eyes and was out instantly.

Sam began, "You know that is really not enough for us to go on."

"Well, you know the location. Can you alert them and tell them the location?"

"I could, but I'm not going to. I have told them about a crime about to happen and that should give us credence enough."

"They didn't believe you, did they?" Sheryl asked.

"Not a word. But I'm going to call them back and let them know where it is, and when it happens, we'll be right."

Sam made the call, explained to the detective on the phone about the circumstance and the detective took it under advisement. He ended the call and told Sheryl, "I told them, and they said they'd send a car around. I doubt they will. I guess we did our part."

In St. Louis a detective asked, "Meier, who was that on the phone?"

"Is it really any of your business O'Keefe?"

"Well, we are partners. Yeah, it kinda is."

"You won't believe it."

"Try me."

"Well, there's this Lieutenant in Arizona, on a reservation, the Navajo National Police. He had information on a murder about to happen at Northwest Plaza. He said a guy dreamt about it."

"That sounds farfetched. How would a guy in Arizona know about a murder at Northwest Plaza?" O'Keefe asked.

"He says some chick gave her brother some peyote, and now he sees this shit in his dreams. You believe that crap?"

"We've seen some weird shit in our day, so seriously I don't put anything aside. Let's take a ride over there and see if there's anything to this."

"I think it's a waste of time but what else have we got? Well, we got that drive-by on Lindbergh, and we got the QT robberies, and we got the murder in

Bellefontaine Neighbors. Not much going on, no."

"Shut up, who's driving?" Meier asked.

"I'll drive that way; you can do the shooting if anything happens. Yeah, 'cause I'm a gunslinger that kills shit every day."

They walked quickly to the car and peeled out of the precinct parking lot to Lindbergh Boulevard, heading north to the plaza.

Stewart was quickly back to sleep and watching the crime unfold.

The three Italian guys stayed behind while Tony took off to an upper parking level. He got out of the

Lincoln and waited to hear the car approach. He heard faint rap music then it got louder and louder. He could tell they had arrived because the music ended abruptly. He got into the Lincoln, started it up and headed slowly to the meeting. He was rolling down the ramp. No one noticed him. The Italian guys had the product in the back of the SUV, and the Black guys had a suitcase filled with cash. They were standing at the back of the SUV doing the deal.

Tony stopped the Lincoln, opened the door, didn't shut it, took off his shoes and began walking slowly toward the scene. All seven men were behind the SUV when Tony opened fire. With an Uzi in each hand, he mowed down the four black men. Then, he instructed the Italian guys to move the dead guys over to their car. They agreed and began dragging the dead guys. All three of them stood over their respective dead guy, and Tony open fired again, killing the Italians. He threw the cash in the back of the SUV and drove back to the Lincoln. He parked the SUV a hundred feet away or so, ran to the Lincoln, took out the rest of the weapons and ran back to the SUV. One of the weapons was an RPG, and he fired it at the Lincoln and then at the other car. He climbed back into the SUV and headed out of the parking lot.

Over the police scanner, O'Keefe and his partner heard "shots fired in the Northwest Plaza parking lot." They turned on their sirens and stepped on it. They were still ten minutes away.

Tony exited the parking garage and made his way across the empty parking lot to Old St. Charles Rock Road, turned left and then another left onto the acceleration lane on Lindbergh and headed south.

When O'Keefe and Meier arrived on the scene, it was a fiery, bloody mess. Seven were dead, and two vehicles were destroyed and on fire. O'Keefe quickly called Sam, "Lieutenant, you were right. The crime just happened. It looks like everyone is dead, though, seven guys, right?"

"No. There was an eighth one," Sam said.

"Shit, where'd he go?" O'Keefe asked.

"I don't know. My guy is asleep watching it all. Lemme wake him and see what's up. Stewart, wake up," Sam said.

"We gotta slap him. I got this," Sheryl said.

Sam giggled and said, "You kinda get some pleasure out of this, don't you?"

"No, not really," Sheryl said, lying and smiling.

"They did it, he did it, Tony shot them all, he's on the run. I think he's headed south on that main four-lane road. He's in the black SUV."

Sam relayed the information to O'Keefe, and O'Keefe and Meier jumped back in their cars and raced out of the parking garage, across the same path as Tony and out onto Lindbergh.

Meanwhile, Tony had turned East on Page Avenue and then pulled into the Courtyard at Marriot's parking lot. There was a Toyota Rav4 waiting. He parked next to it, opened the back and emptied the contents into the Rav4. He placed an incendiary device in the back seat that had a timer set for fifteen minutes and headed back to Page Avenue. He went north on Lindbergh to the airport. He parked the car in the long-term parking lot and took the cash as his carry-on. Once inside the airport, he found the lockers. He put the suitcase in the locker, locked it and went to the gate to fly back to Chicago. Stewart saw none of it. He was awake.

Tony sat, waiting for his flight. He opened the burner phone and called the boss.

"Tony, is it done?"

"It is done, boss."

"Did you take your cut?"

"No, sir, I left it in the locker."

"Okay, good, come by, and I'll pay ya. Oh, and Tony, excellent job. You got 'em all right?"

"Yes, sir. All the rats in the henhouse, now the chickens are fine. The chicken feed is in the Toyota. Number A-three-forty-seven."

"It'll be a long time, won't it, Tony?"

"Yes, sir, long-term goals, for sure."

"Thanks, see you later."

"Yes, sir, thanks for the business."

"You're welcome, bye."

Tony bent the phone backward until it snapped. He rose from his chair and went to the bathroom. On his way, he dropped the phone in the trash. No one saw him.

O'Keefe cried to Sam, "Where is he now?"

"I can't tell you; Stewart is awake."

"Tell him to go back to sleep."

"Okay, I will."

Stewart closed his eyes, but he didn't fall asleep. His heart was racing, and his head was hurting. Sam and Sheryl sat patiently. Stewart kept opening his eyes.

Finally, Sam said, "Can we give him more peyote?"

Sheryl answered, "We can try. I'm not sure what he'll do or if he'll ever wake up again. I have never doubled up on the dose."

"We gotta try something," Chee said.

"Stewart, can we try some more peyote?"

"I'm game. We have to catch this guy," Stewart responded.

Stewart ingested the peyote and fell into a deep sleep. Sam called O'Keefe in St. Louis and told him Stewart was asleep.

"Did he say anything else? Does he know where he went?"

"No, nothing. Last he saw he was on a four-lane road headed south."

"Well, we just got a report of a black SUV that exploded nearby at a Marriot parking lot. Three people driving by were injured. It might be the truck."

"I'm sorry, he didn't see that when we woke him up."

"Great, can we give him a little time and wake him again? Maybe we can get some clues?"

"Sure, I'll give him a few minutes."

Looks like we're at the airport. My guess is we're headed back to Chicago. Yes, we are on Southeast Airlines flight number twenty-two-seventy-two. Okay, guys, wake me up. Come on, wake me up.

Sheryl and Sam tried to wake Stewart. He would not awaken. He was limp, and his breath was weak. Sheryl was worried she may have overdosed on him. They slapped him, put water on his face, shook him, but nothing worked.

Can I talk in my sleep? Maybe I can ask them in my sleep to wake me. Great, we're boarding. Seat B-twenty-six. Okay, no luggage. I'm sitting. Eyes closed. Now Tony is sleeping. That was fast. I guess killing a bunch of people is tiring. I see nothing. I'm just like that sergeant in Hogan's Heroes. I see nothing. Super. I guess it's rest time for me, too.

"Could you wake him?" O'Keefe asked.

Sam answered, "No, the last dose of peyote really did him in."

"Okay, well, thanks for your help. If you hear anything, anything at all, please let us know."

"You know I will."

Sam and Sheryl tried every few minutes to wake Stewart, but nothing worked. Eventually, Sam tired of his feeble attempts and decided to leave.

"Thank you for your help, Sam," Sheryl said.

"Sheryl, you helped more than I did. I was just the messenger."

"We were all messengers, Sam."

"You know, if he wakes and you hear anything, let me know."

"I will. I'm going to bed. When he wakes, should I call you?"

"Good idea, then we'll call O'Keefe and give them the lowdown."

"Yeah, let me walk you out."

"I know my way," Sam said as he headed to the stairs.

"I know you do, but I have got to secure the door."

"Gotcha. After you, my lady," he said.

"Thanks again, Sam."

They made their way up the stairs, and she locked the door behind him. She went down the stairs and looked over at Stewart, snoring away on the couch. She went down the hall to the closet, took a blanket out and went back to cover him. He didn't move a muscle. She returned to the hall and into her room. She left the door open, shed her clothes, put on a T-shirt and climbed into bed. She thought for a minute about the day's events until she was fast asleep.

Tony slept until the plane began to descend. His ears began to hurt, and he opened his eyes. He looked around and stretched his jaw, opening his ears. He closed his eyes and went back to sleep. The plane landed, and the noise level increased, waking Tony.

Looks like we're here. Midway or O'Hare? Oh, Midway. Wake up. That's right, the peyote is super strong, and I'm not waking up until it wears off. I guess I'll just watch and learn. What next, my murderous host? You go ahead; I'll just narrate my journey in your head. I think I need a drink. Hey Tony, are you thirsty? Oh look, we're stopping in the shop. Water! Really? Was that power of suggestion? I wonder. Oh, he is thirsty, drinking before paying. Paying? He's a criminal, right? Will he pay? Yes, okay, we are paying.

Yeah, Milky Way bar, too. Yummy. Oh, here's something: I get to eat fancy, delicious food and not gain weight. Go for it, tiger; let's have two. Wait, he's going back for another. Maybe this power of suggestion is working, and we're opening it before paying, okay? Wholly cow, that is good. Man, this peyote has heightened my senses. The best candy bar ever. Hey, cool, we paid. I feel high. I'm sleeping, I'm watching this douchebag through his own eyes, and I feel high. I wonder if he feels high. Shouldn't he be like I am? Who knows? Hey Tony, let's go pee. Okay then, we're going to pee. That's three-for-three in the power of suggestion arena, or was it just a coincidence? I guess guzzling the water made us have to pee. Damn, I'm seeing a penis again. Why does he have to look at it all the time? Yup, zip, wash. No wash, what's wrong with you? Yeah, buddy, we're eating the second Milky Way. Ew, we didn't wash our hands. Yuck, really dude, piss on your fingers and yuck. Well, it still tasted awesome. I love the Milky Way. Over that way, that looks like the exit. Uh-huh, he's listening. Cab, Of course, a cab.

"Take I-fifty-five to South Bollingbrook Road. There's a Denny's there. That's where I'm headed," Tony told the cabbie.

The cabbie responded, "You bet." Then off they went.

Another boring car ride. Yeah. We're looking around. Looks like we're leaving the city. Oh cool. Toon blast. Pick that one. No. Pick that one. No. You're not listening. You lose. Oh, yeah, let's play again. Super. Can I please see something else? No, toon blast it is.

A half hour and several lost games later, they arrived at Denny's in Bolingbrook. Tony paid the cab driver and then walked into Denny's. He was seated. His server came over immediately, a forty-something, heavyset woman with dirty-looking brown hair. She smiled and asked, "Whatcha want to drink sugar?"

"Coffee and a grand slam. Eggs scrambled, bacon and blueberry syrup, please."

I love it when he eats. I get the taste without the calories. Yum, I always forget about the blueberry syrup.

The server brought the coffee. Tony nodded in approval. She didn't smile. Under her breath, as she walked away, she said, "You're welcome asshole." Tony didn't hear her. *I heard that. She is right. This guy is an... a number one asshole. Better be careful, Betty. He'll put a cap in your ass. That's okay; she's likely to spit in his food. Oh, here she comes with it.*

"Here you go. Is there anything else I can get you?"

"More coffee, please."

"Right away."

It looks fine. Hot, smells good. Pancakes first; they always get cold fast. Ahhh, yeah, that's good, blueberry syrup. Wow, this is good. More syrup, thatta boy. I love it when he listens. Ewww, that's good. Don't wolf it down. Slow down. Come on, Tony, where you gotta be? Pancakes gone. Bacon gone. Eggs gone. Okay. We're done here.

Tony threw a twenty on the table and walked out. The server came over to the table hurriedly, saw the twenty, smiled and relaxed her shoulders. She watched as Tony walked to an empty parking lot across the grass to the construction company gate. She moved closer to the window and kept watch as he opened the gate, walked to the Range Rover, got in, started it and drove back to the gate. She saw him lock the gate up and drive away.

I wonder if the police in Chicago would be interested in the fingerprints on that lock. I need to tell Sam about this. In the meantime, let's drive back into the city. We should be home and in bed in an hour. Let's go, champ.

It was after three in the morning, and there were only a few vehicles on the road. Tony sped past an unmarked highway patrol car. He looked in his rearview mirror, and the light came on. He wondered where his arms were. He did an assessment of what his reaction should be, and then he pulled over. The trooper stopped and exited his car. He slowly came up to the driver's side of the car with his hand on his pistol. Tony put his window down, and the trooper said, "Good morning, sir. Do you know why I pulled you over?"

"No sir, I don't."

"Did you know the speed limit on this stretch of I-fifty-five is fifty-five miles an hour?"

"No sir, I thought it was sixty-five."

"Then why were you doing eighty-three?"

"I want to get home to bed, sir."

"Okay, we'll work on that. May I have your license, insurance and registration card, please?"

"Of course. Here you are." Tony handed them to the trooper.

"Thank you. I will be back with them in a few minutes, but first, do you have any firearms in the vehicle?"

"I'm not sure that's relevant. But, no. I don't believe in firearms."

The trooper took a flashlight and shined it into the back of the vehicle. "Then I suppose you won't mind me searching your car."

"I didn't say that."

"Where are you coming from?" he said, looking at his license.

"The Denny's down the road."

"Um, Mr. Palumbo, if you don't mind, you live about twenty miles from that Denny's, and you probably pass four on your way home. Why is it that you would go to that one?"

"A friend works there. Do you know Betty?"

"No, sir. I do know most of the wait staff there, and there's no Betty. Might there be another reason you chose Denny's," he said, unlatching his gun.

"The truth is, I call her Betty, but her name is Melissa. You might know her. She's a little heavy, has brown hair and calls everyone 'Sugar.' We went to high school together. I work nights delivering organs. I had to go to visit a friend in St. Louis. I flew back tonight; she had my car, so I took a cab there. I had some breakfast, and now I'd just like to go home and go to bed. So, if you're going to give me a ticket, please do it so that I may be on my way."

"Mr. Palumbo, I'm going to have to ask you to step outside the car. Keep your hands where I can see them."

"Why?"

"Well, Mr. Palumbo, there is no Betty or Melissa at that Denny's, so there's no way anyone there would have kept your car when you were at the airport. The airport is out of the way of Denny's compared to where you live and likely where you work. Your behavior is agitated, which tells me you're not being truthful to me, and your job does not seem to reflect the type that would allow you to own such a vehicle. I haven't run the plates on this car, but I suspect it is stolen. So far, your lies tell me you won't be telling me any truths. Now, I asked you nicely to exit the car with your hands where I can see them."

"Officer," Tony started, then was interrupted.

"It's a trooper."

"Okay, trooper, if you'll just run the plates, you will find the car belongs to me. I just flew in on the red eye. I'm very tired and maybe confused; there's no reason to ask me out of the car." The trooper called in the license and asked for backup at his location. Then he waited by the rear of the car for information. The dispatcher told him the car belonged to one Anthony

Palumbo, but Stewart didn't hear his address or any other information pertaining to Tony. Anthony Palumbo had no record. His driving record was clean, as was his history. The trooper wondered why Tony would lie, so he gave him one more chance. He walked up to the back of the driver's door. Tony had taken his nine-millimeter out and was sitting it on his lap. The trooper said, "Okay, Tony, I'm going to give you one more chance to tell me the truth. Tell me the truth."

Just shoot him, officer.

"I just came from Denny's, and you're right. I don't know the waitress there. A friend took me to St. Louis, and I left my car at the construction company next to Denny's. I flew back from St. Louis on flight twenty-two-seventy-two. I arrived about two-thirty and took a cab to Denny's where I had something to eat, a grand slam with blueberry syrup and a coffee. I got my car out of the gated lot, I had the combination, and now I just want to go home and go to bed."

Just shoot him, officer. He's a murderer. He's got a gun, and he will shoot you if you give him a chance.

"Now, was that so hard? Why did you lie."

"I'm really tired, and I didn't want to go through all this discussion. Can we just get this over with?"

"You know I can arrest you for doing twenty over the speed limit."

"Okay, then do that."

"Well, since there's nobody really on the road and your record is clean, I'm going to let you go with a ticket for seventy-four in a fifty-five. Give me a minute to write it up."

Seriously man. We can nail this guy, and you're letting him off. Shoot him. He is really a bad guy.

The trooper wrote the ticket, gave it to Tony to sign, and Tony signed it. He gave Tony a copy and went back to his car. Tony sped off at a reasonable speed. He had averted a catastrophe. Tony picked up his cell phone and called the boss. He just spoke, *Boss,* into the phone, and it dialed.

"Tony, you back?"

"I'm on the road from Bolingbrook. Had a delay, but I'm almost there."

"There's no need to come tonight. I'll have a courier bring your cash by later today after the sun rises. Just go home and get some rest. You deserve it. You've been a good garbage man. We'll talk real soon."

"Okay, boss."

"Oh, and Tony, you can call me by my first name."

"Thanks, boss. Imma leave it the way it is if you don't mind."

"I don't," he said and ended the call.

Tony set the phone down and continued driving. He arrived at his parking garage without looking at the front of the building again. He got into his apartment without looking at the door number again, and so Stewart still had no idea where he lived. Tony got to his bedroom, dropped clothes from the door to the bed and was asleep after three sighs.

Okay, now I need to wake up. I need to tell Sam Tony's last name. Come on, wake up. I can't. I need rest.

*I...*Stewart lost full consciousness.

Chapter Twelve: Ashley

Sheryl called Sam and asked him to be there when Stewart woke up. He arrived a little after ten in the morning. They exchanged pleasantries and Sam sat on the couch waiting for Stewart. Sheryl went into Stewart's room and woke him. He needed a shower, so he went to the bathroom to get cleaned up. Sheryl went back out to the living room and offered Sam some coffee.

He accepted. She made the coffee and sat with Sam as Stewart readied himself.

Sam said, "Did he say anything?"

"No, he just said he needed a shower."

"O'Keefe called me three times this morning to see if we knew anything."

"I bet they have a big mess on their hands over there."

"He said it was the worst ever recorded at a single location in his county. Then again, he said since they've been keeping track of those things. Battles notwithstanding, the same goes for the shooting here. It was the worst we'd seen in recorded history. I didn't tell him about that."

Stewart emerged from his room with wet hair. He sat next to Sheryl on the couch and began, "The first and most important thing that you need to know is his last name. If it is real, it is Palumbo, Anthony Palumbo. There is a state trooper who gave him a ticket this morning for seventy-four in a fifty-five outside blooming something, Illinois. Tony took flight twenty-two seventy-two from St. Louis on flight twenty-two seventy-two and landed at about two-thirty this morning. He then took a cab to Denny's in Blooming, whatever, I can't remember. There's a waitress there who would remember him. She flirted with him, and he was an asshole to her. He was the only person in the place at three in the morning. Then he went next door to the construction company and retrieved the Range Rover. The combination on the lock was seven, seven, four, six, five. He somehow got away with lying to the trooper and exceeding the speed limit by twenty-eight miles an hour, and he only got a ticket for nineteen over. He was supposed to meet the boss any minute now, but when Sheryl woke me up, he was still sleeping."

Sam called O'Keefe, put him on speaker phone, and relayed the information. O'Keefe was quite angry when he heard that he landed in Chicago. O'Keefe said, "Now, somebody has to call the FBI. I hate the fucking FBI."

Sam responded, "I would, but it is your crime."

"Oh, I know, and it was my jurisdiction. Now it's gone interstate, and the damn FBI has to be involved. I'll call them. I'll let you know what they say. Mind if I give them your number? They might have questions for Stewart."

"Go ahead."

"We'll talk soon, later."

"Okay, bye."

"Stewart, maybe you should go back to sleep so that you can see the boss," Sam said.

"I could try, but you guys won't know when I see something."

"True. Maybe you could wake yourself up since you've already rested."

Sheryl got up off the couch, and Stewart lay down. He closed his eyes and then jumped back into a seated position. "I can see."

In unison, both Sheryl and Sam said, "See what?"

"When I close my eyes, and I'm awake, I can see what Tony sees."

Sheryl, "What the fuck, are fucking kidding me, that's so fucking cool."

"Sheryl, I haven't heard you talking like that in a few days," Stewart said.

"Yeah, Sam was around."

Sam said, "I got news for ya, Sheryl, that's not illegal."

"I know, it was outta respect. Stew, what the fuck? Tell us more."

Stewart closed his eyes, and he could see. He began talking, "He is driving. They like to meet at a diner, but I never see the name of the diner. The boss sometimes is in a strip club, and other times he's fuck, what's the place? I forgot. Right now, it's daylight there, and he's on a four-lane road with traffic lights. I can't tell which direction he's headed. It is dinner time, oh wait. He just turned into Pizzeria Uno's parking lot. He's parking. Yeah, he's going inside Uno. He's looking around. I think he sees the boss. Yeah, we're walking toward him. He's in the back corner of the place. This is much cooler than the ones I have been to. It looks like the boss is getting up. Shit, I can't see his face. Striped, pin-striped suit. Yeah, Tony is going to the same booth. We're sitting down. The boss left an envelope on the bench. It's money. Lots of money. Lots of hundreds. I bet there's two hundred of them here. The waitress is coming over. She asked if the other guy was coming back. Tony said no. She asked him... is this important?"

Sam answered, "No."

"Okay," he ordered.

"Nothing is happening. Can I open my eyes?"

"Yeah, this is remarkable. Now, you can give us a play-by-play of his every move."

"Must have been that double peyote batch I gave you yesterday. This is so cool," Sheryl quipped.

"We have to keep you awake to watch Tony's every move," Sam said.

"I'll give him a half hour to eat, then get back to him," Stewart said.

"Okay, I'm going to step outside and call O'Keefe and give him an update."

Sheryl nodded, and Stewart waved. They sat in silence. Sheryl felt a sense of importance and achievement, and Stewart was frightened by their newfound spiritual skills. Sam came back to the living room, looking even more concerned.

"O'Keefe has asked us to fly to St. Louis. He wants you to show him everything you saw. Then, he wants to go to Chicago and do the same. He has contacted a detective in Chicago to collaborate with. If you can identify the boss, maybe you can take down the Chicago Syndicate once and for all. The problem, he said, is that there are a lot of dirty cops in Chicago. He said he's not even certain if the one he knows is not dirty."

"I'll go."

"Stewart, this could be very dangerous," Sheryl said concerned.

"How? He doesn't know I exist or that I see anything at all."

"That's what I'm saying. The Chicago police might inform the mob boss, and then they will be gunning for you. If they find out anything, you can see God knows what or who they will send after you," Sam said.

"It looks like I don't have a choice in the matter."

"You do. The good news is the FBI will be footing the bill for this whole thing. They will be protecting you and Sheryl, as well."

"Me, why me?" Sheryl asked.

"Well, you have to go too," Sam said.

"I can't go. I have to pack my things and get ready to move to New Jersey."

"You will have time for that later. This should only take a few days."

"You hope so," she retorted.

"Come on, sis, this could be fun. Tony slept during the day. We might be able to see some sights or have some fun. It'll be a bonding experience. There's that arch."

"Ha ha, yeah, we've been doing a lot of that," she answered.

"I should close my eyes and see what he's doing. Okay, he's done eating and on the move. He's driving. Looks like he is back at his place. It's hard to tell. We usually do this at night."

"See if you can see any street signs or landmarks."

"It's just city streets. He's not looking at street signs or at places of interest. It's like he has tunnel vision. I do think we'll need to go there. Wait. I just saw six-forty on the building. I think it is his address. Will that help?"

"It could. I think you are right. Like in St. Louis, we need to drive you around so you can see things. Maybe you can find him."

"We're in the parking garage. I recognize it."

"Terrific, I'll tell O'Keefe."

"If you don't mind, am I done for now?" Stewart asked.

"No. No, that's fine."

"I still don't know why you need me in St. Louis," Sheryl said.

Sam responded, "I'll talk to O'Keefe about that too," they continued their discussion about travel plans until Sam's phone rang.

He answered, "Lieutenant Chee."

"Lieutenant, this is Special Agent Mullens of the FBI. We are here in Flagstaff. We drove in from L.A. and would like to meet you and your witnesses."

"It's witness."

"Right, witness, what's his name?"

"Why don't we meet, and we can discuss the details."

"Well, we wanted to run some preliminaries. Can you give me his name, please, date of birth and home address?"

"Agent Mullens, did you say? Can you do me a favor? I'm not in a place right now where we can discuss this. There was no caller identification on this call. Will you give me your number, and I'll call you back in a few minutes."

"I'm at the hotel here in Flagstaff. We'll be leaving here shortly. I'll just call you back in a little while."

"Sounds fine." He clicked the phone to the end. "I need to call L.A. and see if there's an agent Mullens from there."

"Why are you suspicious about that call?" Sheryl asked.

"He didn't seem legit. Gimme a minute to make this call."

Sam left the room and came back a few minutes later. "It is just as I suspected; there is no Agent Mullens with the FBI, not in L.A., not anywhere. Guys, it's already starting. Someone in Chicago has been tipped off, and they're already coming to get us. I'm not sure if they are really here in Flagstaff or if that was a call from Illinois, but they know. I got in touch with O'Keefe. He's expecting all of us tomorrow. Sheryl, I think you'll be safer with us. I'm pretty sure these guys can figure out who you are and where you live. If they have any reason to believe you can make the peyote or that Stewart will come to your aid, they will snatch you up in an instant and use you to get to him."

"Okay, I will join you in St. Louis."

Just then, Sam's phone rang again, "Chee here."

"Chee, this is Special Agent Timkons with the FBI. I have been assigned to the case you are working on.

My partner, Agent Kronke, and I will meet you in St. Louis at the County Police Station on St. Charles Rock Road tomorrow morning. O'Keefe will pick you up at the airport. There is an FBI jet there waiting for you at Pulliam. Do you know where that is? Agents Barnum and Reynolds will be your escorts. I suggest you contact O'Keefe to verify this."

"I know where Pulliam is, yes. What time?"

"The jet leaves when you arrive. Reynolds will be calling you in a few minutes. I'll see you in St. Louis."

"Meet me in St. Louie, Louie?"

"Very funny, Chee. Goodbye."

"Bye," he hung up and called O'Keefe.

"Sam, is that you?"

"Yeah."

"Agent Kronke called me a few minutes ago. He said you guys are flying on an FBI jet to St. Louis."

"That's what his partner Timkons told me a minute ago. So, this is on the up and up."

"Yeah, why?"

"Well, a few minutes before, another guy posing as an FBI agent called asking for Stewart's contact information."

"Oh damn, we've been made in Chicago."

"That's what I was thinking. Mike, what are we going to do?"

"Let's let the FBI take the lead in Chicago. They should be able to hook us up with the right guys there. They will put you guys somewhere safe, and don't you worry, as confidential informants, your people will be paid handsomely for putting away the mob boss in Chicago."

"One thing at a time, Mike. Let's not go to trial until we have a suspect or two in custody."

"I'm a forward-thinking kind of guy."

"Okay, so what's the weather like in St. Louie?"

"First, Sam, don't call it St. Louie. Second, it's rainy and in the fifties. Dress for snow and for summer. You'll be fine."

"Gotcha! We'll be in touch when we're almost there. Wait, snow in April?"

"Well, not often and copy that. Safe travels. Later."

"Uh-huh, bye," he said to O'Keefe then he turned to Stewart and Sheryl. "Time to pack. He said, pack for fifties temperatures with the possibilities of snow and summer."

"Sounds less than delightful," Sheryl said.

"Okay, will do," Stewart said.

"Also, Sheryl. Make sure we have extra peyote, just in case."

"I think I have plenty for a week. I'm not sure he needs more."

"Make it a month. I'll talk to Jonathan and let him know what's happening here at the house, and they'll make arrangements to help you move."

"I don't want some stranger touching my stuff."

"I'll insist that nothing get touched while we're gone." "If you can guarantee that, it'd be great."

"Okay, now you guys need to pack. I need to get my stuff ready, too. Crap, I'll be back in an hour and a half."

Sam ran out of the house to his car. With squealing tires, lights and sirens, he was on his way. Sheryl began packing, and Stewart, well, Stewart, put the few things he had purchased into a little suitcase he had picked up. Stewart was not ready for the coming temperatures, and he realized he needed to go shopping.

He was hollering from his room, "Sheryl. Sheryl."

She came quickly, "What? What's the problem?"

"I don't have clothes for this trip."

"You have the clothes you arrived in from the airport."

"Right, but we haven't washed them."

"Ew, well, give 'em to me, let's get that done quickly. Can I dry them in the dryer?"

"Yes."

She ran off and put the clothes in the washing machine. A few minutes later, they were in the dryer.

Stewart finished his packing and laid back on the bed. He fell asleep. Tony was asleep, so he didn't see anything. He rested.

Two hours passed, and Sheryl woke Stewart. "Here are your clothes. Sam is here. We need to go."

Stewart yawned, stretched and dressed. He was out in the living room with a little bag before Sheryl could bring her bags to the bottom of the stairs. Stewart grabbed hers and his and headed up the stairs. Sam led the way empty-handed. When they all reached the top of the stairs, Sam said, "I made the calls to the FBI headquarters and verified the agents. I told them we'd be there in about an hour from now. We have time to stop for a quick bite at Momma's if you guys want a burger."

Sheryl responded, "I'm not hungry."

Stewart said, "I can eat."

Sam said, "Good, because I'm hungry. I'm fairly certain there's not going to be a stewardess on an FBI jet, so there's likely no meal, no snacks and maybe even no drinks."

Sheryl then said, "I can eat."

Sam replied, "Is Momma okay with you guys?"

In unison, they answered, "Perfect" and "Uh-huh."

Sam loaded his Expedition with the bags, Sheryl took the back seat and Stewart shotgun. Sam turned around to Sheryl and said, "Did you bring more peyote?"

"I made a fresh batch, and it's in my bag."

"Great, here we go."

The three walked into Hangar Twelve, where a dozen FBI agents mulled around. Agent Timkons met Sam first. "I'm special agent Timkons. This is my partner, Special Agent Kronke; thank you for your prompt response. We hope to have you in St. Louis before too long. The pilot is a career FBI flyer who has flown in missions over Afghanistan and Iraq for the Air Force. The jet you are flying in is equipped with evasive maneuvering capability. It is armed, and he has the authority to shoot down anyone who you may encounter in the air. It looks like your normal Gulfstream G650, but rest assured, this baby hauls ass and shoots like a F-16. He gave us a test flight a few hours ago, you will not be dissatisfied. Climb aboard. When you arrive, Agent Reynolds will be your contact. He will show you around and get you to your hotel. Don't worry, it is secure."

Sam answered, "Thank you." Sheryl and Stewart nodded in agreement. They were both frightened. They boarded the jet to see extreme luxury. Sam stayed outside talking to Timkons. Big ivory-colored leather tufted seats, about a dozen seats, leather walls and plush carpeting filled the cabin. Deep-colored wood trim lined the walls like a chair rail. The same wood framed the seats. Stewart thought this was pure elegance.

Towards the back of the plane, a female voice said, "Your seats are the third row facing the front. Stewart, you are on your left, seat five, and Sheryl is on your right, seat six. We have a few more passengers expected shortly. They were on-call waiting for you. When we got the heads up an hour ago, we called them, and they should be here soon. I'm your flight attendant. I know you can't see me. I'll be up there to introduce myself in a minute."

They sat down in their respective seats. Sheryl looked out over the wing and watched a guy put the bags in the cargo bay. Nothing was suspicious. She looked around and then played with the seat back into a reclining position, almost lying down as she reclined a seat pad raised under her calves. Then she raised the seat back up; cool.

Stewart watched her as she played with the seat and giggled to himself. Then, outside his window, a Mercedes limousine pulled up. The driver opened the door, and four men stepped out. They were all in suits, and Stewart thought, I guess I'm underdressed.

Each one entered the cabin, and one by one, they filled the four seats ahead of him. They didn't introduce themselves. They kept to themselves. With six seats left, Stewart wondered, is there anyone else?

Four of the agents that had been mulling around boarded the plane. Three of them passed Stewart and Sheryl, and the fourth one stopped and went to one knee and said, "I'm special agent Watkins, John Watkins. The four of us are from the US Organized Crime Task Force. We will be working in the shadows behind you and the other agents in St. Louis and Chicago. We've heard we have a problem with law enforcement in Chicago. We've identified the officer that O'Keefe talked to and everyone he might have spoken to in Chicago. Apparently, your story seems far-fetched, and they had a good laugh at your expense. One of the officers within earshot of that laugh put the word out that you may have seen something. Now you are in danger, and it is our job, me and my partners, to keep you safe. Has anyone explained what we'll be doing in St. Louis and Chicago and where this might all lead?"

Stewart answered, "Not really; our friend, Sam, is outside right now. He has been handling this for us so far."

"Oh, do you mean Lieutenant Chee?"

"Yes."

"Well, Lieutenant Chee is staying here. We will be taking over from this point. Our goal is to find these guys and get this Tony guy to meet with the boss. Get another job, then catch him before he does anything. If we can do that, maybe we can get him to turn on the boss. Then we'll go to trial, and you may or may not be needed from there."

Stewart then said, "The way you put that, it sounds easy."

"It's not."

"And, what if Tony doesn't testify?"

"We put a killer behind bars. You get your life back."

"Really? I get to go back to normal; they never chase after me?"

"No, you and your sister go into witsec."

"Witsec? What's that?"

"Witness protection program. New identity, new place to live, new job, you know, new life."

"Sheryl, we should get off this plane right now and forget about it."

"Now, Stewart, don't jump to conclusions."

"Stewart, did they not already contact Chee and try to find you?" the agent said.

Stewart gave him a look, as did Sheryl, and they relaxed back into the seat.

Stewart leaned forward and asked, "Who are the four guys up front?"

"They are not with our agency but here to help should things go sideways."

Sideways, it better not go fucking sideways, Sheryl thought.

"Let's just all relax and enjoy this ride. Ashley, our attendant, will be taking care of us."

Ashley? How many Ashley's are there in the world? Stewart thought.

The cargo door was closed and then the passenger entrance door. The pilot started the jet, and it began to taxi. Within a few minutes, it was in the air. Ten passengers on the plane, one attendant, the pilot and the copilot were all accounted for. The cruising altitude for the jet was just under thirty thousand feet, and it reached that height in fifteen minutes. Once at thirty thousand feet, Ashley made her way from the rear of the plane. Unlike a commercial jet, she didn't have a cart she was pushing. She came to Sheryl first. With her back to Stewart, she asked if she could get Sheryl something to drink. She told Sheryl there was a well-stocked bar and plenty of snacks. Sheryl thought for a minute and then said, "Do you have Ultra?"

"Yes, of course. Would you like Snyders pretzels with your low-carb beer?" she said with a smile.

Sheryl smiled back, "No, thank you. The beer is fine unless you have roasted peanuts."

"Indeed, one moment," then she turned toward Stewart, and he could not believe his eyes. It was Ashley. She didn't recognize him, but he was certain it was her. The years did nothing to her appearance and in his mind, she looked as stunning as the last time she saw her some thirty years earlier.

"Stewart, what would you like?"

"I'd like to ask you a question."

"Surely, I may be able to answer."

"Are you Ashley Jett from Edgewater, New Jersey? Leonia High School Class of Ninety-two?"

"No, I'm sorry, Stewart... Stewart Miller, it was ninety-three. How the hell are you? What are you doing on my plane? Damn, I haven't seen you since you were a dick to me in high school. Really, no hard feelings, broken heart a little, but no hard feelings. Fuck, who am I lying to? I fucking hated you for a long ass time. Shit, listen to my language, see what you did. I'm going to bring you a beer; you hate beer. I bet you still do."

"Ashley, wait. I thought you were dead."

"What?"

"I'm sorry about high school; I never got a chance to apologize. I was so lucky to have had you interested in me. Now look at you, this impressive lady on a jet. Do you think we can catch up?"

She was stunned that Stewart was being so nice to her. She remembered a different guy; she turned to Sheryl and asked, "After I have attended to the other passengers, might I ask you to exchange seats with me?"

"Gladly, my brother has told me so much about you, including you were dead."

"Really? I can't wait to hear," she said, walking to the back to retrieve their drinks.

"I thought you said she was dead," Sheryl asked Stewart.

"Hey, that's what I heard. Here she comes; be quiet."

"So, Stewart, are you still living in Edgewater?"

"Yes, I live in my parent's old home."

"Oh wow, how are they?

"They both passed away some time ago. Mom got MS, and Dad got lung cancer. I moved back in with them to help Dad take care of Mom."

"Oh, wow, I bet that was tough. I'm so sorry to hear. Yeah, my folks have been dead for a good number, let's see, wow, fifteen years. Did you see the house caught fire?"

"Well, as a matter of fact, I did. I thought you were there then."

"I was visiting. I'd gone out with Nancy, you remember Nancy Puddlijeske, don't you?"

"I do, yes, puddles. How come the word got out that you had died in the fire?"

"I can't tell you that. Not now, anyway. Here are your drinks. I need to attend to other passengers. Be back shortly."

"Wow, Stewart, she's mysterious and sexy and beautiful. I wonder if you can get another shot at her," Sheryl said sarcastically.

"Shut up."

"What, can't take it? Have I turned you into a pussy?"

Stewart turned away.

"Really, no comment. Wow, just fucking, wow."

About a half hour later, Ashley returned. Sheryl and Stewart had been silent, and Sheryl gave up her seat. As she passed Ashley, she whispered in her ear, "Be gentle on him; he's still a virgin."

"No!"

Sheryl whispered, "As God is my witness."

"How could that be?"

"It's a long, embarrassing story; you should ask him."

Ashley sat down and turned to Stewart. She started, "I should begin. I'm sorry to hear that my position here may seem like a normal flight attendant, but I'm not. You see, I work for the government, like everyone on this plane except you. This jet has been used all over the world, and my job is to make sure the passengers are safe. I was trained at Quantico and worked for the FBI up until my cover was blown. I went home to hide; the guys I was chasing found me and burned down my mom and dad's house. I stay on the run on this jet. If they ever figure out where this secret jet is or where it is going, they'll kill anyone associated with it. I do the flight attendant job to keep me busy. I like serving people, and I have to say these FBI guys are mostly gorgeous. I have never been married, don't have kids, and I have seen most of the armpits of the world. I have seen some beautiful places, worked with some powerful people and have lived a fun life. I have been briefed on your case. The crime boss that's after you is in the same syndicate that is after me. The depth of their corruption goes worldwide. Your safety will be easy. Johnny Cotton (Torino), as we call him, is only one leg of the centipede. He's a local Chicago thug and doesn't go much past the Midwest. His boss, on the other hand, reports to the top guy, an ex-politician's wife. If they think you're worth the trouble, they'll chase you down until they get you. It seems you only have this leg. My hope is Johnny Torino will lead us to the top. At the top, there is human trafficking, child pornography, child enslavement and even more disgusting things. I had just about busted them for the children when the shit hit the fan. After they killed my family, I hit a wall. The FBI knew it and gave me this cool job. A secret fucking jet that has the same weaponry as an F-16 and flies supersonic. Should I ask the pilot to kick it up?"

"No, I'm good. The g's we're feeling now are plenty."

"Aw, come on. Maybe a barrel roll or two?"

"Could we do a climb and stall?"

"In aerobatics, it is called a 'hammerhead turn.' You climb straight up until the plane cannot continue, then just as that happens, you turn and drift awhile, then hopefully restart the engines and go back to your maneuvers. I don't know if this pilot has ever done one of those before. The barrel roll I mentioned isn't fun in this jet. It's fun in a WWII plane. So, what does Stewart do for fun back in Jersey?"

"I'm on one of the Price bowling teams."

"Oh boy, got anything else?"

"Well, that takes a lot of my time, practicing."

"You practice bowling?"

His eyes shifted, looking for an answer, "Sometimes I do, I guess."

"Dude, you need some action. I'm going to take you out in Chicago when we get there."

"Don't you have to stay with the jet?"

"Not this time. Since this case is about Johnny Torino and we haven't been this close since Mom and Dad, I'm back in the field with Reynolds and Barnum, the lead agent. I'm assisting. I'll be by your side the whole way. The guys behind you are part of the team. The guys in front are a logistical backup. There are a few dozen agents in both St. Louis and Chicago also working on this. You, my dear, have uncovered something very big. I shouldn't tell you but. Can I ask you?"

"Ask me what?"

"How do you do it?"

"How do I do what? See the stuff I see?"

"Yeah, how does it work?"

"Well, you see, Sheryl made some peyote. It's not like the stuff you heard about in movies. Peyote is a term used by the Navajo Indians for the medications they make. They often mix the medications with chants and prayers for more effectiveness. Sheryl made a peyote that was just supposed to make me more compassionate. She did something wrong, and it opened a portal in my mind. At first, when I dreamed, I saw what this guy was doing. Then she increased the dosage, and I began to smell and taste. So, now I hear, see what he's looking at, I smell, and I can taste. I can't feel what he feels. I can't control his movements or where he looks. She overdosed on me a few days ago, and now, when I close my eyes, just close my eyes, I can see what he sees. Here, let me try." Stewart closed his eyes. She sat in silence, waiting. Ten seconds later, "He must be asleep. I didn't see anything."

"That's too bad. You're lucky."

"I don't consider myself lucky. Why would you say that?"

"Let's start off with you were a major ass-hat before your sister dosed you. You now seem cool as shit, you don't dress the part, but that's easy to fix with clothes and a haircut. You are on this jet with me; you get to travel to places you have never been to and see shit you've never seen. The FBI is kissing your ass, and they don't kiss anyone's ass. They are going to pay you; did you know they are going to pay you?"

"No. Really?"

"Yes, handsomely! You and your sister. First you. You'll get ten percent of every dollar seized. If they collect a hundred million dollars, you, my newfound lost and found friend, will get ten fucking million dollars. You know, the guy who turned in El Chapo made one point three billion dollars. If they find that kind of dough, you are fixed for life plus, you lucky fucker. All you have to do is give us enough information to pin the muthafuckas to the wall and find the money. You are set. Set. Set. Set. Need a bitch who can kick ass on your arm, let's talk. As for your sister, wow, she's got a new career in the building. The CIA is going to want to use her peyote to open some doors. Can it be directed?"

"What do you mean directed?"

"Can you choose who you see in your dreams?"

"I don't think it works that way. Actually, I hadn't given it much thought as to how it works, but I don't think it works that way. Let's go back to the bitch who can kick some ass statement. You wanna hang out after this is all done?"

"Hang out? What are we still in high school? Either we get to know each other as we should have a hundred years ago, or I work for you; you're gonna need security, and your sister is going to need security. I got connections to people who can keep you alive."

"Ashley, I'm so sorry. I misunderstood everything back when we were kids. It really fucked me up. That

Kip Mason guy told me a bunch of lies about you, and it scared me away. It hurts so bad."

"Kip Mason, are you serious? That guy was my stalker before they called them stalkers. My Dad caught him in the tree outside my window. He got caught hiding in the girl's locker room and eventually ended up getting shot and killed by the father of a little girl he tried to abduct. That guy was fucked up. Wait, what did he tell you?"

"I don't remember exactly."

"Paraphrase then, you dickhead."

"Well, when he saw us out at that party, he told me you were a slut, and if I didn't get a blowjob from you, I was a pussy."

"That was a paraphrase?"

"No, that was exactly what he said."

"I was sixteen years old and a virgin; I never, oh, if I could..." She got very angry and then cooled off. "Well, it seems he got what he deserved."

"I suppose you're right. Anyway, that certainly affected me. Then, my mom got ill, and I had to take care of her. Sheryl ran off with an Indian. Dad died, and well, my heart never healed."

"You're a sad sucker. Let's make you rich and change your lot in life. What do you say?"

"I like the idea."

"Okay, well, although this has been riveting, I need to do some stewardess shit, want another beer?"

"Sure."

"Okay, I'll send Sheryl back with your Bud Light, and she can sit back in your lap."

"Thanks, Ashley." *She's still as cool as I remember her.*

Sheryl returned to her seat with two beers. One for her and one for Stewart. They talked about his conversation, finished the beers and took a nap.

Three hours passed, and Ashley announced they would be landing soon. She made a joke about tray tables and seat backs, flotation devices, and parachutes, then came back to Stewart. She squatted down between Sheryl and Stewart. Stewart noticed she had changed her clothing. Her pantsuit was gone, and now she wore a casual skirt, higher-heeled shoes and a white semi-translucent top. She had changed her hair; she had gone from attractive to stunning. "When we get to St. Louis, we're going to the hotel. It'll be too late to meet O'Keefe, Barnum and Reynolds until the morning. I'll be in the room next to you and Sheryl on the other side. The eight guys on this plane will also be on the same floor as us." She handed them both phones, "These are secure phones. If you see or hear anything suspicious, call immediately. I'm gonna need something to eat and a drink when we get there. Do you two want to join me? I heard there's a place right nearby on Fee Fee Road called Pasta House. They are open late. I hear it is really good. I told O'Keefe we're going there. He may meet us."

Sheryl and Stewart looked at each other and then back at Ashley. Sheryl answered, "Sure, sounds good."

The jet landed, and the four security guys got off first. Ten minutes passed, and one came back and gave the 'all clear.' The other FBI agents climbed the stairs to the tarmac and waited. Stewart and Sheryl disembarked, and the FBI agents surrounded them as they walked to the hangar. Once in the hangar, there were three black SUVs in line. Ashley led them to the middle one. They opened the doors and began to get in. Ashley stopped them. "Sheryl, shotgun, Stewart, you sit in the back with me. This is Bob Bohn, he's, our driver. He's a marksman, he served three tours overseas, he's a sniper and will be leaving us after this assignment to join the secret service. The president hand-picked him. Fuck you, Bob."

"I love you too, Ashley," Bob replied.

"Are you planning on sitting out in the Chevy while we get to eat toasted raviolis, bread and all-we-want salad at the Pasta House Company Restaurant?"

"It's not a Chevy, it's a GMC, and no, I'm coming in with you," he said as they all drove out of the hangar.

"Anyone wants music?"

Stewart answered, "I haven't heard any good rock since I left Jersey. What kind of stations do they have here?"

"Really, here goes."

He turned the radio on and tuned to ninety-four point seven, they heard the end of a Metallica song and then the jock, 'Favazz with ya, that was Metallica, Enter the Sandman, coming up on Real Rock Radio KSHE ninety-five we have a Zeppelin triple play, but first we gotta pay some bills.'

The radio played a commercial for Dobbs Auto, A law firm, Imo's Pizza and Bommarito Auto Group, then went straight into the long intro of 'In the evening…'

All four sang along to the Led Zeppelin songs as Bob turned the music up higher and higher to drown himself out. It was a party in the Denali on the way to pasta. They arrived in the same order they had left the airport. The parking lot was empty. The three large SUVs pulled up to the door and parked. One of the men from the first truck got out and went to the door. A manager came out to greet him. He opened the door, and all twelve people got out and went in. There wasn't a soul in the place. Ashley said to the manager, "Thank you for staying open for us. We won't be long."

"You are welcome. It's no problem, and it was a slow night anyway. Is this everyone?"

"I think so. Do you know Mike O'Keefe?"

"I sure do. We grew up together. I'm Kevin. Mike asked me to accommodate you guys, and I'm glad to help out law enforcement however I can. I'm sorry to say we only have a few things for you. We'll start with drinks; who's thirsty for a Bud?"

Hands went up, so Kevin counted and brought three pitchers and nine glasses. He took the other orders for tea; they were the drivers. They sat at a very large round table. It was more of a family get-together than a protective unit. Before long, they were telling stories, laughing and ribbing each other. The food came and went, and it seemed like hours when Kevin came back to the table and said, "Has everyone had enough? Can we do anything else for you?"

"No, Kevin, you've done enough," Ashley said. They all got up and loaded back into the SUVs to the hotel. Ashley got all of the keys, dispersed them then they went up the elevator to the third floor. One of the guys would stand guard. They played rock, paper, and scissors to see who would go first. Chris, a red-headed guy with a bright, kind smile, went first.

Ashley followed Stewart to his room. "Remember, I'll be right next door."

"Okay, should you come in my room and maybe I close my eyes and see what I can see."

"I wouldn't want to do that alone. I might need the whole detail in there, and that could get crowded."

"Oh, yeah. Well, maybe you want to talk a little while longer. It seems a waste for you to look so beautiful for such a short time."

"Awe, that was nice. No, you are not getting into my skirt, Stewart."

"That's not."

She interrupted, "That's not what you were saying, but thinking yes."

"Can you blame me?"

"Not at all, I'm fucking hot in these stilettos. Go to sleep, Stewart. Dream, see some shit and tell us in the morning."

"Okay. Good night, Ashley."

"Good night."

Chapter Thirteen: St. Louis

Stewart woke up with a headache. He didn't remember his dreams. Nothing happened while he was sleeping. *Did Tony die? Why didn't I see anything?*

He lay in bed.

Silence.

The power is gone. Ticking. *Where's the remote? Nah. I don't want to watch TV.* He went to the window and looked out. The skies were grey. He could only see the parking lot. Behind the hotel were trees. He looked further and saw some traffic moving. What time is it? He looked at the clock, nine-seventeen. He closed his eyes, darkness. *Did I lose it coming here? I got nothing.*

He went to the bathroom, relieved himself then undressed for the shower. He showered quickly using the provided body wash and shampoo. He dressed in the same clothes then he picked up his cell phone and looked at the contacts. There were sixteen. Each of the other twelve people on the plane, Sheryl, O'Keefe,

Reynolds and Barnum. He pressed Sheryl's number. She didn't answer. He pressed Ashley's number; she didn't answer. He tried O'Keefe. He didn't. He sat on the edge of the bed, looking at the remaining names, trying to pick one. Before he could dial another, his phone rang, "Hello."

"Stewart, are you okay?"

"I am, who's this," he responded.

"This is Ashley. Didn't you look at the caller ID before you answered?"

"No, should I?"

"Yes. Every time. From now on, every time your phone rings, look at the damn id. Got it?" Ashley answered.

"Yeah, I got it."

"Now, what's up? You called and hung up," she said.

"Me?" he responded.

"Uh, what do you mean?"

"I'm awake. I have showered, I'm wearing the same fucking clothes. I need clothes for this climate," Stewart barked at her.

"We've got clothes coming for you. Don't worry about that. What else?" Ashley responded kindly.

"I didn't see any, I didn't see a thing. I am growing impatient, sorry."

"What?" she asked.

"I didn't see a thing. No dreams. No, nothing," Stewart answered.

"Are you fucking kidding me?" she said impatiently.

"No," he barked.

Ashley rubbed her face, asking, "Have you talked to Sheryl?"

"No, not yet."

She looked around the room frustrated, then said, "Okay, we need to get you some of that peyote."

"I have some bad news for ya," he said.

"What now?"

"We didn't know it wasn't permanent. This is the first time I haven't seen Tony in my dreams. When she gives me the peyote, I sleep like a log. Someone is going to have to be there to wake me up when it gets dark."

"Well, first, we need to take a ride with O'Keefe and help him figure out his mess here. I'll get in touch with him and have him come and get you. Bob will ride along. Bob has the clothing for you. He should be back any minute. Hang tight!"

Half an hour passed and Bob came to the door with a suit, white shirt, and tie for Stewart.

"I can't wear this; I don't have the right shoes."

"Deal with it. We'll figure it out later."

Stewart tried the clothing on in the bathroom mirror, and surprisingly, it all fit. He felt handsome sans the shoes. Bob waited outside the door. Stewart opened the door to tell Bob he was ready and everyone, not just Bob, everyone was waiting outside the door for Stewart.

They all went to the elevators together. Eight went onto the elevators, and eight took the stairs. They all met in the lobby. They went to the breakfast area, grabbed something to go and left. The SUVs were proportioned equally as they drove to the precinct. They were led to a large conference room where Sheryl and Stewart, Ashley, Reynolds and Barnum sat and waited for O'Keefe.

Stewart was thinking, *what have I gotten myself into? This is the most dangerous game, fuck that book about hunting people, that's gonna be me if these guys are even a little crooked. I'm putting my life in their hands, and I'm also about to tell them I've lost my powers. I sure hope Sheryl can, oh here they come.*

O'Keefe followed a handsome guy in his fifties. O'Keefe, too in his fifties, had light brown hair, a thin but muscular build, blue eyes and tanned skin. He began speaking as soon as he approached the table, "My name is Mike O'Keefe, this is Chief Tom Meyer. The Chief has a few words. First, Stewart, will you speak to our artist to make a composite drawing?"

"Absolutely."

The Chief began. "I have not met any of you before, and I'm not sure you are aware of our reputation. We don't tolerate anything crooked. So, I need you to know this man, Mike O'Keefe, is beyond reproach. He is of the highest integrity we have in this police force. I personally vouch for him and his character. This all said we have been informed that an erroneous call was made to Lieutenant Sam Chee of the Navajo Nation Police Department from a phony FBI agent. As you all know, we have only had contact with Special Agent Reynolds and Barnum here in St. Louis County, as well as a detective in Chicago. The detectives in Chicago, O'Keefe, Barnum or Reynolds are the potential leaks to the syndicate in Chicago. Most likely, it was someone in the twelfth precinct in Chicago who was the mole. I will only speak for O'Keefe. On the table here, you have O'Keefe's report, you have the name of the detective in Chicago, Ralph Nillson and his partner, whom O'Keefe didn't talk to, Roger Hernandez. Now, that is our report to you. Shall we sit down and discuss our plan going forward and what you will need from the County Police."

Agent Barnum spoke first, "My name is Special Agent Phil Barnum. I have been assigned the lead here in St. Louis for this case. There are elements of the case that aren't pertinent to the Millers; that's Sheryl and Stewart here. Miller is Sheryl's maiden name, and I will likely be using it regularly. We have some questions for them, and once we're finished, you can take them on the tour to locate the path you believe our suspect took. Any concerns about that?"

No one spoke.

"Okay, I'll accept silence as agreement. O'Keefe, if you would like to question the witness, please proceed."

"Thank you. Mr. Miller, may I call you Stewart?"

"I prefer it."

"Thank you. You witnessed Anthony, Tony Palumbo, shoot four black men during a drug deal. Is this correct?"

"I did, but that's not all."

"I understand. We need to take this one step at a time. Tell us about the shooting of the four black men."

"It was a setup from the beginning. Tony was given instructions to bring drugs to St. Louis from Chicago and use them as bait to bring the St. Louis partners to the parking garage. I believe the place was Northwest Plaza. At this meeting, he was going to kill the four men and then take money back to Chicago. Do you want the details on how he arrived here?"

"No, just the details on what happened here."

"Okay, he met the other three men from Chicago at the parking garage and explained his plan. He would take his vehicle up a floor and wait. When the four black men arrived, he would sneak up and shoot them all when they had their guards down. That's precisely what he did."

"Then what happened?"

"Then he told the other men to move the black guys over to their vehicle, get the cash and give it to him. When they began doing that, he shot them all dead.

Then he took the money and the drugs and left."

"Where did he go next?"

"He took the car they were driving out to the main road; then my sister woke me up. I missed the rest until he was on the plane to Midway."

The FBI agents looked at each other as if that didn't matter.

Ashley asked, "Did he encounter anyone else along the way? You know anyone who could put him here or witness his presence?"

"No, he didn't talk to anyone. He had all of his flight documents in the envelope that was in the Lincoln he drove from Chicago."

O'Keefe interacted, "That was the vehicle we found torched in the parking garage."

Ashley asked, "Could you tell if there is someone waiting?"

"Last I saw, he left the parking garage. Sam and Sheryl woke me up and the next time I was asleep, he was asleep; I think on the plane."

Chief Meyer asked, "Was that it then?"

"Yes, that's it."

"We have nothing more. We don't know where he went. We don't know how he got to the airport. It's a dead end. Mike, take Stewart to see the artist then to the scene, see if he remembers anything else."

"Yes sir, right away," O'Keefe said, leaving the room with Stewart.

The FBI agents together concluded the trip to St. Louis might have been a waste.

Stewart joined Mike O'Keefe in his late model Ford Crown Victoria. They first drove to the scene of the crime. It was the first time Stewart had come to the reality of his visions and dreams. He stepped out of the car, fell to his knees, and cried. O'Keefe didn't know what to do. He went around to the passenger side of the car and waited for Stewart to compose himself. Once composed, Stewart said, "It was real. It really happened. This is where he killed them."

"What do you remember?"

"The SUV with the other three guys got here first, and Tony arrived shortly after. He briefed them on his plan. They were to meet with the dealers and make the exchange, and Tony was going to be hiding. He was going to sneak up on them and do what he did: blow them all away. He drove his car up to the level above. I can show you."

"I don't think it's important."

"Then he rolled the car down the ramp. He somehow snuck up, and they didn't see him. He opened fire. Like I told you before."

"Stewart, I'm just trying to see if there is something we missed."

"Okay, I'll continue..."

Stewart repeated the story, giving O'Keefe no new information. Stewart had become a dead end. They finished the tour and met back at the hotel. Stewart was handed back to the FBI, and the day was finished.

The FBI and the St. Louis County police reviewed hours of security tapes and found the vehicle that Tony had switched to at the Marriot. It was an RAV4, they saw where he went and where it was parked. They also watched it get picked up by a hooded man, and he left the airport. They lost the vehicle in Fergusson. It had been reported stolen two days before the incident, as had the SUV and the Lincoln. The RAV4 showed up again on traffic cameras at interstate forty and Grand Avenue. The St. Louis Police impounded it, and when the County Police inspected it, they found no useable evidence. It, too, was a dead end that took three days.

Before the trail got cold, the FBI, Stewart and Sheryl boarded the jet and were on their way to Chicago. They left before the county police found the RAV4. The trip was quick and painless. When they arrived in Chicago, there was a collection of SUVs waiting in the hangar along with the detectives from District Twelve, Nillson and Hernandez. They had a short meeting without Stewart or Sheryl on the tarmac; the detectives left, and the FBI waited. Two of the agents boarded a helicopter and took off. It was dark outside; Tony was likely awake, so Stewart closed his eyes in hopes of seeing something. He didn't. He and Sheryl waited in the jet. Agent Reynolds took a phone call. He turned and talked to Ashley, and she climbed the stairs and into the jet, "It's time to go."

Barnum drove the middle SUV, Stewart and Ashley sat in the back, and Sheryl was in the passenger seat. Barnum asked, "Let us know when you recognize something."

"Is it important that I recognize something from the airport?"

"Did he talk to anyone or meet anyone there?"

"No."

"Then no," Barnum said.

"He did talk to the waitress at Denny's and the cab driver. I saw both. He talked to the State Trooper. He could help."

"We'll start at Denny's," Barnum said.

"Jett, get in touch with the state and see if you can have the trooper meet us at the restaurant."

"Yes, sir."

Ashley immediately called the trooper. She reported from the call, "He is not on duty but would make an exception and meet them as soon as he could."

Barnum answered, "Terrific, his experience might greatly help."

It took a half hour to get to Denny's. The entourage arrived simultaneously and parked side by side. They stayed in the car until the trooper arrived. Barnum said, "Stewart and Sheryl, you guys go inside with Jett. Have something to eat if you would like; Reynolds and I are going to talk to the trooper."

Once inside, they were greeted by the same waitress that served Tony, Stewart whispered to Ashley once they were seated and ordered drinks, "She's the one who waited on Tony."

Ashley responded, "Perfect." She got up and went back out to Barnum; Stewart watched as she told Barnum and Reynolds. Barnum stayed with the trooper and continued the discussion. Reynolds followed Ashley in then they split. Reynolds stopped at the front hostess desk, and the waitress went to seat him. They stood talking for a few minutes; he showed her the composite picture of Tony, then asked if she remembered him from three nights ago.

"Yes, I remember him. It was about four in the morning. He was the only customer. A yellow taxi dropped him off, and he had a grand slam with coffee. He left without paying me at the cashier's desk, so I ran over, and he tipped me a ten-dollar bill. I watched him as he walked across the parking lot to that construction company over there," she pointed through the front door. Reynolds turned and looked. She continued, "He must've had the combination or key because he opened the gate and then left in a Range Rover, a black Range Rover. I love those vehicles. They're not really cars, are they?"

"Was that it, uh, Tammy, is it?"

"Yes, Tammy. Yes, that was it."

"Thank you. One of the other agents will take your full statement. We appreciate your help."

Reynolds went back out to Barnum and the trooper. They had identified where Tony had lived when he last renewed his driver's license. They had his date of birth and last known place of employment; it was not Acme Medical Supply. The trooper told the FBI agents that Tony lied and didn't give him his present address or his present employer. Their search on the national database didn't reveal an Anthony (Tony) Palumbo in Oak Park. There were several in other parts of the country, but none in Chicago. The FBI had concluded his name was erroneous. It seemed Tony was trying to reenact the historical mobster from the seventies through two-thousand ten. He pleaded a deal and is living in witness protection somewhere. The agents thanked the trooper for his information, and he left. They went inside, sat together and ordered a meal.

Stewart, Sheryl and Ashley were served, ate and waited. When the other agents had finished eating, they convened outside. They told Stewart and Sheryl to stay in the middle SUV, and the rest walked across the parking lot to the construction company. The company was said to be owned by a shell corporation, and they could not identify the directors as part of the established syndicate. It was yet another dead end. The chain-linked gate was locked, and all they could do was look inside the fenced area from outside. Without a warrant and no reason to obtain a warrant, they got as close as they could. They went back to the SUVs, loaded up and began driving into the city.

This time, Stewart was in the front seat directing their travels. He gave directions of where to turn, and after more than an hour, they ended up at what Stewart thought was Tony's apartment building. They got a pass from security to enter the parking garage, and Stewart confirmed they were in the correct location.

They went to the Chicago Marriot on Ogden and rented several rooms. Similarly, to the setup in St. Louis, Stewart and Sheryl were sandwiched between Ashley and Reynolds. Stewart had given them almost everything they needed, so he and Sheryl were to stay at the hotel until they were needed again. They were tired and turned in immediately. A new team of agents sat in waiting in Tony's apartment garage. The surveillance team would be rotated every four hours for as long as it took.

Stewart didn't dream about Tony. His dreams were like the dreams he had had before the peyote started. When he awoke in the morning, he was worried. He called his sister's room.

"Hello," she answered.

"Sis, it's me. Did I wake you?"

She rubbed her eyes and said, "No. I have been up for a while. Do you want breakfast?"

"I do, but..."

She sat up in bed and asked, "But what?"

"We got a problem," he said.

"We do? What's that?" she wondered aloud.

"I didn't see Tony in my dreams. I lost the power."

"Oh shit, you're fucking with me, aren't you?" she answered excitedly.

"No, sis, I'm not. I need some peyote."

"If I give it to you, you will go to sleep," she asked, annoyed.

"I know. I need to see what he's doing. Maybe only give me a little so you can wake me."

"We better talk to Agent Jett."

"Sis."

"What?"

"What if they think I'm a fraud?" he asked concerned.

"Stewart, you've led them this far. They aren't going to think you're a fraud."

"Okay, let's talk to Ashley. I'll call her," Stewart said.

"Fine, meet you down in the lobby in what?"

"A half-hour."

"Okay, I'll be down there."

He called Ashley on the hotel phone.

"Hello, Agent Jett here," Ashley answered the phone.

"Ashley, it's Stewart from next door."

"Really, Stewart?"

He giggled and replied, "Yeah, sorry. We have something important to talk about. Will you meet us downstairs in the lobby in a half hour? I'm hungry."

"Me too, yeah, breakfast sounds good."

Half an hour passed and Stewart was drinking a cup of coffee at a table in the restaurant alone. He had chosen a four-top and looked through the menu. Sheryl arrived next, and a few minutes later, Ashley and Barnum arrived. Reynolds came five minutes after they were all seated. They moved to a round table for six.

Barnum said when he arrived, "Stewart, what happened to your security detail? How did you and Sheryl get down here without them?"

Stewart responded, "I don't know. We came out of the rooms, and they were gone."

Barnum asked, "Jett, do you know where they went?"

"No sir, I don't."

"Reynolds, get on the phone, find them," Barnum barked.

Reynolds took out his cell phone and dialed one of the agents, "Schnaze, where the hell are you?"

Schnaze answered, "Reynolds, I'm in the hallway."

"Where were you ten minutes ago?"

"Dude, really? Why?" Schnaze answered.

"I'm not your dude. Where were you?"

"I was in my room."

"Why?"

"Well, I needed to."

"To what?" Reynolds continued his interrogation.

"Go to the bathroom."

"Why didn't you call someone?" Reynolds asked with an elevated voice.

"I didn't think it would take so long."

"Thanks," he ended the call, "Barnum, you won't believe this, he was crapping."

"Oh my God, get rid of that guy," Barnum said with disgust.

Everyone was quiet until they had been served coffee, and the waitress took their breakfast order. The Barnum said, "So, Stewart, I understand you have something important to discuss."

"I do. You see. Um, well."

"Spit it out, man," Reynolds said, "as you just heard, I have not had a very good morning."

Ashley and Barnum laughed a little.

"Well, I lost my power."

In unison, they all spoke. Different things with Barnum being the loudest and longest, "What the actual fuck?"

Sheryl chimed in, "We didn't know it was temporary. This has never happened before."

"Okay, wait. You are saying you don't see Palumbo anymore?" Barnum asked firmly.

"Right, I don't. I need to get peyote and sleep. He's awake at night. It really won't do much good if I get it now. He'll be asleep."

"We know. He came home about three hours ago. He went to his apartment, we followed him to the ninth floor, and we got off on the tenth. We checked the records, and we now know which apartment is his."

Reynolds chimed in, "We don't need them anymore. We can do this our way. We watch and catch him."

Barnum said, "We'll talk about logistics later. I recommend Sheryl, you give him a big dose of that peyote as soon as you can. Maybe we can wake him up, and he can tell us where Tony is. Finish your breakfast, drug him and then we get together at dark. In the meantime, Ashley, you babysit these two. Be where they can get you if they need you."

"Right."

They finished eating, Stewart went to his room, and Ashley followed. Sheryl went to her room, retrieved the peyote and knocked on Stewart's door. Ashley let her in, she gave him the mixture, and he was out in less than five minutes. He fell asleep dressed on the couch in his room. Sheryl and Ashley picked him up and led him to the bed. Then, they sat on the couch and began talking.

Ashley started, "I haven't been able to think past what you said on the plane."

"What did I say? I'd been drinking."

"No, you had not," Ashley answered quickly.

"Oh. I wanted to."

"We all did. But we didn't. Wait, yes, you were, you were drinking Ultra."

"I was indeed, and I have some next door. Do you want some?"

"How did you get beer already?" Ashley asked.

"I asked the front desk. They brought it to me," she answered.

"Oh shit, did you put it in the room?"

"I did," she said with a grin.

"Barnum's gonna be pissed. You guys are getting away with too much shit. Just ask any of us, and we will get it for you."

Sheryl said, "I'm not sorry. You want one? Or more?"

"Sure, you're the one in trouble. However, we gotta stay sober for when Stewart wakes up."

"You have to stay sober. Me, no, I just have to drug my brother."

"Go get the beer. I got questions," Ashley demanded.

"Okay. Quit being a bitch. I didn't remember you being a bitch."

Sheryl left the room, got the beer and returned with an open twelve-pack. "So, what questions do you have?"

"You told me to be easy on your brother as he was a virgin. How is that possible?" Ashley genuinely asked.

"You are why that's possible," Sheryl said as she opened her beer.

"Huh? What do you mean, I'm why that's possible?" Ashley asked as they clicked the beers together.

"I'm not sure if you noticed, but Stewart lacks confidence with the ladies. He always has. He met you and got the nerve to ask you out. When you accepted, he was quite moved. Excited is one term you might use. He didn't know how to behave, and the fucker didn't want to fuck up. So, he was careful."

"I remember he was very nice," Ashley said, taking a sip of her beer.

"Stewart used to be nice. He told me you two went to a party, and a guy there, Steve Madsen or something like that told him you were a slut. He told him he would be a pussy if he didn't fuck you or at least get a blow job."

"Are you kidding me? Is that what happened? That's what Stewart said. I thought he was fucking with me. Is that why I never heard from him again? You know Steve Madsen died a horrible death. That's not his name, it was Kip. Not that it matters. I guess he deserved it."

"So I heard. So, the trauma of breaking up with you, the only girl he really loved, changed him. He became a crabby asshole. I can see why. I mean, all that sperm built up inside of him, no wonder."

"Oh my God, that's funny. It's not supposed to be, but Sheryl," she said, almost spitting her beer out.

"I know. So, I thought I could help him with his personality, but really, you have more power than peyote," Sheryl said, opening a second beer.

"That's nice of you to say so. You know that incident had a similar effect on me. Now, Stewart's not my type as much as you are."

"Oh snap, motherfucker, don't you say," Sheryl cried out.

"Uh-huh. He hurt me, and a girl in high school made me feel good about myself. I began to see how girls were towards me," Ashley finished her beer, and Sheryl handed her another.

"Well, hell, ya, you are hot," Sheryl said, looking her up and down.

"Shut up," Ashley said before a big gulp of beer.

"So, you ain't had a dick?"

Spitting the beer all over the room, "No, I haven't."

"Fuck me running backward, you and my brother both fucked each other's life up, and neither has had sex with the opposite sex. I guess maybe you two are the only ones who could fix this shit. Or maybe fuck it up even more."

Ashley laughed and regained her composure to say with sadness, “He was the only guy I have ever been interested in.”

“What the actual fuck? My brother?” Sheryl said, gulping the last of her second beer and opening a third.

“Who is being insensitive now?”

“Ok, yeah, I’m sorry.”

“You might be right; maybe this is the only way. Do you think he might still be interested?” Ashley asked, catching up and finishing her second beer.

“You have a captive audience, my dear. He’s asleep. Go fucking jump his bones.”

“What? You are out of your mind; gimme another one of those beers.”

“Well, he’s lying there in the bed. He won’t wake up for a day or so, and you got him from the outside. He won’t even know what hit him,” Sheryl said, grinning and leaning on one elbow on the bed.

“You are one sick bitch,” Ashley responded, thinking maybe she was right.

“If by sick you mean kinky, then yeah, I’m sick, alright.”

“Well, Sheryl, when we started this conversation, I sort of expected it to be above a certain bar. You have dipped. What I glean from this is your brother and I have some unfinished business. I might ask, who do you think should make a move?”

“Did you not hear me? At this point, Ashley, if there’s going to be a move, a shake, a kiss or a fuck, it is going to be you that makes that happen. I know, he’s fucking afraid of you right now. I know I am. You may be turned on, but I wanna fucking jump out that window,” Sheryl said, pointing at the curtains.

“Well, that’d be a bad idea.”

“Why?”

“We’re on the second floor.”

Sheryl got up and went to the window to look out, then stopped, turned around and said, "Oh yeah, that's true."

"And who said I wanted to fuck you?" Ashley said, undressing Sheryl with her eyes.

Sheryl paused, looked over her shoulder coyly, smiled and said, "Well, you said I was more your type."

"No, that's not what I said. After your brother broke my heart, a girl in high school put it back together. I thought that was love. It was. It was a different love that never felt right. Every time we were naked together, I felt dirty. I felt like I was doing something I shouldn't. That same feeling hits me with every woman I sleep with. Men have tried to seduce me; none have been of interest. Well, that's not true, one. Just one."

"Right. My paisley brother," Sheryl said as she sat back on the edge of the bed.

"Don't ask me to explain. I cannot. I just know women may give me an orgasm, but I've never been satisfied. They may be soft and luscious, but they have never made me feel right."

"It sucks to be you," Sheryl said, looking away and finishing her third beer.

"Tell me again, which of you, Millers, is more a mess?" Ashley asked sarcastically.

Sheryl turned her head quickly and glared, then said as she turned her head back around, "That would be me." She set her empty beer on the nightstand, threw her legs up on the bed next to her brother, crossed them and leaned back on both elbows, "My brother is ultra-stable. He is like a rock. When Mom or Dad needed anything, he was always there. Me, I was the flower child. I ran away from home more times than I was there. I lost my virginity way too early. You know what? I'm getting the impression you and Stewart are both virgins."

"No. Not me. I have had plenty of partners."

"Oh, have you? But not dick, right?"

"Well, not a real one."

Sheryl uncrossed her legs, sat up, crossed them again and leaned towards Ashley with her elbows on her knees. Ashley was on the other edge of the bed on the other side of Stewart when Sheryl continued, "Okay then, girl, that makes you a virgin. Back to my plan, you go take down those tidy whities and ride that stallion. Get-r-done bitch."

Ashley stood up, rotated in her shoes and rested her wrists on her hips, "Is that really how you want his first real sexual experience to go? You want it stolen from him?"

"Fuck, no. Are you thinking stealing his woody is what I meant? Well. I did. I'm so kidding. Want another beer?" she asked, getting up off the bed and reaching into the refrigerator.

"Sure, what is this four?"

"You're keeping pace with me, and I'm on four. So, yup. You drunk enough to go wake my bro up and attack him?" Sheryl said, handing her another Ultra.

"I could entertain that idea, yeah," she said with a slight slur.

"I'd help, but that would just be weird."

"I wonder if he's seeing anything in his dreams yet?" Ashley said.

"Oh, so you're changing the subject. I think I will, uh, go back to my, uh, room and leave you here with him," Sheryl said, getting up, taking half of the beers and leaving.

Ashley moved to the couch and sat with the palms of her hands, holding her head up. Her elbows planted on her knees. She was wearing sensible FBI agent apparel and didn't feel sexy. She looked over at Stewart. He was sleeping on his side in the middle of the king-sized bed. He flinched. It was still light outside, so she was fairly certain Tony was still asleep as well.

Stewart's sleep was solid. Nothing about Tony interrupted his regular dreams. Ashley got up from the couch. She stood still for a moment at the side of the bed. Stewart was facing her. She bent over and carefully pressed her palms flat on the comforter he slept on. Her back was bent at the hips, and she lowered her knees to the ground to get a bed-level view of him. Stewart's sleep was quiet, his breathing shallow, and his mouth was closed. She looked at him and remembered the younger version of him. She smiled as she thought about the years that had gone by and how she was so angry with him for taking her heterosexuality away. Now she knows it was not him. She rose and removed her shoes. She kicked off the right and then the left. The right knee was carefully placed on the bed, and then the palms of her hands lifted her weight from the left foot and mirrored the right knee. Her left hand slid up the bed as she fell on her side slowly. Face to face, she laid down. Stewart's arms were crossed, and she reached over and touched his left shoulder. She traced it to his elbow. He didn't move.

Past his elbow onto his hip, she placed her hand. He still didn't move. She kept her hand on his hip and then softly said his name. He didn't react. She slid her body closer. She could feel his breath against her face. She slid down. Her face, even with the collar of his shirt, she put her arm around him. She looked up, nothing. Still no movement. Just sleep. She moved closer to him and pressed her face against his flat chest. She looked up again. Still no movement. She moved her body up to be face to face. She leaned in. Her lips almost touched his. His breath was cool. He smelled clean. She moved in closer and touched his lips to hers. He didn't react. She backed up and rolled onto her back. She looked up at the ceiling, wondering what she was doing. Twenty-plus years as an FBI agent, and never had she crossed any line. She moved and sat up on the edge of the bed. Then she stood. Retrieved another beer, opened it and sat back on the couch and drank it. Stewart rustled and turned to his back and dropped his arms to his side. Ashley inspected him. She looked at his face first, then at his breathing on his chest and down his shirt to his pants. She saw what appeared to be an erection in his pants. She got up to move closer to inspect closer. Standing at the side of the bed, she looked down. She wondered if what she was seeing was true. She wanted to touch him to assure herself. The right knee was raised onto the bed, then the left palm supported her as she slid in next to him. She touched his chest with her flat right palm softly. He didn't move, flinch, or rustle. She allowed more weight against her palm, then began to slide her hand down his stomach across his belt then she stopped. She thought for a few seconds about the many sexual deviants she had arrested. She thought about how each one seemed to justify their sexual behaviors as they considered it an act of love. She removed her hand from his pants. She rolled away from him and lay on her side. Her arms were crossed. Her eyes were open but closing. There were so many things she wanted to do, none she would. She fell asleep.

Stewart's dreams remained null.

Chapter Fourteen: Feels Like The First Time

Ashley rolled toward Stewart in her sleep and threw her arm over him, it woke him. He opened his eyes to see Ashley's face inches from his. It was a vision he had hoped for for as long as he could remember. He didn't know what to do. He said her name softly. She smiled in her sleep. He elevated his voice a little, and her breathing changed. He said her name again, and she opened her eyes. Her blue eyes appeared green. The sun was beginning to fade, and the light in the room was dimming. His eyes were hazel. More green, brown and gold than any other colors. It was a tender moment. It had a time limit. He wondered what he should do. He smiled, and she returned the smile. They both moved closer until their noses touched. She moved again, tilting her head slightly, their lips touched. He mimicked her, and their lips drew closer to a penetrating kiss. *God, I bet my breath stinks,* he thought. She kissed him back. Their mouths barely open until his tongue found her lips, then the tips of her teeth. She stopped moving; she was waiting to see what he would do next. His tongue ran across her teeth slightly, and then he felt the tip of her tongue. The two tips danced slightly between her lips. He slid his arm under her and rolled her over on top of him. She was stunned by his sudden movement but highly aroused. *This was the moment I had been dreaming about all of my life,* he thought.

They kissed as if their tongues were doing a friendly battle. He wanted to take her clothes off, but that was her call. She wanted the same of him, he didn't know how to take this to the next level. He rolled her onto her back, and he was above her. The beer in her mouth blanketed the taste of his sleepy breath. He tugged at his shirt, taking it off. Then he asked, “Is this okay?”

She whispered, “Yes.”

He unbuttoned her white cotton blouse, exposing a white bra. He pushed the fabric to either side to see more of her skin. He took in the image of her as if he had in his dreams for decades. It was everything he had hoped it would be. She whispered, “The clasp is on the front.” He looked down at the junction of the cups and saw the clasp; he carefully unclasped the bra. He let the cups rest; nothing happened. With one hand, he lifted each one of her breasts, releasing them to his vision. He swallowed a gulp. Her nipples were erect, and her areolas tight, he leaned in. He opened his mouth over her right nipple and fit it between his lips. His lips were soft on her. She felt joy and pleasure. He opened his mouth wider and brought his tongue out to touch the nipple. She groaned a small groan. It was a sound he had longed for. He stopped and looked her in the eyes. They connected as neither of them had ever connected. He took a deep breath and then slid up to kiss her. Their kiss was deep and passionate. Their tongues entwined as they shared a kiss like none other. Stewart stopped, and he kissed her under her ear on her neck. She giggled. He licked her with just the tip of his tongue. She writhed slightly. His tongue tickled her to the front of her neck, then he traced it to the right nipple, circling a few times, then under the right breast and across to the left. Under the left and then to the nipple again. He repeated back and forth several times, then he went to the center of her cleavage and began kissing his way down to her navel. As he was kissing her navel, he was undoing her FBI pants. She twisted to the left, then to the right. His kisses were tickling her, and she was moaning. The zipper came down easily, and she raised up. He pulled both her pants and panties down and then off. It was his first real sighting of a woman's naked body in front of him. He sat back and looked at her. All his dreams of her were coming true. Her legs were slightly apart and bent with her feet flat on the bed. She laid on her back, and her hair crowned her face. She was excited and frightened at the same time. He had his hands around her ankles; then he began to slide them up across her shins to her knees. She answered his move by raising her feet to her heels and sliding them toward him. His hands crept up her thighs as his thumbs traced the inside of them, pressing in opposite directions. His pressure opened her legs enough for him to get a full view of her glistening. She took a deep breath as his thumbs made their way up her thighs, past her well-manicured bikini waxing to her tummy. His face moved forward as his hands traveled up her tummy to her nipples. With a nipple in each hand, his fingers circled them. She raised her knees involuntarily and pressed them against his ribcage. He bent his face down and kissed her right knee. Then he began to lick the inside of her right thigh. She answered by letting it fall to the side as he traced down towards her Netherland. She was unable to lay still as he approached her flower. His tongue slid over her labia and across her clitoris, and she winced in pleasure. The slight touches were driving her crazy. He reversed his path past the left labia, inside the thigh and up to the knee. She took a deep breath and smiled at him. He smiled back. He repeated his motion down her left leg, past her left labia to her clitoris again and touched his tongue to her once, twice and then a third time. He took a deep breath of his own and looked up at her flat belly across her nipples to the bottom of her neck as her head was back and her back was arched. She was ready for his complete attention. He extended his tongue out of his mouth flat. Carefully and slowly, he laid it against her vagina and clitoris. She screamed and twisted her hips. He was not sure if she had had an orgasm, so he backed off. She gasped, “No.” He repeated his tongue flat against all her womanhood, then pointed it and felt her wetness. The taste, like no other taste, delighted him. He had wondered all his life what that would be like. He liked it. His tip went into her and then up her clitoris, and she screamed again. He repeated it for the same reaction. Again and again, her moans got greater until they turned to screams and writhing. She held his head hard against her as his mouth encompassed her. His tongue moving in circles, she tightened, she squeezed his head between her thighs, and he stopped. His mouth rested against her wet pussy, and she let all the air out of her lungs and relaxed. He raised himself with his hips against the bed and his palm flat on either side of her. His face glistening from her moisture, she pulled him to her and kissed him deeply yet again. He was surprised.

She whispered in his ear, “It’s my turn, roll onto your back.”

He laid on his back. Ashley straddled him across his hips and sat up. She pulled her bra and top off. She was completely nude. He looked up at her. *Better than I ever hoped.* His eyes moved to her face and then down to her breasts, perfect in size and shape. Her C-cup fit well into his hand as he reached up to hold them. She let him for a few seconds, then pushed his hands aside, and they fell flat on the bed. She leaned forward. Their nipples touched. They were cool and soft against his hairy chest. She leaned in and kissed his neck by his ears like he had done to her. It tickled. He didn’t like to be tickled. A traumatic incident at an early age caused him distress when being tickled. He resisted the pleasure of pain. Her mouth moved from his neck to his chest, and the pain intensified. He said, “Please don’t tickle me like that.”

She didn't know what to do, so she backed off him and unbuckled his belt. He raised his hips as she removed his pants like he had done for her. She tossed them onto the pile where he had tossed hers. She backed up to see him in his nakedness. She was pleased. He was the only man she had ever wanted. He was naked and hers. A rush of warmth came into her, and she reached down between her legs to find that she was dripping. She caught some moisture on two fingers, brought her hand up in front of her in a girl scout sign with wet fingers, then pointed them at him. He got up on his elbows and leaned forward, and she put the fingers in his mouth. He groaned with pleasure, as did she while he was sucking on her fingers. His cock was rock hard and dripping wet from pre-cum. She took the fingers out of his mouth, then with the same hand, she wrapped it around his whole manhood and squeezed. More semen came forward, clear and sticky. She stroked upwards, and more came up, over his head and onto the rim of her fingers. She repeated that motion several times, and he groaned with pleasure. She stopped and looked down at his almost throbbing cock, glistening from her actions. He waited. She breathed. She inhaled deeply. She exhaled deeply. Then she leaned forward and touched her lips slightly against the tip of his penis. There was not enough contact for him to feel it. She did recognize he made no noise. He waited. She opened her lips in an "O" shape and allowed the tip into her mouth. She could taste his pre-cum; it was sweet and salty at the same time. It was slippery against her tongue. She let more of his penis into her mouth, and she stroked him up and down with her hand. His circumcised cock grew in between her lips. She stopped to look again. What was once a light shade of pink had turned purple. She returned her lips to it and took her hand away. With palms flat on the bed, she moved her mouth up and down on him. Each stroke brought him closer to the climax. With each stroke in her mouth, his body released more semen. She had remembered stories from former lovers about how bad it tasted and was surprised that he was not what she expected. His cock grew larger in her mouth as she licked it and continued up and down on it. Then she remembered what she was doing. She remembered the term "suck a cock." So, she created suction on each stroke, and his back arched. His moans got louder. She was not sure how close he was. She didn't know if she wanted him to cum in her mouth, but then, the choice was gone. Without notice, he filled her mouth and throat with his load. Before she knew it, it was down her throat; she had swallowed it. She kept sucking and licking until he could take no more. She released his still-hard cock from her mouth. His breathing was heavy as if he had just run ten miles. She sat up with her legs bent under themselves. She smiled at him and asked, "Are you alright?"

"I can barely breathe, but yes, I'm wonderful. Maybe I can ask you for a favor."

"Okay, what is it."

"I've always wondered what it would be like if you would straddle my face and sort of sit on it. Would you do that for me?"

She wondered for a moment; she smiled and said, "Well, yes, of course."

She positioned herself facing him, and he moved with a pillow under his head. She lowered her pussy to his lips, and he began to lick her. He reached his hands around her and grabbed her ass cheeks, pressing her hard against him. She was groaning loudly. His tongue entered deep inside her, and she moved her hips against him. She moved in circles and up and down against his face. She stopped and turned around. She could see his cock was still a rock. She leaned forward and sucked the remaining cum off it. Then she came herself on his face. While her vagina was throbbing, she lifted herself off his face, turned and positioned his cock against her labia and lowered herself onto him.

Oh my God, Stewart thought. *Is this real? Ohhh, man, that feels so, so, so good.*

She rested her weight on top of him. He put a hand on each hip. *Now what?* he thought. She raised herself slowly. The suction was immeasurably pleasurable. He looked down; what a thing of beauty. *Do that again slowly,* he thought. She lowered herself again, then raised, then lowered, increasing her tempo each time. Then she groaned very loudly and fell forward onto him motionless. She came. *Does that mean she's done?*

"Are you finished," he whispered.

"Are you?"

"No."

"Neither am I?"

"Okay, roll off me onto your back," he demanded softly.

She followed his order. They separated. She laid on her back, he was on his knees in the missionary position, and he guided himself into her. She arched her back and grabbed the sheets under her. He pushed slowly against her. *Nine times slow, then one hard, just like you read.* He followed his own instructions, nine times slow into her, then once hard and deep. She screamed. He repeated it. She screamed again. Her pleasure was a complete turn-on for him. He repeated. Repeated again. Then he held himself deep inside her. She came again. Her vagina pumping his penis, he nearly came. He removed himself from her, rolled her onto her knees and entered her from behind. He counted: *1, 2, 3, 4, 5, 6, 7, 8, 9, bam.* Watching from above was incredible to him. Every slow stroke was felt on every inch of his cock. Her wetness increased, and the friction reduced. It was easier for him *1, 2, 3, 4, 5, 6, 7, 8, 9, bam. Hold it.* He grabbed her hips and held her tighter. He moved his hips in circles, and her groans grew louder and louder. His passion became unbearable as sweat dripped from his face onto her back. He stopped counting and just slid in and out rapidly. Over and over, he fucked her from behind. He was about to cum, and he pulled out. He motioned her to roll over again; he penetrated her in the missionary position again and pounded her quickly. Over and over, she screamed, writhing against him. She pulled the sheets from the bed. *Is there something wrong with me? I can't cum.* He continued, and the minutes turned into what seemed like hours. His tempo would change from slow to fast and back to slow again, and then, as if struck by lightning, the rush hit his groin. He didn't know, *Oh my God, oh, oh, oh.* He came inside of her. He fell onto her, still inside and out of breath. She threw her arms around him and held him close and tight. *I can't breathe.*

"I can't breathe," he said. She let him go, but he still couldn't breathe. He rolled off her and onto his back, breathing heavily. He finally caught his breath. She giggled. He passed out, asleep.

Ashley got up and went into the bathroom. When she returned, she rearranged the bed as best she could with him in it. She stood naked beside the bed. She wondered, Should *I join him? Should I shower and get dressed? I better be ready if Barnum and Reynolds need me. Shower, shit, yeah.*

She went back to the bathroom, looked in the mirror at her disheveled hair and flushed face, and smiled. She turned and started the water in the shower. It warmed in seconds, and she climbed in. Stewart woke. He looked around the room and then heard the water in the bathroom. *I have never showered with a woman.* He approached the bathroom door and knocked, "Can I come in."

She thought, *you already did, that's why I'm in the shower*, she said, "Yes. Do you want to join me?"

Do I? Fuck yeah.

He asked, "Is that alright?"

Is that alright? Fuck yeah! "Uh-huh, come on," she said.

He opened the door and then the shower curtain and found her looking more magnificent than ever. The water cascaded over her hair onto her breasts and across her belly.

"Should I wash you?" he asked.

She watched him climb into the shower, heard him and said out of turn, "Do you know what you're doing?"

He grinned, "Um, using a towel and body wash?"

She looked him directly in the eyes, kissed him gently, pulled back and said, "Okay, go ahead. I have already washed my hair."

Stewart paused, then said, "Let me do it again."

Water rushed over her face as she bent back under the shower. Then she leaned forward, wiped the water away, smiled and said, "Really?"

"Yeah. Do you mind? I have never done that. Can I?" he said, tilting his head slightly.

"No, no. I don't."

He took the shampoo in his hands and lathered them up. He started at the top of her head and then traced down the sides. There was not enough, so he took more and, with his fingertips, began scrubbing her head. She closed her eyes and enjoyed the head massage. The lather grew on her long blonde hair, and he pulled it up to the top and bunched it over and over with his fingertips. She felt like a Goddess. He said, "I think I'm finished with your hair." She leaned back into the water, and that raised her near-perfect breasts up to greet him. He could not resist; he bent down and took her right nipple into his mouth and began to suck. The soapy water rushed across his face, but he didn't mind. She moved forward, and he stopped drowning. He let her nipple free.

She looked at him and asked, "Why did you stop?"

She took the conditioner in her hands and put it into her hair as he took her other nipple into his mouth. She worked the conditioner through her hair, and he worked his tongue around and around her nipple. She could not concentrate; she wrapped her arms around his head and pulled him closer. He held his breath. He could not breathe. She grunted, laughed and released him. He stood up giggling, and then he kissed her deeply. They wrapped themselves around each other, arms and legs entwined. She backed up under the water, and he followed. The water cascaded over both of them as they continued to kiss, holding their breath. He backed up, letting her lips go and taking a deep breath that ended in laughter. They kissed again. Then he asked, "Should I finish you?"

"By that, you meant what?"

"I meant wash you, but maybe you have something else in mind."

"Well, sweetie, I'm kind of sore. I never did that before, and I think I need a minute's rest. Or a few days rest, but yes, you can wash me if it pleases you."

He lathered the washcloth with body wash and gently started at her shoulders. Then he took her arm and lathered it up. He smiled as the washcloth crossed her chest then he washed her breasts slowly. He finished and took her other arm and cleaned it and under it. Then he washed her belly and carefully between her legs. She closed her eyes as he stayed in that spot for a little extra time. He replaced the washcloth with his fingers and rubbed slowly and softly. She moaned quietly, opened her eyes and said, "Still a little sore," with a 'please-go-on-smile.' He washed her thighs and then her feet. He turned her around and, washed her back, and finished at her rear end. Then, she took the washcloth from him and completed the task on herself. She lathered it up again and started to return the favor to him when she heard her cell phone ringing. She opened the curtain, grabbed a towel and tried to wrap herself in it as she ran to the phone on the table, "Agent Jett here."

"Jett, where the hell you have been? I have been calling you for an hour," Barnum said.

"Oh, I'm sorry, my phone must have been on mute. I missed it."

"What are you doing now? Is the subject awake?"

"Stewart is awake. Yes, he is."

"Did he see anything?"

"No, sir. Nothing to report from here."

"Damn it, you gotta get him to go to sleep and give us some information. Everything we have so far is circumstantial."

"Okay, sir. It is still early. Tony doesn't usually start moving until dark."

"Where the fuck have you been, Jett? It's nine-thirty. It's been dark for over two hours."

"Right, but he..."

"Jett. Shut up, Jett. What the hell? Did you sleep with him?"

"Sir, no sir. Why would..."

Barnum Interrupted, "You better not have slept with our witness. You know what that'll look like to the defense if this goes to trial."

"Barnum, you know me better than that. You know I'm gay, right?"

"Jett, I don't need to know what you think you are; I saw the way you were looking at that guy. The way you are so protective of him and how you want to spend all your time with him. I'm not blind, Ashley. Don't do something stupid."

"Don't you worry about me!"

"So, get him to bed and asleep so we can figure out where Tony is and where he's going."

"Yes, sir."

Stewart got out of the shower, dried off and went into the main room. He was very tired and very happy.

"Stewart, we have to talk."

"Okay, sure," he responded.

"Look, we, I mean I, need to remain professional through this whole thing. What we just did was a big mistake. You are a witness in multiple homicides and maybe even more. Your testimony cannot be jaded by a tryst."

"A tryst? Ashley, I have waited all my life for this, what you called a tryst. Is that what it meant to you," he said with a slightly elevated voice.

"No, well, no, of course not. That was not what I meant. What I mean is, I don't know what I mean. I'm so confused right now. This was never going to happen, and it did, and Stewart," she kissed him and continued, "and I loved it. I loved it all. It was just like I had hoped. All those years wondering, and it was." She stopped and realized she was confessing her desire before knowing it was safe.

"It was what?"

"Stewart, I jeopardized our investigation. If you need to rest," she realized she was repeating herself, and she changed her direction. "You should sleep. If you can sleep, maybe you can see him in the dark of night, and we can bring these guys to justice. You should get dressed and go to bed. While you're dressing, I'll fix the bed."

"I see," he said, crushed by her words.

She contained her emotion and straightened the bed as he dressed. She sat on the couch, and Stewart leaned down to kiss her. She turned her head, "I'm sorry. We need decorum. After this is over, yes, defi," she interrupted herself, "Stewart, please."

He backed up. Turned around and got into bed. He was asleep instantly.

She began to cry.

Chapter Fifteen: Another Night

Sheryl knocked on the door, and Ashley answered, "Come on in, he's sleeping."

"How long has he been out?"

"Oh, I don't know. I guess it's been a good hour or so."

"Really? Did he wake up before?"

"Um, yeah, he woke up for a few hours."

"I thought so. Good, he was awake when you fucked him."

"Sheryl, I would rather not-" she was interrupted.

"What? You'd rather not talk about how you fucked my brother," Sheryl said snidely.

"It wasn't like that, and a good girl doesn't kiss and tell. Especially to his sister."

"Okay, I'll shut up, but only after one question. Do you like dick now?"

Ashley turned her head in disgust, then looked back at Sheryl, "Really?" Then she couldn't help but smile.

"Okay, case closed, that's what I thought. You two were so stupid to let that little high school fuck up waste your lives. Well, at least you found each other now."

"Getting down to business. We need to get inside his brain and find out what's going on."

"We cannot. We just wait."

"We wait?"

"Right, he should sleep through the night, and then we can get some information. You are on your own. I wanna go out and see what this town has to offer. Do you think the entourage will allow me some fun? Will they escort me into the world out there?"

"If you intend on leaving, yes, they will tail you and make sure you are protected. They are not your party boys. They will try to dissuade you from any activities, but they will not stop you."

"Well, sitting here babysitting my brother as he sleeps may be all that to you, but, girl, that shit is a no way for me. See ya."

Sheryl walked out the door to be met by two FBI agents, "Where you headed, ma'am."

"Well, young man, I'm headed out for a little Chitown fun. Are you my escort, or is there someone else that's gonna tail me?"

"Well, ma'am, we suggest you stay in your room."

Interrupting, "Yeah, yeah, yeah, I get it. Lemme ask you, how many times you think this girl's been to the windy city."

"I would not know, ma'am."

"Right, never. So, if you don't mind, I wanna see what all the hype is about. You coming?"

"Yes, ma'am, I will be with you the whole way."

"Cool, you gonna drive, hop in the taxi or follow the taxi wherever I go."

"Technically."

"Right, I got it, you are going to follow me, suit yourself. Let's go."

Sheryl left the room, and Agent Jeff Schnaze followed behind closely. Jeff was a six-foot-something large man in his fifties. He was bald with kind eyes and a large scar on his forehead. He had been through much in his career, and even though he was relegated to surveillance and security most of the time, Jeff didn't mind it. Jeff walked with a gate as he followed behind Sheryl, to the elevator. His dark blue suit, white shirt and blue and gold tie were the ideal uniform for an FBI agent. Unlike most FBI agents, Jeff was married with children. He and his wife of thirty years endured many tribulations, but they always stuck together. She was a master poker player, winning millions in Las Vegas. She knew Jeff's job was his first love and she accepted the time he dedicated to it. Even with the millions she won while in Vegas, Jeff would continue to work as long as he could.

Once on the elevator, the two rode silently to the lobby. Across the lobby of the Marriot, they went to the valet desk outside. Jeff handed the valet a ticket, and he left for the parking lot. Sheryl wondered, *Are FBI agents supposed to valet park their cars?*

She kept that thought to herself. The car arrived, and Jeff tipped the valet. He took the driver's seat and drove around the parking lot to position himself to follow Sheryl's taxi. She thought, *He really is going to make me take a taxi.*

She hailed a taxi, and the driver sat while she got in the back. The taxi driver was a thirty-something black man in a sweatshirt. His hair was cut short, and he wore wireframe glasses. He turned to Sheryl, "Where to ma-am?"

"I'm not sure, young man. I'm looking for a place to go that might be exciting, fun and safe for a fifty-year-old woman to get a drink."

"Do you like Martini's?"

"I can do that. Why?"

"Well, there is Cheek's Martini bar. A lot of ladies like to go there."

"Do men go there?"

"Usually to meet the ladies."

"Am I dressed appropriately for that place?"

He looked in his rearview mirror and said, "Ma'am, you look lovely; it would be their honor to have you visit the place."

"Oh, don't you think complimenting me is going to get you a better tip, young man? It will, but don't you think it will? Keep 'em coming."

"So, Cheeks?"

"Why not? Oh, and don't lose the guy following us. He's my security detail."

"Yes, ma'am," he said and drove off.

A few minutes later, she exited the cab and entered Cheek's Martini Bar. Before she walked in, she noticed the multi-colored neon sign over the door. It was so bright it could be seen from miles away. The word 'Cheeks' was in red with a white martini glass outline and amber letters that spelled out 'martini bar.' Inside, more neon lined the ceiling. More neon martini glasses and drink shapes decorated the walls. There were mirrors and chrome everywhere; the ceiling was black, and the floor was black and white checkerboard. The bar sat in the center of the building in an oval, and it was surrounded by booths along the outside walls. Music was playing songs from Motown in the sixties, and a few people danced on what looked like a dance floor. She felt like all eyes were on her as she made her way to the bar. She found a stool between two women about her age and ordered an Ultra. Once the crowd looked her over, they were satisfied to go about their own business. Seven women were in a line at the bar, and she was planted in the middle. No one addressed her. She finished her first Ultra and ordered another. Then another, then another. The music changed; she tapped her foot and sang along a few times as she enjoyed her night out in the big city. After her fourth beer, she was approached by a man. He was a few years her senior, handsome with a full head of gray hair. He had a straight nose, blue eyes and a slender build. He was wearing a blue or black sports coat with a white tee shirt and jeans. He had been off to Sheryl's left, out of sight, until he walked up to her.

He spoke quietly; Sheryl leaned toward him, "Excuse me, pretty lady, I would like to buy you a drink and maybe converse a little. Do you think you would join me in my booth?" he said, pointing in the direction of an empty booth.

She thought for a second, then answered, "Well, sure."

Jeff watched carefully as they changed positions in the bar. Sheryl sat across from him, and he introduced himself, "My name is Timothy. May I ask you, yours?"

She responded, "Pleasure to meet you, Timothy, and I'm Sheryl."

"The pleasure is mine. Are you from around here?"

"No, I'm here on business from Arizona."

"Oh, well, that explains your lovely tan."

"Thank you. I guess right, we do get a lot of sun."

"What kind of business are you in?"

"I'm in retail. I came here to shop," she said, giggling.

"Oh, what are you shopping for tonight?"

Sly Fox. "I'm shopping for another beer."

"Oh, that's right, I promised you a beer."

Timothy slid out of the booth and over to the bar.

Sheryl watched him.

Jeff came over to Sheryl and leaned in, "Miss Sheryl, I don't think this is a good idea."

Timothy turned to look back and saw Jeff talking to Sheryl. He could tell that Jeff was armed, and so he walked away from the bar and out the door.

"Jeff, look, I haven't had a man interested in me in decades. Can you just give me a break?"

Jeff backed away from the table, and Sheryl looked back up at the bar where Timothy had been standing. She saw that he was gone. She slid out of the seat and walked to the door, hailed a cab and went back to the hotel.

Stewart was sleeping. Ashley watched him closely to see if his dreams would present movement. The minutes turned to a little more than an hour, and then Stewart flinched. Tony had awakened, showered, dressed and driven to his job. The FBI had followed him, but he didn't take notice. He sat in the waiting room for hours until his cell phone rang. "Hello."

"Tony, this is Paul Jackson. I'm with the Chicago police department. We both have friends in the same places. I cannot go into the details, but we have reason to believe the FBI might be on your trail. We believe you are being followed. At eight in the morning, someone you know will pick you up at your place of employment, you know, where you are now. There will be five identical vehicles. Follow that friend. There will be five other people dressed identically to you. They will all get into separate vehicles and go in five different directions. The FBI won't know which way you went, and they will bring you to rendezvous with me. I will do my best to explain what is going on. See you then." He ended the call. Tony sat undisturbed for the next seven hours in the waiting room. At seven-thirty, a man in a black suit walked in. At seven thirty-five, the man in the black suit walked out, and two men in black suits dressed identically to the first man came in, and the first man walked out. Five minutes later, two more men came in, and one went out. At 7:55, a fourth man came in; he took off two jackets, an extra white shirt and an extra pair of black pants. He gave them to Tony, and Tony dressed the same as the other men. The men put on wigs that mimicked Tony's hair, which made each man look the same. At eight o'clock, five black SUVs pulled up, and a man in the same suit got out of each SUV. They went inside, and all ten came out together. Tony followed his friend Rick into the middle SUV. All five started off together, and the FBI tail followed behind. They called for help, but before they could respond, the five vehicles split up, and the tail could only follow one. The SUV they followed stopped at a Catholic Church, and the two men got out. They had removed their wigs, and the FBI knew they had followed the wrong car. They had lost Tony.

Stewart saw Tony with his friend Rick in the back seat of the. The car pulled up to a 'stop sign', and Rick said, this is where we get out. The two got out, and Rick led Tony to a red sports car parked on the opposite side of the street. He clicked on his key and opened both doors. Tony took the passenger seat, and Rick drove the opposite way of the SUV. There were no working cameras on that street corner to see them switch cars, so Rick drove out of the city and onto Interstate fifty-five towards St. Louis. He got off at Cicero Avenue and went south to Forty-eighth Street. He turned right at forty-eighth and then turned left at the alley. He pulled over into the parking lot of Mayahuel Restaurant. There was a sedan parked in the empty parking lot, and he pulled up next to it.

"This is where you get out. That's Jackson. He will take you to the safe house and let you know what's happening."

Stewart watched and listened as Rick explained the details; Tony got out of the sports car and took his place in the passenger seat of the city-issued Crown Victoria. Rick drove through the parking lot and back onto Cicero Avenue, heading south. Jackson introduced himself and told Tony not to say anything until they got to the house. Tony nodded, and Jackson drove off into the alley, back to forty eighth and took a left. He took a right at Central and then back to the interstate and headed south. He exited the interstate at county road seven thousand. Stewart saw the sign for Gardner; they were in farm country. They turned onto highway forty-seven and passed Mc Ardle Grain. A few more roads and a right turn onto a private road to a farm. They parked behind the house and walked into what looked like guest quarters.

"This place is safe. The owner of this farm died a month ago. Has no living relatives, so no one is expected here. As you can see, with the corn, you can't see for miles. If someone finds you, it is because they are psychic," he laughed. They went into the old farmhouse and found the kitchen table. Each took a chair. Then Jackson began speaking, "Tony, you've been compromised. We don't know how, but you will need to stay here until things get figured out. The boss has high hopes for you and your skillset, so apparently, you are valuable enough to keep alive. I thought you guys were a dime a dozen. So, there's plenty to eat here. There is cable television; believe it or not, there is a ton of meat in the freezer, and there is the internet. Here is your new phone. Give me your old one." He said, handing Tony a flip burner phone. He opened the back of his iPhone and removed the sim card. Keep these things separate. If they are tracking your phone, we're fucked. Let's keep it that way. Without the sim card, this phone is a paperweight. When this all cools, you can have it all back. We have a guy inside the FBI working on the how and where to figure out why you have been flagged. Don't call anyone with that phone. It is for incoming calls only. Ima leave, you never met me. Someone will be here later with some clothes for you. I think the boss said he was going to send you a bitch to fuck around with while you're here."

"Really?" he asked with enthusiasm.

"No, that part was a lie. Get some rest. If you need to, only out of necessity, I mean life or death; if you need to, there is a car in the garage. The keys are hanging by the door. Remember, if you leave and fuck this up, the boss will, in fact, kill you and you never saw me."

"Got it."

Jackson left. Tony looked around the kitchen and opened the refrigerator to find it stocked with his favorite things. There was a shelf dedicated to Busch bottled beer. A drawer filled with bologna and turkey. Some bread and, in the freezer, DiGiorno Peperoni pizzas. Tony left the kitchen and walked down a short hallway past two small bedrooms to a large room with a king-size bed. He dropped his clothing on the floor and climbed into bed. He fell asleep instantly.

I have to wake up and tell the FBI where he is. Wake up, wake up. Shit, I can't wake up. I gotta pee. That always works. I do. I gotta pee. Wake up.

Ashley had fallen asleep on the couch and woke in pain. She looked over at Stewart asleep, got up from the couch and went to the bathroom. When she came out, Stewart was still asleep. She walked to him and touched his shoulder. He didn't move. She shook him slightly. He still slept.

If I fake this sleeping thing, maybe she'll do something cool.

"Stewart, come on, get up," she said.

Hold out.

"Stewart. Stewart. Stewart, are you okay? You are not breathing. Oh shit, What's my emergency? My friend stopped breathing..."

Stewart opened his eyes; her face was inches away from his.

"I knew it. I knew you were fucking with me. Stop it. We got work to do. What did you see last night?" She picked up her phone and looked at it. She had five new text messages from Barnum. "Shit, Stewart, they lost Tony. Barnum will be here," she looked at her watch, "in twenty minutes. You better get ready. I'll go grab something from the restaurant down in the lobby. Go, brush your teeth. I want a kiss."

"You want a what?"

"You heard me. Go, we are running out of time."

Stewart went to the bathroom. Ashley texted Barnum back, asking for an extra twenty minutes. Reynolds responded, "Barnum is driving; meet us in the hotel restaurant."

She responded, "Affirmative."

Stewart finished brushing his teeth, came out and kissed Ashley passionately. She pushed him back, "Get dressed, we have to go."

He quickly dressed, and they headed to the elevator. When Stewart reached the elevator, he said, "Wait, what about Sheryl?"

"I guess she can sleep in. We don't really need her right now."

The door opened, and they entered. Ashley put her arms around his neck and continued the kiss she interrupted in the room. She pushed him back just before the door opened. "I thought you weren't going to do that anymore?"

"So did I."

They walked through the lobby to the restaurant, where they found Barnum and Reynolds sitting at a table for four. They said their hellos and sat down.

Barnum started, "Okay, Miller, we lost Tony. I'm not going to lie; the way we lost him was seriously orchestrated. Someone in the Chicago police must have tipped Tony off. What did you see?"

"Well, he was sitting in the waiting room at Acme Medical when a guy in a black suit came in, then two more and one left, then two more came in. One of the men had a duplicate of clothing on; he removed it, and then Tony changed his clothes. Five guys dressed the same came in, and all ten went out. Two guys got into each of the five SUVs, and Tony was in the middle one. His friend Rick was with him. They split up, lost the FBI tail and went to an intersection where they got out of the SUV and into a red sports car. I think it was a Porsche. Then Rick drove down interstate fifty-five and got off at Cicero. They met a guy in what looked like an unmarked police car. He said his name was Jackson. Jackson drove Tony to a farmhouse and left him there. He said the owner had died a month earlier. It seems the house was in probate, so no one was there. They stocked the frig and left Tony there alone. Tony is asleep now."

"Do you think you could lead us there?"

"Take fifty-five to forty-seven, go north, pass one road then there is a driveway on the right with a farmhouse way off the road. Go between two pine trees; you will see the three or four silos on the left; the house is surrounded by trees. The kitchen is at the back of the house. He entered there. Then pass through the kitchen, and at the end of the hall is the bedroom he is asleep in."

"Is that all?"

"That is everything I know."

"If you close your eyes, do you see what he sees?"

"No."

"How did you do that?"

"My sister gave me a double shot, but it put me to sleep for a day and a half."

"Have some breakfast, then go up to your sister's room and have her double you up. We'll try to wake you tonight to see what he sees."

"I don't think he's going to do anything. They have him there to protect him against you guys. Jackson said they have a guy in the FBI."

Barnum raised his voice a bit, "They what? Okay, Stewart, finish eating and go up to your sister's room."

"Do I need an escort?"

"No, not this time."

They sat and made small talk until Stewart finished and walked away. Then Barnum began, "Reynolds, who knows about this case?"

"Well, there's the three of us, Schnaze watching over Sheryl, there is Eckhart and Ballard. I think that's it."

"How well do you know Eckhart and Ballard?"

"I only met them in Arizona before the flight to Saint Louis."

"What about Schnaze?"

"Before you, he was my partner. Then he got injured. He's not the type."

"Well, we got a mole. From now on, all information comes through me. You two got it."

Ashley nodded, and Reynolds said, "You bet."

Stewart arrived at his sister's door and knocked. She didn't answer. FBI agent Schnaze was not outside her door. Stewart knocked again. Still no answer. He went to his room and called his sister's phone. She didn't answer. He used the house phone and called her room but still had no answer. He ran out of his room down the hall to the elevator, it opened and down he went. He got off and ran to the FBI agents still at the same table.

Stewart was out of breath and panting, "She's gone. Sheryl and the guard, they are gone."

"What?" Barnum said loudly.

"She's not in her room. I tried her phone, her room phone. I knocked three times, and the guard is gone from outside."

"Schnaze wasn't in the hall?"

"No, I didn't remember him being in the hall when we came down the first time."

Barnum looked at Ashley, "Did you see Schnaze when you came down before?"

"I don't remember, sir."

"Great, we have no idea where they are or when they left. Jett, go look at the security footage for the floor and see if you can see what happened. Meet us back in Stewart's room."

Ashley Jett went to the manager's office, and the others went to the elevator up to Stewart's room.

The manager obliged; she watched the footage and then had him send it to her email. She went to Stewart's room, where Reynolds and Barnum met her. She opened her laptop and then started the video immediately showing Schanze following Sheryl out at around eleven o'clock and then following her back at two thirty-seven. The video shows a couple stumbling down the hall at three fourteen. The man fell into Schnaze then Jeff fell to the ground. The couple opened the hotel room door, dragged Schnaze in and closed the door. At three twenty-seven, they escorted Sheryl out of the room, keeping their heads down, past the security camera. Stewart exclaimed, "They got my sister. You have to do something. What are you going to do?"

"Stewart, calm down. You and Ashley stay here. Reynolds and I are going to the office and see if we can get any facial recognition on either of them."

"Reynolds and I."

"Shut up, Reynolds."

"Right."

They left. Stewart started in on Ashley, "Why would they take her and not me?"

"My guess is they thought it was you in the room he was guarding, so when they drugged him, wait, he might still be in the room. Hold on."

She ran to the door, opened it and screamed down the hall toward the elevator, "Hey, what about Schnaze? He might still be in that room."

They turned around and ran back. Reynolds arrived at the door first, and with one quick kick, the door was open. Schnaze was on the floor. Jett reached down to check his pulse while Reynolds and Barnum cleared the room. Schnaze was gone. He was cold.

Barnum and Reynolds both looked at Jett. Jett shook her head.

Barnum dialed the emergency number, "This is special Agent Barnum of the FBI. We are at..." He finished his call then said, "We have to get these guys now, more than ever. We know it wasn't Schnaze. Fuck, Reynolds, stay here. Deal with this; I'm going into the office. Damn, Sheryl's gone. Stewart only has one more night's sleep to catch this guy. If they kill Sheryl, we'll never get 'em. Reynolds. We can't even send anyone to watch Tony. They will be noticed on forty-seven. Reynolds, contact the satellite division let's get eyes on that place. Who can we trust in Chicago? I don't know."

Reynolds responded, "Me either. We have to use Washington D.C. or New York if we're going to trust everyone."

"I know everyone in L.A. John, this is terrible. We're going to have to be a step ahead of everyone. We need to be side by side with the analysts to figure this out. We have to do this here. I'll call the director on the way to the Chicago office."

Barnum ran to the stairs and then down. He ran to his car, and with tires spinning, he was gone. On the way, he told the director's assistant the whole story. He finished his call, and he arrived at the Chicago office. He ran in, flashed his badge, and jumped through security to the third floor. Once on the third floor, he found Rosemary Nettles. She was an expert on facial recognition for the Chicago region. He explained the situation, and they went to her office.

"Agent Nettles, is it okay if I call you Rosemary?"

"My friends call me Rose. I know, it is an old name. I was named after my Mom's Mom. You can call me Rose."

"Rose, we have two killers on this tape. They kidnapped a key witness to the local crime syndicate hitman. We need to find out where they have taken this woman in the tape."

She opened the email and began the tape. She patched into the rest of the hotel's feed and got two good images. She ran facial recognition and came up with a woman named, "Kelsey MacMillan, wanted in Louisiana for attempted murder, wanted in Florida in a triple homicide and wanted in Texas for a double homicide. The other individual was Oscar Tines. Mr. Tines is also wanted in Florida for the same crime. Tines is wanted in New York, and Interpol has three separate crimes they want him for. He's a British nationalist, and she's from Kansas. He specializes in accidental deaths, and she looks like she's the interrogator. She's a real hard ass. Why would they bring them in to do this job? Who is this woman? She looks so meek."

"That's not important. Can you see where they went?"

"Well, they were driving a blue Toyota Four Runner. They headed south on Ashland to Roosevelt and then waited. They went to the Roosevelt Collection Mall. They went into the parking garage, and I lost them. It's less than a half mile from here."

He got up and began running to the stairs; he turned and said, "Get me back up at that location." Down the stairs and out to his car. He was there in less than five minutes. Once in the parking garage, he found the Four Runner; the hood was still hot. He looked around for cameras, but there were none in that portion of the garage. His backup arrived a few minutes later; it was Eckhart and Ballard. He told them to look for the suspects in the mall and then he left back to the field office.

Back at Agent Nettle's desk, they looked at more security tapes of vehicles leaving over the past half hour and found fifteen vehicles, each one with only a driver. Six men and nine women. No two vehicles went the same way on Roosevelt together. It appeared to be a dead end. Barnum said to Nettles, "If you come across anything at all, get to me immediately."

"Will do, sir."

He picked up his phone and called Eckhart, "Jason, this is Barnum. Did you guys find anything at the mall garage?"

"The four runners were stolen yesterday at the airport. Another car parked right next to it was stolen at the same time. It was a white 2014 BMW 325i; it was seen here at the garage by the attendant. The guy happens to have a hard-on for BMWs. It has gold wheels and low-profile tires. I don't know if that is an issue; wait, hold on, someone is screaming. I'll call you right back."

"No. Just... shit. Just leave the line open. Fuck."

Barnum went back to Nettle's office, "We have another lead. A white 2014 BMW 325i was stolen at the airport yesterday. Look and see if you saw it going to the mall or leaving."

"Copy that." She scanned the videos, "Here it is, it left the garage and went East, hold on, then south on Clark."

"Yeah, this is Barnum," he said, answering his cell phone, "Uh-huh, okay. Thanks. Nettle's look for a Sliver 2013 Ford Mustang convertible. It was just stolen in the last hour from the same mall."

"Okay, which car should I follow?"

"Right, stay with the BMW for now."

"Okay, it went down. Clark turned left, sorry, East on Cermak, that's weird, then went and backtracked North on State Street. It cut over to Michigan Avenue, then continued North. Got onto forty-one and stopped at Lincoln Park. I lost it there. Should I go back to the Mustang?"

"Yes."

"Okay, the Mustang went straight down Roosevelt to forty-one and then North. It's still on forty-one, from what I can tell. Just passed the Navy Pier. In a few minutes, it will be at Lincoln Park, and we'll lose him."

"So, they must have sat in the parking lot for a few hours then left... How long will it take me to get there?"

"Nineteen minutes, maybe seventeen."

"Call the local authorities and tell them to hold those people at the park. Get the Chicago police there and anyone else that can prevent this from getting out of hand."

"Got it, Phil."

"Thanks, Rose, great job."

Phil Barnum ran away, down the stairs and out to his car. He was onto Roosevelt and headed to Lincoln Park. He needed to get there before they dumped these cars and found new ones.

Waiting in Lincoln Park was a 2019 Black Lincoln Continental. The BMW parked next to the Lincoln. The woman driver got out of the car and opened the trunk. She had a gun on Sheryl as she climbed out of the trunk. She escorted her to the Lincoln; the suicide door opened, and she climbed in back. The man in the back said, "Kelsey, we're done for now. Please stay in Chicago in case I need you."

Kelsey nodded and turned away from Lincoln... "Hello, Sheryl. It is a pleasure to meet you. I'm so sorry about all this scary stuff. Excuse me. Billy, drive. You see, I heard you can do some special stuff, and I have heard you can help people see things they shouldn't. I want to know how you do it and who they can see."

"Where to boss?"

"Billy, just show Miss Sheryl downtown Chicago. We are going to have a nice conversation. Now, Sheryl, tell me what you do."

"I don't understand, sir. I work in retail in Arizona."

"Are you going to play games with me? I know you don't know who I'm, and I know you don't know my business but sufficed to say I usually get what I want. If I want you to tell me something, I will figure out a way to get it. Capishe' my darling?"

"I get it, yes, but I don't really know what you want from me."

"Well, let me tell you what we got from your friend back in Arizona. You know that good Lieutenant Chee. Well, we got him to tell us that you made a peyote that opened your brother's mind to see what one of my employees was doing for me. Am I right so far?"

Sheryl nodded.

"Miss Sheryl, where I'm from, we speak, so I will need you to say yes and no and answer my questions. No nodding and no shaking your head, you got it?"

"Yes, I got it."

"Okay, great now. What I know from your departed friend Lieutenant Chee is that your brother saw a few tricks a guy named Tony did. Now, Tony is a professional, and no one has ever seen his face except your brother. Now, you can tell me what I need to do to stop your brother from seeing Tony again or well, let's say the two of you won't have such a pleasant visit to Chi-town. Again, do you understand?"

"Yes, I do. If I don't tell..."

Interrupting, "Eh, eh, eh, did I ask you for a recap?"

"No."

"Okay, so long as you understand, then we can do some business. Now. I have a few choices. I can use you to see other things, or I can just end this. What would you like to do?"

"Well, boss, can I ask a question or two?"

"I would rather you didn't."

"Who do you want me to give the peyote to?"

"Oh, well, not me. We can start with my driver, Billy."

"Okay, well, do you mind waiting about thirty hours for the results?"

"What do you mean thirty hours?"

"It takes thirty hours of sleep before the patient sees anything. It may not happen the first time; I don't know. My brother didn't see that guy the first night, and he slept twenty-eight hours. He saw him on the third night, but I increased his dosage."

"Can you speed that up?"

"No sir, I cannot."

"Oh, well, I suppose we will just have to live with that. Billy, go to the JW Marriot; you are going to take a nap. Also, call the boys and have us meet them there. Now, Sheryl, we are going to be in a public place. We know where your brother is. We have people there right now. He's not safe unless you cooperate. Do you understand this?"

"Yes, I do. Can I make a suggestion?"

"Again, I would rather not, but if you must."

"Well, Johnnie, might I suggest you have me administer this for a few of your guys so that you can see the varying degrees of success. I mean, after all, if we are going to do a scientific experiment, we should have a few test subjects."

"You know, that is not a bad idea. Billy, have Molly order us five rooms. We need three of the boys to participate in this experiment."

"Yes, sir." Billy made the call.

"Miss Sheryl, I'm not sure why you proposed this and or why you intend to help me. Oh, and how did you know my name?"

"I knew your name because I heard the FBI agents talking about you. They know Tony works for you. They know what you had Tony did in Saint Louis and they know what Tony has done here in Chicago over the last few weeks. What they don't know is how to pin it on you. Tony is more of a liability to you than Stewart is. Everything Tony does, Stewart sees as long as he is sleeping. His dream memory is phenomenal. Tony is the real problem, not Stewart. I proposed this because I can see how it works with the brain. I would like to find out if it works the same way for other people. Maybe there is some research to do, and maybe there is a business venture here."

"That is unexpected. We abduct you from your hotel room, and your answer is you want to work with us on a business venture. I must say I didn't see that coming. Also, Tony is of value to me, your brother. No, he is a liability."

"Honestly, John, I'm more interested in the results from this peyote than you are. I have only tried it on my brother, and I'm not sure if this is a one-off. It wears off, and as long as Tony is out of the picture, my brother is safe. So, if we can determine the validity of the procedure, maybe we can make some money off it."

"Sheryl, I cannot at this time guarantee your brother's safety. You know who you are dealing with. Sometimes, we are honorable, and other times, we will stab you in the back. That is no secret. I will say if I see loyalty and I can trust you, it will be the former in place of the latter."

In other words, as soon as he has what he needs, I am dead. I have to play this out until they can figure out where I am, she thought.

They pulled into the parking garage of the JV Marriot. Molly had already checked in, and they headed straight to the rooms. They were met at the elevator by several suited Italian-looking men. They all took the elevator to the twelfth floor. The top floor offered the greatest view of the city. It offered the best escape route from the roof with a helicopter, and it had twenty-nine suites. Five suites in a line were rented and opened by the hotel staff. Each suite would be inhabited by two men, and Sheryl's suite by her and a woman, who had yet to arrive.

Johnnie escorted Sheryl to the largest suite and then introduced her to the test subjects. Each one would get a dose of the peyote, and they would monitor their sleep. After the first night, Sheryl would increase the dose upon Johnnie's determination. Each subject would report their dreams, and the data would be collected.

Johnnie introduced Matthew. He was a twentysomething young man in excellent shape. Brown eyes and dark, almost black hair. He stood a few inches less than six feet and had broad shoulders. Sheryl asked him, "Do you dream much, Matthew?"

"Well, ma'am, I do have dreams, yes. I remember some of them."

"I think you will do fine next."

Sly was next. He was in his fifties, overweight and sloppy. He was a loyal member of the syndicate since birth. Sly volunteered because he wanted to meet the guy using his head. Sly was grey-haired and bald on top. His teeth were cracked in the front and yellow from drinking too much coffee. His breath smelled like yesterday's trash, and his shirt was wrinkled and partially untucked. She noticed his shoes were dull and his suit was not clean. She wanted another subject like Matthew, but when she asked, "Do you remember your dreams."

Sly responded, "I have very vivid dreams. Some of them are quite fun. Oftentimes..."

She cut him off, "He'll do fine."

The last subject is another male, Pete. Pete was reluctant but knew his life counted on his participation. Pete was the oldest of the participants, in his sixties, maybe even seventy. He was thin and sickly looking. Pete was not the typical mobster of the day, but maybe in the past. Pete probably had stories that, if he could remember, would put Johnnie in the ground. Sheryl asked Pete the same question about his dreams, and Pete responded, "Miss, If I could remember my shoes, I might wear them every day. As for dreams, I will do my best."

"Johnnie, I don't think Pete is right for this."

"That's okay, Sheryl, just do him."

"Alright. Gentlemen, allow me to..."

Johnnie watched intently as Sheryl prayed and chanted and administered the peyote to each of them. A few minutes later, the men began to get drowsy, and Sheryl recommended they adjourn to their rooms. They left the room, and Johnnie told her to settle in as it would be a while.

Chapter Sixteen: The Dream Weaver

Barnum got to Lincoln Park and found one of the two cars abandoned. He called for forensics, and when they arrived, he instructed them to comb the cars for any evidence they could find. He hurried back to the field office distraught, thinking he had let his informant get abducted.

Kelsey nodded and turned away from the Lincoln. The Mustang arrived, and she got in. The two left the park at the north exit and got back on forty-one. They were stopped by the Chicago police and taken into custody to be brought to the FBI field office. Each was sitting in a separate interrogation room waiting.

Reynolds met Barnum as he approached Nettle's office.

"Phil, we got the assassins. The local guys caught them on forty-one. They are in rooms three and seven. Do you want me to talk to either of them?"

"No, let's do it together. Let's start with the brit. What's his name?"

"Oscar Tines."

Barnum slowly opened the door and walked in; Reynolds followed. Reynolds leaned his back against the wall, and Phil pulled out the chair opposite Tines. Tines had no fear; he had been at the interrogation table more times than he could count. He had been tortured to near death. He had been questioned by mercenaries and by heads of state. He was thinking this interrogation would be a farce.

Barnum opened his file and looked at Schnaze's picture, dead on the floor. He turned the picture towards Tines and began, "Does this look familiar to you?"

"Never saw that."

"Is that all you have to say?"

"Yes."

"You might need to say more than that. You see, we have you on video surveillance leaving the room where Agent Schnaze's body was found. We have you on video surveillance bumping into him and him falling to the ground, then dragging him into Sheryl's room. We have your partner, and you escort our key witness out of the Marriot. We have you driving to the same park and picking up Miss Kelsey MacMillan, then we picked you two up. We have witnesses at the park who will testify that they saw Kelsey take our witness out of the blue four-runner and put her into another car. We have enough evidence to put you away for murdering an FBI agent, and that's the death penalty or life in prison. It all depends on where we try you. For now, you can do one of two things. You can be quiet and go to the gas chamber, or you can speak up and maybe walk away someday."

"You are a funny fellow officer."

Barnum interrupted, "That's Agent Barnum."

"Yes, fine, Agent Barnum. I know you know this is not my first time in a room like this. In fact, you chaps have been more than accommodating compared to my last event of this sort. Oh my, at that time, those fellows had me dead to rights. You simply have videos of someone who looks like me with a woman I have never met. What did you say her name was, Stacy or Sally? I just don't know."

"So, Oscar, if you know how this works so well, perhaps you will just skip all of the bullshit and tell us what we want to know and be on your merry way."

"I would assume, Mr. FBI agent, that you would like to know who I work for."

"There you go, that's a start."

"Well, sir, I'm a business consultant from Nottingham in England. I'm here on business. I came to Chicago to try to acquire some new clients. My company does life coaching, and I was planning on visiting some of the bigger corporations, but you have stalled my progress. I should indeed demand my freedom to go about my business. Do you know what it costs to cultivate life coaching clients in a foreign land?"

"I was just joking about you going on your merry way. We're planning on selling you to the highest bidder; you are wanted all over this big blue ball we call Earth. You might as well give up your dealings here as it matters to us and less to the five other countries after your head."

"Five, I'm up to five. Isn't that dandy? All along, I thought I was only in high demand from local corporations looking for life coaches. Do tell me who wants me. Please tell me, I'm quite astonished at my popularity."

"You, too, are a funny fellow, Tines. Offer us up what we ask for, and let's end this game of chit-chatter."

"I do believe I will restrain on speaking of my business here in your city of windy as you call it."

"Windy city, but that's okay." Barnum turned toward Reynolds, "We're done here. Contact Interpol and Florida, let's get rid of this scum."

They left the room to Tines laughing. Then, she went to the other interrogation room and opened the door to see Kelsey with her head down on the table.

"Wake up!" Barnum said. "I'm agent Barnum, and this is agent Reynolds. We have been authorized to give you a pass on this. Reynolds, should we tell her what we know or just ask her to tell us?"

"I say, let her open up."

"Well, there you have it. Reynolds wants to hear your pretty little voice sing like a bird."

She lifted her head from the table and looked at both of them standing in front of her. Then she put her head back down on her crossed arms.

"Well, Reynolds, it doesn't look like she's interested. So… we ask questions. Miss MacMillan, what were you doing at the Marriot hotel this afternoon?"

"I wasn't at any hotel today. I went to the park to visit a friend, and we were about to take a ride when the cops arrested us."

"We have video surveillance of you in the Marriot. We have video of you kidnapping a woman and video of you with Tines killing an FBI agent."

"Whatever video you have is not me."

Barnum looked at Reynolds, then back at the top of her head, "We have video of you driving a stolen car from traffic light cameras; at least we have that. Then there are the warrants for your arrest. Maybe you can work with us, and maybe you can work with the other authorities. You give us Johnnie, and we might be able to give you your freedom."

"You know you are lying. You can't make a deal on my outstanding warrants. You can only deal with a stolen car that I didn't steal. You can't prove anything, so I'm not talking."

"Well, Kelsey, we don't care about a stolen car. We care about kidnapping our witness' sister. We want to know what you did with her and where she is."

"I have no idea what you are talking about. I didn't kidnap anyone."

"We have video of you escorting Sheryl Benally out of the Marriot, likely at gunpoint."

"You might have a video of her and some people, but it was not me. Are you guys new at this? You should try some new tactics; this softball FBI shit may work with some suspects but not with seasoned operatives."

Barnum looked back at Reynolds and changed positions with him. He pulled out the chair and sat, "Hi again, I'm Agent Reynolds. My partner likes to go easy on our suspects. Me? Well, I have a little different approach. My plan is to give you a new identity and throw you into the general population at the federal prison. We'll make sure all the inmates know you are a baby murderer. That way, you won't live more than a few days. They will beat you to an inch of your life and keep you there just so you feel the pain until you can no longer take it and die. Your British friend gave me that idea. You won't even make it to trial. You will die before you get indicted. We will be done with you. Or you can tell us what we need to hear."

"Are you the king of idle threats? You can't do that."

Reynolds turned to Barnum, and he nodded. "Okay, have it your way. In a few minutes, you will be booked and sent to the Cook County prison. Give me a minute, and I will get your file. I'll be right back."

Nettles handed him a file outside the door. He returned and said, "That was fast."

"As fast as it will be when the killers in Cook County get a hold of you," he opened the file and read the name, "Wow, Kelsey Wingate. You are accused of drowning your children. Five-year-old Marcy, look at that lovely little child. and three-year-old Jacob. You did it in your boyfriend's toilet, how appropriate. You held each child's head under piss water until they died. You must be some kind of crackhead, evil bitch. Those bitches at the county are gonna love you to death. I'd be surprised if you made it a week. But you ain't going there yet. We are going to get the press involved, and we're going to make it look like you really did this. Nothing a little television can't fix. We're tired of fucking with the likes of you. You are going down, woman."

Reynolds got up and headed for the door. Barnum walked in front of him, and they left. A few minutes later, a booking agent came and took her to be booked under the name Kelsey Wingate. She was photographed and placed in a holding cell.

The story was built, and the next morning, they took her to a different interrogation room. A video was started with the local news reporting of a woman who murdered her two children, a crack addict on the southside. She watched it as they showed her picture in the news and her mug shot. Then Reynolds said, "Now tell us, Kelsey, do you want to talk, or do you want to go see what the Cook County prisoners have in store for you?"

She looked him in the eyes and said, "I didn't think you could pull off such a good version of extortion. I must say I have to weigh my options."

"You got five minutes. I'll get you a pop if you want."

"No thanks, I know what I'm going to do. Take me to the county."

Reynolds stood up and walked out. Barnum had been behind the mirror and met him in the hallway.

"Todd, that bluff didn't work."

"I was sure it would," Reynolds said.

"Me too. She's a tough bitch," Barnum said with a grimace.

"Yeah, now what do we do? I played all my cards."

"It was a bluff; she saw that. We cannot use any of it. I suppose we let her stew a little while longer and see if she breaks." Barnum began down the hallway.

"You know she won't."

"I do, but what else do we have besides giving her to the other jurisdictions."

"That's probably all," said Reynolds, "I got it. We change her file back to MacMillan. She won't know it, then we will take her to the county. She won't know it is a bluff, she won't know which identity she has, and she'll see her end in sight."

"That just might work. Let's get a detail to process her."

"We should take her to county ourselves," Reynolds continued.

"No, we have to use the Marshals."

"Right, she knows too much. She'd be on to us. Okay, I'll call the Marshals."

The Marshals arrived and began escorting Kelsey to the van to move her to the county.

"Hello, Miss Wingate, I'm Marshal Rogers, and this is Marshal Becky Wills. Together, we will be taking you to County."

"I want a lawyer."

"That's nice, and I want a beach house," Marshal Wills said.

"Seriously, I know my rights. I want a lawyer."

"Have you been read your rights?" Rogers asked.

"I have."

"Good, then you know you also have the right to remain silent, and if you know what is best for you, you will exercise that right until we get you to the county. Once you are there, they will make arrangements for you to see a lawyer, but they are going to process you first. Sometime tomorrow, you should be given your opportunity."

"Tomorrow? I want a lawyer now!"

"Remember, I want a beach house. Now, who do you think will get what they want first? You will, but we've got things to do with you first. Until then, be quiet."

"Lawyer. Lawyer."

She kept repeating, "Lawyer." The entire ride to Cook County Detention Center. Once they arrived at the detention center, she stopped saying "Lawyer" and said, "Okay, it was Johnnie, Johnnie Torino, he hired us."

Rogers said to Wills, "Did you hear something?"

"I did. But, Rogers, I don't think it makes a difference anymore since Tines gave up this information already."

"Fuck Tines, he's the one who killed the FBI agent. He stuck him with that shit in the hall of the Marriot. I was just there to ask her questions. I never did shit. He's the one who killed him."

"Did you get all that Wills?"

"I did. I got it all. Now the question is, can we keep her alive long enough to take Torino down?"

"Can you guy offer me witsec?"

"We can," Rogers said. "Are you going to give us some more dirt on Torino?"

"No, this was my first job at Torino. He's only a cog in the family. I can give you New York, Las Vegas, Florida and more. You set me up with a great gig, and I'll spill all the beans. You guys will be able to clean up the country."

"We will believe it when it happens. For now, we head back to the FBI field office. We have to let them decide what to do with you; it's their case."

"I thought you said you'd get me witsec?"

"That's what we said, but it's their game," Wills said. "Fuck you guys double-crossed me."

"That's what we do to career criminals like you. If your intel is good and these guys go down, well, then you get to win the lottery. You become a confidential informant, and you get ten percent of all the cash they take in. You have to put your tail on the line, though and testifying ain't enough," Rogers said. "The alternative is we put you on the stand without protection, and no one goes to jail, but you go to the worms. Or everyone's least favorite option; you don't testify, you rot in jail for murdering an FBI agent, or you get the death penalty."

Wells turned around and looked her square in the eyes, "What's it going to be, sweetie?"

"I think I'll take what's behind door number one, witsec."

"Good choice. We did our job, Wills."

"Yes, we did, Rogers, I'll phone ahead to Barnum." Rogers and Wills arrived at the field office and brought Kelsey to a conference room where Barnum and Reynolds were waiting.

"Thank you, Marshals, we'll take it from here and great job. Kelsey, have a seat."

"Are these cuffs necessary?"

"They are for now. We must get a few things straight. Relax, and if we all agree, we will remove them. Before we begin, you need to know we will be recording this. Now, first, who were you working for?"

"Here in Chicago, I was contracted by a lieutenant of the Torino family. His name is Billy Valente. He is Johnnie's driver. He told me and Tines where to find Stewart, but he was wrong. When we got into the room, we found Sheryl instead. Tines had already killed the agent in the hallway. It was funny; she didn't even scream. I asked her where her brother was, and she said he was in the next room with five FBI agents. We figured five agents against us two was, uh, bad odds, so we grabbed her. I asked her how Stewart knew so much about Tony, and she proudly told me she gave him some peyote, and now he sees everything Tony does when he's asleep. Then she told me all he had to do was close his eyes. She was very cooperative with a knife to her neck. I phoned Johnnie and told him what she said, and he told us to bring her to the park. We had extra cars in the parking lot here but not at the park, so that was why you squeezed us on Forty-one."

"What happened to Sheryl when you met Johnnie," Barnum asked.

"I gave her to Billy, and he put her in the back seat with Johnnie. What happened after that is a mystery to me."

"What kind of car were they driving?" Reynolds asked.

"It was one of those newer Lincoln Continentals, a limousine, I think."

Barnum asked, "Where were they going?"

"They didn't tell me. They paid us, and we left in the Mustang."

"Reynolds, stay with Kelsey. I'm going to see what Nettles has on that Lincoln."

"Got it."

Barnum ran to Nettle's office and instructed her to look at the traffic cameras for the Lincoln. "See if you can tell where they were going or where they went?"

Nettles immediately had the Continental on her monitor and traced it to the JW Marriot. It went into the parking garage and left ten minutes later. Then it went back to Torino's residence.

"So, they went to the hotel or Torino's house."

"Sir, I wouldn't expect Torino to take her to his house; that's not his M.O. It is more likely they went to the hotel or they traded her into another vehicle."

"Do we have to get the footage from the Hotel."

"That is a tough one. That hotel manager doesn't give that up without a warrant. If you like, we can get to work on the warrant. It is a Friday, and Judge Callahan may be available."

"Nettles, we need to see that footage. Do whatever you need to do."

"I'm on it."

Chapter Seventeen: New Dreamers

The next day, Johnnie arrived at the hotel by helicopter and made his way to the central room where Sheryl was held captive. Sheryl had been cooperative and acted more like a guest than a prisoner. Johnnie was impatient and wanted to hear from his "boys."

Sly woke up first. He phoned Sheryl's room and told them he would be there shortly. He dressed in his usual attire and arrived in less than ten minutes for his debriefing. Room service had arrived with some breakfast and a large thermos of coffee. Sly poured a cup and then sat on the couch across from Johnnie.

"Boss, I remember my dreams like I've never remembered them. So, boss, I was in China, I think. Maybe Taiwan or even Japan. There were a bunch of chinks around me, and I didn't understand a word anyone said. Boss, I woke up a little after I fell asleep here, and I was there. It was so real."

"Who were you?"

"Well, as far as I could tell, I was a little boy."

"So, you were a little Chinese boy?"

"Right, yeah. I went to school. I rode a bus. I ate weird-looking food. I couldn't move anything; all I could do was watch. It was as if I was in his head. Wherever he looked, I saw. I could taste and smell, but that was it. Man, that little boy ate some nasty shit."

"Okay, Sly. Thanks, we're done, go get Pete."

"Yes, sir."

Sly left and rapped on Pete's door. Pete didn't answer. Sly went back to Sheryl's room, knocked and let in by Billy.

"What's the matter, Sly? Where's Pete?" "He didn't answer. We should call him."

"Billy, call Pete's room!" Johnnie barked.

"On it." He dialed. One, two, three rings, "No answer, boss." Four, five, six rings. "Six rings, boss, still nothing." Seven, eight, nine, "JW Marriot, how can I help you."

"I was trying to reach my friend in room... he's not answering."

"Sir, perhaps he's in the restroom or bathing. Would you like us to send someone up to check on him?"

"Boss, should they send someone up to check on Pete?"

"Yeah, you and Billy meet 'em in the hallway."

"Yeah, that's good; we'll meet ya in the hallway."

"It will be hotel security."

"Boss, it will be hotel security."

"Sly, that's fine. Hang the fucking phone up."

"Okay, yeah, that's good, bye."

"Now, you and Billy try Matthew, wake his ass up and then wait for security."

"Gotcha boss. Come on, Billy."

They left the room and knocked on Matthew's room. He came to the door dressed.

"Is the boss ready for me?"

"Yeah, Sheryl's room."

"Right."

Matthew went to Sheryl's room, and Sly knocked on Pete's room again, to no avail. They stood in the hallway, waiting for security.

Paulie let Matthew into Sheryl's room. Mathew grabbed a Red Bull from the breakfast tray and sat on the couch with a great big grin on his face.

"Matthew, are you alright?"

"Boss, you won't believe what I dreamt about. I was a showgirl in Las Vegas. I performed on stage. I danced with the Rockets or Rocketts or whatever they're called. I was in a fucking burlesque show. I had awesome titties, and I shook 'em around like a stripper. After the show, I went into the dressing room and I changed. I watched the other girls change. I cleaned off my makeup and did my hair; then, I took a shower. Damn boss, my body was tight."

"Okay, Matthew, that's enough."

"Thank you, Sheryl, that was an amazing night's sleep. I've never felt this rested. Damn, it was fun. Boss, do I get to keep this?"

"Thanks, Matthew. Now, go help Sly and Billy in the hallway."

Matthew joined Sly and Billy as the security guard opened Pete's door. The four men walked into Pete's room to find him dead in his bed.

Sly said, "Shit the boss' gonna be pissed about this."

Matthew said, "Wow, he looks so peaceful. I always thought ole Pete was gonna go in his sleep. I wonder what he dreamt about."

"Who were you, Matt?" Sly asked.

"Dude, I was a Rockette in Las Vegas. I saw all the Rockettes naked and fucked some dude. It was awesome, what about you?"

"Fuck you."

"Wait, what about you?"

"Fuck you; I was a little Chinese boy. I couldn't understand a thing anyone was saying, and he ate some nasty ass shit. Like bats or something gross. It was a terrible experience."

Matthew was laughing out loud, and Billy said, "Shut the fuck up, you too, Pete is dead, we gotta go back and tell the boss."

The security guard had already called the police. So, the three men left the room. Back in Sheryl's room, Matthew began speaking, "Boss, Pete is dead. Seems he had a stroke or heart attack. He died in his sleep."

"Are you fuckin' kiddin' me? We gotta get out of here. Okay boys, load up, we're leaving."

Before the police arrived, Johnnie, Sheryl, Billy and Maggie were in the helicopter and gone. Sly, Matthew and Paulie took the elevator down to the lobby got to each of their SUVs left. Billy called Matthew as he went down the elevator and told them to go to Gioia's for coffee and wait for instructions. They did as they were told.

Judge Callahan signed the warrant, and the FBI collected the video. They watched the Lincoln enter the parking garage. They saw Sheryl get out with Johnnie. They watched as Pete, Matthew, Sly, Paulie and Billy joined them in the elevator. They watched them go to a room together and watched as the five men left the main room. Then they saw Maggie arrive and Johnnie leave with Billy.

In the video from the next morning, they saw Johnnie and Billy arrive, watched Sly enter the room, watched Sly leave the room and knock on Pete's room. Matthew go into the main room, come out with Billy and Sly and then the security guard go into Pete's room. Then they saw all of them leave the hotel. They took note that no one entered or left Pete's room and concluded he died of natural causes.

Satellite images showed the helicopter going to an office in downtown Chicago and letting off two men and two women. It looked like Sheryl may have become a willing participant. The helicopter stayed atop the office building.

Barnum Barked, "Get a team to that office building, now!"

Reynolds and Barnum ran out of Nettle's office, down the hall to the stairs and skipped stairs to get to the bottom and out the door. Once in the car, they called for backup with the local police. FBI and Chicago police rushed to the scene. Barnum and Reynolds ran inside the office building to find Sheryl standing in the lobby surrounded by law enforcement.

"Sheryl, are you alright?" Barnum asked quickly.

"Yes, I'm fine. I have met a nice gentleman, Mr. Torino and he gave me a ride on his helicopter. I'm fine, yes, just fine."

Barnum was stunned, "You took a ride with him. He didn't kidnap you; you've been gone for two days. Stewart is going crazy worried about you?"

"Oh, no, that's ridiculous," she said with an odd look, "we should probably go, I'm sure Stewart is worried."

Reynolds chimed in, "Yeah, that's what he said, Sheryl, come with us."

They cautiously walked out of the building across the long concrete entrance. Reynolds opened the back door, and Sheryl stepped in. He closed the door behind her, went around the back and climbed in the other door. Barnum took the driver's seat, started the SUV and pulled away. Then he asked, "Is there something you want to tell us?"

"I could not talk there. They have ears everywhere in that building. Yes, they nabbed me. They wanted me to try the peyote on three of their guys. One of them died in his sleep. I guess the dreams were too much for him. Torino offered me the potential of a lot of money from making peyote for people. I don't think it is illegal, but then again, I'm not sure if it is legal. There aren't any drugs in my product, just herbs. It is a shame about Pete dying. He was very old, and I suspect what he experienced must have been pretty fucking outrageous. That was how I got out of it all. He expects me to work with him. So, I can be your inside person. Everything I learn along the way, I can inform you. I'm sure he won't tell me much since he can't trust me. To me, that's a win-win situation. You guys get your criminal, and I launch a business changing people's minds."

"Sheryl, what do you know about Tony?"

"I don't know a fucking thing about that scumbag."

They arrived at the field office and went to the conference room where Stewart and Ashley were waiting. Stewart jumped up from his chair and hugged his sister. She was shocked. They all made a place, and Rose Nettles came in to join them.

Barnum started, "Stewart, do you have any updates on Tony?"

"The only thing is he is held up alone at the farmhouse. I don't want to tell what he's been doing with himself."

"Well, that's good. Nettles, can you get someone to take Stewart to another room for a few minutes?" Barnum asked.

Nettles nodded and hit a number on her phone. She said a few things, and an agent arrived at the conference room. She left to get Agent Westall.

Between times, Barnum asked Sheryl, "What do you know about Torino?"

"He didn't tell me a fucking thing. He took me to the hotel; I gave his guys the peyote then he asked me a few questions."

"How did you leave it with him?"

"He knew you were going to be there to get me the next morning and that we only had a few minutes. He knew you would eventually make it to the hotel. At the JW? After Pete died, he panicked and had to get away, but we hadn't finished our conversation. We couldn't talk in the helicopter, so once we made it to the office building, we talked a little more."

"What did you talk about?" Barnum asked.

"He wanted to know what ingredients I needed. He wanted to know if anyone could take the peyote and if it could be packaged. I told him I didn't know."

"Did he ask you about Tony or Stewart?"

"No, he didn't seem to care about either of them."

"Weren't they after Stewart?"

"They never said to me who they were after."

"Is that all you got, Sheryl?"

"Well, yeah, I guess."

"Did they give you any idea what was next?"

"No, no idea at all."

"Good morning, Agent Westall. Will you escort Sheryl and Stewart to the cafeteria for a beverage?"

"Yes, sir. Y'all wanna come with me?"

Agent Gregg Westall was a Southern gentleman born in a small town in Kentucky. He was the first FBI agent to come from his town. Westport is a tiny town of under three hundred people along the Ohio River. Most of the roads along Covington Ridge Road are private. More than half of the town is water, as it is only one and a half square miles. Gregg's uncle owned the Knock on Wood Mercantile and Café while his cousin owned the Boat Docktor, which was a boat repair company. You can see Indiana across Ohio, but the nearest bridge is almost ten miles away, as crows fly, and Louisville will take you over a half-hour's drive. Gregg's single mother held the family together after his father died in Afghanistan. She taught Gregg to be a proud young man, proud of his country and to be proud of his father. He stood over six feet with broad shoulders. He wore an off-the-shelf suit that was not tailored to his body, and his shoes were soiled with mud. His tie was loosened at his neck, and his shirt had last month's wrinkles. Sheryl could tell with one look he was a single man. She thought, *with a haircut, shave, and an iron, this guy would be a hottie,* as she followed him out of the room.

The country boy FBI agent escorted his New Jersey friends down the hall to the elevator, where they entered and rode down to the second floor. Sheryl smiled at him, and he smiled back. He seemed a slight bit intimidated by Sheryl. Gregg was not a field agent. He was an analyst with perfect vision. His dirty blonde hair was showing some grey and his blue eyes showed some sadness. At that moment, he smiled; he felt something, he thought to himself. He turned away smiling, and Sheryl noticed. She saw his smile, and she giggled to herself. They exited the elevator, and he stood by the side of the door, waiting for Stewart and Sheryl to walk ahead. Then he realized they didn't know where they were going, "Oh, excuse me, y'all just follow along. I'll have us there in a bit."

Sheryl melted in his accent. She was speechless. She just followed behind him far enough to watch his movements and gait. Something was stirring inside of her that had not happened since she met her late departed husband.

As they moved across the empty cafeteria floor through the maze of tables with multi-colored barrel plastic chairs, there was a man coming towards them in a hurry from the left. He was an Italian-looking man, well-dressed and clean-shaven. His hair was slicked back against his olive-colored skin. He hurried to Gregg. Gregg saw him coming and increased his pace to the counter. The Italian man increased his pace to the counter until they both began to run. Gregg made it to the counter first, and they both started to laugh. Gregg turned back to Stewart and Sheryl as they caught up to the counter. He said, "May I introduce to you my best friend, Carmelo Calandro."

"Eh, hem, that's Agent Calandro."

"Oh yeah, special, and I do mean special agent Carmelo Calandro. The two of us have been assigned to keep watch on you. Carmelo, this is Stewart and his lovely sister Sheryl."

"Pleased to meet you both. How are you guys holding out under the stress of FBI protection?"

Sheryl answered, "Did you hear about the last two days and my abduction?"

"I did, so I suppose we haven't done very well at protecting you two."

"That's laughable in a sick kind of way, Carmelo. I was taken, Schnaze was killed, and then the mob boss got me to administer peyote to his guys. Now, both of us are marked for another abduction, so you two seriously have your work cut out for you."

"As long as we are here, you are safe."

Stewart responded, "Oh great, we live out the rest of our lives in FBI custody in a cafeteria in Chicago. That was my plan, yes, it was."

Gregg gave Stewart a look of disgust and said, "Sir, we are doing our very best."

"I'm sure you are," Sheryl answered with a smile. "Maybe you could be more hands-on. Gregg cocked his head, smiled and said, "Perhaps we could try that. Yeah, hands-on sounds good."

"Excuse me, you two," Carmelo said, then whispered to his partner, "Gregg, stop it. This is your first field assignment in years, don't fuck it up. You know you can't do that."

Gregg looked back at Carmelo, *I don't care.*

Carmelo then said, "Folks, we should just have a seat, some coffee, a Danish or something to eat. We're not staying here. We are just waiting until the brass tells us where we are going next. If we can keep you from Torino until we pull this off, we'll all be good."

"Nice pep talk, Agent Cal... whatever. You aren't the one hunted by the mob," Stewart said.

"Guys, guys, guys, calm down. Can I have a few minutes alone with my brother?"

Westall answered, "Sure, we'll just go over there for a bit." He said, pointing to a table on the other side of the cafeteria, "Great, thank you."

The agents got up and moved to the furthest table, and Sheryl turned to Stewart and said, "This Torino guy is gunning for you. He trusts Tony too much, and

Tony is too valuable to let go. It's you, not him. These guys are our only hope. Torino told me he wanted to make peyote until one of his guys went and fucking died. Now, I'm not sure. He wanted to partner up, but I think I can get a better offer from someone legal. Look, the government is going to take good care of us. They are going to pay us for the time we spend here, and they will give us part of what they get from Torino if we help them. You need to concentrate and see if there's something you can help them with. You know, like anything Tony may have done that could get him behind bars."

"I didn't see anything last night. I think the peyote might have worn off."

"No, I gave you plenty. It might be he has a different schedule. Now they know about you, and they know you can see him. They don't think dreams are good for a court of law. Fuck, I don't think anyone will go along with that. You just have to stay in hiding because Tony is useless as long as you cannot tell the FBI what he is up to. He may burn out, and then maybe the mob will take care of him on their own, and you'll be free to go about your life."

"That's funny, Sheryl. You know the mob isn't going to let that happen. Either we take them down, or I'm dead."

"I guess we'll just have to see what these guys come up with. Speaking of coming, uh, up with. Tell me, how did it go with your old flame?"

"I should probably keep that to myself."

She leaned in and whispered, "This was your first time, right? Is it not killing you to tell the world?"

He looked around the room, leaned into her and responded, "Well, kind of."

She leaned back, flailed her arms in the air, rested back and said loudly, "So spill the, ha, ha, ha, beans."

He paused, thought and said, "There's not much to tell."

She laughed, leaned forward and demanded, "Details, bro, details, did you fuck her?"

"Why you gotta be so crass?" he said, sitting back and looking away.

She smiled proudly, "You did, you fucked her."

He whispered, "Well, yeah, but that wasn't all."

She smiled larger and said louder, "Oh, did you get her to scream?"

He stopped and glared at her, "Shhh, I did."

She said softly, "Did she write?"

Proudly, he responded, "Well, haha, yeah, she writhed."

"Good for you, bro, you got her to orgasm. Fuck yeah, good for you," she looked around and looked back at him with her arms crossed against her chest.

Even more proudly, he said, "I think I did like five times."

"Outstanding, you stud. You gonna fuck her again?" she said louder than Stewart wanted.

He looked around to see if anyone had heard her. Then asked, "Sheryl, really, do you need to say fuck."

"Well, I don't need to. I like the word. Fact, I wanna fuck that Agent Westall myself."

"Okay, sis. That was a need-to-know thing, and I didn't need to know."

"Well, it ain't fair you gettin' some FBI sex, and I don't. These fuckers are hot as shit. I just don't like how serious they all are. They are pushy and demanding and think their shit doesn't stink. Except that Westall guy, he's got it going on. I wanna lick him all over."

"Okay, I'm calling them back, so you stop talking like that."

"Fuck you. Didn't you want to lick Jett all over?"

"I did."

"You did, you fucker, you licked her all over."

"Shut up, I wanted to."

"You didn't? What the fuck. What's wrong with you? You better lick her all over next time."

"Okay, sis, I will next time. Now, can we talk about how we're going to get out of this mess?"

"I want details. You need to tell me so I can live vicariously through you."

"What, eww, no. You can do anyone you want. Leave my sex life out of it. Besides, I see her as more than just a sex toy."

"Let's hope she sees you the same way."

"What's that supposed to mean?"

"Well, she thought she was a lesbian because of you. Now you better have impressed the pussy licker out of her."

"Oh my God, Sheryl, really?"

"Well, once you had it, you don't wanna switch, do ya?"

"What the hell happened to you? I have never wanted to switch; she's been on my mind for almost thirty years. She's all I ever wanted, and it was everything I dreamed it would be. She was heaven-sent. I have fucking loved this girl since puberty."

"That-a-boy, now you're sounding like me. Gimme some emotion."

"Seriously, Sher, I never thought I would ever see her again. I knew that the chances would be so very slim. I had no idea where she lived, what she was doing or anything, and I was never going to fucking hunt her down. That would've made me a stalker."

"Funny, the line between, that's fucking awesome, and that's fucking scary. Good thing this turned out fucking awesome. I am. I am," she got choked up, "I am, huh, okay, sorry, I am very happy for you. You do deserve to be happy, she stopped, took a breath, then continued, “At least since I fixed your fucking broken personality.”

With tears on his cheeks, “Thank you, Sheryl. You don’t know how much I appreciate what you’ve done for me. I wish I had not waited so long to get to know you again. I think Mom would be proud of you. Dad was a douche.”

They laughed together.

“Dad was a douche, for sure, and he never gave you another chance. You deserved that. You deserved another chance.”

“Thank you, bro. You ain’t so bad, either. Again, since I fixed you.”

They laughed again.

Chapter Eighteen: Getting Torino

Kelsey summoned me to the office building. She entered the building at the front door, made her way to the security guard's desk, and announced herself. He pointed to the furthest elevator, "Today's access code to the top floor is..."

She followed his instructions and exited the elevator to the sixty-fourth floor of the Prudential Tower building. She entered the room marked TGE, and the receptionist told her to go to the conference room behind her. Kelsey stood in the window looking down at all that was Chicago. She was nearly a thousand feet up. She had never felt so small and never felt so unsure of herself. She was at a moment where she would be betraying the very people who had given her the life she had. She owned anything she wanted. She traveled the world on a whim. She could shop for days and never run out of money. She had cars, land, and money tucked away on the islands she had only dreamed of visiting. She stood in the window, and she saw her reflection. Her face was sad. Her eyes looked heavy. Her shoulders drooped. She could not fake a smile. She could not imagine what her future would be like. She had spent her entire adult life on the wrong side of the law, and now she would betray, bite off the hand that fed her. She tried to think of another way. She had not slept, so she was trying to devise another plan. So often, she could fabricate solutions to the hardest problems, but not this one. They had her. Her biggest concern was Tines. He was still in FBI custody, but she was free. How would she explain her freedom? She knew Torino would ask. She feared he would not ask. She knew her life was over no matter what. Either Torino would kill her, have her killed, or she would never be herself again under the protection of the government. She weighed it one last time. Was their plan the best plan? It was too late; Torino was behind her.

"Kelsey, so glad to see you. Please have a seat. This is Robert Brenner; he will be asking you some questions. If we don't hear what we need, we'll use another room at a different location, which will not be a pleasant experience. Just so you know, he is a forensic expert on the truth. We already did a full body scan of you while you were on the elevator. We know you are not wearing any listening devices. If you had been, well, let's just say we would terminate the discussion. So, shall we begin, Robert," Johnny said as he was sitting down.

"Miss MacMillan, would you please have a seat across from me? Now, when I ask you a question, I want you to answer with words. Please, no grunts, nodding or head shakes, got it?"

"Yes, I got it. I will say I don't understand this."

"Rest assured, we are all looking for understanding, Miss MacMillan. May I call you Maggie?"

"Yes, you can. How did you know..."

"I will be asking the questions. Now, your mother's name is Patricia and your father, well, he's Michael, how quaint, Pat and Mike MacMillan. Can you tell me where you were born?"

"I was born in Boston. I grew up in Revere, Mass."

"Thank you, just answer the question, no elaboration, please. We don't have time for storytelling unless we ask you to tell a story. Why did you take the name Kelsey?"

"I was a fan of Kelsey Grammar in Cheers when I was growing up, so to hide my true identity..."

"Thank you. That is enough. How old are you?"

"I'm forty-two."

"Thank you. Where do you live now?"

"I have several places, but my main location is in Hilton Head Island, South Carolina."

"Fine. Again, please keep your answers brief. Who hired you for the position with TGE?"

"That would be Billy, the driver of Mr. Torino."

"Great," he said, looking at Johnny, "Now what was your role supposed to be."

"We, Times and I, were supposed to get Stewart Miller and bring him to the park where we would meet. Johnny."

"Why did you bring Sheryl instead?"

"Our intel was incorrect. We were told the agent that Tines killed was outside Stewart's room. It seemed the guy was pacing, and we found him outside Sheryl's room."

"Why didn't you just go to Stewart's room when you figured you were in the wrong room?"

"Well, Sheryl..."

"Excuse me. Are you about to tell me something your captive said?"

"Well, yes. I was about..."

"What the fuck Maggie. You listened to the sister of the guy you went to kill." Johnny screamed.

"When you put..."

"Shut up, that was not a question." Robert continued. "So, you and Tines brought Sheryl to Mr. Torino in the park. Is that correct?"

"Yes."

"What did you do next?"

"Tines and I left the park."

"Did you leave the park together?"

Shit. This is where they are going to hang me.

"No, he left in the Mustang, and I walked to the nearest bus stop, then I took a bus back to the mall where we started and drove off in one of the cars we stole earlier."

"Mr. Torino, you might want to take Ms. MacMillan away now."

"Wait, why?" Kelsey screamed.

"Well, Ms. MacMillan, you told me the truth all the way up to that point. You and Tines left the park together. You were stopped by the police and returned to the FBI field office. Tines is still there, and they released you. Now, why did they release you? Don't answer that; it will only be a lie. Ms. MacMillan, you are about to die. Do you have anything you'd like to say to Mr. Torino before it happens?"

"Uh, I'm sorry. Please don't do this. I won't say anything else."

Johnnie said, "I'm very disappointed in you. Now, you and your family will have to die. You had such a promising career with us."

"Wait, can't we work this out."

"Kelsey, Maggie, whoever, you know how this works. We can lie, but you must tell us the truth. I know, I know, it's a double standard, but I'm the boss."

Barnum called Reynolds, "Where is she?"

"Not sure. She got on the elevator, and I lost all communication with her."

"Shit, fuck, are you kidding me?"

"I wish I was Phil. They must have some sophisticated jamming system in the elevator. What do we do now?"

"Well, we got nothing on them. How attached are we to her?" Barnum asked.

"What'ta mean?"

"I mean, do we send in a team and extract her?"

"Don't we owe that much to her?" Reynolds asked.

"I don't know what we owe her. I didn't really like her. She isn't much of an asset. She'll end up costing the government a ton. We could save her or save money. What do you think?"

"I have never heard you debate a life before; we have to go in there."

"I know, but if she died, it'd be one more bad guy off the payroll."

"Phil, you gotta give the order."

"I know. How long's it been?"

"We've been in the van for about fifteen minutes. You, well, you just got there, slacker. She's been up there about ten minutes, and her coms have been down for five."

"Well, okay, let's send in the calvary. All units, take the building, go to the top floor."

Twenty-two FBI agents ran into the building. Reynolds was first through the door and to the security desk, "I'm special agent Reynolds. We need to get to the top floor. and now, give us the code."

"I'm sorry, sir; without a warrant, I'm not allowed to give anyone the code."

"Look, rent a cop, a girl's life is in danger. We'll hold you as an accessory to her death if we don't get there before they kill her."

"It's bacon."

"I'm sorry, what?"

"The code is 'bacon.'"

"Ain't that special, let's go boys."

"Agent Reynolds, the maximum in the elevator is twenty-five hundred pounds, and it is the last elevator on the left."

Eleven guys got onto the elevator. Reynolds punched in "Bacon," and up they went. The receptionist got the message, "Bacon."

She called Johnnie, "Sir, the police are on their way up the elevator."

"Thank you, Sissy. Robert will take Maggie here down the private elevator in my office. Robert, follow me. Do you have Maggie's coat? Ask Priscilla to put it on and then take the stairs to sixty-three, where she can get the elevator to the lobby. Tell her to just go out the front door and hail a cab. She needs to take a cab and go home. You have..."

"Yes, sir, I know, sir, about two minutes, you better go."

Maggie began to fight. Robert pulled something out of his pocket, a syringe, and he stuck her. She fell to the ground, and he picked her up and carried her to Johnnie's office. Robert looked sickly to Maggie, so she thought he would be a pushover. Robert was no pushover. He was a former collegiate world champion wrestler who never lost his muscle tone even in his fifties, now fifty-nine. You would see Robert in the gym every morning between four and six. Underneath his Armani suit was a brick shithouse.

Robert put Maggie down in the elevator, and Billy joined him. They went to the third-floor garage, where two other guys were waiting. Robert and Billy passed Maggie off to the other guys, and they carried her to a nearby Cadillac. One of the guys opened the trunk while the other dropped her in. They left the parking lot and headed to the farmhouse.

The FBI got to the sixty-fourth floor, and Sissy greeted them, "May I help you, gentlemen?"

"Where is she," Reynolds barked.

"I'm sorry, sir, you will need to get more specific. We have about thirty women who work for our company."

"I'm looking for the young woman who came up the elevator about ten minutes ago."

"Oh, you mean Ms. MacMillan. She left a few minutes ago. You must have missed her in the lobby."

Reynolds said, "Clear this floor."

"Sir, I'm sorry, without a search warrant, you will not be able to get past this lobby."

Reynolds took his phone out of his pocket, "Get a battering ram up here immediately. Keep an eye out for Kelsey leaving the building. She is in a khaki raincoat. She has auburn hair about shoulder length. Find her."

He turned to Sissy, "You need to understand, I will go anywhere I choose on this floor. Either you open the doors, or I will break them down."

"Suit yourself, sir, but I'm not allowed to open any doors without Mr. Torino's approval."

"Do you want to go to jail for obstruction?"

"Sir, I'm sorry."

"Somebody cuff her and read her her rights. Arrest her for obstruction of justice."

Pricilla passed by the guard in the lobby and winked at him. He smiled back. She headed out the front door and was in a cab before a single FBI agent realized. The guard stopped one of the agents a few minutes later once the cab was out of sight, "Excuse me, were you looking for that MacMillan woman?"

The agent answered, "Yes."

"Well, she just caught a cab at the curb. She's gone."

The agent called Reynolds, "Agent Reynolds, it's Harmon. I'm in the lobby. The guard down here said MacMillan just caught a cab outside. We missed her."

"Fuck, there are more than seven thousand cabs in Chicago. We'll never find her," Reynolds said.

Harmon ran outside to try to see if he could make out any of the cabs, but it was too late. Kelsey woke up tied and gagged in a chair at the farmhouse. She was tied and gagged. Tony was in the other room watching the local news. He heard her move and went into the cleared bedroom where Maggie was tied.

Tony said, "Do you know why you are here? That's right, you are gagged, hold on." He removed her gag, and she said, "I'm guessing you are the enforcer."

"You are right. So far, I have a few dozen kills under my belt, but many still call me a rookie."

"Oh, so you are Tony, the reason this all started."

"Right, I have been given free reign over you. I can do whatever I want. I have never been a rapist, but you, well, you might be my first. Wanna have some fun?"

"Fuck you, you slimy motherfucker, you stay away from me. Kill me if you want, but, oh fuck, stay away."

"Potty mouth, I like that. Torino told me he was going to send me a playmate. I had no idea it would be such a feisty one."

Tony crossed his arms and undressed her with his eyes while she screamed obscenities at him. He laughed and then left the room, closing the door behind him.

Reynolds got his battering ram and broke down the main door to Johnnie's office. Johnnie was calmly sitting behind his desk when the door crashed open. He was talking to his lawyer and handed the phone to Reynolds.

"This is Special Agent Reynolds of the FBI. To whom am I speaking."

"This is Arthur Golden of G, P & R. We represent Mr. Torino, and we demand you cease and desist. We demand you vacate the property, or I'll have Judge Callahan on the phone, and he'll stop you."

"You do that. A woman's life is in danger, and I will do whatever I need to save her."

"Fine, I assume Judge Callahan has your phone number?"

"I believe he does."

"Well, then do what you need to do. He'll be in touch with you shortly."

The agents continued their search when Reynold's phone rang, and he answered, "Reynolds."

"This is Judge Callahan, Todd. You have to stop. I'm sorry you cannot continue searching. You may have probable cause, but since the guard saw her leave..."

"Your honor that was a decoy."

"That may be true, but the guard witnessed her departure and that's all I need to tell you to stop."

"Fuck."

"I know it sucks, but the law is on his side again."

"Okay, your honor. Goodbye."

Reynolds clicked his phone off, then spoke into his walkie-talkie, "Stand down, all units, stand down and desist. We're done here." He dialed Barnum. Barnum answered, "Tell me you got her."

Todd responded.

"No, Todd... No, what happened?"

"The story the guard down in the lobby is telling us is she waltzed right out the front door under our noses. Somehow, she took another elevator down and out, grabbed a cab, and she was gone."

"I'll get Nettles on the cams outside and see if we can track her down. Have the team stand by. We might get eyes on her and give you a location."

Stewart and Sheryl watched breakfast turn into lunch, and the crowd grew wain, and they disappeared. They had more FBI cafeteria food than they wanted while Westall tried to woo Sheryl. The afternoon was coming, and they wanted to leave, but the agents kept them where they were.

It only took Nettles a few minutes to track down Priscilla and give the address to Reynold's team. Nettles pointed out that the house belonged to an employee of TGE one, Priscilla Knight. Nettles showed the picture of Priscilla to Barnum, and he knew they had been hoodwinked. Reynolds and the team still went to Knight's home.

Reynolds went to the door, and Knight opened it. "I'm Special Agent Reynolds of the FBI," he asked, "Were you at work this morning?"

"I was, I am ill, so I just got home. What's the problem, uh, agent?"

"You were seen wearing a suspect's coat. Where is that coat."

"I'm sorry, sir, I have no idea what coat you speak of."

"Okay, then, Miss Knight, is it? You're under arrest for obstruction of justice. Turn around. You do know it is illegal to lie to a federal officer, don't you? I'll be adding that to your charges."

"What? Why? I just work there in the accounting department. What's the problem? I left the coat in the cab. I gave the guy twenty bucks to get rid of it."

"Well, that was fast," he said, pushing his way into her house. "Sit down, Priscilla, we're not done here."

He called Barnum, "She left the coat in the cab."

"Nettles, get on with the cab company, stop the cab driver."

"Right, sir."

"Reynolds, bring her in."

"You got it."

Reynolds said to one of his team, "Cuff her, she's coming with us."

Nettles got the cabbie to stop, and Reynold's and his team caught up to him, got the coat and his statement and took Priscilla back to the field office.

Sheryl and Stewart were still bored in the cafeteria.

Tony went back into the room where Maggie was sitting. "So, tell me, girl, what's your specialty?"

"Oh, some small talk before you fuck me and off me, huh?"

"Hey, don't make it sound so gross. We'll have some fun together; you know you and me."

"You know, under other circumstances, you might have been my type, but knowing you'd rape me and kill me is kind of a turn-off."

"Come on, you know every bitch has a rape fantasy. You ain't different."

"That's bullshit, guys who rape made-up. Can you imagine some dick you don't want in your ass? Can you imagine being sodomized by some hairy motherfucker without even a kiss?"

"Shut up."

"I mean, really, is that who you are? You don't look like a pervert. You don't look like a bitch slapper. You do look like a killer, though; I will give you that. Me, I'm not a killer. I'm the interrogator. I do what you think you'll be able to do to me. I could teach you some shit, but no, your job is to fuck me and kill me. Asswipe!"

"Don't be so shitty. This doesn't have to go that way."

"No? It doesn't? You gonna go against the boss's orders?"

"Well, no, but it doesn't have to be that ugly."

"Just get it over with."

"I haven't been given the go yet. He said to wait. So, we wait. Are you hungry? You want a sandwich or something?"

"That'd be nice."

"I'll pop in a DiGiorno, how's that sound?"

"Delish."

Nettles called Barnum "Agent Branum. It turns out a car went to the farmhouse a little while ago. Two men delivered what, from the satellite could tell, was Kelsey MacMillan. She's at the farmhouse."

"Thank you, Nettles, great work."

Nettles smiled, clicked to end the call, then noticed it was ringing.

"Nettles."

"Yes sir."

"Why did you hang up?"

"I thought we were done."

"No. Who is available to send there?"

"Reynolds and his team are in the field at the office building downtown awaiting a warrant from Callahan. Westall and Calandro are downstairs babysitting Stewart and Sheryl. Timkons, Kronke, Portell and Kleinhoffer are at the JW still looking for evidence. We have a few guys here that could go. But, sir, I doubt they would be able to handle Palumbo and MacMillan."

"Nettles, they took her there to kill her. That's all Palumbo does. She might be dead already."

"Wait, sir, Mark Moran, the analyst watching, said she just escaped out the back and ran into the cornfield. Tony didn't follow her."

"Send a helicopter. I'm going there myself. Do me a favor, call Reynolds, and have him and Harmon get over there, too. I'm going to take Calandro with me. We can't let Palumbo know we know where he is."

Tony brought Maggie the pizza, and she kicked it into his face, covering his eyes. She picked the chair up, turned with the legs facing him, and ran backwards into him, knocking him into the wall, hitting his head and making him fall out cold. She slammed the chair into the wall a few times, breaking it and loosening the ropes around her hands. Then she untied herself, took his handgun from his belt, pointed it at him then stopped. She put it in her pants and ran through the house and out the back door. Ahead of her was the cornfield. Six to eight-foot-high corn plants with rows of openings gave her shelter from her assailant. Tony was out for more than fifteen minutes, which gave Maggie, a former track and field player, a mile-and-a-half head start. She came to a small creek, almost dry and ran to her right. She could hear the roar of the road as a truck went down. In two minutes, she came to West Stonewall Road. She looked left and then right. She went right. Another two minutes brought her to highway forty-seven.

Moran reported to Nettles, who relayed to Barnum, "She's in the ditch at West Stonewall Road and Highway forty-seven. No sight of Tony coming out yet."

Tony woke up to find a destroyed chair and a gash on his forehead. With blood across his face, he could not see. He went to the bathroom and grabbed a towel and wiped the blood away, then took the towel and ran out the front door. He looked around and then went to the back of the building and into the garage, where the car was parked. The keys were inside the house. He ran back inside, took the keys off the key holder and flew out the back door to the garage. The first attempt to start the old car failed. He pumped the gas pedal and tried again. On the third try, it turned over. With dust flying in every direction, he spun the wheels and squealed his way to Highway forty-seven. He turned right. He was going in the opposite direction from Maggie.

"Barnum, Palumbo just left the farmhouse. He went south on forty-seven away from MacMillan."

"Is there a local officer in the area that could pick her up before Palumbo finds her?"

"I'll contact the sheriff. I think she found a hiding place. She's at Huffton Transportation. No, I'm wrong, she is back in the cornfield behind Huffton. We have the deputy on the way."

"Okay, good. Where is Tony?"

"He just turned around on forty-seven, headed back to the farmhouse."

"Any idea when a deputy will be on scene?"

"I'll ask."

"Is Kelsey still on the cornfield?"

"Affirmative, still in the cornfield walking south. Deputy, ten minutes out."

"Is there any way, in your opinion, that Tony would be able to see her?"

"No, sir. I believe she is safe."

"Good. Keep an eye on Tony. I'm still at least a half hour from there. Where's the fucking helicopter."

"Phil, I think you'll get there before the helicopter."

"Terrific! Have someone take Torino into custody and bring him to the field office. We need him to be out of communication with everyone in his organization. Arrest him for whatever; just get him gone from his office."

"You got it."

Barnum drove in silence of his thoughts for nearly twenty-five minutes. His phone rang, "Yes. Go ahead."

"Agent Barnum, this is Judge Callahan. You know, whatever you have on Torino is going to fail. We might even have a false arrest charge, and that's going to make it harder for you to pin anything on him. I suggest you let him go right away."

"With all due respect, your honor, and you know I respect you above all the others, I cannot do that. If I let him go, both Palumbo and MacMillan will be dead in an hour. I need both of them in custody with him. I do have forty-eight hours, right?"

"No, you have until his lawyer can file an injunction."

"How long is that?"

"You might have four hours, give or take."

"I'll take it. Can you help me stall?"

"That is with me helping."

"Oh, wow, okay. Hey, judge. Thank you, you just saved my case."

"Phil, you better make a case this time."

"Judge, I appreciate it."

"Good luck, stay safe."

"Thanks. Talk soon." He didn't wait for the judge to end the call or speak again; he ended the call. He looked over at Calandro and almost spoke. He kept the conversation to himself. He dialed Nettles, "Tell me some good news."

"Sir, MacMillan is still on foot. The helicopter is circling overhead. Tony is in custody, and one of the deputies is closing in on Kelsey as we speak."

"I knew I could count on you."

"Sir, it's your operation. I'm just here to help."

"Nettles, we all deserve credit for this one."

Barnum pulled up to the farmhouse where Tony was in custody. A deputy car followed him into the driveway. Barnum was first inside, and the deputy was immediately behind him. Once inside, they found Palumbo face down on the floor, handcuffed, and Kelsey sitting in a chair. Kelsey had given the deputy Tony's gun. Palumbo was spouting off angrily at Kelsey and ignored his rant. Barnum asked two deputies to pick up Tony, but Calandro and the first deputy did it. Once on his feet, he was escorted to Barnum's car and placed in the back seat. Along the way, he asked the deputy if they had frisked him and if he had mirandized. The deputy said yes, but to Barnum, it was not convincing, so he told Calandro to take Tony out of the car and lean him against it. Calandro agreed and complied, and then Barnum frisked Tony. He found nothing and felt assured that everyone at the farmhouse was clean cops. He instructed Calandro to Mirandize him, and he did. Then Calandro put Tony back into the back of Barnum's car. Just then, Reynolds and Harmon arrived along with the crime scene units.

Barnum told Reynolds to escort Kelsey back to the field office, and he helped her into the back seat. The two cars with prisoners left, and the deputies followed.

Calandro drove as Barnum took the passenger seat. He turned to Tony and said, "You know your rights, correct?"

"Yes. I'm-m-m not s-s-s-saying a-a-a-anything."

"I didn't know you stuttered."

"I d-d-d-don't, shit."

"Oh, you have Tourette too."

"No, I d-d-d-don't. Fuck!"

"Sounds to me like you do. Does it sound like Tourette to you, Calandro?"

"It does, boss."

"So, Tony, you can relax. You don't need to get all worked up. You can stop stuttering because you can get out of everything."

"How c-c-c-can I d-d-d-do that?"

"Aw, come on, you have to know what we want."

"No, I d-d-d-don't."

"Tony, no one believes that. We know who you work for, and we know why you were at the farmhouse. Kelsey told us you were going to kill her, that that was your job. We caught you there. We found her nearby after she escaped, and she told us you had already started beating her. She has the injuries to prove it."

"I d-d-didn't t-t-touch her."

"All I can say is the rape test will prove you raped her too."

"Now w-w-wait a minute. I m-m-m-may have hit her a few. Fuck."

"See, Tony, I already got you admitting you hit her. Admit it all; you could be free if you just give us what we need."

"I-I-I-If I s-s-s-s, say any t-t-t-thing, I'm a d-d-d-dead man."

"Oh, come on, you know we can protect you. Do you know how many informants we have in witsec? Don't answer, I ain't got time, we got thousands."

"I was j-j-j-just at the f-f-f-farmhouse v-v-v-visiting a f-f-f-friend."

"Right, okay, you wanna play that way. We have a witness that can identify every person you've killed in the past month. You'll get the gas chamber unless you give us Torino."

"Who?"

"Oh, you gonna be like that. Calandro takes the next dirt road. We're gonna take care of this scum ourselves."

"You got it, Phil."

Calandro found a dirt road and turned. He drove about a half mile off of forty-seven cornfields surrounding them. He stopped the car. Barnum got out of the passenger side and opened the back door and pulled Tony to his feet, and then began pushing him toward the cornfield. They went down a row and deep into the field. He told Tony to get down on his knees. Tony was looking up at him when he pulled a glove out of his pocket, put it on his right hand, and then pulled up his pant leg, exposing a snub-nosed thirty-eight. He pulled the hammer back and pointed at Tony. Then he said, "There's no one gonna stop me from taking justice in my own hands. I took this gun from one of your buddies when we arrested them. When the ballistics come back, it will look like a mob hit. No one will know any better. So, you have exactly fifteen seconds to start talking, or you will be dead, 15, 14, 13."

Tony was clearly frightened when he said, "I t-t-t-told you I-I-I d-d-d-don't know any-t-t-t-thing."

Barnum continued, "Ten."

Tony wiggled on the ground, trying to inch away on his knees, "P-P-P-Please, d-d-d-don't d-d-do this."

"Five, four, three, two."

Tony screamed, "Ok-k-k-kay, s-s-s-stop. M-M-M-My boss is Torino. I-I-I d-d-do what you think."

Barnum, clearly impatient, screamed, "Fifteen more seconds, that was not enough."

Tony screamed back, "S-s-s-stop c-c-c-counting."

Barnum filled in for Tony, "Tell me you killed..."

Tony began confessing with his head down, "I did, I killed them all. I was hired to kill them all."

Barnum grabbed him under the elbow and began to lift him, "Okay, get up. We're going in."

Barnum led Tony back to the car and put him back in the back seat. He turned to Calandro and said, "You take his statement when we get back. He just told me he killed... So, Tony, you hungry?"

"Yeah."

Calandro then asked, "I thought you had a DiGiorno at the farmhouse."

"How'd you know that?"

Calandro answered, "We know everything, Tony. We'll get you a Portillo's dog when we get there. Whatcha want on it? Wait, no, I bet you want an Italian beef."

"I do like the Italian beef, that's great."

Calandro continued, "Well, you spill the beans, and we'll get you the Italian Beef. Deal?"

Reluctantly, Tony said, "Deal."

Calandro looked him in the face and sarcastically said, "Interesting, you only stutter when you are nervous."

Barnum and Calandro brought Tony to interrogation room four and set him down. They told him they would be back shortly and left.

Barnum returned to his office, where an attorney who claimed to represent Tony met him.

The attorney asked, "Agent Barnum, I presume."

"Well, you are in my office," Barnum said in an unimpressed voice.

"I'm Robert Golden. I represent Tony Palumbo. I insist you release him immediately."

"You can insist all you want. He confessed to me, and we're getting his statement right now."

"His statement will be inadmissible as I'm his attorney, and I was not present during his testimony."

"I'm so sorry about that. I believe it is too late for you to stop him."

"Take me to him, now!"

"Right this way," Phil said as he led him down the hallway to the interrogation room. He opened the door to a room with just Tony. He was pissed. He let Mr. Golden in the room, then slammed the door and screamed, "Where's Calandro? Where the fuck is Calandro!"

Calandro heard Phil screaming and came running with a bag from Portillo's in his hand. "Yeah, boss, whatcha need? I got the beef."

"Are you fucking kidding me? You didn't get his statement? You got him a sandwich. You fucking idiot, he lawyered up, and now we got shit. Nettles, Nettles, where the fuck are you, Nettles?"

Nettles came running, "Yes, Phil, I'm here. What do you need?"

First, get ears in that interrogation room, then call someone to send Calandro to the fucking moon. How the hell did... Never fucking mind. Calandro, just go home."

"I'm so sor..."

"Calandro, don't speak. Get lost before I fucking shoot you."

"Okay, I'm going."

In exasperation, he said aloud, "Reynolds, where are you?"

Nettles responded, "Reynolds is in seven with MacMillan. But, bad news, boss, she's got a lawyer too."

"What the, what does she need a lawyer for?"

"She is recanting her whole story, says it was taken under duress."

"Are you saying after we just saved her ass, she's double-crossing us?"

"Sir, yes sir, there's no loyalty among thieves."

"Who is the lawyer?"

"He's from the same firm as..."

"Golden, fuck, they are good. I'm going in."

Barnum stormed into the interrogation room and told Reynolds he was taking over. Reynolds stood up and put his back to the wall. Barnum began, "Okay, Kelsey, I realize you have a lawyer here, but I have one quick question: do you realize the lawyer you have is the same law firm as Palumbo and Torino?"

The lawyer chimed in, "What's your point, agent, uh?"

"It's agent Barnum, and I'm in charge here in this office. My point was to your client: as soon as you get her released, she's dead. They were about to kill her when we saved her ass." He turned to Kelsey and said, "Girl, you'd be dead if it wasn't for us, and now you are falling right back into their trap. Go ahead and side with them, but you won't see tomorrow morning."

She sat and stared at Barnum. She was silent.

Barnum stared back. The lawyer began talking. Barnum told him to be quiet, and he complied. Barnum and MacMillan continued staring at each other. They sat in silence for almost five minutes until Kelsey said, "Agent Barnum, I will keep my deal with you. Steve or Roger or Paul or Ringo or whatever your name is, take a hike. I won't be needing your services."

The Lawyer rose, gathered his things and left.

"Now that he's gone, tell me everything," Barnum said.

"You know they snatched me in Torino's office. They drugged me and took me to the farmhouse. Tony told me that Torino told him I was coming to be his playmate. He said he could do anything to me as long as I ended up dead. Then he told me what he intended and slapped me a few times. I had been in that chair before, but I don't think he knew what he was doing. He was too soft. He asked me if I was hungry, and when he returned with pizza, I used that moment to get free. I knocked the hot pizza into his face, broke the chair and cracked him over the head. That was when I ran. I have no idea how you guys found me."

"That's not important. Just know you won't get far if you try and run."

"I know my life of crime is over. Now I just want to put the sons of bitches who wanted to kill me behind bars. I got dirt on a whole lot of the mob."

Barnum looked over at Reynolds. Reynolds tilted his head. Barnum said, "Well, you are going to have to give us a lot." Then Barnum got up and motioned to Reynolds to follow him out of the room. Out in the hallway, he said, "If she can give us what she says she can give us, then we might be taking down the whole syndicate. How the hell are we going to keep her alive? Reynolds, get in touch with the attorney general's office in D. C. We need to move this there. We have to make it difficult for Torino and the mob to find her. Tell Nettles to contact Judge Callahan so we can keep Torino here. If Kelsey goes before the grand jury, it should be done remotely. Have Nettles ask if that's possible."

"Got it," Reynolds said, and then he took off down the hall. Barnum stood in the hall for a moment and then went back into the interrogation room.

"Agent Barnum, do we have a deal?"

"We're talking to the attorney general right now. Now, it's time for you to start writing. Start from the beginning."

"Hold on, Hoss. I need to see my immunity in writing for all of my previous crimes. All wiped clean, and I'll tell you everything I have done since my fist snatch and grab at the candy store at age eleven."

"Okay, then wait. Look, we're going out on a limb for you. I'm asking the judge for some seriously special considerations to keep you alive. When this is all over, you will get what you deserve, and they'll all be hanging or on their way to a lethal injection. We gave

Tony a chance to come clean, he told me a bunch of shit, and then the lawyer turned him around. Stick with us, kid, and we'll take good care of you." Barnum put his hand on the doorknob and began opening it.

"Barnum, thanks."

"You bet."

He stepped out and thought, *she's gonna fry too.*

Chapter Nineteen: Here Comes the Judge

Barnum, Reynolds, Sheryl and Stewart entered the judge's chambers. When they came into the room, they saw a large conference table with ten chairs. It was a dark office with wood-paneled walls and wainscoting stained cherry red. His cherry red desk was almost against the far wall, and behind him, a door. He picked up a remote from his desk, and with a single press, the dark room turned to light. The shades automatically opened, and the light went up all the way. He excused his clerk, Janice and rose from behind the desk. He was a tall man in his fifties. His square chin was covered in a reddish-brown beard hair that met his handlebar mustache and rose to his temples. From there, he was shaven. He sported broad shoulders and a rotund belly. He was expectantly well dressed in a heavily starched pinpoint Oxford cloth shirt and striped tie. Red, white and blue told the world who he was. His suit coat hung from a valet to his left. He grabbed it, slid it on and made his way to the conference table. He waved his hand towards the table to instruct his guests where to sit. He took the head seat without sitting, Reynolds and Stewart on his left, Sheryl and Barnum on his right, respectively. He stood and waved to his guests to sit. They all sat, and he towered over them.

He began to speak with a southern accent, "I appreciate y'all coming down here to visit me. I'm going to ask some questions to see if we have somewhere to go here. I know these two guys," he said pointing with both hands a t Reynolds and Barnum, "but who do we have here."

There was a knock at the door. Janice opened the door and let Jett in.

"Sorry, I'm late. I got distracted by a call."

"Agent Jett, we could have done this without you, you know."

"I do your honor, but I have been with this case since the beginning and..."

"Enough, sit down. Now, Barnum, tell me about the case."

Barnum began speaking, and Callahan paced the room.

"Okay, I think I have heard enough from you. Sheryl is it alright if I call you Sheryl," he said with a small grin. It was his first sign of emotion in the fifteen minutes they had been at the conference.

"Yes, yes, you may your honor."

"So, let me get this right. You gave your brother this peyote and now you, Stewart," he turned and looked at Stewart. Stewart nodded, he continued, "And now your brother can see everything Mr. Palumbo does while he is dreaming."

"That is correct, your honor."

"Stewart, you saw this Tony Palumbo kill people?"

"I did your honor."

"Well, y'all, this is very hard to believe. In fact, it is so hard to believe that it is paving new ground, and I think it is inadmissible in court. If I allow this testimony, I will be the laughingstock of the judicial community and maybe even tossed. I can't have any of that."

Stewart spoke up, "Your honor, might I make a suggestion? This might seem, well, rather extreme, but what if you tried it yourself."

There was silence. The judge stared at Stewart. He looked at Sheryl, then at Reynolds and Barnum. His eyes fixed back on Stewart for a few seconds, and then he turned to Sheryl. "Can you do that?"

"I can, your honor. Would you like to try?"

"What does this mean?"

Sheryl started, "Well, sir, we go to your home. I administer the peyote and say some prayers. Honestly, I'm not sure which works, the peyote or the prayers. I use them both."

"Excuse me, Sheryl, is it okay if I call you Sheryl?"

"Of course, your honor, you asked that already."

"Great, then you call me Randall. Will you do that?"

"I will, Randall."

Reynolds and Barnum looked dismayed at each other. Both were thinking the same thing. I had never heard him tell someone to call him by his first name.

"Okay, so Sheryl, what does this take again? Please continue."

"Well, like I was saying, I administer the peyote and say some prayers. I say them out loud, and then you'll begin to get sleepy. You may feel like you have been drinking. You will need to be close to a bed because you will fall asleep rather quickly, and then you will sleep for maybe a whole day."

"A whole day, are you kidding?"

"No, Randall," she said, feeling uncomfortable using his first name, "While you are asleep, the person you, well, connect with might be asleep too. You might see their dreams instead of your own, and then, well, when they are awake, you will see through their eyes. You might smell what they smell and taste what they taste; you will hear what they hear. You will not have any control over movements, nor will you be able to speak."

"Astounding." He sat back in his chair. "I guess I need to clear my calendar. We'll need to postpone all my appointments tomorrow. I will need all of you at my house with a doctor while this is going on. I did hear one of your subjects died, did I not."

"Yes, your honor, sorry Randall, he was in very poor physical condition, and I can, um, tell, you are, uh, not."

"I get it. Okay, tonight, everyone, come to my house for dinner. We'll have some drinks, some conversation, and then we'll do this." He got up from his seat, opened the door and exclaimed, "Cancel everything I have for tomorrow. Get in touch with my chef and tell him six more for dinner tonight, make it special. Also, get in touch with my doctor and tell him to send someone to my house around ten tonight. Someone who can stay with me, monitor my sleep and be there in case some emergency arises. Got it"

"Yes, your honor."

"Okay, it's set, be at my home at six. Dress comfortably; I feel it is going to be a very long night for y'all. Oh, and bring your appetite. Fitzgerald is an amazing chef."

They pulled up to a cast iron fence that had to be over one hundred years old. The gate opened without announcement. Two SUVs pulled in and followed the pavement for almost a half mile up to the circle driveway. They exited the SUVs onto cobblestone pavers that had been recycled from the riverfront in Saint Louis. Randall Callahan was the fifth-generation owner of what appeared to be a castle in the middle of Chicago. The tall trees and fencing kept strangers from seeing the home. His great, great, great, great grandfather was a mason who was brought to the United States as a slave in the early eighteen-hundreds. He was freed under the Emancipation Proclamation, went to school, and became a lawyer and a police officer. His son followed and became a lawyer, and the family moved from Saint Louis to Chicago in 1886. They purchased the property that the home stood on and, over fifty years, amassed the castle. Randall's wife left him in 1997, and he had sequestered himself in his home. He was the last of the Callahan's. Randall Callahan was appointed federal judge by President Bush just before the Twin Towers fell in two thousand one.

He stood barefoot in khaki pants and a pink polo knit shirt, the open door awaiting his guests. A woman a few years older than him stood a few feet behind him. She was in a plain-looking dress with an apron. On either side of her were young men in black slacks, white shirts and black bow ties. Behind them stood several others, male and female, all in waiting. When the party arrived at the door, the judge turned and walked in. His crew of workers parted, and his guests followed. The inside of the castle was grander than the outside. He had left the décor the same as it had been for almost one hundred years in the foyer. The group followed him to a parlor with a massive chandelier and pool table in the center. High-top bar tables and stools surrounded the pool table. Past the pool table was a monumental oak bar in the shape of an "L." It terminated on a wall. Across the floor was a slight step up that appeared to be a stage. The room was large enough for as many as one hundred visitors.

Adjacent to the terminus of the bar was a door, and it opened both ways in the middle. The two young men with bowties exited the door, bringing hors d' oeuvres on silver platters. The woman who stood behind the judge took her station at the bar. The judge waved at the servers to halt, and they stopped. He turned and addressed his guests, "Welcome to my home. Many of you will be impressed with the likes of this place, but I must assure you it has been in my family for generations. The son of an Irish slave built this place with his father and his sons and their sons. I enjoy the fruits of their labor, and I also enjoy the cost of upkeep." They all laughed. He had lost his Southern accent. "I will tell you all: I don't often share my home.

Back in twenty seventeen, I had an inauguration party when Trump was sworn in. It was me and a few of my colleagues. Prior to that, well, hell, who gives a shit? So, I offer my home to people I trust and to people I want to know better, and yes, I have chosen all of you. In case you are wondering, the Southern gentleman thing plays well in the courtroom. I'm truly a Chicago boy through and through. Let's get this party started. Eat, drink, and laugh, please. This house needs some laughter."

His guests were surprised at how accommodating the judge was. The bar was filled with spirits, wine and beer, and his staff was generous and kind. He turned on some eighties rock music and even danced for a while. Dinner was served; they ate, told stories and enjoyed each other's company. Randall paid a great deal of attention to Sheryl, and Sheryl reciprocated. They were getting along well, then the doctor's assistant showed up, and it was time to start the procedure. Sheryl, the physician's assistant and the judge, retired to his bedroom. The rest of the party played pool, drank and enjoyed the music.

Across the hall, up the grand spiraling stairs, down a hall and as far away as one could get from the parlor was the master suite. When Sheryl entered, there was a sitting space. It looked like a living room with a couch, two side chairs and a coffee table. She turned to see if there was a television on the wall, and there was. Past the couch was a California king-sized four-poster bed. The walls had deep mahogany wainscoting like his courthouse office, halfway up and a pale beige paint above. The ceiling was capped with mahogany crown molding. She felt it odd that there was no window in the room. The flooring was a plush carpet, and the furniture was Old English.

The judge suggested that Sheryl sit on the sofa as he passed it. She complied. He went to a server to the right of his bed and unveiled his private collection of adult beverages. He offered her a drink, and she gently refused. He gently handled a tall bottle with a monochromatic image of a southern gentleman in glasses smoking a cigar. He poured the brown gold into a glass. It was less than a shot. He lifted it toward her as one last chance for Sheryl to join him. She shook her head. He sipped it as he walked to the couch to join her. She sat on the right of the couch with her elbow resting on the arm. He looked at the couch and then sat in the chair next to her. The P.A. seemed almost invisible to him until he waved his hand toward the other chair and sat down.

"Sheryl, would you mind if we got a little better acquainted before we begin?"

"Not at all."

The judge asked, "Are you sure you wouldn't like a cocktail?"

"I am, thank you, though," she said nervously.

"Will we need her services yet?" he said, waving toward the Grant, the P.A.

"I would hope not. Is she here all of the time?" Sheryl asked.

"Well, I have a medical provider with me at all times. It is one of my neurotic tendencies."

"I see, okay."

"Does he make you uncomfortable?"

"Well, no, it's not that. I just..."

"Just what?"

"No, nothing," she said, shaking her head.

"Would you be more comfortable if Grant left for a bit?" she nodded, "Grant, can you leave us, please."

Grant rose and walked out. He made his way to a room set up for the medical providers next door. In his room, there was a queen-sized bed, a desk, a file cabinet, couch, coffee table and another television. He dove onto the bed, took his phone out of his pocket and entered his own world.

Sheryl turned toward Randall, "How could you tell I was uncomfortable?"

He softly and assuredly answered, "It is my life's work to read people. In court, it is almost never what someone says as much as it is their demeanor. I will know when I hear the truth. I know when I don't. I often times want to tell the jury to ignore a comment or even a whole testimony. That's not my job. I will call the attorneys to my chambers and express my disdain if things come to that. I think most of them know this. Damn, did I just go off on a diatribe?"

Laughing, she replied, "Yes, you did, that's okay."

"I think you'd rather I sat next to you," he said.

"You do, do you?"

"I did. Was I right?"

"You might have been."

He moved to the other side of the nine-foot leather tufted couch. "Is this what you mean?"

She slid over closer to him. "No, this is more what I meant."

"You know a judge has to maintain a certain decorum with anyone who might take the stand in his courtroom. Person feelings, personal action and any connection other than professional is strictly prohibited."

She took the glass out of his hand, then drank what was left of his Pappy Van Winkle and said, "Is it?" Then she put the glass down on the table and slid closer.

"Strictly prohibited." He moved closer, and they kissed.

She asked as she pulled away, "Was that prohibited?"

He took her face in his hands and pulled her closer and kissed her deeply.

She pulled back and said, "Randall, I cannot do anything that might affect your ability to judge this case."

"Anything?"

She giggled, "Yes, anything, you know what I mean."

He sat back and looked away, then looked back, "Sheryl, you may think I do this kind of thing all the time. I don't. You are the first person I have had in my bedroom in years. I'm a bit of a recluse. I work. I come home, and like most Americans, I watch the news. I watch some cop shows. I watch science fiction or superhero movies. Aside from my work life, my lonely life is pretty much like anyone else. I used to have friends I played golf with, then it seemed like everyone wanted a favor from me. I was approached by people who wanted to do me favors and there were always strings. Did you want a favor from me?"

"I was thinking we might share favors."

"As nice as that sounds, I would be remiss if I did."

"No, you'd be a fool if you didn't. Then again, I'm not pushing," she said as she slid back onto the other side of the couch and then stood up. She went and gathered her things and said, "Maybe we should get the treatment started."

"Don't be like that. Sheryl. Sheryl. Um, Sheryl, I'm very much interested in you in that way. I just cannot."

"I get it. Let's do what we gotta do, and then, well, maybe after this whole thing is over."

"Yeah, maybe after this whole thing is over."

Dejected, she got out the peyote and portioned it. She held the treatment in a small spoon and told him to open his mouth. He complied, and she dropped it on his tongue. She said, "Don't swallow. Hold it on your tongue. Let it dissolve. Then, once the parts that dissolve are gone, swallow the rest." She began praying out loud in Navajo. The judge could feel it beginning to work, so after she finished the prayer, he rose from the couch and walked to his bed. He dropped his pants on the floor and then his shirt. He was wearing boxers and a V-neck T-shirt. He climbed under his covers, put his head on his pillow and was asleep. He didn't swallow as the leaves stayed in his mouth. As he slept, he, like Stewart, would swallow the leaves. Sheryl took the glass she had finished, then poured more Pappy almost to the rim. She walked out of the judge's room and knocked on Paco's door. Paco came to the door, "May I help you, Ma'am?"

"Ma'am? Fuck that! Do I look like a ma'am to you?"

"Sorry."

"I just wanted you to know that the judge is asleep already."

"Are you kidding me? He usually takes an hour to fall asleep."

"No, I'm not fucking kidding. He's out like a fucking sack of potatoes."

"Okay, I will monitor him."

She took a sip of the Pappy and then walked to the stairs. She stopped. She thought I should go get the whole bottle. She continued down the stairs and back to the pool room. It was quiet. Stewart was waiting, "Sheryl, are you going to give me some peyote tonight?"

Barnum chimed in, "I don't think that is necessary."

Sheryl responded, "I agree."

Stewart looked at Ashley and grinned. He got up from his chair and said, "Well then, I guess I'll turn in."

One of the judge's workers came over and said, "I'll escort you to your room."

Barnum said, "Why don't you show us all to our rooms? Then you guys can call it a night."

"Thank you, sir. Right this way."

They all followed, and he showed them to their quarters for the night. Barnum, Jett and Reynolds met in the hallway after being shown their rooms.

Barnum started, "Someone needs to be on the lookout overnight. Who is it going to be?"

Ashley answered, "Rock, paper, scissors?"

They engaged in a childish game to conclude that Jett would be watching for the night. Barnum and Reynolds turned in and Jett found a chair to sit on at the top of the stairs. A few minutes later, Stewart dragged a chair out of his room and joined Ashley. They stayed up all night talking about life and the things they had missed.

Chapter Twenty: Don't Judge Me

The judge began dreaming about fishing. He was on a lake with his friend John, whom he hadn't seen in many years. They were in a canoe, and a large wave was coming at them. They began paddling to get away from the wave, and it picked them up and threw them; the judge landed in a chair across from his ex-wife. He was having lunch, and she was the age she was when he met her. The server offered a bottle of wine, and she responded she wasn't old enough to drink. Then, she began to age in front of him. She turned thirty, then forty and then fifty. She wrinkled and shriveled and turned to dust. The judge told the server, I guess it'll just be one glass of wine. Light came gently through a window, and he opened his eyes.

A clock, it's seven, must be morning. No alarm. Did I hear an alarm? No. This must be. Wait, a sheer lace canopy. Cherry wood dresser. Mirror, look in the mirror. No. I'm putting on a robe, okay, arms, female arms. Oh wow, I'm a woman. Slippers, of course, fuzzy slippers. Looking back at the bed, There's a man in the bed. I guess that's my husband. Looking into a dark adjacent room, walking, okay, light switch, bright light, wow, that's bright. Eyes. Adjust eyes. I see the floor.

This is exciting. I seem so conscious. This must be working. Okay, I have seen, whoa, mirror, I'm gorgeous. Who am I? I think I have met this woman. Wait, yeah, that, I, we are, District Circuit Judge in London, Jamie Adams. I met her a few years ago. Yes, I know her. Oh, I cannot see this. She, I'm disrobing. Close my eyes. I cannot close my eyes. I have to see this. This is so inappropriate of me. Wow. Okay, look away. Alright, no more mirror. Shower, fine, shampoo. Soaping arm, oh my, breast. I'm so glad I cannot feel that. Soap smells good. Leg, lovely leg. Foot, other foot, other leg, belly, yikes, wow. Okay, rinsing. I have seen enough. Oh, she's turning the shower off. I have often wondered how women do the towel-on-the-head thing. Now she's drying. I'm invading my favorite British Judge's privacy here. Okay, then back to the mirror. More drying. No more thinking. I'm just going to try not to watch. I cannot. Okay then. Shoulders are dry, arms. Yup, gotta lift up the breast and get underneath. Belly, back, in between the legs, of course, oh foot on the sink, that's a view I didn't expect. Thank you, Jamie. You are well-groomed there, too. Perfect, all dry. Oh, of course, lotion. Let's start with the arms, then the shoulders. Can't miss the breasts. Oh, a bonus: your nipples are erect. Belly, there goes the foot on the sink again. Lotion on the thighs, calves, and ankles. Okay, yeah, the other leg. This is just wrong. How did I get someone I knew? Please stop. Oh, she's not stopping, oh, good she is. No, we're checking to see if the husband was her husband, I don't remember, he is still asleep. Oh good. No more mirrors, I hear moaning. I cannot see anything, my eyes must be closed, good. More moaning, wait, that was almost a scream, muffled scream. Maybe we're done. That was quick. If ten minutes is quick, was it ten minutes? I have no idea how much time is elapsing. Oh God, mirror again. Jamie, you certainly are beautiful. I guess we're done in the loo, so let's go get dressed, shall we? Panties, yes, of course, panties. Those are nice. Pink and light blue with lace. Oh, we have a bra to match. That was fun, I had never put on a bra before. Closet, yeah, a light would help. Noise. What was that? Looking. Looks like my husband is stirring, is he her husband?

"Jamie darling, where are you? Are you done in the loo?"

"In the wardrobe, Paul, it is nearly eight, and I'm running late. The alarm clock failed yet again. Maybe we could find a working clock soon. I have court at ten.

I mustn't be late. Perhaps you'd be a gem. Call Justin and make sure he's privy to my tardiness so he might rush me to my chambers."

"Gladly, my love."

"You are a peach. Should I wear a black skirt or a black skirt?

"Will you be pairing a white blouse with either?"

"How on earth did you ever know?"

"You are adorable, my love. And, just so you know, I heard you in the loo a minute ago. That was a quick one. Next time, do ask for help."

"Dear, you know I'm running late, and you so often belabor the event. With all that lapping you insist on doing. I just needed to shed some stress and be off. Perhaps tomorrow, that dreadful clock will work, and you can take my stress away."

"I'll be off to the market today to fetch a new one should that promise be kept."

"I promise, dear, you know how I love you so."

"Brilliant, then it is a date."

Randall thought, *are you kidding me? Does she have his approval to do that? What kind of relationship is this, and can I get one too? What was with the white blouse and black skirt thing? All I saw were white blouses and black skirts. It must be her uniform or something.*

She walked past the bed, and Paul grabbed her hand and squeezed it. Randall saw Paul lying naked, uncovered on the bed. *Ewww.* She went back into the bathroom and brushed her teeth, and Randall saw her gross morning habits. She put on make-up, brushed it, and dried her hair. She flossed her teeth and drooled onto the sink without wiping it away.

She made her way again, passed the bed and Paul's naked body, out the door and down a short hallway to a cast iron spiral staircase. She descended into a kitchen where a younger version of her dressed in a navy-blue suit and high heels was pouring a cup of coffee into a to-go cup. She handed it to her mother along with a small sack and said, "Good morning, Mum. Your biscuit and egg are wrapped up for your travel. Your coffee is to your liking as usual. I did hope for a minute to chat, but I see that was unavailable. Would you mind if I rode with you to the courts and got a lift to the firm?"

"Sweetie, you are always welcome with me in the car. Justin is probably outside right now."

"He is. I took him a cup of coffee, too. Shall we go then?"

"Yes, let's be off."

They walked out of the kitchen to an open foyer to a large oak door, then down some stairs to a circle drive off a busy street.

Nice, a Rolls. She does travel in style.

Justin met them at the rear door of the Rolls Royce limousine. He opened the door, and they climbed in. He closed the door behind them and drove off.

"So, darling, what did you want to chat about?"

"Well, Mum, Peter Ballanger has asked me for a date. You know him, right? He's the son of that land baron, Roger Ballanger. He's been pursuing me for weeks now. I have put him off time and time again, but he is persistent. He would like to take me to Covent Garden. That place is delightful, but I don't feel it appropriate as I have little interest in him."

"The Ballanger's are a pretentious lot. What happened to that stud Wallace McDermott you were seeing?"

"Oh, the Irishman? He was incorrigible. Stud in bed, yes, mummy, but a halfwit in conversation. He looked good on my arm but didn't understand proper English. The man never had a tea, for God's sake."

"Oh, my, that is news to me. Best you moved along from that train wreck. You silly girl. Have you seen

Paul? I cannot carry on a conversation with that sack of muscle, either. I keep him nearby just for the fun of it all, and most of the time, he does not know how to satisfy me. I do love his body, though."

"Is that why you haven't married?"

"Oh dear, I have no intentions of marrying him. I simply call him my husband to make him feel desired. I thought you were aware it is to maintain decorum. I do love an Irishman, though. For some reason, this morning, I had a thought about an Irishman I met some years back, Randall Callahan. While I was in the shower, he seemed to have entered my head. It was so very strong. Like he was right there with me."

"Tell me about this Callahan fellow."

"There is not much to say. We met at a conference in New York City. I was there while he was one of the keynote speakers. He was from Chicago, I believe. He was a well-dressed man, but that didn't matter. He was rugged, soft-spoken, but boisterous at the same time. His smile is so very fetching. He has kind eyes and a lovely laugh. We had a drink together. Paul interrupted us, and so it came to an abrupt closure. I wanted to ring him up but felt it was inappropriate, given my status with Paul. It is odd today, I feel like he is with me. Even now. I must say it is overwhelming."

"That is odd, Mum. When was this?"

"Oh, my, it could have been five years ago."

"No, it was seven. We did more than just have a drink. We went for a walk in Central Park. You said you had never been to Central Park. We had lunch together, and we spent most of that October day together. In the evening, we did meet up with Paul. He had been at the gym all day while you and I skipped some of the breakout rooms to break out on our own. I haven't forgotten our time together; in fact, I had always had a hope we would meet again. I never in my wildest dreams thought it would be this way."

"No, no, it was seven years ago. My memories are coming back. We didn't just have a drink. No, we went for lunch in New York and a walk in Central Park. He was such a beautiful man. Paul was at the gym as usual, so I had met Randall for the rest of my life. We both knew it would not amount to anything as we lived so far apart. Dear, I'm saddened by these thoughts. Sweet as they may be, they sadden me."

"Sorry, Mum, perhaps you should look this Randall Callahan up?"

"I may."

"This is your stop, Mum. Don't cry. Here, take a tissue, I have a whole packet in my bag."

"I have not cried for him in years. We seemed so right together. I must go."

Justin opened the door on a one-way street to the sidewalk, and Jamie carefully stepped out. She was met by her assistant, who was holding an umbrella to protect her from London's misty morning outside a grand Portland stone archway of the courthouse. On either side of the door were signs that read "Central Criminal Court." On top of the sixty-seven-foot-high dome, a 12-foot gold leaf statue was placed of a "lady of justice" holding a sword in one hand and the scales of justice in the other; she is not, as is conventional with such figures, blindfolded. Over the main entrance to the building, figures were placed representing fortitude, the recording angel and truth, along with the carved inscription, "defend the children of the poor and punish the wrongdoer." It was nine-thirty and Jamie had but thirty minutes to be prepared for the day.

This courthouse is magnificent. The open spaces and the architecture are stunning. *Wait, why am I thinking about that? Did you hear what she just said about you, Randall? I never realized she felt that way. What do I do with this? Oh, lovely chambers. Very*

British Judgelike. I like how her side door goes out to her courtroom. I wonder what we have on the docket. Shh, she's talking.

"Anne, will you do me a stand-up? I'm looking for anything you can get on a judge in Chicago, Illinois, USA. His name is Randall Callahan. Find out the marital status, how close he might be to retirement, his net worth and well, whatever the hell he might be interested in."

"Certainly, Mum, I will ask Bert to do some digging," Anne responded.

"No, I'm not looking for official details. Well, yeah, ask Bert, but ask him to see me before he starts digging," the judge asked.

What the hell? I should call her when I wake up. Damn, but how will I explain how I know about her. This is weird and really cool. Now what. What's on our plate for today? I wonder if I'll influence her decisions.

"Anne, can you come in here please," Jamie ordered.

Anne came through the door. Jamie motioned for her to sit in the chair in front of her.

"According to my calendar, we have council meetings at ten, then again at one. Are there any changes?" Jamie asked.

Sitting down, Anne continued, "No, Mum. These are settlement meetings, plea bargaining in the first and sentencing in the second."

Jamie looked out the window as Anne was talking as if she wasn't there, then said, "Is that all we have today?"

Anne was puzzled. The judge is usually attentive, "Yes, it is light."

Jamie smiled like a schoolgirl, "Well then, what time is it in Chicago?"

Anne fumbled for her phone. She tapped a few things, then answered, "I believe it is three in the morning."

Snapping her finger in a swooping motion in front of her, she said, "Oh drat, far too early to ring up Callahan. Wouldn't that be a surprise for him?"

Anne said, surprised, "Sorry, mum, is that your plan?"

Jamie poised to speak, then stopped. Her eyes went to the upper corner as she tilted her head, smiled and then said, "I'm not sure yet, but that man has definitely been on my mind."

Anne was confused, so she asked, "Is there anything else, mum?"

Jamie sat in silence for almost a minute, looking at Anne. She looked out the window. Got up from her chair and went to the window. Anne watched her as she paced, then asked again, "Mum, is there anything else I could do for you?"

The judge stopped. She crossed her arms on her chest, sighed and said, "No miss, you go on now."

Anne left the room. Jamie sat back down at her desk, opened the file in front of her, and began preparing for her meeting in less than twelve minutes.

A plea bargain. Looks like the perp robbed a sixty-three-year-old lady and beat her to death. Nice guy. His lawyer is asking for manslaughter for a guilty plea. It looks like he was on PCP at the time, and they have tried temporary insanity to no avail. Now, he has remorse and wants a light sentence. That's a tough one, Jamie. I think I would deny it. I think this should be tried, and let the jury decide.

Jamie sat back and looked out the window on her right. She was thinking about many cases like this. She thought about those who were given leniency and if they became repeat offenders.

"Mum, the counselors are here. Shall I show them in?"

"Yes, miss, I'm ready."

She stood up and met the two lawyers and the client at the door. The accused was handcuffed with his hands behind his back. She guided them to the conference table, where she took one side, and the rest took the other. A constable accompanied them, as did the court bailiff. The constable and the bailiff took seats at the back of the room, and the perpetrator took the center seat between both lawyers.

"Gentlemen, this is a formal meeting to determine a plea. I will be asking a few questions. I would like concise answers, no stories unless I ask for stories and only facts. I will ask the accused directly and expect him to answer directly without interaction from your counselor. Is that clear?"

They all nodded.

"Okay, we don't have a court reporter present because someone didn't ask for one." She looked at the accused, "Sir, do you wish to have these proceedings reported? Sorry, I mean recorded?"

He looked at his counselor; he shook his head. Then said, "No, your honor."

"Okay, this is for your counselor. Your name is St. James, am I correct?"

"Yes, ma'am."

"Mister St. James, that implies you expect these proceedings to go your way, and not hearing no is not your expectation. I do hope for your client's sake you have calculated correctly. Now, Mister Spangler, you are the prosecutor, correct?"

"That is correct, your honor."

"Brilliant, now allow me to introduce you to my bailiff. This is Bull. John Bull, if you are taking notes. Next to him is Constable Wilson. Both of these fellows are here to keep order. I assume everyone will stay civil. Is that correct?"

They nodded.

"I will need vocal answers for that question, as nodding is insufficient."

They all spoke, "Yes."

Keep it up, Jamie. You are doing very well. I love your style.

She smiled for no reason and looked away. The lawyers didn't understand her sudden smile. "Now, Mister Floyd, you have been charged with armed robbery, resisting arrest, failure to adhere, assault on a constable with the intent to kill, assault and battery and murder. Which of these will you be pleading guilty to?"

Mister St. James began speaking, "Your honor, if I may."

She interrupted him, "I do love how these meetings get dragged out by defense attorneys. At the onset, Mister St. James, I insisted that your client answer the questions, and it would please the court if he answered the questions alone."

"Well, your honor, I don't believe I'm guilty of any of these crimes. I was not even on that street that night."

"Are you kidding me? Constable, remove the accused."

They all got up.

"No, the rest of you stay here."

The constable escorted the accused out of the room and down the hall to a bench and sat him down. Then he muttered to himself, "Dumb shit."

"Gentlemen, I expected this. Mister St. James, your client agreed already to be guilty of every charge except murder. You have lost the insanity case, and now, what is his deal? Does he not know the seriousness of this meeting? Don't waste my time any longer. This case goes to trial. Good day, gentlemen."

Whoa, Jamie, that was fantastic. Just like I would have handled it, it's no wonder we share this mind. Bring on the next session.

Jamie pressed the call button on her phone, "Anne, any word from Bert?"

"No, Mum. Not yet. I did get you a number, but it's not even three thirty in the morning there."

"Thank you. No interruptions until Bert comes or calls."

Jamie stood up and walked to the window. She looked down at the street and watched the two counselors talking, then separated them and walked in different directions. She watched the different cars on the street, the cabs, and the people walking. The rain had stopped, and the sky was blue. She looked up to see a cloud-free sky.

She pressed the call button again, "Anne, I will be heading out. I feel a need to capture some air. Care to walk to Old Smithfield Gardens with? Call ahead to Gascon to reserve a table for two at 11:30."

"Yes, mum, I would be delighted. Thank you for your generosity."

"It will be my pleasure. We don't spend enough time together; you can tell me all about your recent holiday. Oh, and if Bert can get me the information I desire, then make a spot for him as well."

"I will."

Sitting at her desk she picked up a picture frame of her and Paul. There was a picture of the two of them in the Alps. There was a picture of them in Paris and in Germany. There was a picture of her, Paul, her daughter and her son. She thought about the times she took Paul with her on holiday. How, over the last seven years, he was nothing more than her coat tail. She set the picture down, rested her chin in the palms of her hands, closed her eyes and wept. She whispered to herself, "I just want someone who understands me.

Someone to confide in, to converse with, someone who gets me."

I understand, Jamie. That's what I have wanted since my wife died. We got divorced, but it seemed like a death to me. It is too bad we have this pond between us. Damn, I almost messed up with Sheryl last night. Bert met the two ladies at the restaurant, sat down, and Jamie offered him the drink menu. The server arrived.

She asked, "May I fetch you a beverage, sir?"

"A Theakston would be nice."

"Right away. Ladies, are you well?"

Jamie answered, "We are."

The server scampered away. Bert looked at Jamie and said, "I have everything I could find on your mystery man and mum. He is no longer a mystery. He is a fifth-generation colonialist, a second-generation judge. He had been married for a decade; she left him for the prosecuting attorney. He had hired a private dick to follow her, and so she got nothing from him. That didn't matter, though she was well off before they came together. They had two children. He won custody of them both and dedicated his life to making sure they were great people. His son is a partner in a technology company in California, and his daughter is a doctor and the wife of a doctor in Chicago. Both of the kids have been out of the house for several years, and he has not had a female in his life. He has been waiting for it for twenty years. He is a federal judge. He lives alone and has hired some twelve people to help maintain his mansion. Rumors say he only needs two of them. He keeps the rest on the staff because their families have served his family for generations. He is a tough judge but fair and kind to everyone. How was that?"

"Now I need a relationship counselor. Maybe this feeling will subside. I need another drink," Jamie said

"Judge, may I remind you that you still have that other meeting this afternoon," Anne said.

"Postpone it. I think I need to think. I'm not getting younger. Something has come over me, and I need time to sort things out."

This is not good. I should not be having this effect on her. This is not fair. I cannot have a relationship with someone so far away. If she calls, I will have to ignore the call. I cannot wait, and then she will think bad of me. I don't want that either. I wish I could see her face. I feel so distraught. I hope I wake up soon.

Judge Randall Callahan didn't wake up soon. He continued watching Jamie's day, and then she arrived home. She had been thinking of him all day, even close to calling him, and then she saw Paul.

"Paul, we need to talk," Jamie said.

Paul had seen this day for over five years. He was a stable boy when she plucked him from the life of a ranch hand. He trained her to ride and helped her break her horse. He had loved her in every way he could but knew she didn't feel the same way about him. Even though he was short on college degrees, he could see the angst in her eyes. He knew that his time with her was coming to an end that very morning. He saw it in her face when she would not look his way but for a second. She left without kissing him goodbye, and she didn't touch him in the morning.

"Yes, dear, I'm at your service."

"You see, Paul, that's it."

Shit, don't do this, Jamie, not because of me. We haven't talked for what, eight years.

"Paul, you know I like you, and in so many ways, I love you."

"Where are you going with this, Jamie, darling?"

"Paul, I will always admire you. I woke up this morning."

No, Jamie, don't.

"When I woke up this morning, I saw you in bed, but I felt so alone. I want so much more from a relationship than what we have. I know you do, too. Our future together, well, there really was never a long-term future."

Oh, maybe this isn't all about me. Good.

"You met someone else, did you, did you meet someone else? Was I not satisfying you? I could try harder."

"Paul, you are groveling. That is unbecoming of such a man. I'm taking off tomorrow. I will be gone for a few weeks. I will let the staff know when I will be back. Please be moved out before I return. I have made arrangements for you to have an apartment on the East side of London. It is near the water. You will like that. I have paid the rent for a year. I found your work. There are stables nearby, you will recover. It is a nice place. You will like it. Tonight, you have a room at the Treehouse. Justin is waiting for you in the limousine. He will take you to the hotel. Then tomorrow he will bring you back to collect your belongings. He will make arrangements to have your items sent to your new place. Now go! I wish you well."

"That's it? No discussion?"

"No, no discussion: I have made up my mind, and it will not be altered. Be on your way now!"

Paul wanted to throw things. He wanted to act up, but that was not his style. He took his phone and a bag filled with necessities, and he left. He met Justin at the limousine. He opened his own door, and Justin spoke, "Sir, I'm sorry for your situation, but I have been instructed to close the enclosure between you and me and not converse. I will tell you that all of the joint accounts you were attached to have been closed in your name. Mum has ordered you a new debit card; you have some pounds in an envelope in a bag in the bonnet. You start your new job next Monday, and the information about it is also enclosed in the bag. You can choose to follow this protocol or do your own thing, but if I were you, I would take on the gifts that Mum has given you. You will be well cared for if you accept. There is a document for your signature. It has been drawn up; it, too, is in the bonnet. You will have three days to sign it and contact me for retrieval. If you don't sign it, then you lose all of the benefits except the cash in the bag. Do you understand?"

"Justin, I'm stunned."

"I'm sorry, sir, I have been instructed to ask you one question and then close the window. Do you understand what I just told you?"

"Yes, but..."

The window went up, and Justin put the vehicle in gear and drove to the hotel. He parked at the turnaround of the hotel and waited for Paul to exit the limousine and retrieve the bag from the trunk. Paul sat with a sad face, realizing seven years of his life had just come to an abrupt end. He heard the click of the door lock, reached for the handle and stepped out. He went around to the rear of the car and lifted the lid to the trunk. He took the two items out, closed the trunk, and the Rolls drove away. Justin looked in the rearview mirror as he was leaving and saw a stunned Paul. He fixed his eyes forward and continued his drive back to the judge's home.

"I would like to book a flight from London to O'Hare in Chicago. I need a hotel near downtown, and I need to leave as soon as possible. Come on, Anne, I know it's late. You'll be bonused. You will need to postpone all of my meetings unless I can video conference. I'm packing, and Justin will be taking me to the airport as soon as you can get me the details. Do airlines still have the Concorde?"

What is she doing? That's a suitcase. Right, Captain Obvious.

"Mum, the Concorde flights ended in the eighties."

"Really? They were very fast."

Did you not hear? She's coming here.

"Apparently, they were too loud and inefficient. The jets closed the speed gap. Sorry, Mum, but nine hours will have to do. I have you booked to leave in two hours. Justin has your itinerary and will drop you at the gate. He will be there in seventeen minutes, according to the GPS monitor. You will have a driver in Chicago. He will be your chauffeur for the duration. His name is Duane. We have you booked at the Plaza de Chic. Your security detail will be flying with you as well."

"Anne, I don't require a security detail."

"Mum, it is standard court system protocol. Parliament requires it as of late with all the civil unrest happening in the colonies these days."

"Right. Yes, Chicago does indeed have a criminal element and blemish on the name. I do hope I can extract Randall from that deprived place."

"Mum, have you considered he is not a stable boy? He is a staunch judicial presence in the federal government of the United States. I would say he is likely an immovable statue."

"Naysayer, no time would be better for him than now. I will get my way."

"Yes, mum, you always do."

"Oh, Anne, Justin is here, cheerio."

"Cheerio mum, Godspeed."

I cannot stop her. I'm asleep. Wake up, wake up, wake up. Shit. She wants me to move to London. What about her moving here? She hasn't seen my home yet.

Jamie boarded the plane and settled into her seat. The security detail sat nearby. She closed her eyes and fell asleep.

Randall began dreaming his own dreams and lost contact with Jamie.

Chapter Twenty-One: The Eagle Has Landed

Randall Callahan had slept for eighteen hours, he woke up and looked at the clock; it was two in the afternoon. He leapt from his bed, ran into the shower, he quickly shaved, showered, dressed and exited his room.

He was met by agent Barnum. “Your honor, we must speak.”

“No time. Jamie will be here in an hour.”

“I’m sorry, sir, what?”

“I don’t have time to talk. I must get to the airport. Jamie will be here in less than an hour.”

“Again, your honor, not following.”

“It is no concern of yours. I must get to the airport,” he said as he was making his way towards the front door.

“Sir, can I ask, did the peyote work?”

“Barnum, ride with me. Have Reynolds follow and have him give you a ride back. I’ll tell you in the car.”

“Yes, sir. Can you…” The judge was out the door and into the back seat of his limousine. “Oh, I guess not. I’ll call him from the car.”

“You know where you’re going, right?”

His chauffeur said, “Yes, your honor, British Airways arrivals.”

“Perfect, we have about an hour; how will we do.”

“We should be fine.”

“Great.”

Barnum asked, “Your honor, can I ask, what is this about?”

“You asked if the peyote worked. I can unequivocally say yes, it did. Seven years ago, I went to a conference in New York. I met a judge from

London. Her name is Jamie Adams. We had a lovely day together. Not a day has gone by that I haven't thought about her. I never thought that she felt the same way as me and with our differences in locale, I assumed we would never be together. I went to sleep last night, had my own dreams for a while, and then she woke up, and I was in her head. I could see what she saw. I could taste what she tasted. I could smell the same things as her. I was in some way communicating with her, and she decided to hop on a plane and come to Chicago at that moment. Jamie Adams is set to arrive at O'Hare Airport in an hour. Then there's customs and baggage claim. I think I have less than two hours to meet her."

"Sir, how will you explain why you are there?"

"I will explain what happened, and better yet, if this case is to continue, we will ask her to try the peyote as well. I'm hoping she sees me."

"Your honor, I'm. Well, I don't know what to say. This is indeed a strange turn of events."

"With all due respect, Agent Barnum, your opinion in the matter is unnecessary. I have an old flame to connect with if you will. I have some, well, a lot of catching up to do, and if you don't mind, your commentary will not be accepted."

"Okay, your honor. So, I suppose you will agree to Stewart's testimony?"

"Yes, yes, I will. It is better than an eyewitness as he not only was there but could see everything that Mr. Palumbo did. I will also want the jurors to agree to the process, and if they don't, we will find jurors who will. I want Palumbo to go down."

"Sir, please, we are after Torino."

"Oh, that's right. I got so excited by this whole thing. Right, we're using Palumbo to get to Torino. Indeed, when the jurors know that Stewart is telling the truth, there will be no option for Palumbo but to turn on Torino. I suggest we give him two options. One before trial that says he gets witsec and another that he goes to jail with Torino."

"You honor, he is new to this game. I believe he will take witsec."

"Then maybe we will not have to employ Ms. Benally to process the jurors."

"That should expedite things. Sir, if it's okay with you, I can get out here and just have Reynolds pick me up. He's only five minutes behind us."

"Certainly, driver, please pull over."

"Barnum, go get 'em. This is an exciting case. You will certainly get an attaboy for this one, probably a promotion and who knows where this will take you.

Good job."

He opened the door to the sidewalk, "Thank you, sir, for coming from you. That means a lot."

"Wait, I'll be putting in a good word for you and Reynolds. You both deserve commendations, no go, you're holding things up," he said with a big smile.

It was the first time he had ever seen Judge Callahan smile. He climbed out of the limo and onto the sidewalk. He took a big, deep breath and rested his shoulders. He looked in both directions. No one was nearby, and no one could see him. He humped up, screamed, "Yeah!" then dropped to one knee and did a hockey pump. He stood back up, elated, smiling and relieved. Reynolds arrived three minutes later. Barnum told him everything.

The judge made a few calls and found out who the transport company would be for Jamie. He found out which hotel she was staying in and where she would meet her limousine driver. He instructed his driver to pull up to the same parking lot. They found the driver and were able to move the judge's limousine in front of Jamie's. They parked. Two men appeared at the limousine. Jack, the driver, opened the back door, and the judge emerged. He addressed the men, "Hi, guys.

Dan, how's your wife been?"

"She's well, thank you, your honor. The baby is almost three months now."

"Is he keeping you up all night?"

"Oh, no, Erin takes care of him. She's such a trooper."

"You got my gift, right?"

"We did, thank you, sir. Erin is a little slow on the thank you letters, sorry."

"No need. I know you are very busy. Dave, how are you?"

"Your honor, I'm well."

"Good, anything new with you?"

"Not much. I do appreciate you calling on me for this extra job."

"Well, son, it isn't much of a job. I need you and Dan to scout out a passenger coming in on British Airways. Her name is Jamie Adams. I want you to go ahead and find out when the plane lands, where the baggage claim is and then Dan, I want you to be at the baggage claim and walk out that door," he pointed to the exit just outside of arriving flights, "so we... no, I can see when she arrives. I want to be standing outside this limo when she walks out. We'll tell her security detail to ride along with you. Got it, boys?"

"Yes, your honor," they said in unison.

Randall got back into the limousine and waited. He was nervous, excited and sweating. He resisted the urge to repeat his grade school habit of biting his fingernails. His leg swayed, and his fingers tapped on the armrest. His eyes were fixed on the door.

Dave reported to Jack, "Jack, Dave here. The plane is late. It is about an hour late. Will you tell the judge, please?"

"I will." He turned back to the judge and said, "Your honor, we have some news on Judge Adams. It seems the plane is running about an hour behind. That means it will not be here for two hours. What would you like me to do?"

"Let me think for a minute." He sat and pondered. A few minutes later, he said, "Driver, what's your name?"

"I'm sorry, sir. I should have."

Interrupting, "No apologies necessary, I was remiss in asking you."

"Sir, its Jack."

"How long have you worked for the government?"

"Sir, I'm a private contractor. I work for Studio Limousines."

"Studio Limousines? Who called you?"

"Sir, I'm unaware of the identity of the person who contacted us. Apparently, I was the only limousine in the area that could meet your request."

"I see, thank you, Jack, for your perseverance. This is my first experience with this sort of thing. What advice would you give me?"

"Well, sir, this is the most romantic thing I have ever witnessed. I could not give you advice beyond what you have already done."

"Stop. Stop blowing smoke up my ass. Come on, man to man. What do you think? It looks like we have an hour or two, you hungry?"

"Excuse me, sir?"

"Are you hungry? Maybe we lock the limo up and go inside and see if we can get a dog or a burger or something. You up for that?"

"Well, yes, your honor. I will contact the others; I have been instructed to stay with you and make sure your security detail is with you at all times."

"Since when?"

"Umm, I'm not sure, your honor. I understand there is an eminent threat on your life."

"My life? Since when, oh yeah, you won't know that either. Okay, call the guys, I'll wait."

The FBI agents, Sheryl and Stewart, were loaded into black GMC Yukons, and they left the judge's house. An hour or so later, they arrived at a small airport and drove out to the tarmac. There was a jet waiting. Jett recognized her jet immediately. Everyone climbed in, and she took over as the flight attendant until Gretchen came in. Gretchen had been Ashley's trainer, and she had authority over the FBI air fleet attendants. Gretchen got up in Ashley's face and said, "I'm taking this flight, honey. You are my passenger. If I need you, I'll ask. For now, enjoy the ride."

Ashley turned away from Gretchen and sat next to Stewart. Stewart looked at her and said, "If you'd like, I could move, and you could have the window seat."

She barked, "Stop being a pussy. I'm not sure I like what Sheryl has done to you; it is almost like she castrated you."

He was shocked. He turned away from her and to the window. He watched as the ground crew loaded the jet. He was hurt. He had nothing to say. She was right.

Sheryl sat across from Ashley. She was reading a magazine. Westall took the window seat next to Sheryl. The rest of the plane was filled with familiar FBI agents. There were several seats empty. The door was still open, and Sheryl looked up as they heard a noise out on the tarmac. Reynolds and Barnum were in the front seats, so they got up and went out to meet the passengers. The first on the plane was Kelsey, then Oscar, then Tony, Johnnie and finally four US Marshalls. Oscar, Tony and Johnnie were hand and ankle-cuffed, but Kelsey was not. The handcuffs had six inches of chain between the wrists. The Marshalls sat each prisoner in a seat and rearranged the handcuffs. They wrapped one side of each cuff through the armrest and then back on the other wrist. This gave them a slight range of movement. Then they detached one side of the ankle cuffs, strung them through the frame of the seat and back on the ankle.

Kelsey was seated out of sight of the other criminals and surrounded by FBI agents. Agent Harmon sat next to her. They were behind Stewart and Sheryl. Stewart could see her.

The door on the jet closed, and it taxied to the runway. Stewart braced himself as usual, and then, in seconds, the plane was in the air. Gretchen brought a drink cart by and offered Ashley a soft drink and Stewart anything. He took an Ultra. Before he could finish it, the jet touched down. It taxied to a hangar and sat. The door opened, and several of the FBI agents disembarked. They left the hangar and went out onto the tarmac through a single standard-sized door.

Ashley had gotten out of her seat and was outside the jet. She told Stewart and Sheryl to stay put until they were asked to get off. Sheryl had found a book to read and was absorbed in the story. Stewart closed his eyes and fell asleep.

When they landed, it was daytime, and when Ashley woke Stewart up, the sun had set, and night had fallen. Stewart and Sheryl joined Ashley and Gregg as they exited the hangar and boarded a helicopter. They lifted off, and it revealed a place neither was familiar with.

The chopper rose several thousand feet and cruised for no more than twenty minutes, then put down on a building in a downtown area of what seemed like a small city. They left the chopper on the roof and went down some stairs into a hallway through a door and into a room that felt kind of like a restaurant. There was a bar on one wall connected in an "L" shape to a kitchen counter on an adjacent wall that held the door to the roof. There was a double door that had steamed-up windows. It appeared to be the kitchen. Next to the doors were self-serve glass doors with beverages and ready-to-eat cold snacks. Behind the bar was a generous stock of alcoholic beverages and glassware. Oak cabinet doors separated the glass coolers and the bourbon wall behind the bar. Every imaginable bourbon bottle was present, as well as a few other types of spirits. At the far end of the bar was another door that housed some of America's best wines.

The seating areas were more than comfortable. Round, square and rectangular tables of all sizes filled the space with barrel-type seating. On one wall opposite the kitchen were two doors. One door at either end, and in the middle were several large couches with associated coffee tables and side tables. This part of the room resembled a coffee shop or a living room.

Sheryl and Stewart were met by a woman in her mid-thirties with dark black hair and bright red highlights. She had a piercing in her eyebrow, and she wore black eyeshadow. She extended her hand to introduce herself to Sheryl, and Sheryl noticed her black fingernails. She accepted as she said, "I'm Melissa. I'm the host of this establishment, which we would like to call the FBI South Hotel. There are five such places in the country. Y'all will be waiting here until the trial starts. I'll show you to your rooms individually. Or, if you like, I will take you together, your choice."

Sheryl said, "What the fuck, yeah, we can go together. Don't separate us."

Melissa responded, "You do want separate rooms, don't you? I thought..."

Interrupting, Sheryl said, "Fuck yeah, he's, my brother."

"Right, okay, right this way," she said, leading them to the door on the left wall.

They exited the restaurant area and entered a hallway that immediately came to a wall. They then turned left. She was walking in front of them and turning and talking every few steps.

"The area we are entering is the guest living quarters. There are more than thirty rooms with varying accommodations. The coolest thing about the rooms is they are adorned with decorations from FBI seizures over the years. Each room has its own theme. One of the rooms, not either of yours, has Al Capone's bedroom set in it. It is fantastic. I'm sorry, I cannot show that one to you. Maybe if you ask nicely, Barnum will show you. He gets that room. Did you know Barnum is a big shot now? Y'all have made him a Rockstar. He was a *nobody* until this case, and Miss Sheryl, you catapulted that dude to superstardom. I wonder if he can handle the pressure."

They arrived at Sheryl's room. The door had a sign on the wall that read "Bonnie's room."

Melissa opened the door and spoke, "Although the furnishings in this room didn't actually belong to Bonnie Elizabeth Parker, they do come from the period when she and Clyde Barrow did their damage across the country. They mostly stayed in shacks and people's homes while they were on the run. Her notorious behavior is felt in the room. Not really."

The walls were reclaimed barn wood to a chair rail and flowered 1920s-looking wallpaper above. The lighting was Tiffany-style lamps on tables and sconces on the walls, four lamps in all. The poster bed had a lace canopy and was French Provincial, painted antique white with antique brass handles on the side tables. There was a massive, knitted rug underfoot and partially under the bed. There was an armoire against a wall that was closed and a dresser next to it all matching, with a large flat-screened television sitting atop it. There was a door off to the left that led to a private bathroom.

"Sheryl, the furnishings in this room actually come from a furniture store in Knoxville, Tennessee, that was a front for illegal whiskey distribution during prohibition. All the assets were seized, and most were sold. Both the Bonnie and the Clyde rooms adorn these decorations. You will find that the armoire and dresser are filled with clothing that will not only meet your size but also your style. We employ a personal concierge to address all of our guests' needs. They have studied both you and Stewart and have supplied you with items I'm sure you'll love. You will get to keep everything as all the rest of your belongings in Arizona have since been stored. I apologize that we will not be able to retrieve them until this entire matter is concluded."

Sheryl went into the room and closed the door behind her. Melissa waved her hand forward, and they walked to a room labeled "Scarface." She opened the door, revealing a look similar to the Miami Vice television show. One wall was covered with bamboo halves, while another had a mural of a beach, and the other two were painted Robin egg blue. The furnishings were rattan, and the motif was a beach with shells and a sand-colored floor. The ceiling had a sky painting with clouds and seagulls. Stewart was pleased with the choice for him until he noticed there was not a door to a bathroom, "Where's the bathroom?"

"I'm sorry, Stewart, some of the rooms don't have private bathrooms. All of the ladies' rooms do, but the men's quarters don't. At least you have a private room. You will notice your room has all of the newest game counsels and many games for you to occupy yourself with. We have also included a desktop computer with limited internet access. You cannot email anyone as it leaves a trial. We cannot let anyone know where you are as you may end up in witness protection after this ordeal ends. You can, however, enjoy surfing the web. We know you like porn, so feel free to be the pervert you were before we met you."

He looked at her and squinted in displeasure, "Hey, I'm not judging. Look at me; I have my quirks. Just a warning that stuff will rot your brain. Your bathroom is a shared bathroom, sorry. You and the agents all use the same room. Well, not Barnum or Reynolds, they have their own bathrooms since they are rock stars. It's nice; there are private showers and stalls, and it's more like a country club than a barrack. When you leave the room, continue to your left. It's marked Men's room. Oh, and another thing I forgot to tell Sheryl is that there are cameras in every room. They are there in case something happens. You know, for your protection. No one will be watching; they are there to record in case we need the video. So, go ahead and whack away if you need to. Oh, I forgot to tell your sister that there are no visitors in your rooms. Remember to tell her, please."

Stewart responded, "Cameras that no one is watching and no visitors, but I can masturbate as much I feel the need to. That is terrific; maybe I'll get started right now. Can you excuse me?"

She gave him an odd look and then left him alone. He sat on the edge of the bed and dangled his feet. He looked around the room and took it in like it was a resort hotel room. He was pleased. He stood up and checked his armoire. He opened the doors and revealed two black suits. One navy jacket, several pressed white shirts and several dress slacks in an assortment of colors. There were black and brown shoes appropriate for the suits and some casual shoes and sneakers. He opened his top dresser drawer to find his brand of underwear, dark and white socks. He opened the second drawer to find jeans and t-shirts of a multitude of colors and a few hooded sweatshirts. I wonder how long we'll be here. I'm hungry.

He found a suitable change of clothes, changed and went back to the restaurant area. When he arrived, everyone from the plane was in attendance except Tony, Johnnie, Oscar and Kelsey. Stewart went to the table where his sister and Ashley were sitting. Ashley was drinking iced tea, and Sheryl was drinking an Ultra. Reynolds met Stewart at the table and said, "Stew, you thirsty?"

"Yes, I'm."

"Okay, let me show you how this place works. Follow me."

He walked over to the counter, down to an opening and went behind the counter. He started to explain, "These doors lead to the kitchen area. Every day, Melissa and her crew will put together a menu. Some of the things don't change from day to day. Either she or another girl, I forget her name, will take your order and they will deliver it to your table. This first glass door is frozen stuff. It's where the ice is kept if you want some in a drink. The second door is cold drinks like pop or beer. The third door is stocked with fruits and cut vegetables; we eat healthy shit here, so can you. In this section, you'll find melon and cherries or pineapple. Oh, plus sandwiches. There are dollar roll sandwiches. She even has pimento cheese sandwiches like down in Savannah. We got it all. Melissa has a theme each day for dinner. What's today? Friday, right?"

"I seriously have no idea."

"Yeah, it is Friday. I think tonight is seafood and fish. She used to be a good Catholic girl and still respects the Friday, no meat thing. Anyway, check out this bar. Wholly cow, we have every imaginable bourbon in the world and a few others. Isn't that odd?"

"The only reason I could think is that we're in Louisville, Kentucky," said Stewart.

"Well, wherever we are, it's bourbon country."

"Yes, it is, and I think I'll have some Wild Turkey."

"Sounds good, enjoy. I'm on duty," Phil responded.

"When are you not on duty?"

"Hmm, well, when we leave here, I guess."

"That sucks."

"It does. Stewart, we are on high alert right now. We have to be ready for anything. Even though no one knows where we are, we cannot expect that to remain. Fortunately, this place, like the other five the FBI has, has never been compromised. We have an unblemished reputation, and I'm not one to tempt fate, but this is one of the six safest places in this country."

Stewart poured a tall glass of Wild Turkey 101 and added a handful of ice. He went back, and he came by the bar and by the counter and opened the door to the sandwiches. He took out one with a label marked "Turkey and Swiss." He followed Reynolds over to Ashley and Sheryl and put his sandwich down. Then he asked, "Ladies, while I'm up, would you like something? Should I go to the kitchen and place an order for you? I could grab the menu?"

Sheryl answered, "Thank you, Stewart. No, I have an order for shrimp, scallops, and new potatoes with asparagus."

Ashley answered, "That's sweet. Do not sit down; enjoy your sandwich."

Stewart responded, "I may put this back and get what she's having. That sounds fantastic."

Ashley said, "Do it."

He turned around and carried the sandwich back to the cooler. Put it back and met Melissa on her way out the kitchen door, "Can I get you something, Mister Samuelson?"

"I'd like the seafood special."

"Do you want the Lobster and the scallops or the Lobster and shrimp combo, or the Shrimp and scallop combo? Or, one more, all three."

"Well, if I can have all three, I'll take all three."

"Fine, new potatoes, rice, Fettuccini Alfredo or garlic mashed potatoes?"

"Well, Fett, please."

"Perfect, Asparagus, broccoli, snow peas and mushrooms or creamed spinach?"

"How about the spinach and the asparagus."

"You got it, one more thing. Salad; garden or Caesar?"

"Caesar, no croutons, please."

"Coming right up." She turned around and went back into the kitchen, out of sight.

Stewart sat down with his drink and toasted, "To life, with all its mysteries, with all the ups and downs, with all the uncertainties, may it bring us joy and may the people we share it with be filled with love." The three took a sip of their drink and put the glasses down on the table. Then Stewart said, "One more thing. Thank you to both of you for bringing back my lost smile, for bringing me my heart, for bringing me happiness and joy and for being here with me."

Sheryl looked at him and said, "What the actual fuck? Who the hell took over my brother's body? Whoever did, well, fuck them, what the fuck?"

Ashley looked at Sheryl and said, "You turned him into a pussy. He was an asshat before now he's a fucking pussy. I kind of like how much he cares, but he's over the top a pussy."

Stewart said, looking right at her, "Hello. I'm right here."

"I know dipshit. I think your sister should reverse part of this compassionate Stewart. Dial the fucker back a bit."

"Shut the fuck up, I like it. Finally, my brother is a man. If you don't like it hit the bricks bitch."

"Sheryl, there's no need for that. Ashley and I have just started to get reacquainted. Give us some time."

"Fine. I need another drink anyway. Anyone since I'm going?"

Ashley looked at her watch. It was 7:35, and she said, "Pour me one of what Stewart is drinking. Smells like one oh one."

Stewart looked at her, cocked his head and then said, "How'd you know?"

"Naïve, I saw you pour it. Wow."

"Sheryl, bring her some peyote too. She needs to soften those edges."

Sheryl looked back, shook her head and walked further away.

Ashley leaned in and said, "I don't need any peyote. I need to lay with you. We're not going to be able to do that here with these fucking cameras everywhere."

"That's funny, and Melissa told me I could jack off any time I wanted. She said I have porn on my computer and a big screen to watch it with."

"You better not. I have no idea what the deal is here. I'm sure she was fucking with you. If you jack off on camera, God knows what they'll do with that. You know we're not going anywhere for months."

"Months, really? They can't keep us."

"You want to die?'

"No."

"Then you'll stay put."

They continued the night with bourbon and more bourbon, and then Melissa brought out some microphones, and the whole crew joined in on some singing...

Stewart and Sheryl got toasted and had to be helped to their rooms, and they passed out immediately.

Back at the airport in Chicago, Jack radioed ahead and was told to stay put. Dan and Dave came out of the exit together a few minutes later, they locked the limousine up and went inside as a group. The first place they came to was O'Brien's Bar and Grill. They went in, were seated immediately, ordered drinks and food, and ate. A little while later, Dave left for the gate to check on the progress of the plane, and Dan stayed with the judge. Dave reported the plane had landed and so the three men made their way back to the limousine. Dan escorted the judge to the limo and then went back into the airport baggage claim and waited for Jamie.

The judge sat in the seat; he was excited and nervous. He recalled the feeling from high school when he asked Michele O'Leary to the winter dance. She had to have been the best girlfriend he had ever had. He remembered being nervous, and she eased his fears. The girl was down to earth, kind, and, oh, what a smile. She was another one that got away. That was fine. He heard she was living near Hilton Head Island and happily married to some guy from Saint Louis. Randy was tapping his foot, shaking the limo. Dave announced, "The gates have opened, and passengers are headed to baggage claim. I have eyes on the subject."

Dan responded, "I'm set in baggage claim. I see her coming."

Randy could barely contain himself. He went over the things he would say, and none of them seemed right. Over and over in his mind, he tried to figure it all out. He was running out of time to prepare. He could not retreat to his chambers and pause the world; she was about to exit the airport into his presence.

"Judge Adams has collected her baggage and is moving to the door. Her estimated exit is less than one minute," Dan said.

Judge Randall Callahan opened his door, got out, adjusted his pants, straightened his shirt and pulled his jacket sleeved down. He crossed his hands in front of his pants. He took a deep breath, looked up, exhaled and then locked his eyes forward.

As if in slow motion, Jamie Adams came out of the airport. She looked towards the line of limousines. She was expecting to see her name on a placard. She looked left and then right. It was at that moment that she stopped, and Randy had a chance to view her for the first time in almost ten years. She was wearing a navy-blue overcoat. The sun danced off her light brown hair, with blond highlights falling onto her shoulders. She wore a pink and teal flowered skirt and a white silk blouse.

Her legs were exposed just above her knee to her elegant high heels. She put on her sunglasses as she exited, covering her blue eyes. Randy stood up straight and took a half step towards her. She noticed the movement and then fixed her face in his direction; she removed the sunglasses she had just placed over her eyes. Randy took another step towards her. Other passengers exited and went around her, some of them obstructing each other's view. She stood motionless as he took another step. He could see a smile growing on her face. At the same time, he saw a puzzled look. It combined with a smile. Dave had instructed her security detail of the plan, and they acquiesced, so Dan and Dave were at her side. Dave leaned in over her left shoulder and said, "Ms. Adams, we're with Judge Callahan's security detail. If you'd like, you can leave your bags with us and go to him."

She looked over her left shoulder at Dave, then to her right at Dan, behind them her detail, then she dropped the bags and ran the fifteen feet to Randy. She stopped short of him for a half second, then lunged into his arms. He picked her up with his arms wrapped around her and twirled in a circle twice, with their eyes locked. He put her down, she asked, "How did you?"

Before she could finish, he took her words with a kiss. He kissed her passionately for what she thought was an hour. They stopped kissing, and he responded, "Please join me in the limousine, and I will explain."

"But what about me?" she began.

He interrupted and said, "We sent them off. We are at your service."

"But, but, but how on earth, who tipped you?" she said, and then he interrupted again.

"Allow me to explain. We are working on a very strange case. Please, forgive me," he opened the back door and allowed her to get in. She got in and slid across the seat to the other door. Dan had one bag and Dave the other. They placed the bags in the trunk and then made their way to their vehicle with her security.

He continued, "We have a very unusual case. I must admit it has surprised me. Even more, it has excited me. You see, this may seem unbelievable. No, it is unbelievable unless you experience it for yourself. Wow, it is so good to see you. You look so beautiful, just as I remembered."

"And you, Judge Callahan, are as handsome as I recall. What has it been? Seven years? It, indeed, has been far too long. I cannot wait to catch up, but I'm most curious about your presence at the airport and how you summonsed me here today."

"I'm not sure about my summonsing you, but I will continue. In this case, we have a Mafia hitman who, wait. Let me start with a woman named Sheryl," he continued telling the story for the next thirty minutes until he got to, "so, I woke up this morning knowing you would be coming out that very door and here we are."

"My, oh my, Judge Callahan, have you misplaced your marbles?"

He laughed, "No, dear. I think I may have found them." He smiled, she smiled back, and he leaned in and kissed her again.

"Jack, will you take us to my house, please."

"Oh, Judge Callahan, you cannot expect a lady to come into town and then just sleep with you in your own bed. This is a holiday for me. I would like to feel pampered, so I have chosen a hotel to care for me. If you would please take me there, I can freshen up should you want to escape into the evening together. I was in no way ready to see you. I must look like a truck hit me."

She pointed to her forehead and said, "Does it say MACK up there?"

He laughed and said, "No, miss, you look more adorable than I remember," then he kissed her again on the forehead, "Jack, change of plans. I believe the lady is staying downtown at the Marriot."

"No sir, it is the Hyatt Regency. I was at some other Chic palace, but this seems more appropriate, so I changed it while I was flying. The inflight magazine gave it a wonderful recommendation."

"Very well Judges." Jack pulled out, and Dave followed.

"So, do tell me more of this peyote."

"It seems if you induce a double quantity, you can see while you are awake just with your eyes closed."

"What does she call this peyote?"

"Good question. I don't believe she has named it. She originally thought it would make her brother more compassionate. It did do that, and that seems permanent, but the mind transference is temporary."

"Oh, so if you fall asleep and I'm awake and naked. You, oh, you saw me naked this morning," she raised the pitch of her voice.

"Wait, wait, don't get..."

"No, Randy, that takes all of the... oh no, you saw everything this morning. I'm so embarrassed."

"Please don't be embarrassed. I never knew you and I would connect like that or this, but now that we have. Jamie, try to understand, it was just like a dream. I could not feel you or touch you like right now."

"But Randy, you saw me. You saw me. You saw me doing. You saw me."

He looked out the window at the passing buildings. Then he turned toward her and said, "Would you like to know what my thoughts were?"

"Yes, yes I would, perhaps that would help, yes, tell me."

"Like I told you before, you are so beautiful to me. I got such a special glimpse of you; I will treasure it in my mind forever, but my darling, having you next to me is ten thousand times better than a vision in my head. It will be our combined pleasure to be completely acquainted with each other. I must admit, you have been on my mind since two-thousand twelve, November eighth, two-thousand twelve, around nine-forty-five in the morning. The sight of you leaving that night, the last night for you in New York, well, it tore my heart out. You took it with you, you know. You have been carrying my heart around for almost ten years. The last time I saw you was at eleven fifty-two that night. I recollect it to be the very best day of my life. Then, the worst. I have never recovered. Now, maybe I can."

"Perhaps I should not reveal this at this Moment. I will, though. I felt the very same way. I never wanted to leave you. We both had such enormous careers, and neither of us could abandon them. You were just appointed to your court, and I was about to be. That choice. Oh, how that choice hurt. I suffered every day with you clasping at my heartstrings. I may have carried your heart, but you had mine. I kept busy for the likes of need with Paul, but Randy, it was you I desired. You, what of you, was there someone?"

"No one. I'm a person who compares. It is a flaw. I admit. I would meet someone and then compare. No one was you. I thought I would be alone forever. I gave up, in fact. Subtle things would remind me of you. I would watch a bit of NYPD Blue, and they would be at the park, and you and I would be hand in hand even though we were never hand in hand. I would try to forget, to no avail. I almost, I should stop."

"No, no, please. Please continue. We shared similar thoughts."

"Did you watch NYPD Blue?"

"Silly, I have never heard of that. No, but every movie with the park would bring me back. You yank like that park for movies."

"Yes, we do. I would order a shrimp cocktail, and you would leap into my thoughts. Some mornings, I would roll over in my bed, and I think you are there. There have been many nights that I would wake up and wonder about you. I would just sit up and think of you. It was odd. It always seemed to be around one in the morning."

"Hmm, wait, the time difference. What is it? Well, is it not seven hours? That would be eight in the morning. Yes, of course. I would wake at seven, then around eight, well, I would think of you. Often, it was strong that with which I thought of you. My days would be better after those thoughts."

He stared at her as she finished speaking. A little smile filled his face. It was the satisfaction of a long-awaited journey, and it was a pleasure from a long-expressed emotion trapped in his inner mind. No one knew his thoughts, but she felt his presence even seven hours away. She could read his mind, and he could tell her. They knew now that it was more. It was mind-sharing.

The End.

Acknowledgments

For me, acknowledgments are for those who have impacted my life in ways that made my writing possible. For the average reader, this will be meaningless. For those named, it will mean much. Don't be dissuaded by this personal note to these wonderful people.

Since this is my second book and the first book is out of print and may someday see the light again. I thought it fitting to put the names of those who have helped shape me in black and white. Each and every personal friend had some part in this book. Some are not mentioned here as they have not been forgotten but simply not mentioned. It is likely their names will appear in the text in the future, and I will acknowledge them at that time.

First and foremost, Michele, no one has ever believed in me as much as you, I have not ever been loved as much as you do. I revere you above all else with love and compassion. Thank you, baby, for being you. I love you so much, but you already know that.

William, I am so proud of the man you are becoming. You are so fun for me. I wish you everything you ever wanted.

Breandan, right now, you are still but a boy, trying to be a man and I appreciate your humor and love. I know you will be a great man someday. You and your brother will always be my reason for being.

My sisters: Wendy and Cindy. Kim. Brothers: John, David. Pat.

Our best friends are Joe and Diane Jennings, Clayton and Gretchen Davey, Tyler Harwood and mostly Tricia Evegan. I will immortalize y'all in my books—count on it.

Randy Wingbermuehle is a better friend than I knew. Thank you for all your kind words and support.

Mike O'Keefe, for the greatest quote I could never think of, gunslinger!

Gregg Westall, for being so cool in school that you elevated my standing.

Mitch Harmon, for being a friend when I needed you.

Steve (Joe) Bonansinga, the first reader to give me amazing feedback. He's credited for the term "reads like a movie..."

Bob Ducar, Bob Tucker, Pam, Brad Durant, Debbie and Pete Stephenson, Eric and Delighlia Brehm.

There are many more. You are not forgotten.

About the Author

Hello, thank you for taking a moment to read about the author. He's a private person who believes his work will entertain you. He considers the concepts you're about to read to be completely original. Any similarities to something else you may have seen are strictly coincidental. Future episodes will reveal more about the author.

www.ingramcontent.com/pod-product-compliance
Lightning Source LLC
Chambersburg PA
CBHW070426170726
48291CB00002B/377

9781917095433